"'Nearly ten years. I've waited long enough to finish what I started on the Blue River Ranch. This time no one will be there to save you. This time you will die.'"

Gabriel cursed. "You got this, and you still came here?"

Jodi shrugged, tried to make it seem as if this didn't have her in knots.

"This proves my father is innocent," she said.

"No. A copycat could have written it. Or your father could have paid someone to do it."

"But I have to believe it wasn't a copycat. It's either that or accept that my father murdered both of your parents, attacked me and then left me for dead." She paused, shook her head. "Of course, no one in your family had trouble believing it."

"Neither did a jury," Gabriel pointed out.

"My father was convicted on circumstantial evidence," Jodi said, though she was preaching to the choir. Because as the sheriff and the son of the murdered couple, Gabriel knew the case better than everyone else.

Everyone but the real killer, that was.

PERIL ON THE RANCH

USA TODAY BESTSELLING AUTHOR

Delores Fossen

AND

Nicole Helm

Previously published as *Always a Lawman*
and *Wyoming Cowboy Protection*

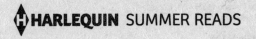 **HARLEQUIN** SUMMER READS

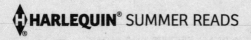 HARLEQUIN® SUMMER READS

Recycling programs
for this product may
not exist in your area.

ISBN-13: 978-1-335-17995-1

Peril on the Ranch
Copyright © 2020 by Harlequin Books S.A.

Always a Lawman
First published in 2017. This edition published in 2020.
Copyright © 2017 by Delores Fossen

Wyoming Cowboy Protection
First published in 2018. This edition published in 2020.
Copyright © 2018 by Nicole Helm

This edition published by arrangement with Harlequin Books S.A.

For questions and comments about the quality of this book,
please contact us at CustomerService@Harlequin.com.

Harlequin Enterprises ULC
22 Adelaide St. West, 40th Floor
Toronto, Ontario M5H 4E3, Canada
www.Harlequin.com

Printed in U.S.A.

CONTENTS

Delores Fossen, a *USA TODAY* bestselling author, has written over seventy-five novels, with millions of copies of her books in print worldwide. She's received a Booksellers' Best Award and an RT Reviewers' Choice Best Book Award. She was also a finalist for a prestigious RITA® Award. You can contact the author through her website at deloresfossen.com.

Books by Delores Fossen

Harlequin Intrigue

The Lawmen of McCall Canyon

Cowboy Above the Law
Finger on the Trigger
Lawman with a Cause
Under the Cowboy's Protection

Blue River Ranch

Always a Lawman
Gunfire on the Ranch
Lawman from Her Past
Roughshod Justice

HQN Books

A Coldwater Texas Novel

Lone Star Christmas
Hot Texas Sunrise
Sweet Summer Sunset
A Coldwater Christmas

Visit the Author Profile page at Harlequin.com for more titles.

ALWAYS A LAWMAN

Delores Fossen

Chapter 1

She had died here. Temporarily, anyway.

But she was alive now, and Jodi Canton could feel the nerves just beneath the surface of her skin. With the Smith & Wesson gripped in her hand, she inched closer to the dump site where *he* had left her for dead.

There were no signs of the site now. Nearly ten years had passed, and the thick Texas woods had reclaimed the ground. It didn't look nearly so sinister dotted with wildflowers and a honeysuckle vine coiling over it. No drag marks.

No blood.

The years had washed it all away, but Jodi could see it, smell it and even taste it as if it were that sweltering July night when a killer had come within a breath of ending her life.

The nearby house had succumbed to time and the elements, too. It'd been a home then. Now, the white paint was blistered, and several of the windows on the bottom floor were closed off with boards that had grayed with age. Of course, she hadn't expected this place to ever feel like anything but the crime scene that it had once been.

Considering that two people had been murdered inside.

Jodi adjusted the grip on the gun when she heard the footsteps. They weren't hurried, but her visitor wasn't trying to sneak up on her, either. Jodi had been listening for that. Listening for everything that could get her killed.

Permanently this time.

Just in case she was wrong about who this might be, Jodi pivoted and took aim at him.

"You shouldn't have come here," he said. His voice was husky and deep, part lawman's growl, part Texas drawl.

The man was exactly who she thought it might be. Sheriff Gabriel Beckett. No surprise that he had arrived since this was Beckett land, and she'd parked in plain sight on the side of the road that led to the house. Even though the Becketts no longer lived here, Gabriel would have likely used the road to get to his current house.

"*You* came," Jodi answered, and she lowered her gun.

Muttering some profanity with that husky drawl, Gabriel walked to her side, his attention on the same area where hers was fixed. Or at least it was until he looked at her the same exact moment that she looked at him.

Their gazes connected.

And now it was Jodi who wanted to curse. *Really?* After all this time that punch of attraction was still there? She had huge reasons for the attraction to go away and not a single reason for it to stay.

Yet it remained.

At least on her part anyway. That wasn't heat she saw in Gabriel's eyes. Not attraction heat anyway. He was riled to the bone that she was back at the scene of the crime.

Gabriel hadn't changed much over the years. He was as lanky as he had been a decade ago. His dark brown hair was shorter now, but he still had those sizzling blue eyes. Still had the face that could make most women do a triple take. Simply put, he was one hot cowboy cop.

"Is it true?" Gabriel asked. "Are you actually remembering more details from the night of the attack?"

She'd expected the question and heard the skepticism in his voice. Skepticism that she deserved. Because her remembering anything else was a lie. "No. I told the press that because I thought it would draw out the real killer."

He gave her a look that could have frozen the hottest parts of hell. "That's not only stupid, it's dangerous. You made yourself a target."

"I'm already a target," she mumbled under her breath. And because she thought they needed a change of subject, Jodi tipped her head to the house. "I'm surprised it's still standing. Why haven't you bulldozed it?"

A muscle tightened in his jaw. "There's a difference of opinion about that in the family."

Yes, Jodi had heard about some of those *opinions*. One of his sisters had wanted the place to remain standing, though Jodi had no idea why. She couldn't imagine any of them wanting to live in the house again. Still, maybe it was hard to demolish a childhood home even when that place was now a reminder of the nightmare.

"It's not a good time to be out here," he growled as if delivering an order that she would jump to obey. "And not just because you put out that lie to the press."

Jodi stayed put, and she darn sure didn't jump. "I was hoping if I saw the place again, it actually would help me remember, that what I told the press would no longer be a lie."

He aimed a scowl at her. Then, another scowl at the house and the spot where he'd found her bleeding and dying nearly a decade ago. "Why the heck would you want to remember that?"

He had a point. But so did Jodi. It wasn't a point that would likely make sense to Gabriel.

"I want to see his face." She shook her head. "I want to *remember* his face."

Ironically, it was one of the few things about that night that she couldn't recall. That particular detail was lost in the tangle of memories in her head. She could feel the slice of the knife as it cut into her body.

The pain.

Jodi could remember the blood draining from her. But she couldn't see the man who'd been responsible for turning her life on a dime.

"Why come back now?" Gabriel demanded. "Why tell the press that you're remembering after all this time?"

Good questions. And she had good answers.

"I got an email." Jodi figured that would get his attention, and it did.

Gabriel turned those lethal blue eyes on her. "What kind of email?"

She took out the printed copy from the front pocket of her jeans and handed it to him. Jodi didn't need to see what was written there. She'd memorized every word.

Nearly ten years. I've waited long enough to finish what I started on the Blue River Ranch. This time, no one will be there to save you. This time, you will die.

Gabriel cursed again. "You got this, and you still came here?"

Jodi shrugged, tried to make it seem as if this message didn't have her in knots. It did. But then, she'd been in knots for a long time now. For ten painful years. In some sick way, maybe this meant there'd be a showdown, and the knots would finally loosen.

"This proves my father's innocent," she said and waited for Gabriel to blast that to smithereens.

It didn't take long before he attempted that blast. "No. A copycat could have written it. Or your father could have paid someone to do it."

Both could be true, and she acknowledged that with a slight sound of agreement. "But I have to believe it wasn't a copycat. It's either that or accept that my father murdered both of your parents, attacked me and then left me for dead." She paused, shook her head. "Of course, no one in your family had trouble believing it."

"Neither did a jury," Gabriel pointed out.

It was true. A jury had indeed convicted her father, Travis, of two counts of murder and also of her own attack, and the jurors had given him two consecutive life sentences without the possibility of parole. He was rotting away in a jail cell, exactly where the Becketts wanted him. Of course, it could have been worse. Travis could have gotten the death penalty, but thankfully the DA had backed off on that because of some weaknesses in the case.

No eye witness to put Travis at the scene, and the fact that her father couldn't recall what'd gone on that night.

"My father was convicted on circumstantial evidence," Jodi said, though she was preaching to the choir. Because as the sheriff and the son of the murdered couple, Gabriel knew the case better than everyone else.

Everyone but the real killer, that is.

"My father didn't have the murder weapon on him when the cops found him," she went on. Yes, Gabriel knew that, too, but she wanted to remind him. "And the wounds to your parents and to me were made with a unique knife."

"A skinning knife with a crescent-shaped blade. Is this going somewhere?" he continued without hesitating. "Because it doesn't matter that your father claimed he didn't own a knife like that—"

"He didn't," she interrupted. "I was the one who cleaned the house. Cleaned his room. The barn. You name it, I cleaned it, and I never saw a blade that resembled anything like a crescent."

It wasn't easy for her to talk about the knife. But even when she didn't talk about it, the image of it was still clear in her head. Not from that night, though. Jodi hadn't actually seen it, but the FBI had shown her photos of a skinning knife. And they were certain that's what had been used on her because the tip of it had broken off during the attack. The surgeon had removed it from what'd been left of her spleen.

"That doesn't mean Travis didn't have that knife hidden away," Gabriel countered. "And I don't care if he says he didn't. Nor do I care that he claims he can't remember anything from that night because he had three times more than the legal limit of alcohol. The bottom line is that he had motive, and my father's blood on his shirt."

Blood that someone could have planted there when Travis was passed out drunk by the Blue River, where the deputies had found him hours after the murders and her own attack.

Jodi couldn't have argued that her alcoholic father hadn't been in any shape to murder two people, one of them sheriff at the time. That's because the DA had successfully argued that Travis could have gotten drunk afterward.

And yes, her father did have motive.

Bad blood between him and the Becketts. Feuds over land and water rights that had been going on before Jodi was born. It had created the perfect trifecta for law enforcement. Her father had had the means, motive and opportunity to butcher two people and then turn that knife on Jodi when he thought maybe she'd witnessed what he had done.

She hadn't.

Because of the blasted tears she'd been crying over Gabriel's rejection, she hadn't seen anything. She'd barely had time to hear the footsteps before her attacker had clubbed her on the head and started stabbing her.

"Have you considered the reason you don't remember your attacker's face is because you blocked it out?"

Gabriel asked a moment later. "Because it was too traumatic for you to see the face of the man that you thought loved you?"

Jodi had to take a moment to try to tamp down the panic rising inside her. No way could she believe that.

"My father never confessed to the murders," she pointed out.

"That doesn't mean he didn't do it," he countered and then huffed. No doubt signaling an end to an argument they'd been having for a decade. He looked at the email again. "You gave a copy of this to the FBI?"

She nodded, annoyed that it was a question. "Of course I gave it to them since they're the ones who handled this investigation. With you and your brother's help, of course."

In fact, Gabriel's brother, Jameson, had pretty much spearheaded the case in the beginning. Not that anyone had been dragging their feet. No. Everyone seemed to be racing toward any evidence that would result in her father's conviction. But Jameson had been a key player in getting that guilty verdict.

"I just wanted to make sure you didn't withhold anything from the FBI," Gabriel added. "Because they need to see any and all threats, so they can put a stop to them."

Jodi's annoyance went up a notch. Gabriel was talking down to her. Talking to her as if she was a criminal. Or an idiot. "I know you don't think much of what I do for a living, but I'd have no reason to keep something like that to myself."

He handed her back the email, his gaze connecting with hers again, and she got another dose of his doubt.

Gabriel definitely didn't think much of what she did.

Consultant for Sentry, a private security firm. Many cops thought that Sentry toed the line when it came to investigations.

And sometimes they did.

"I don't wear one of these," she said, tapping his badge, "but that doesn't mean I'm not out for justice just like you, Jameson and your deputies."

"Justice at any price," he argued.

She shrugged, trying to make sure she didn't look as if that'd stung a little. "Repeating my boss's motto— the law isn't always justice."

"Hector March." Gabriel said her boss's name as if it were profanity. To him, it was. "Is he out of jail yet?"

That was another jab. And another sting. "Yes. And for the record, what Hector did was definitely justice. The illegal video surveillance he set up eventually led to the arrest of a pimp who was known for beating up his girls. He used his fists to do whatever he wanted, and now he's been stopped."

There was too much emotion in her voice now. Too much emotion inside her, as well. It was hard to rein in the feelings of being powerless against a much stronger attacker, but Jodi had had a lot of practice doing just that.

"The pimp would have gone to jail eventually through legal means," Gabriel growled.

It was probably the truth. Probably. But Hector had made it happen a little sooner than the cops could have managed it.

"If I can save one woman from getting beaten or killed, I'll do it," Jodi insisted. "And yes, I'm overidentifying."

She waved off any other part of this discussion that

might happen because she'd admitted that. It was obvious Gabriel and she were never going to agree when it came to Sentry, Hector or her job. Jodi also didn't want to keep talking about something that couldn't change. She'd nearly died. Had the scars to prove it. Nothing was going to undo that.

"You blame me for what happened to you." Gabriel threw that out there like a gauntlet.

She turned toward him so fast that her neck popped. Jodi wanted to say no, that she didn't. Better yet, she wanted to believe it. But she didn't. Not completely anyway.

"I know in here it wasn't your fault." She touched her fingers to her head. "But everything that happened that night has gotten all rolled into one tangled mess inside me. A mess that involves you, me…and the killer. I don't want to include you in that nightmare, but it did begin with you, and I can't just forget that."

"Yeah," he said and looked away. Gabriel always looked away whenever the subject of attraction or sex came up between them. And despite her near murder not actually being about sex, it was sex that had started it all.

Or rather, lack of sex.

"You were nineteen," he reminded her. "Too young to be with me."

Obviously, his mind had hitched a ride on the exact train of thought as hers. "I was an adult."

"Barely. You were also one of my kid sister's best friends. And I was five years older than you. There's a world of difference between a nineteen-year-old college student and a twenty-four-year-old deputy sheriff.

Legally, you weren't jailbait, but that still didn't make being with you right."

It was his old argument that she knew all too well since it was the same one he'd used the night of the attack. She'd been staying in the Beckett house, a guest of Gabriel's sister Ivy, who at the time was also her college roommate. Around 10:00 p.m., Jodi had walked the less than a quarter of a mile distance between the Becketts' and Gabriel's place, the house left to him by his grandparents. And Jodi had done that for the sole purpose of seducing Gabriel.

It hadn't worked.

"You turned me down," she said under her breath. Thankfully, it didn't sound as if she still carried a decade of hurt. But it had certainly hurt then. Simply put, Gabriel Beckett was the only man she'd ever wanted. It was ironic, though, that after the night of the attack she'd never wanted him or another man again.

She silently cursed. That was a partial lie. A lie she could feel now that she was standing so close to Gabriel. Much to her disgust, she still wanted him.

"Sex is a commitment," she mumbled. "That's what you told me when you turned me away," Jodi huffed. "Which wasn't the truth since you had sex with half the women in town, and you didn't *commit* to any of them."

He said something under his breath that she didn't catch. Then, something she did catch. Bad profanity. "Why did you really come here? Because I'm not buying it that you're here just to remember. Are you trying to draw out the person who sent you the email?"

She didn't deny it. Jodi did indeed want to draw him out in the open and put an end to this once and for all.

"He could just shoot you," Gabriel reminded her.

"I don't think so. I think he wants his hands on me again." Just saying it nearly made her gag. "I won't be the victim for the rest of my life."

"Then start by not being here." Gabriel paused and glanced around. The kind of glance that a lawman made as if checking to make sure no one else was there. "You're not the only one who got a threatening email."

Everything inside her went still. "Who else? *You?*"

Gabriel nodded. "All three of my siblings, too. Jameson, Ivy and Lauren."

Jodi hadn't needed their names. She'd grown up next to the Becketts and knew them well enough to know their birthdays. Now, of course, they were her enemies. Enemies who'd apparently gotten death threats.

"What'd the emails say?" she asked.

Gabriel drew in a weary breath. "Almost the same as yours. Except for mine. The threat was, well, more explicit. Probably because I'm the sheriff now."

Jodi tried to process that. "What possible reason would my father have to send threats like this?"

"I've given up trying to figure out why killers do what they do." He hesitated again. "But I'm leaning more toward a copycat. There are a lot of sick people out there, and the story got plenty of press. With the tenth anniversary coming up in three months, I believe it's bringing out the lunatics."

"So, you think the emails are empty threats?" Jodi hated to sound disappointed. Hated even more that she was disappointed that it might be true. It sickened her to think the truth had already played out.

And that her father had left her for dead.

"Copycat threats aren't always empty," Gabriel corrected. "That's why I don't want you out here. Not alone anyway. If you want to try to jog your memory again, call me, and I'll have someone meet you."

Jodi probably should be insulted because she was an expert marksman and trained in hand-to-hand combat. She could protect herself.

Probably.

And it was the fact that the *probably* was not a certainty that kept her up at night.

She turned, ready to head back to her car, but something caught her eye. Some movement in one of the second-floor windows. Gabriel must have seen it, too, because he stepped in front of her.

And he drew his gun.

Jodi pulled her weapon, too. "Should there be anyone in the house?" she asked.

"No." That time he absolutely didn't hesitate, and Gabriel started toward the porch. "Before you jump to conclusions, it's probably just a teenager out for a stupid thrill. Or maybe a reporter. Either way, you should go to your car now."

"Just in case it turns out to be something more than a teen or a reporter, I can back you up if you're going inside."

Which he apparently was.

Gabriel didn't turn down her offer of backup. Didn't order her to her car again, either. Maybe because he figured she could be attacked while heading to the road. It was obvious he was thinking this was more than just a false alarm. Of course, after those threatening emails, Jodi doubted there was anything false about it, either.

Mercy. Was the killer here?

That sent her heartbeat racing, the sound of it throbbing in her ears. The memories came. Too many of them too fast. She had to force them back into that little box she'd built in her mind. This was no time for a panic attack. Not in front of a killer.

Not in front of Gabriel, either.

He took slow, cautious steps, his gaze firing not just to the window but all around them. "I'm Sheriff Gabriel Beckett," he called out. "You're trespassing. Come out with your hands in the air."

Nothing.

It was hard to hear because of her racing pulse and the breeze rattling through the live oaks, but Jodi thought she heard someone moving around inside. There were plenty of windows on the back part of the house that the intruder could use to escape. But maybe he didn't have escape in mind.

Maybe this would turn into another attempt to murder her.

If so, she was ready.

"Stay behind me," Gabriel insisted. "And watch our backs."

She did, and Jodi continued to keep an eye out as they made their way up the steps to the porch. But as soon as Gabriel reached the top step, he stopped.

Then, he froze.

Jodi was near enough to him to sense the muscles tensing in his body. And she soon realized why.

Her heart jumped to her throat. "Oh, mercy." Jodi shook her head and inched closer. Not that she needed to be closer to realize what she was seeing.

A knife.

With a crescent-shaped blade. The tip was missing. And there was blood on it.

Chapter 2

Even before he saw the knife. Gabriel had already had a bad feeling. He'd gotten it the moment he laid eyes on Jodi because she should be nowhere near this place. Now, that bad feeling turned to something much worse.

Hell.

Just to be sure his eyes weren't playing tricks on him, he took another look at what someone had left on the porch just about two feet to the left side of the door. No tricks. It was the knife all right. Or rather, *a* knife.

"That blood on it isn't dry," Jodi pointed out. Her voice was trembling just a little, but Gabriel had to hand it to her because she was holding herself together.

On the outside anyway.

On the inside, he figured it was a whole different story. If it was indeed the knife that had killed his parents, then it was the same one the killer had used on Jodi.

"It could be fake blood," Gabriel reminded her.

There was no way he would touch it to find out, though. Since the tip was missing, this was either the actual weapon that had killed his parents or else someone had broken off the end of the blade so that it would resemble it.

But there was a problem with that.

The missing tip that the surgeon had removed from Jodi's body hadn't been mentioned in any of the police reports. Nor was the fact that the killer had taken his father's watch and his mother's necklace. Those were just a few of the little details that the FBI had left out in case some nutjob tried to confess to the crime. So, either someone had hacked into those actual reports, or…

Gabriel didn't want to speculate about an *or* just yet.

While keeping his attention on their surroundings, Gabriel took his phone from his pocket and texted Jameson. He told him that he needed his help and for him to call a CSI to come and take custody of this knife. Jameson was at his house and could be there in a couple of minutes.

Bringing in his brother was better than waiting for the deputies to come in from the sheriff's office. Besides, Jameson was a Texas Ranger and the best backup Gabriel could have. Once Jameson arrived, maybe they could keep Jodi out of this. Of course, the problem was that she was here and therefore already in the middle of it.

Whatever *it* was.

This could still be a prank, and Gabriel was holding on to that hope. Over the years the house had become a magnet for daredevil kids, ghost hunters and pretty much anyone warped enough to want to see an old crime scene. That's how the windows had gotten broken and the boards sprayed with graffiti.

Gabriel tested the doorknob. Locked, just as it should be, and he used his key to open it. He pushed open the door, had a look around and got an instant punch of the musty smell and the dust. An instant punch of the memories, too.

He hated this place.

Hated that it still felt like an open, raw wound. A cut so deep that it would never heal. It was no doubt the same for Jodi. Even though she hadn't lost her parents that day, it had been just as costly for her.

In plenty of ways, she'd lost herself.

For just a moment he got a flash of another memory. Of the smiling nineteen-year-old who'd shown up at his house that night. She'd been wearing cutoff denim shorts, a snug red top and had looked far better than a girl had a right to look.

He pushed that memory aside, too. He'd lost himself that night, as well. Because he hadn't protected her. He hadn't saved his parents, and while Jodi had lived, he darn sure hadn't saved her, either.

Gabriel didn't see anyone in either of the two rooms just off the entry. Nor did he hear anyone. He ducked under the crisscross of boards, his back scraping against the rough wood. He moved just far enough inside for Jodi to step in behind him. Even though she didn't say anything, he could hear her breathing. Which was too fast.

There were no signs of an intruder here. No footprints in the dust on the hardwood floors.

The furniture in the living and dining rooms was still draped with the sheets that his sisters had put on them years earlier. It hadn't felt right to move anything after the CSIs had finished with it, so they'd covered everything, locked and boarded it up. Now, it was like some kind of sick time capsule.

"Anyone up there?" Gabriel called out.

He didn't expect a response and didn't get one. But what he did hear was something he didn't want to hear.

A footstep.

Yeah, someone was definitely upstairs. And judging from the weight of the step, it wasn't a raccoon or some other animal.

Jodi moved as if ready to barge right up there, but Gabriel leaned in front of her and shot her a scowl. "We'll wait here for Jameson. Once he arrives, I'll go upstairs. Alone."

She huffed, clearly not pleased about that. Maybe because she wanted to confront the person who'd left the knife. Of course, she thought it was the same person who had attacked her, but Gabriel was sticking to his guns that her father had been responsible for that.

"We should at least check the back door," she suggested. "That might be how he got in."

Yes, either that or a window. The place wasn't exactly a fortress, though the doors and windows should have at least all been locked. That wouldn't have stopped someone from breaking one of the panes and getting inside, though.

Gabriel went to the center of the foyer, and he volleyed his attention around the rooms and the stairs. He still didn't see anyone or anything out of place. Definitely no more blood to go along with what was on that knife, and if he had seen so much as a drop, he would have stopped and gotten out of there since this could potentially be a crime scene.

Again.

But thankfully there was nothing other than the bad feeling that continued to snake down his spine.

"Stay here," he warned Jodi.

Whether she would or not was anyone's guess, but Gabriel went into the adjacent family room so he could peer through to the kitchen. No one was there, but the rear door was open. The wind was causing it to sway just enough to make this whole ordeal even creepier than it already was.

Gabriel was about to lose patience with himself and whoever the hell had broken in, and he probably would have just charged upstairs if he hadn't heard a sound that he actually wanted to hear.

"What the hell?" someone asked and then added a string of profanity.

Jameson.

He'd probably seen the knife. Or maybe the cussing was for Jodi. Not that Jameson had anything in particular against Jodi, but he would have known it wasn't a good idea for her to be here.

"Someone's upstairs," Jodi said to his brother.

With his gun already drawn, Jameson came into the house, stepping around her, and his attention went straight to Gabriel. "Did the intruder leave the knife?"

"I'm not sure." But Gabriel was about to find out. "Stay here with Jodi."

"The CSIs are on the way," Jameson told him as Gabriel started up the stairs. "I called Cameron, too."

Cameron Doran. A deputy and family friend. Cameron would have been at his own house on the ranch grounds, and while Gabriel appreciated the double backup, he hoped it wouldn't be necessary.

With his gun aimed, Gabriel went up the stairs, pausing after each step to listen for any footsteps or movement. He didn't hear anything other than that damn creaky door downstairs.

At first anyway.

Then, there were definitely footsteps, and they appeared to be coming from his parents' bedroom. No more pausing for him. Gabriel hurried up the stairs and to the landing so he could pivot in that direction.

No one was in the hall, so he went toward the bedroom, passing several others along the way. He kept watch around him. The doors were all closed, but that didn't mean someone wouldn't open one of them and start shooting. Or running anyway. He was still hoping this would turn out to be nothing.

By the time Gabriel made it the forty or so feet to his parents' room, he'd worked up a sweat. And it wasn't helping his temper. This was not how he wanted to spend his afternoon.

He kicked open the door, and he nearly fired when he saw the movement. But it was just the white gauzy curtains fluttering in the breeze.

"He's out back, and he's getting away!" Jodi shouted.

Hell.

Gabriel hurried to the window to look out, and the first thing he spotted was the ladder propped up against the back of the house. But there were no signs of the person who'd put it there.

However, there were signs of Jodi and Jameson.

He saw them run into the yard, such that it was.

Once it'd been a manicured lawn, but now it was overgrown with weeds and underbrush.

"Stop or I'll shoot," Jameson called out.

Gabriel saw the guy then. He was dressed all in black, like some kind of ninja, and he was running into the woods. There were plenty of places to hide there and even some old ranch trails where the guy could have stashed a vehicle. Gabriel wanted to stop him because he had some answering to do about that knife.

Jameson and Jodi went after him, and that sent Gabriel hurrying, as well. He didn't go down the ladder because that would have made him an easy target in case the intruder was armed. Instead, he barreled down the hall and stairs and hurried out the back door.

Jameson and Jodi had gotten way ahead of him by now and had disappeared into the woods. With any luck, they were on the intruder's heels. Well, hopefully Jameson was. Gabriel didn't like it that a civilian was in the mix of things. Especially *this* civilian. Despite Jodi's attempt at trying to keep her composure when she saw the knife, Gabriel knew it caused her to have a slam of bad memories.

Once he was in the backyard, he had to hurdle over some of the underbrush, and it took him several long moments of hard running before he spotted Jameson and Jodi again. He'd hardly gotten a glimpse of them before Gabriel heard something else that caused his heart to jump into overdrive.

A cracking sound.

A shot being fired through a silencer.

Gabriel cursed again because neither Jodi's nor Jameson's guns were rigged that way. That meant the shot had come from the intruder. Well, that blew his theory that this was all some kind of sick prank. If the idiot had come here armed, then he meant business.

But what kind of business exactly?

If he'd wanted to kill them, he could have done that when Jodi and he had been talking earlier.

Jameson and Jodi thankfully ducked behind some trees, and using massive oaks as cover, Gabriel darted behind them as he made his way to Jodi. Jameson was only several yards away, and both of them had their guns and attention directed at a thick cluster of bushes and weeds.

Jodi was breathing through her mouth, but other than that, she was holding it together. And she looked like the trained security specialist that she was.

"Did you get a look at his face?" Gabriel wanted to know.

She shook her head and spared him a glance. Gabriel saw it then. The fear. But he also saw the determination to get her hands on this guy.

"Do you see him?" Jameson asked.

Gabriel peered around the tree for a glance. But he didn't get much of a look. That's because a bullet smacked into the bark just inches from his head. A second shot quickly followed.

He cursed and pulled Jodi to the ground. Gabriel hadn't intended to land on her, but that's what happened. The front of his body right on her back. They'd never been lovers, but being pressed against her gave Gabriel a jolt of attraction. A jolt he quickly shoved aside so he could adjust his position in case he got a chance to return fire.

The intruder fired again, and Gabriel tried to pinpoint the shot. Hard to do with the silencer, but he was pretty sure he knew the guy's general area.

"Stop shooting and come out with your hands up," Gabriel shouted out to him.

He didn't expect the intruder to do that.

And was stunned when he did.

"I'm coming out," the man said.

Jodi went stiff and practically shoved Gabriel off her so that she could get to her feet. Gabriel did the same, and he muscled her behind him just in case this was some kind of trick.

But it wasn't.

The man stood, his hands raised in the air. In addition to the black clothes, he was also wearing a ski mask and gloves.

"Where's your gun?" Gabriel snapped.

"On the ground near my feet."

Gabriel didn't want it anywhere near this fool. "Walk toward us. Slowly. Don't make any sudden moves, and remember that part about keeping your hands in the air."

The guy gave a shaky nod, and he started toward them. Jameson came out from cover, his gun trained on the guy. Gabriel and Jodi did the same, and the moment he was close enough to Jameson, his brother hurried to the man, put him facedown on the ground and frisked him.

"Keep watch around us," Gabriel told Jodi.

Her eyes widened a moment, and she must have realized that this man might have brought a *friend* or two with him.

Gabriel went closer to the guy, too, and handed

Jameson a pair of plastic cuffs that he took from his pocket. Jameson immediately put them on him.

"Who the hell are you?" Gabriel asked the man.

Gabriel stooped down and yanked off the ski mask. His head was shaved, and there were several home-made tattoos on his forehead and neck. Definitely not someone Gabriel recognized, and judging from the way Jameson shook his head, neither did his brother.

"I'm not saying nothing until I talk to my lawyer," the guy answered. He sounded pretty defiant for some-one who'd just surrendered.

But Jodi had some defiance of her own. She got right in the guy's face. "Where did you get that knife?"

He smiled. A sick kind of smile that had Gabriel's insides twisting. He wasn't sure what the heck this was all about, but he intended to find out.

"I'll take him to the sheriff's office," Gabriel said. "He can call his lawyer, and I'll question him." Then, he turned to the guy and hoped he could change his mind about clamming up. "Just so you know, you're looking at three counts of attempted murder."

The guy smiled again. Gabriel sure didn't. He si-lently cursed. Because they could be dealing with someone who was mentally unstable. If so, they might never get answers. But Jodi clearly wasn't giving up on that just yet.

She was right at the goon's side as Jameson started leading him back to the house. "Tell me where you got the knife."

Gabriel doubted the guy was about to blurt out any-thing, but just in case, he went ahead and read him his rights. Jodi waited, the impatience all over her face, and the moment Gabriel finished, she repeated her demand.

Nothing. Well, she got nothing other than the smile that Gabriel wished he could knock off the idiot's face.

"He's too young to have been part of your attack," Gabriel reminded Jodi. This guy was barely twenty, maybe still in his teens. He would have been just a kid a decade ago.

"He could still know something about it," she pointed out just as quickly.

"Yeah," Gabriel admitted. "That's why I'll handle this. You should go home, and I'll let you know if he says anything."

That earned him a glare. He'd expected it. She wasn't about to back away from this, but Gabriel had to keep her at bay because he didn't want her compromising his investigation.

"Need some help?" someone called out.

Cameron. The deputy was hurrying around the side of the house toward them. He, too, had his weapon drawn.

"Did you come here in your cruiser?" Gabriel asked him.

Cameron nodded. "Who is this guy? And why is the knife on the porch?"

Good questions. "I'm hoping he'll tell me once we've booked him." Gabriel tipped his head to the woods. "This clown left a gun out there. Keep an eye on it until the CSIs get here to collect it, and then I'll need Jameson and you to drive him to the sheriff's office. I'll be right behind you as soon as I've talked to the CSIs."

And after he'd had a look around.

Something more than the obvious wasn't right.

Jameson headed to the cruiser with the prisoner, and Cameron started for the woods. Jodi didn't budge.

"I want to be there when you question him," she insisted.

"No." And he wasn't going to compromise on that. At best he would allow her to watch from the observation room, but Gabriel was sure even that wasn't a good idea.

Gabriel looked at her, and that's when he saw that she was trembling. Jodi realized he'd noticed, too, and she cursed under her breath.

"I'm fine," she snapped. Her blond hair was damp with sweat, and she pushed it from her face. Her face was beaded with sweat, as well.

They stared at each other, until Jodi glanced away. "Sometimes, I have panic attacks," she said.

He figured she had to be close to one now to admit something like that. It didn't go well with her tough Sentry employee image.

"The water is still on in the house since it comes from a well. I wouldn't drink it because there might be rust in the pipes, but it might help if you splash some on your face."

But the moment he made the offer, it occurred to him why he still had that niggling feeling in his gut. Gabriel's attention zoomed to the back door.

"What?" Jodi asked when she followed his gaze.

"The ladder's there, but the back door was open when I went into the house."

She made a sound to indicate she was giving that some thought. "Well, the guy used the ladder to escape. Jameson and I saw him running from it when we got to the backyard."

Yeah. So, maybe the open back door had nothing to do with their perp. Still, Gabriel intended to check it out. When he'd run through the house to go in pursuit, he hadn't looked around to see if anything else had been...disturbed.

Gabriel started toward the porch with Jodi following along behind him. Part of him wanted to tell her to stay put while he checked it out, but it might not be safe for her to be out here alone. Of course, she would believe she could take care of herself, but if that idiot had indeed brought help, there could be more gunfire.

He didn't slow down until he reached the back door, and then Gabriel paused just to take in the room. The gray tile didn't show the dust, which meant it didn't show any footprints, either. That didn't mean some weren't there, though, so he used his elbow to open the door as wide as it would go, and he stepped to the side.

Jodi stayed in the doorway, but they seemed to spot something at the same time. She made a slight gasping sound.

Because the thing they spotted appeared to be drops of blood.

Gabriel reminded himself that it could be fake. Just like the blood on the knife. But that didn't stop the tightness in his chest.

"Come inside but stay back," he told her. He definitely didn't want her following what appeared to be a trail of blood drops. Drops that led right to the pantry.

The door to the pantry was ajar but not open enough for Gabriel to see if there was anyone or anything inside. With his gun ready, he went closer, and behind him he could hear Jodi shifting her position, as well. No doubt getting ready in case they were about to be attacked again.

As soon as he was close enough, Gabriel gave the door a kick with the toe of his boot. He took aim.

Then he cursed.

Hell.

There was more blood here, pooled on the floor amid the toppled cans. And in the middle of all that blood was what appeared to be a dead body.

Chapter 3

Breathe.

Jodi kept repeating that reminder to herself.

She couldn't keep taking in those short bursts of air that could cause her to hyperventilate. She needed normal breaths because that was her best bet right now at staving off a panic attack.

Gabriel certainly wasn't doing anything to put her at ease. He was seated at his desk at the sheriff's office building on Main Street in Blue River, and he was on his umpteenth phone call since they'd arrived two hours earlier. Jameson and Cameron were in the squad room, and they were doing the same thing.

Obviously there was lots to do now that this was a murder investigation. In addition to the calls and fielding questions from his deputies, Gabriel also kept glancing up at her.

Not that he had to glance far.

Jodi was pacing across his office while she tried to keep herself together.

What Gabriel wasn't doing was questioning their suspect. The bald kid who'd fired shots at them. Maybe a kid who had committed the murder, too. And had also left the knife on the porch. But Gabriel wouldn't have a chance of confirming any of that until the kid's lawyer arrived. Whenever that would be.

Gabriel finally finished his latest call, and immediately started making some notes on his computer. "You should go home," he said. And since Jodi was the only other person in the room, that order was obviously meant for her. "I can have one of the reserve deputies drive you and stay with you until this is all sorted out."

"I'm staying here," she insisted.

Then, she huffed, a little insulted that Gabriel had thought she couldn't take care of herself and needed a deputy. His doubt about her abilities probably had to do with that look that kept crossing her face, the one indicating she was about to have a panic attack. Jodi hated that it was there. Hated that it felt as if she might lose it at any moment, but that wouldn't stop her from defending herself if someone came after her again.

"What did the ME have to say about the body?" she asked.

His eyebrow came up, maybe to show her that he was surprised that she'd known he was talking to the ME. She hadn't heard anything the ME said, but she had been able to tell from Gabriel's questions who'd been on the other end of the phone line.

"He's a white male in his mid-to late thirties," Gabriel answered after a short hesitation. "There was no

ID on him. Cause of death appears to be exsanguina-tion from multiple stab wounds to the torso."

Breathe.

That felt like a punch to the chest. Because just hear-ing the words caused the memories to come. Memories of her own blood loss from stab wounds.

Mercy.

She'd lost so much blood that night that her heart had stopped for a couple of seconds. The medics had brought her back, but it could have gone either way. She could have ended up like the dead man in the Beck-etts' house. Or like Gabriel's parents who had died on their kitchen floor.

"Is this never going to end?" Jodi said before she could stop herself.

Gabriel cursed, got up from his desk and took hold of her arm. Good thing, too, because she suddenly wasn't too steady on her feet. He put her in the chair and got her a bottle of water from the small fridge in the corner.

"This is why you shouldn't be here," he insisted. "This is too much for you."

"It's too much for all of us."

He certainly didn't argue with that, but he did sit on the armrest and stare down at her. She saw it all in his eyes. His own battle with the nightmarish memories. His unease at her being there.

Except it was more than unease.

Oh, no. It was that attraction again. Anytime they were within breathing distance of each other, the heat returned. Thankfully, they were both in a place to shove it away. It wouldn't stay gone. But for now, they could keep it at bay.

"How do you think he got the knife?" Jodi pressed.

Gabriel lifted his shoulder. "Maybe he found it. I would say it's a duplicate, but there's the problem with only a handful of people knowing about the broken tip. Of course, a handful is more than enough for the info to leak and get to the wrong person. If so, he could be just some nutjob copycat."

All of that made sense, but it didn't exactly soothe her raw nerves. Too bad Gabriel didn't have a theory that would clear her father's name.

Gabriel gave a heavy sigh. "Look, I don't know what happened, but if this guy confesses to sending the threatening emails and committing the murder, then maybe this will put an end to it." He added another shrug when she stared at him. "Well, for everyone but your father."

Yes. Her father would get a different kind of ending. This wouldn't do a thing to get Travis out of jail.

Jodi looked away from him at the exact moment she felt Gabriel's hand on her shoulder. She didn't jump out of her skin as she usually did from an unexpected touch. In fact, it felt far more comforting than it should.

And that's the reason she stood and moved away from him.

That got his attention. Something she hadn't particularly wanted to get right now. Gabriel was giving her the once-over with those lawman's eyes, and he was obviously waiting for an explanation.

"I just have trouble being touched sometimes," she settled for saying.

A lie. She had trouble with it *all the time*.

He drew his eyebrows together. "Uh, have you gotten help for it?"

She nodded. That wasn't a lie. She'd attempted to get help by seeing a string of therapists. "In my case, help didn't work."

He kept staring at her, clearly still wanting more. She'd already told him far more than she'd spilled to anyone else, and Jodi didn't want to get any deeper into it. He probably wouldn't understand that the only thing that eased the demons was the knowledge that she could now defend herself.

Thankfully, she didn't have to add more because there was movement in the doorway. Jodi automatically reached for her gun, but it was just Cameron.

Cameron had lawman's eyes, too, and he slid a glance between Gabriel and her. The corner of his mouth lifted a fraction and for just a second. A dimple flashed in his cheek.

"You two always did have a thing for each other," he drawled.

Heaven knew what Cameron had seen or sensed to make him say that or to make him give that half smile, but it caused Gabriel to scowl. Unlike most people, Cameron didn't seem to be affected by that particular expression from the king of scowls. Probably because he'd had a lifetime of scowls tossed at him. After all, Gabriel wasn't just his boss, but they'd been friends since childhood.

"Do you have a reason to be here?" Gabriel snapped.

Cameron gave them that lazy smile again, and he handed her a cup of coffee and a small white bag. "It's some doughnuts from the diner. Thought you might need a sugar fix right about now."

She wasn't hungry in the least. In fact, Jodi wasn't sure she'd be able to hold anything down, but Cameron's gesture touched her. "You remembered I have a sweet tooth," she said.

"Hard to forget it. I remember having to wrestle some chocolate cake away from you once when we were kids."

Jodi nodded. "And I had to wrestle them from Lauren and your sister, Gilly."

She caught the slight change in Cameron's expression and knew she'd hit a nerve. Two of them, actually. From what Jodi had heard, Gilly had died during childbirth, and Cameron was raising her child. Since that'd happened only a few months earlier, the grief still had to be raw.

However, there was another rawness, too. One that might never go away, as well. Once, Cameron had been in love with Lauren. And vice versa. But again, those feelings of young love had all been shattered the night of the murders because Cameron had been a deputy then, and Lauren had blamed him for not preventing her parents' deaths. It probably wasn't logical for Lauren to feel that way, but those sorts of raw feelings weren't always logical.

"Yes," Cameron said as if he knew what she was thinking.

His smile stayed in place a moment longer before his attention shifted to Gabriel. "The CSIs are processing the knife right away. We should know soon if the blood belongs to the victim and if there are prints that match our suspect.

"Sorry," Cameron added to Jodi. "This kind of talk doesn't exactly go well with coffee and doughnuts."

"It's all right. I want to know what's happening with the case. Has the kid said anything?" she asked. "Or has his lawyer arrived yet?"

Cameron shook his head to both of her questions. "Nothing from him, but you do have a visitor, and he's demanding to see you. It's your boss, Hector March."

Gabriel shot her a glance, one that seemed like an accusation. "I didn't call him," Jodi insisted. And she looked to Cameron for answers. "The murder is already on the news?"

The deputy nodded.

Good grief. That hadn't taken long at all, but then, she hadn't expected it to stay quiet. Still, she hadn't wanted to deal with Hector when her nerves were this close to the surface.

Jodi stood, trying to steel herself up by taking some deep breaths and flexing her hands. "Where is he?"

Cameron hitched his thumb toward the squad room. "I had him wait out there. Something he's not very happy about. Apparently, he's not the waiting-around sort."

No, he wasn't. But if Jodi tried to put Hector off, that would only make him dig in his heels even more. She reminded herself that Hector had been the one to help her get back on her feet when she'd been just nineteen and devastated from the knife attack. He'd been the one to offer her a job and train her. She would probably be in a psych ward somewhere if it weren't for him.

She put the coffee and doughnut bag on Gabriel's desk and went out in the hall and toward Reception. Gabriel was right behind her, of course. And Hector was exactly where Cameron had said he would be. Her boss was dressed in his usual black cargo pants and black T-shirt. He'd once been special ops in the Marines, and he still looked as if he were in uniform.

Hector immediately went to her, ignoring Gabriel's

scowl. Heck, Cameron was scowling now, too. Apparently, neither approved of Hector's shades-of-gray approach to his business and justice.

Hector didn't touch her. He hadn't in years, since she usually went board stiff when someone put their hands on her. But he did get close enough to whisper, "Are you all right?"

She managed a nod. "Neither of us were hit, and Gabriel has a suspect in custody."

Hector turned to Gabriel then and extended his hand. "I'm Hector March, owner of Sentry Security."

Gabriel didn't shake his hand. "I know who you are."

Hector gave a crisp nod. "And I know who you are, too, Sheriff. Why the hell would you let Jodi get anywhere near that house after we got those threatening emails?"

That grabbed Gabriel's attention. "*We?* You got an email, too?"

"Yes." Hector frowned as if annoyed that he would have to take the time to address this. "It came this morning. But Jodi got hers the day before yesterday, right after she told a reporter that she was remembering some more details of her attack. I'm sure she explained that to you, and that's why you shouldn't have let her go to the house."

"I didn't let Jodi do anything." Gabriel's voice was as crisp as Hector's nod had been. "When I saw her car, I stopped to see what she was doing. She trespassed onto private property and then stumbled onto a crime scene."

Suddenly, all eyes were on her. Even the emergency dispatcher at the reception desk and the other deputies were looking at her. Maybe they were waiting for some kind of logic from her that they would understand. But it wasn't something they'd be able to grasp. Because they'd never been left for dead in a shallow grave.

"I wanted to see if being at the old house would trigger any other memories of the night of my attack," she admitted. Best not to tell them she had also wanted to draw out the snake who'd knifed her.

Hector pulled back his shoulders, clearly not approving of that. "And did it? Are you actually remembering new details?"

"No." In fact, the only thing it had accomplished was nearly getting Gabriel, Jameson and her killed along with giving her a new set of nightmarish memories.

All that blood on the pantry floor.

Mercy, another dead body.

She prayed the man wasn't dead because of her, but Jodi had to accept that he could be.

"Did you give the FBI the email you got?" Gabriel asked Hector at the same moment that Hector asked him, "Is Jodi free to go? I can drive her to her apartment in San Antonio."

"I don't want to go home," she insisted. "I want to listen when Gabriel talks to the suspect."

Hector's mouth tightened. It was yet something else he didn't approve of. Tough. She was staying put.

"And yes, I gave the FBI the email," Hector answered Gabriel, but he kept his attention on her. "Apparently, it's not traceable since the person who sent it bounced it around through several foreign internet providers."

Not a surprise. Jodi hadn't figured it would be so easy to find out who was doing this. But then maybe their suspect would spill it all. Not just about the emails but about the person who'd hired him.

"You think the guy in custody is the one who attacked you ten years ago?" Hector asked.

She didn't jump to answer. Because she wasn't sure how much Gabriel wanted to reveal about this investigation.

"No," Gabriel finally said. "He's too young. Plus, I believe the man who attacked her has already been caught and is in prison."

Hector made a quick sound of agreement. He always did when it came to her father. It was the one thing he had in common with the Becketts—they thought her father was guilty.

"Several other people got threats," Hector went on. "Apparently, all of you did." He glanced at Gabriel, Jameson and then her. "But so did Russell Laney and August Canton."

Judging from the soft grunt of agreement Gabriel made, he was already aware of those last two. Jodi certainly wasn't, and she looked at Gabriel for him to provide some details.

"There are probably others who got the emails, too," Gabriel said as Cameron stepped away to take a call. "The FBI figures some folks just deleted them as a hoax. But, yes, I suspect anyone connected to the initial investigation was on the receiving end of the threats. Russell and August got theirs the same day I did."

Jodi knew both Russell and August, of course. Both had been suspects in the Beckett murders and her attack.

Them, and Jodi's own brother, Theo.

It was public knowledge that the police and then the FBI had questioned all three. Theo, because he'd been a hothead at the time and had a run-in that day with Gabriel's father, Sherman, over some horses that'd broken fence. Russell had gotten caught up in it simply because Jodi had ended her short relationship with him the week before the attack. August was her dad's half brother and had been just as much of a hothead as Theo.

And the cops excluded them all as suspects.

After they'd found her father passed out drunk with Gabriel's father's blood on him.

"August thinks the threatening emails prove that Travis is innocent," Hector went on. "In fact, he's already taking all of this to Travis's lawyers in the hopes that it'll help with his last-ditch appeal."

August was probably the only other person in Texas who believed her father was innocent. Despite that, it never had felt as if August and she were on the same side. That's because August had never approved of her friendship with the Becketts. It didn't matter that the friendship had ended the night of the attack. It was a drop in the bucket, though, to what August held against Jameson. Because Jameson had been the most vocal of the Becketts in professing her father's guilt.

"Theo might have gotten a threatening email, too. Have you been in touch with him?" Hector asked her.

"No. I haven't spoken to him in over a year. I don't even have a phone number for him."

Nor did she know who to contact to get one. As a DEA agent, Theo spent a lot of time on deep-cover assignments, and if the copycat/killer had managed to send Theo an email, then he or she was well connected with insider Justice Department information.

Not exactly a comforting thought if it was true.

"We have an ID on our young suspect," Cameron announced as soon as he finished his latest call. "We got a match on his prints because he's a missing person. His name is Billy Coleman."

Jodi repeated that a couple of times to see if she recognized it. She didn't.

"He's a runaway," Cameron continued. "His parents filed a missing person report about a year ago. Not for the first time, either. He's run away at least two other times. He's seventeen, and judging from his juvie record, he's paranoid schizophrenic. My guess is he's probably off his meds."

Gabriel cursed. And Jodi knew why. Billy was no doubt going to plead mental incompetence, and they might never get answers as to why he'd committed this horrible crime.

But something about that didn't sound right.

"Billy called a lawyer," Jodi pointed out.

"Yeah," Gabriel agreed, and he cursed again. "And he had the name and phone number of the attorney when he got here to the sheriff's office. Not something a runaway teen would necessarily have."

"Especially since he's not from a wealthy family," Cameron supplied. "His parents both work at blue-collar jobs."

So, that confirmed that someone had likely put Billy up to doing this, and if so, that meant he was just another victim of this tangled mess.

"What about the dead guy?" Gabriel asked Cameron. "Any ID on him yet?"

"No. His prints weren't in the system, so we'll have to try to get an ID by searching through missing person reports and getting his picture out to the press."

That might take a while. Especially if the man was homeless and no one was looking for him.

"I really think you should let me take you home," Hector said, turning back to her. "Gabriel can fill you in on anything that happens, including whatever the suspect says in the interview."

She was shaking her head before Hector even finished. "I'm staying here." And she didn't leave any room for argument in her tone.

Hector gave a heavy sigh and looked at Gabriel as if he expected him to force her to leave. "I'm not sure it's a good idea for Jodi to be out anywhere right now," Gabriel answered. "She'll be safer here."

Jodi was more than a little surprised that Gabriel had backed her up. Then she realized why he'd done that. Because she was almost certainly in danger from the person who was manipulating Billy. Gabriel probably didn't want to be a part of another attack that could leave her dead.

"Just go," Jodi told Hector. "I'll be fine."

He obviously knew that "fine" part was a lie. Was also obviously not happy about being dismissed. But he didn't get a chance to voice that unhappiness. That's because Jameson finished his phone call, and he got up from his desk, making a beeline toward them.

"There were prints on the knife," Jameson said, "and the CSIs got an immediate hit." He snapped toward Jodi, and that definitely wasn't a friendly expression he was sporting. "Is there something you want to tell us?" he demanded.

Jodi shook her head, not understanding why Gabriel's brother looked ready to blast her to smithereens.

But she soon found out.

Jameson turned to his brother to finish delivering the news. "It's Jodi's prints on the knife."

Chapter 4

Gabriel had hoped there wouldn't be any more surprises today, but this was a huge one. Since Billy had been wearing gloves, Gabriel hadn't expected there to be any prints at all on the knife.

Especially not Jodi's.

Judging from the stunned look on her face, Jodi hadn't expected it, either. Her attention slashed from Jameson to Gabriel, and she shook her head. She also opened her mouth as if ready to blurt out some kind of denial, but the denial and anything else she might have said died on her lips because she groaned and sank down into the nearest chair.

"Jodi was obviously set up," Hector jumped to say.

Gabriel hated to give the man even a slight benefit of doubt, but Hector could be right. Of course, there was another possibility. One that wasn't going to help ease that stark expression on Jodi's already too pale face.

Gabriel moved closer to her, lifting her chin so they could make eye contact. Like the other time he'd touched her, she tensed, making him wonder just how many "scars" she had from the attack a decade ago. Probably plenty that she wouldn't want to discuss with him.

"Do you remember ever touching the knife?" Gabriel asked. He'd chosen his words carefully. No need to say aloud that he wanted to know if she'd taken hold of the handle when her attacker had been trying to end her life.

Jodi ran her hand through her hair and shook her head. "I honestly don't know." She shifted her attention to Jameson, and even though the paleness and nerves were still there, she straightened her posture and took a deep breath. "Is the fingerprint pattern consistent with me having grabbed it while I was being stabbed?"

Jameson lifted his shoulder. "There are two clear prints. Your right index finger and thumb. The other prints are smeared."

"That means nothing. Her attacker could have been wearing gloves." Hector again.

It riled Gabriel that Jodi's boss had taken on the role of defending her. Then again, plenty of things riled him about Hector. Including the fact that Jodi had turned to him and not Gabriel after the nightmare ten years ago. Hector considered himself some kind of victim's recovery advocate and had come to visit Jodi in the hospital shortly after the attack. She'd allowed him into her life—while excluding Gabriel.

"Does Jodi need a lawyer?" Hector asked, glancing at both Jameson and Gabriel. "Are you accusing her of something? Because it certainly seems to me that's what you're doing."

Well, it hadn't been certain to Jodi. Her eyes widened, and she shook her head again.

"I know you didn't stab yourself," Gabriel said before she could speak. But that was only the tip of the iceberg. There was another component to this situation.

The most recent murder.

Jodi seemed to understand that even before Gabriel could bring it up. "I also didn't kill that man and plant the knife on the doorstep so I could clear my father's name." Jodi's voice was stronger now, and she got to her feet to face him. She repeated the part about not killing the man.

Gabriel believed her. Yeah, it was stupid to take her word at face value, especially since he'd hardly seen her in years. He wasn't sure of the woman she'd become. But he seriously doubted that Jodi had become a killer.

"The FBI wants to talk to you," Jameson told her. "They're sending an agent from their San Antonio office."

Which meant the agent would be there soon, since San Antonio was less than an hour's drive away. That might not be enough time, though, for Gabriel to get answers from their suspect. He hoped that didn't mean the agent would take her into custody.

"If this is a copycat killing," Gabriel volunteered, "then the FBI doesn't have jurisdiction. I do." That was splitting legal hairs, but it might stop Jodi from being whisked away and put through what would no doubt be grueling interrogations.

Hell.

Gabriel frowned, then silently cursed himself. He

wasn't thinking with his head now. He was thinking like the twenty-four-year-old deputy who had turned Jodi away that night.

He was also thinking like a man.

One who was still attracted to a woman who shouldn't be on his attraction radar. But she was. And there didn't seem to be anything he could do about it.

"I'll get you a lawyer," Hector told her, already taking out his phone.

"No, don't. Not yet anyway." She turned back to Gabriel. "Any idea when Billy's attorney will be here?"

Gabriel had to shake his head. "But it should be soon. We've already bagged his clothes and tested his hands for gunshot residue. There's residue, by the way, and coupled with the fact that he attacked us, that'll be enough to charge him. Well, at least it's enough to charge him for shooting at us."

Jodi continued to stare at him. "You doubt that he killed that man in the house?"

Gabriel really didn't want to get into the specifics of what he thought or didn't think. Not with Hector right there. Not before he'd had a chance to try to work it all out in his head.

But there was a problem.

And Gabriel didn't believe it was his imagination that Jodi wanted to keep Hector out of this, too. Partially out of it anyway, since she'd refused to go with him and had even asked her boss to leave.

"Come with me a minute," Gabriel told her. He motioned for Jodi to follow him and headed toward the hall. He wanted her in the observation room next to where they were holding Billy.

However, Jodi didn't get far because Hector stepped

in front of her, blocking her path. "You're not questioning her," Hector snapped, his glare on Gabriel.

The man knew how to test every rileable bone in Gabriel's body. "I can and I will." He tapped his badge in
case Hector had forgotten that he was the one in charge
here. Of course, Gabriel didn't have an interrogation in
mind, but he didn't intend to tell Hector that.

"I'll be all right," Jodi told the man, and she stepped
around him.

That put some fire in Hector's eyes. "It's not a good
idea for you to talk to the sheriff without your lawyer
present. He's abusing your childhood friendship. Hell,
you might not even be able to trust him. Remember,
he's the one who helped convict your father."

That stopped Jodi, and for several moments Gabriel
thought she might change her mind about going with
him. She took in more of those deep breaths. The kind
a person took while trying to fight off a panic attack.
Or a fit of temper.

"Go home," Jodi finally said to Hector. Her voice
was as tight as the muscles in her face. "I'll call you
when I'm done."

Oh, that didn't please Hector. That fire in his eyes
turned to a full blaze. "I'm not going anywhere. I'll be
waiting right here when you're finished."

In addition to being a pain, the guy was also mule-
headed. Normally, Gabriel would have been pleased
that Jodi had someone like that on her side, but this
wasn't a normal situation. And Hector wasn't just an
ordinary boss. He was someone who cut legal corners
to suit his needs.

"Sorry about that," Jodi mumbled as Gabriel ushered her into the observation room.

There was a two-way mirror, and Gabriel immediately spotted Billy seated at the table in the interview room. He appeared to be asleep, his head resting on his folded arms.

Gabriel shut the door just in case Hector decided to follow them. Of course, Jameson and Cameron likely wouldn't allow that to happen. They both knew about Gabriel's low opinion of the man, and they had equally low opinions of Jodi's boss.

"Hector's protective of me," Jodi volunteered.

"Yeah, I can see that." He hadn't intended to make that sound like some kind of question, but it did. And that question was—why?

"I owe Hector," she said, answering that unspoken question. "He was there for me after, well, after."

"Only because you didn't let any of us be there for you," Gabriel pointed out.

She didn't disagree with that. Couldn't. Because she'd refused to see him, Jameson or his sisters, Ivy or Lauren, when she was home from the hospital. After that, she'd disappeared and hadn't resurfaced until eight months later at her father's trial. By then, she'd already started her association with Hector. Just how deep that association went, Gabriel didn't know.

It was possible they were or had been lovers.

Jodi didn't look away. She met his gaze head-on. "I'm stating the obvious here, but when I was recovering from my injuries, my father was charged with murdering your parents. For a while, my brother was a suspect as well, and you and Jameson were looking to put someone—*anyone*—behind bars for what happened. It didn't seem like a good idea to see you and cry on your shoulder. Plus, you had your hands full with the investigation."

"So, you cried on Hector's instead." Gabriel didn't bother cursing himself that time, but it was definitely something he shouldn't have thrown out there. He hadn't brought her in here to dig up the past, but they were certainly doing just that.

"I cried but not on anyone's shoulder," she informed him. "Wait. You're not thinking I turned to Hector because of some romantic feelings?" She cursed, made a face and didn't wait for him to respond. "It's not like that between Hector and me. Or any other man."

Her mouth tightened as if she also had said too much. Now, she looked away, dodging his gaze, and everything in her body language signaled to him that this part of the conversation was over.

Good. It was time to move on, and he tipped his head toward Billy. "There was no blood on his clothes. Nor any visible on any part of his body."

It didn't take her long to process that. "That's why you don't believe he killed the man."

Gabriel nodded. "There was blood everywhere in that pantry, and the guy had been stabbed multiple times. An organized killer could have possibly avoided spatter, but I'm not sure Billy's anywhere near organized."

She stared at the teenager on the other side of the glass. "He could have changed his clothes and cleaned himself up after the murder." But Jodi quickly waved that off. She huffed, but it wasn't exactly a sound of frustration. There was something else mixed with it, too. "You really do know that I wouldn't do something like kill a man, don't you?"

"I know." There was something else mixed with his response, too. Empathy. Hell. More than that. Sympathy. Something that she darn sure wouldn't want him to feel. "And you do know if I'd had any suspicions ten years ago about what was going to happen, I wouldn't have let you leave my house?"

She nodded, sighed. Jodi looked up, their gazes connecting, and for just a split second, it seemed as if the last decade melted away. He caught a glimpse of the girl. The very one who'd had a thing for him. That *thing* was still there; Gabriel could feel it, but it was buried beneath the scars and the pain.

He got another flood of memories then. The heat in his own body. He'd never told Jodi that he'd wanted her that night. Wouldn't tell her, either. Because it wouldn't help. In fact, it could make things worse with them going through the "what could have been" scenarios.

Their eye contact continued, and Gabriel could feel that old attraction becoming a simmer again. Thankfully, the simmer turned chilly when he heard voices in the hall.

"I need to see the sheriff and my client now," a woman demanded. It wasn't a shout but close enough so that Gabriel had no trouble hearing her.

She was no doubt Billy's attorney. Good. That meant Gabriel could get on with the interrogation.

Gabriel threw open the door and came face-to-face with Cameron and a brunette who was dressed to the nines. She had a briefcase on the floor next to her pricey shoes. She certainly didn't look like someone who worked cheap, and that piqued his interest, and suspicions, even more. There was no way Billy could pay someone like this.

So, who was footing this bill?

"I'm Mara Rayburn," she said. Her voice had low-ered a couple of notches, but she didn't sound very happy about this visit. "You're Sheriff Beckett?"

Gabriel nodded, but before he could say anything, she took his hand and slapped some papers in his palm. "That's a court order to transfer my client to a psychi-atric facility where he belongs."

Heck, that was pretty fast for a court order, so Ga-briel looked through it.

"It's legit," Cameron provided, sounding as suspi-cious about all of this as Gabriel felt. Jodi, too, because she hurried to Gabriel's side to look over the docu-ment, as well.

"How'd you get this?" Gabriel demanded. "And who's paying you?"

Mara gave him a blank stare. "I got the court order through normal channels, and as your deputy just pointed out, it's *legit.* As for who's paying me, I'm not required to divulge that information. However, you are required to comply with that court order and release my client. There's a marshal waiting outside to escort Billy to the facility, and I don't want to waste any time. Billy's a very sick young man."

"How so?" Gabriel pressed, though he already knew at least part of the answer.

Mara whipped out yet more papers from the brief-case and handed them to him. "That's a report from the psychiatrist. Billy is paranoid schizophrenic. He not only needs medication, but he also needs to be under medical supervision since he's a danger to himself."

"And others," Gabriel quickly provided.

"He fired shots at us," Jodi added. "And it's possible he killed a man."

Mara's only reaction to that was an eye roll. "Please don't tell me you're going to fight this court order. Because it won't work. Billy will get the help he needs whether you stonewall us or not."

Gabriel hitched his thumb toward Billy. "I've got a dead body, and your client is the only person who can give me answers about that."

"That's your problem, not mine, Sheriff," Mara snapped.

She motioned for someone, and a few moments later, the marshal walked up behind her. Gabriel knew him. Dallas Walker. He was a good marshal, definitely not someone who would be on the take, but he would follow through on his job. And his job would be to make sure that court order was carried out.

"Sorry about this," Dallas mumbled to Gabriel.

"No need to apologize." Mara, again. "Just get my client out of here." She turned as if to leave but then stopped and snared Gabriel's attention. "Anything my client might have said to you isn't admissible because he isn't mentally competent."

Maybe, but the jury was still out on that. "You're not doing Billy any favors by covering for the person who's manipulating him," Gabriel told the woman. "Because the person manipulating him is likely a killer. A killer who's got you on his payroll."

If she had a reaction to that, Gabriel didn't see it, because this time when she turned, she walked away. "Bring my client to the car," she added over her shoulder to the marshal.

Dallas issued another apology, and Cameron led him

to the interview room. It didn't take long before the marshal was escorting him out.

Billy had a reaction all right. He smiled. "You two should be real careful," he said like a threat.

Gabriel had to rein in his temper. After all, this idiot could have killed them when they were chasing him. Plus, there was no telling what would go on in that psychiatric facility. Billy could end up not doing any time whatsoever.

"The lawyer didn't ask who I was," Jodi said under her breath.

Yeah. Gabriel had noticed that. Maybe because Mara hadn't cared enough to ask, but it could be because she already knew every single player in this. Whatever the heck *this* was.

"I'll make some calls," Cameron told them as they watched Dallas whisk Billy away. "We might be able to question him while he's at the facility."

It was a long shot, but at the moment it was all Gabriel had. Especially since they didn't even have an ID on the dead guy.

"Find out all you can about the lawyer," Gabriel told Cameron.

The deputy nodded, left to no doubt get started on that, but as Cameron was walking away, Hector was coming toward Jodi and him.

"My people just sent me a preliminary report on Mara Rayburn." Hector had his phone in his hand and appeared to be reading something on the screen. "She's thirty-two and works for a law firm in San Antonio. A reputable one."

"That doesn't mean she's reputable," Gabriel argued.

Hector made a sound of agreement and handed Gabriel his phone. Gabriel scrolled through the report, though he wouldn't take anything there at face value.

"There are no red flags," Hector concluded. "But I might be able to get financials on her."

"No." Gabriel didn't have to think about that, either. There was no legal way for them to get something like that since they didn't have probable cause on Mara. He darn sure didn't want Hector cutting corners on this and therefore compromising the entire investigation.

Jodi moved closer to Gabriel, her arm up against his as she leaned in to read the report, too. It was thorough for something classified as *preliminary*. Mara's address, phone number, educational background and even the cases she'd tried in court. As detailed as it was, Gabriel had to agree with the no red flags part. There had to be one, though, somewhere.

"Now that Billy's gone, are you ready to go home?" Hector asked her.

Gabriel looked up from the report and realized that Hector was scowling. And the man had his attention nailed to the arm-to-arm contact between Jodi and him. Jodi had said it "wasn't like that" between Hector and her, but clearly her boss had a different notion about that. Because that was pure jealousy in Hector's eyes.

Jodi noticed the jealousy, too, and the scowl. She eased away from Gabriel. "I want to stay here a little longer and see what we're able to find out."

That didn't ease Hector's expression. "You can use the resources in the office to learn anything that the sheriff can."

She lifted her shoulder, stayed put. However, Hector stayed put as well, and Gabriel thought he might

have to order the man to leave. He didn't get a chance
to do that, though, because he heard yet another voice.

One that he recognized this time.

Jodi did, too, and she groaned, stepping out into the
hall with Gabriel right behind her. "August," she muttered like profanity.

It was indeed August Canton, her father's half
brother, and he wasn't a stranger to the sheriff's office. Nope. August deemed himself as his half brother's
champion of justice and was doing everything possible
to get Travis out of jail. Gabriel had his own label for
August—pain in the neck.

August wasn't a typical-looking uncle. For one
thing, he was only a few years older than Gabriel. He
was the offspring of his father's second marriage, and
when his parents had been killed in a car crash when
he was twelve, Travis had raised him. More or less.
Travis hadn't been much of a parent to either August
or Jodi, but that hadn't stopped August from standing
by his brother.

And riling Jodi.

Gabriel had only heard August's side of the story
on this, but according to him, Jodi wasn't doing nearly
enough to clear her father's name. August apparently
wanted a lot more from her. August had money, a trust
fund left to him by his mother's family, and he was
using a lot of his cash to pay for private investigators
to dig for anything they could find. Rumor had it that
it rankled him that Jodi wasn't putting in as much time
and money as he was. But Jodi didn't have a trust fund.
Probably didn't have the time, either, because of her job.

"What do you want?" Hector snarled at the man.
Apparently, Hector knew Jodi's uncle, as well. And

evidently there also wasn't any love lost between them because August's eyes narrowed to slits when he looked at Hector.

August ignored Hector's question, put his hands on his hips and studied Jodi a moment. "I heard somebody tried to kill you. You okay?"

"I'm fine." That had to be a lie, but no one challenged it. "Why are you here?" Jodi asked.

A muscle flickered in August's jaw, and he slid a glance at Hector. "I'm here because of him. Because of your boss." Definitely no friendly vibe coming from August. That tone and glance was all venom.

"Because of me?" Hector challenged.

"Yeah," August verified. "I know you're the one who nearly killed Gabriel and Jodi today."

Chapter 5

Jodi groaned. She was so used to hearing August make stupid accusations that she didn't even consider taking that one seriously.

But judging from his expression, Gabriel did.

Of course, the reason he might be doing that was because Gabriel despised her boss. However, August hadn't shown much disapproval of Hector in the past so she couldn't understand why her uncle had just accused Hector of a serious crime.

Attempted murder—of Gabriel and her, no less.

Hector stepped forward. So did Gabriel, and Jodi got in between the three of them. Not easy to do since all three were obviously primed for a fight. She was as well, but Jodi didn't think it would do any good to aim any suspicion at Hector.

"What the hell are you talking about?" Hector demanded.

Gabriel didn't say anything, but his glare should have been enough to prompt August to get talking.

"We're all in danger because of him." August tipped his head to Hector. "He's been having us watched. Followed," he added. "And he's doing that because he's afraid Jodi's remembering the truth that would blow all of this wide-open."

"What truth?" Hector spat out. Jodi wanted to know the same thing.

"The truth that will set Travis free, and if he's free, that means somebody else did those crimes. Somebody you're protecting. Don't you dare say you don't have friends or criminal informants you're trying to protect. Friends who could have killed Gabriel's folks and tried to kill Jodi."

It was so far-fetched that Jodi wanted to laugh.

"It isn't just you, me and Gabriel," August went on ranting. "Hector's had Russell tailed, too. He's on his way here now to make Hector stop."

Jodi scrubbed her hand over her face. She definitely didn't want her ex-boyfriend in on this, especially since this was all some paranoia on August's part. She turned to Hector to get him to assure August that he would never do anything like that.

Hector folded his arms over his chest and aimed a defiant stare at August. "I didn't have anything to do with the murders, and I'm not trying to protect anyone who would have done them."

What Hector didn't do was deny the other part of August's accusation, and it felt as if someone had dissolved the floor and ground beneath her feet.

No.

Hector couldn't have done that.

Gabriel cursed. "You're having us followed?" he snarled.

It took Hector several long moments to answer. "Not you. I figured you'd spot a tail right off, but I've had men on Jodi, Russell and August."

"You what?" That was all Jodi could get out because her breath suddenly got very thin.

"It was for your own safety." Hector took his hands from his hips and reached for her, but Jodi stepped back.

"Explain that," she said, and she thought her glare might match the ones August and Gabriel were giving her boss.

Hector huffed. "The person sending those threatening emails is dangerous. The murder today proves that. I figured the violence would escalate, so I wanted to keep an eye on not just you but on the most likely suspect—August."

August charged at Hector, but he didn't land the punch that he threw because Gabriel caught on to August and put him against the wall.

"Why follow Russell?" Gabriel asked Hector.

"Because he's been getting threats, too, and I thought August or someone he'd hired would go after him. You have to admit that killing Russell would be a way to shed some doubt on Travis's guilt. And August might have an easier time killing Russell than his own niece."

"I didn't try to kill anyone," August fired back. "I just want everyone to know the truth, and that truth is my brother is innocent."

Gabriel ignored August and turned to her. "Did you know anything about Hector's spying?"

"No. Of course not. And if I had, I would have put an end to it. You had no right," she added, aiming her index finger at Hector.

She wasn't sure what riled her more—that Hector had had her followed or that she hadn't spotted the person he'd hired to do that.

"Have you forgotten that you nearly died?" Hector said. "Not just ten years ago but today, too. You're in danger, and it's not very smart to rely on the local sheriff to make sure you're safe."

Jodi stared at him. "I'm not relying on the sheriff *or you* for that. I can take care of myself. Now, call off your dogs. Not just the ones following me but the ones on August and Russell, too."

"That's not wise," Hector warned her.

"Do it!" Jodi snapped.

Hector hesitated several long moments, but he finally took out his phone to make the call. However, Gabriel stopped him.

"Did you have a tail on Jodi today?" Gabriel demanded. He didn't continue until Hector nodded. "Then ask him or her if they saw anyone go into my old family home. Anyone besides Jodi, me and a teenager wearing a ski mask."

"He didn't see anyone," Hector assured him. "I had one of my best men on Jodi. Frank," he added to her.

Frank Mendoza, former black ops. He was indeed one of Sentry's best, and it explained why she hadn't noticed him.

"Frank was positioned up the road from where Jodi

parked," Hector added, "and he said he didn't see anyone go into the house except Jodi and you."

That meant the killer was there before she arrived.
Watching them. Maybe committing the murder while
Gabriel and she were just yards away. So much for her
stellar training. She hadn't been able to sense something like that practically under her nose.

"I'll call my people now," Hector said.

"How did you find out Hector was having you followed?" Gabriel asked August the moment Hector
stepped into an interview room to make his call.

"One of the PIs that I'd hired noticed it. I have security cameras everywhere—in my home, my office.
Even in my car. When the PI reported to me that it appeared I was being followed, I told him to run a check
on the guy and find out who he was. Imagine my surprise when I learned the tail, Rusty Millington, worked
for Hector."

Of course, Jodi knew Rusty, too. He wasn't as good
as Frank, but the PI must have been top-notch to de-
tect Rusty.

"Did you report this Rusty and Hector to the cops
or the FBI?" Gabriel continued.

August frowned. "I'm reporting it now, to you, and
I want you to do something about it."

"I will…if there's anything to be done. It's not a
crime to follow someone, and Hector could just say he
was looking out for your safety."

"Right." August didn't bother to hide the sarcasm,
either. "Hector would like me out of the way so that he
has Jodi completely isolated and all to himself."

Jodi was so surprised by that accusation that she
flinched.

"You know it's true," August went on. "Hector's in love with you."

She shook her head. "I don't know that at all because it's not true." At least she hoped it wasn't. Hector had certainly done a lot for her, and she wanted to think it was because she did a good job for him, but she had to admit that Hector wanted more than just to be her boss. That said, she doubted he'd go to these extremes to get it.

"Am I interrupting anything?" someone asked.

Jodi had been so deep in thought that she hadn't heard the footsteps. But Gabriel clearly had because he'd already stepped in front of her. Now, he put his hand over his weapon in his side holster. But it wasn't the threat that Gabriel was gearing up for.

It was Russell.

It'd been at least six years since Jodi had seen him, but he hadn't changed much. Same blond hair and muscled body. In college, everyone had called him the golden boy because of his looks and because he excelled at sports. A city boy. The opposite of Gabriel, the cowboy cop.

But there was a different edge to Russell than there had been back in college. She knew he'd spent three years in the army, and it seemed to have hardened him a little. Put some more muscles on him, too.

"Jodi," Russell said when his attention landed on her. He went to her, his arms already reaching for her, but she motioned for him to stop.

"Uh, I don't hug," she said.

Of course, it sounded rude, but maybe Russell would get it, especially since he'd seen her in the hospital shortly after the attack. She'd had trouble with even the doctors and nurses touching her then, and in fact, Russell had been there for her first panic attack.

Plenty more had followed. And touching and hugging were triggers that she'd learned to avoid.

"Sorry," Russell said. He shook hands with August and then Gabriel. "August told you about Hector having us followed?" he asked Gabriel.

Gabriel nodded. "I also understand you got a threatening email?"

"I did, and I gave it to the FBI." Russell's forehead bunched up. "What I don't understand is why would a copycat or even Travis include me in this? Jodi and I weren't even together when your parents were killed and she was attacked."

"Lots of people are getting the threats," Jodi explained. "Who knows why? Maybe the killer thinks I told you something that could reveal his identity."

Russell glanced at Gabriel, then back at her. "So, you still think your father's innocent?"

"He is," August interrupted.

Jodi wasn't nearly as enthusiastic about that as her uncle was, but she did make a sound of agreement.

What she didn't do was offer up any details about the recent murder, about maybe it being tied to what had happened to her and Gabriel's parents. But if that knife did prove to be the murder weapon, then maybe there was some kind of DNA evidence on it to give them a suspect other than her father.

Russell kept his attention on her. "How are you? I'm guessing what happened today shook you up?"

"Some. I'm okay," Jodi lied. "How about you? I understand you got married?"

Russell flashed that golden-boy smile that had first

attracted her to him, but there was no trace of that attraction now. She thought that was mutual, too. "I married a wonderful woman four years ago. I met her not long after I left the army. And I'm a dad. Our son is six months old." The smile faded. "My wife and son are the reason I'm so upset about that threatening email. I don't want anyone going after them because of what went on between us."

Jodi heard the anger just beneath the surface. Anger maybe aimed at her because if he hadn't gone on three dates with her, then none of this would be happening right now. But the anger was warranted because Russell was no doubt concerned about this monster going after his wife and child.

"San Antonio police know about the threat," Russell continued, "and August encouraged me to beef up security. I did. I had a new security system installed, and I've told my wife not to go out of the house without me." The muscles in his face got tight. "Obviously, I don't want to have to live like this much longer, so just how close are you to catching this dirtbag?" He directed that question to Gabriel.

Gabriel shrugged. "There is a suspect. Once I'm able to question him, I'll know more."

"I want to talk to him," Russell said, and it was a demand. August nodded in agreement.

Now it was Gabriel's jaw muscles that got tight. "Not a chance. Unless you two become law enforcement officers, you're not getting anywhere near him. I don't want anything to compromise this investigation. Because if that happens, this guy could be guilty as sin and still walk."

August opened his mouth, probably to argue with

that, but he didn't have time to say anything before Hector came out of the interview room.

"I've called off the surveillance for all of you," Hector said, "but there's a problem." He paused. "Someone broke into Jodi's apartment."

Her breath froze, and she felt the instant slam of fear. "When?"

"I'm not sure, but he sent me this." Hector handed her his phone, and she saw the photo on the screen.

It was a selfie from the looks of it. A sick one. Because the person was wearing a ski mask identical to the one their teenage suspect had on when they'd found him. In the background, she could see her bedroom. The clothes that she'd left on the bed. The coffee cup on the dresser. She could also see something else.

The knife the man was holding up in his left hand.

It was a crescent blade with a broken tip.

She choked back a gasp just in time, and if Hector hadn't taken the phone from her, she might have dropped it. Gabriel snatched the phone from Hector, looked at it and cursed.

"When's the last time you were home?" Gabriel asked.

It took her a moment to gather her breath and her composure. Jodi felt the panic fade, replaced by the anger of having someone do this. "Early this morning. He must have gotten in after I left for work."

Russell and August looked at the picture, too. "Or maybe this creep was in your place ages ago," August pointed out.

Jodi had to shake her head. "No, those are the clothes that I put there this morning, and that's the coffee mug I used."

"The FBI is headed to your place," Hector explained. "They'll process the crime scene. And this photo."

Yes, because sometimes there were bits of hidden data in digital pictures. Maybe they'd get lucky. But she doubted this intruder had been sloppy enough to leave a trace of himself behind.

Gabriel glanced at Hector, then Jodi. "How the hell did he get past your security system?"

Good question. Because she had a good system. The best, as a matter of fact—complete with motion detectors and cameras. And she looked at Hector to see if he had an answer for that since he'd been the one to install it.

"Any chance your hired spy gave the intruder the code so he could waltz right into Jodi's apartment?" August asked Hector.

Hector's eyes were narrowed to slits when he turned to August. "No. Any chance your PIs could have found the code and given it to him?"

Oh, no. This was about to get ugly.

"Or maybe you gave that thug the code," August added, and yes, he aimed that accusation at Hector.

"Why the hell would I do that?" Hector snapped.

"To send Jodi running to you. To make her believe that you're the one who can protect her."

That went back to August's theory of Hector trying to isolate her from everyone but him, but obviously it was a theory that ticked off Hector. Since she didn't want punches thrown, she stepped between them again. However, that didn't stop Hector. He just charged right past her, and it might have come to blows if Gabriel hadn't taken hold of Hector. Russell did the same to August.

"I'm not going to stand here and have this moron accuse me of junk like that." Hector's voice was past the anger stage now, and the veins in his neck were bulging. Jodi had never seen him like this, but then August was a pro at pressing hot buttons.

"You," Gabriel said, pointing to August. "Leave now. You two, as well," he added to Hector and Russell.

Russell gladly obliged. In fact, he looked plenty sorry that he'd even made this trip. August, however, didn't go so easily. He spat out some profanities, looking at Jodi as if he wanted her to intervene on his behalf.

She wouldn't.

"You need to go," she told him.

That didn't please August, and it earned her a few choice curse words from him, but her uncle finally stormed out. It didn't surprise her, though, when Hector stayed put.

"You can't go back to your apartment," he said.

Of course, Jodi knew that, but there'd been so much info for her to process that it took her a couple of moments to realize the next thing Hector was about to point out—that she had to go somewhere safe.

But where?

She'd been trained to fight and shoot, but that wouldn't stop someone from gunning her down. Or worse. It wouldn't stop a monster from killing Gabriel, Russell or someone else just to prove a point. Exactly what point, she didn't know, but anyone who'd gotten a threatening email was at risk. She couldn't protect them all. Neither could Hector or Gabriel.

"I want you to come to my house," Hector insisted. "Or to the office. I can have both guarded 24/7."

Jodi was shaking her head before he even finished.

Maybe the unease she was feeling was because Hector had had her followed without telling her. Or maybe nearly being killed had created this edgier-than-usual feeling inside her. Either way, she wasn't going with him.

"Thanks, but no thanks," she answered.

If this snake had managed to get someone into her apartment, he could get to her anywhere. Including the fortress that Hector called home.

Hector's stare turned to a glare that he shifted from her to Gabriel. It was the exact reaction she expected. Some anger mixed with disappointment. Hector wasn't stupid, and he had to have known she was picking sides. A side that would help her get to the bottom of this while not being killed.

And that *side* was with Gabriel.

Hector turned to leave but then stopped. "Gabriel didn't save you ten years ago. Just remember that," Hector said like a warning before he walked out.

Jodi waited to see if Gabriel was going to respond to that. He didn't. He just stood there, hands on his hips, watching as Hector went out of the building.

"I didn't tell Hector that I went to your house that night ten years ago," she explained. "He didn't know I'd come on to you and that you'd turned me down."

Jodi didn't want Gabriel to think she had poured her heart out to Hector. She hadn't. She hadn't poured out her heart to anyone.

Gabriel's silence continued for several more moments before he looked at her. "How exactly did you meet Hector?"

She'd expected questions, just not that one, and she didn't miss that he'd used his lawman's tone to ask it.

"He came to the hospital about a week after the

stabbing." It wasn't hard to recall that meeting. In fact, those days, and the physical pain, were as fresh as if it'd just happened. "He said he'd read about the attack, and he wanted to offer me help getting back on my feet."

Gabriel made a sound of sarcastic disapproval, probably because she hadn't accepted any assistance from him, his sisters or her friends. Including Russell, who'd told her he would be there for her in any way he could. But Hector had offered her something no one else had.

"Hector said he could train me in self-defense, that he could teach me to use a firearm. A knife," Jodi softly added. "Everyone but the FBI was skirting around my attack, but Hector talked about it head-on. He said once I was trained that I could work for him, and that no one would be able to hurt me like that again."

There it was in a nutshell. Jodi would have trusted almost anyone who'd made her believe that she could not only recover but that she would also never again be a victim.

She wouldn't be, either.

The next person who tried to put their hands on her was going to pay.

"And you didn't believe it was suspicious that a stranger would show up and make an offer like that?" Again, he sounded like a lawman, one who had his own doubts.

"What are you asking?"

"If you think Hector could have orchestrated this," Gabriel answered without hesitation.

"No. He didn't know me before the original attack—"

"You're positive?" he snapped.

Well, she had been until now. After giving it some

thought, she had to shake her head again. "Hector's not connected to your parents…is he?"

"Not that I know of, but you can bet I'll be checking to see." He looked at her again. "Someone must have given the intruder the code to get past your security system. I'm not saying Hector did that," he quickly added, "but it could have been one of his employees. Someone who's close to both Hector and you."

A person who might have tried to kill them today.

And that someone might have murdered his parents.

"I know you've gone over every case file your father had worked on," she reminded him. "Were you able to exclude everyone connected to his investigations?"

"No." He cursed and rubbed the back of his neck. "There was a file with notes about Hattie Osmond that didn't make sense."

"Hattie?" she asked. Jodi knew the woman. Or rather, had known her. Hattie was a widow and had owned a big ranch not far from Gabriel's. She'd stayed pretty much to herself until she'd passed away a couple of years ago.

"My dad thought Hattie was being swindled or else blackmailed," Gabriel explained. "She was selling off her livestock and was making weekly trips to the bank."

Yes, that would have been out of the ordinary for her. "Maybe she was sick or wanted to spend her money on her family."

"That's just it. She didn't have a family. I'm talking no heirs except for some distant cousins who didn't even know her. Anyway, when she died, her estate was valued at a fraction of what everyone thought she had, and she'd destroyed a lot of records that people normally keep."

Jodi tried to figure out where he was going with this. "You think Hector was involved in that?"

"Maybe. But your father could have been, too. Or August. Hell. Anybody could have been. It might not even be connected to anything. It's just a loose end, and right now loose ends are all I've got to figure this out."

"Yes," she softly agreed. "And it might be hours or days before you can get in to see Billy Coleman."

Hours that she could be using to find out who'd gotten into her apartment and if Hector did indeed have any old ties that she should know about. While she was at it, she could maybe sneak in to see Billy.

"Do you still have a break room here in the sheriff's office?" she asked. "Because my nerves are a little shot, and I could use some rest."

Gabriel stared at her as if trying to figure out if that was the truth. It wasn't.

"I need my meds," she added, since it was obvious he wasn't going to buy anything other than the truth. Jodi went with a half lie. "I came really close to a panic attack earlier, and the meds are the only thing that'll help. Unfortunately, they sometimes make me drowsy."

More staring, then he nodded and tipped his head to the left side of the building. "The break room is still there. I'll let you know if I hear anything about Billy or the knife."

The knife. She certainly hadn't forgotten about that. Especially since her prints were on it. But that was yet another reason for her to get the heck out of there. The FBI might try to take her into custody while they got that all sorted out. No way did she want to spend hours waiting in an interview room.

Jodi made her way through the building, one that

she knew like the back of her hand. That's because she'd come here often enough with Ivy. First, just because Ivy's dad would give them money for ice cream. Then, later, Jodi came so she could flirt with Gabriel.

Not that he'd flirted back.

But she hadn't given up. Not until that night ten years ago anyway.

The break room was just as it had been the last time she was there. Same old leather sofa. Same fridge from the looks of it. Judging from the smells in the air, someone had recently eaten pizza and had coffee.

There were two ways out—the emergency exit and a window. The door had an alarm on it. It was nothing fancy—just something to alert the lawmen if it opened. Since Jodi didn't want to do that, she checked out the window. No obvious wires or sensors to indicate it was connected to the security system, so she unlocked it and lifted it a fraction.

No alarm.

If it had gone off, she could have told Gabriel she just needed some fresh air. At least now she wouldn't need to lie to his face.

Jodi lifted the window the rest of the way up, pushed out the screen and shimmied outside. She started running the moment her feet landed on the ground.

She didn't get far. The moment she rounded the corner, she smacked right into someone.

Gabriel.

"Back inside," he snarled. Before she had a chance to protest, he took hold of her arm, his grip hard. "You're under arrest."

Chapter 6

This was the first time that Gabriel had brought some-one in his custody to his family's ranch. Of course, it was also possibly the first time he'd arrested someone because he was pissed off at them.

It'd been stupid—along with being dangerous—for Jodi to try to run from him, but he'd known from the moment she said she needed a nap that she was going to try to sneak out of the sheriff's office. And if he'd let her out of his sight, she would have tried it again. That's why he'd arrested her, so he could hold her as a witness in his criminal investigation.

Even though Gabriel wouldn't want to have to ex-plain himself to a judge, he was on solid legal ground. As the sheriff, he had a right to compel someone to give a statement if they'd witnessed a crime. He could do that by detaining them, and while detention and protective custody might keep Jodi alive, it wasn't winning him any brownie points with her.

Not that he wanted points, that is.

Gabriel would settle for her just not glaring at him. And for her being safe. God, he needed for her to be safe.

If he'd trusted Hector, that might be the best place for her, but there were too many questions about the man. Taking Jodi there could be walking her right into the lion's den. Although Gabriel wasn't doing much better by her. He was taking her back to the scene of the crime.

Less than a quarter of a mile from it anyway.

"I shouldn't be here," she said the moment he pulled to a stop in front of his house. It didn't help that it was late, and the muggy heat was practically smothering them. Conditions that were almost identical to that night when she'd been left for dead.

From his truck window, she looked up at the bright moon. Yet another thing that had been in place during the attack. Too bad it hadn't given her enough light to have seen her attacker's face. If she had, then she might be convinced that her father was a killer. Of course, that wouldn't help them with a copycat, but now that Billy was locked up, at least they didn't have to worry about him.

He hoped.

"It's just for tonight," Gabriel assured her. "I can make other arrangements for you tomorrow." Along with having one of the deputies get her car. Right now, it was still parked on the road near the old house. He definitely didn't want to go there tonight.

"*I* can make other arrangements," she insisted.

"Yeah, I'm sure you can, but I didn't think you'd want to be alone."

Jodi didn't argue with that, though that's likely what she wanted to do. After all, she could have reminded him that she lived alone and had for the past decade. But this wasn't an ordinary night.

"I know you don't want anyone to realize that you seeing the knife and the dead body shook you to the core," he went on. "That's probably because you think I'll take it as a sign of weakness. I wouldn't," he assured her.

"Yet you felt I was weak enough to bring me here," she huffed, pushing her hair from her face. "And I was weak enough to let you do it."

Now, Gabriel huffed. Definitely no brownie points. "Come on in. You can grab a shower, rest or eat. Whatever you want. I'll call and see if there's an update on the knife."

Some of the anger eased in her eyes when she looked at him. "Thank you."

Well, it was a start, and Gabriel took that as a green flag to get her moving out of the truck and onto the porch. Every step had to be a trip down memory lane for her. That's why he hurried and got her inside. There shouldn't be any of those memories of that night in the house since they'd had their short conversation on the porch.

The conversation where he'd turned her down.

He looked at her just as she looked at him, and he saw that she was reliving that little chat, too. And judging from the way her eyebrow lifted, she was maybe waiting for him to say something about it. But what he could say? Nothing that would make this better, that's for sure.

"I thought I was doing the right thing that night," he finally admitted. "I thought I was doing you a favor."

She laughed. Not from humor. Because there wasn't anything funny about what he was saying. Ironic that doing what he thought was the right thing had nearly gotten her killed.

Gabriel wouldn't be able to forget that. Ever.

Jodi went past him and into the living room. She glanced around, maybe noticing that he'd had the place redecorated. It was more him now and not just the house he'd inherited from his grandparents.

"Is the downstairs guest room still where it used to be?" she asked.

He nodded, and she immediately headed up the hall toward it. Only then did Gabriel release the breath he'd been holding. She was staying, for now, but just in case she decided to climb out the window, he set the security system. All the windows and doors were wired to sound the alarm if someone opened any of them. However, the only sound he heard was when she turned on the shower.

Gabriel went into the kitchen, put some sandwiches together and got started on checking for updates.

Nothing.

Well, nothing good anyway. Billy had been checked into the facility and wouldn't be evaluated by the psychiatrist until tomorrow morning. Heaven knew how long it would be before Gabriel could see him after that. Maybe not at all if the shrink deemed him incompetent.

That left Billy's lawyer and the knife.

There was no proof yet as to who was paying the attorney, and the knife was just as much of a puzzle as it had been when Gabriel had seen it on the doorstep of the old house. Jodi's prints combined with the dead guy's blood. Definitely not a good combination.

The broken tip appeared to be a match for the weapon used to kill both his parents and the man they found, but the lab would have to test both to be certain. Maybe during that testing, the techs could confirm whether Jodi's prints had been left there that night or if they'd been planted on it later. And he was certain if it was the latter that someone had indeed planted them. Because Jodi wasn't a killer.

Gabriel had just taken a bite of his sandwich when he heard a strange sound. A gasp, maybe. Definitely not something he wanted to hear. He ran to the guest room, praying that nothing was wrong. He knocked and tested the knob to find it locked. He was just on edge enough to break it down, but that wasn't necessary because Jodi opened it.

The lights were off in the bedroom, the shower still running in the adjoining bathroom, but Jodi was there. She hadn't run away after all, though she certainly looked ready to bolt.

Along with only being partly dressed.

Her jeans were on the bed, no doubt where she'd tossed them before taking her shower. Even though her top was long enough to cover her panties, Gabriel still noticed plenty of her bare legs. Jodi didn't seem to notice since her attention was on the other side of the room. Judging from her stark expression, something had spooked her.

"I thought I saw someone." She had a firm grip on her gun, but she took him by the hand and practically dragged him to the window. Not that she had to work hard to do that. Gabriel headed there while drawing his own weapon.

She didn't go directly in front of the window but

instead stood to the side and peered out. Gabriel did the same.

And he cursed.

He rarely went in this room and hadn't realized it had a view of the old house. The moonlight was glinting off the tin roof of the place. It was like a beacon in the night and looked more than a little creepy.

"It might have just been a shadow," she said, her voice a breathy whisper. A whisper that was filled with nerves.

Gabriel tried to pick through the darkness and see if he could spot anyone. There used to be plenty of shrubs that lined the path between his place and the house. He'd had a lot of them cut down after that night because Jodi's attacker had used them to sneak up on her. He hadn't liked the idea of keeping something like that around. But over the years, some cedars had popped up. They were full and bushy, making them a perfect place for someone to hide.

"I don't suppose Ivy, Lauren or Jameson would be out there at this time of night?" Jodi asked.

"No. Jameson built a big log cabin by the river." It was a good half mile from here, and besides, he was still at work. "Ivy left the week after our parents were killed and hasn't been back to the ranch. Lauren didn't come back after she went off to college." He paused. "I figured you knew about Ivy since you two were so close."

Jodi's shoulders stiffened. "No. I haven't seen or heard from her."

Too bad. "Other than the occasional Christmas card and email, she hasn't stayed in touch with anyone. She left around the time that she and your brother broke up."

"Yes," she said under her breath. "They were in love. Or at least they thought they were. Theo blamed Ivy for not believing he was innocent of the murders. He thought she'd put you up to bringing him in for questioning."

Ivy hadn't, but then she hadn't exactly jumped to defend Theo, either. Gabriel wasn't sure why, but in the end Theo's name had been cleared, and he'd gone on to be a DEA agent. All had worked out as well as it could for those two. But Gabriel knew his sister was still broken in some ways. Maybe clinging to the past, too, since Ivy had been the one to insist they not tear down the old house. Of course, she'd insisted that years ago, so maybe it was time to revisit that issue. He didn't like having the nightmare staring him right in the face every day when he drove past it.

His folks would hate that he hadn't been able to keep the family together. Would hate even more that Gabriel hadn't tried too hard to bring his sisters back home. But in the moments when it ate away at him, he rationalized that they had their own lives. Maybe not especially good ones since both Ivy and Lauren had lost their partners.

Yeah, his dad and mom wouldn't care for him not stepping up to the parent role. But Gabriel hadn't seen any reason to drag them back to a place where the memories might be more than his kid sisters could handle. Hell. Sometimes, it was too much for him to handle.

Gabriel continued to look around, also glancing at Jodi to make sure she wasn't about to go into panic attack mode. She wasn't. But her attention kept going back to that section of the trail where she'd nearly died.

"I remember so many things about that night," Jodi said, breaking the silence. "Except for his face."

He remembered plenty of things, too, even though there were times when he wished he didn't. Gabriel certainly remembered finding Jodi. Later he'd had to piece together what had happened to her when she'd left his house that night.

After her attacker had cut her up, he'd dragged her just off the trail and put her in a makeshift "grave" that he'd dug out with his own hands. It really was just a couple of inches of topsoil that the person had scraped away, and then he'd tried to cover her body with some dirt and leaves.

It'd been a miracle that Gabriel had even seen her, especially since by then he'd gotten the frantic call from Ivy to let him know that something "bad" had gone on at the house. After hearing Ivy say that, his focus had been on getting to the house.

Fast.

Gabriel had started running immediately after Ivy's call, and if he hadn't looked down at the exact moment he did, he might not have seen the blood on the ground. He might not have even looked at the grave where the killer had put Jodi.

She could have died right there in that spot.

"I guess it was a false alarm," she added several moments later. "I don't see anyone out there."

Neither did he, but he didn't budge. Jodi did, though. She went into the bathroom to finish getting dressed, but as soon as she'd done that, she hurried straight back to the window.

"Did you get any new info on the investigation?" she asked.

"Not yet. Maybe by morning we'll have something, though." He paused. "You should know that I'll be investigating Hector, to see if he had any connection to our dead guy. Any connection to Hattie, as well."

Jodi didn't seem to have any objections to that. Maybe because she was still upset at her boss having her followed. "August knew her, too, of course."

True. Hattie had lived just up the road from Jodi's family. Gabriel had looked for anything obvious to link August, and anyone else, to Hattie. Now, he needed to dig even deeper because, so far, he hadn't found anything.

"You think August could have killed your father because he was investigating him," she said. It wasn't a question, but if it had been, the answer would have been—it was possible.

"At the time of the murders, August was twenty-eight, broke," Gabriel explained. "He didn't get his trust fund until he was thirty, two years later. He could have milked money from Hattie to pay for all those things he couldn't afford. August always had expensive tastes in cars, women and clothes."

All of that was purely circumstantial, though, and it didn't mean Travis was innocent. Travis could have still murdered Gabriel's parents, and August could have been an accessory.

It could have even been August who'd attacked Jodi.

She tipped her head to the bathroom, probably to say that it was time to put an end to this impromptu surveillance and finish getting cleaned up, but she didn't speak. Something had caught her eye. Just as it'd caught Gabriel's.

There was some movement on the road in front of the old house.

Not a shadow. It was either a deer or a person. The knot in Gabriel's stomach told him it wasn't a deer.

"Wait here," he told her. "I'll get some binoculars."

He didn't remind her to stay back from the glass because Jodi was already doing that. But he did hurry. Whatever he'd seen wasn't coming their direction, but that could change. He didn't have any night goggles and made a mental note to bring a pair to the house, but he had the standard ones that his dad had used for hunting. Gabriel brought them back to the window and had a look at the spot where he'd seen the movement.

"Nothing," he relayed to Jodi, and he handed her the binoculars so she could check it out for herself. Several moments later she made a sound of agreement. That sound was coupled with some relief, too.

Gabriel took out his phone. "I'll have one of the deputies go by the place just in case."

Even though the CSIs had already processed the pantry and kitchen, he didn't want any thrill seekers trying to get a look at the crime scene. He also didn't want to leave Jodi alone so he could do it himself.

"Wait. It's a man," Jodi said, quickly passing him back the binoculars. No relief now. There was an edge and an urgency in her voice. "He's by the cluster of trees just up the road from your parents' house. He's wearing a ski mask."

That knot in his stomach had been warranted after all, and he had a look for himself. Yeah, he saw someone all right. And the person was on the move. Not leaving, either. The guy was coming in the direction of Gabriel's place.

He handed Jodi the binoculars so he could text Cameron, and he warned the deputy to approach with caution. Since this clown had on a ski mask, this might not be a prank situation after all. It could be the person who'd put Billy up to killing a man and then attacking Jodi and him.

"He's got a gun," Jodi blurted out.

Gabriel had just finished the text, and he pushed her away from the window and against the wall. She automatically pushed back and brought up both her knee and hand as if to fight him. Gabriel eased away from her, hoping it would lessen the panic he suddenly felt in her. The panic hadn't come from the guy with the gun, though. It had come because he'd touched her.

Now, Gabriel had a whole new reason to hate her father. Or whoever the hell it was who'd gone after her with that knife. The attack had left her this way, and after all these years, it might be permanent.

"I just didn't want you in this guy's line of sight," he reminded her.

She nodded and lowered both her knee and her hand. At least she hadn't tried to shoot him. With her training and skills, she might have managed to get off a shot before he could stop her.

Gabriel went back to the window, only glancing at Cameron's text response that he was on the way. It took him a moment to spot the guy again. He was definitely coming toward the house, and he was running now. It would be only a couple of minutes before he got there.

He weighed his options and doubted he'd be able to convince Jodi to hide in the bathroom. That meant Gabriel just had to protect her as best he could.

"Go in the living room and disarm the security system," he told her and rattled off the code. "Otherwise, when I open this window, the alarm will go off, and I won't be able to hear."

Gabriel especially needed to hear if this guy had brought a partner in crime with him. One that was even closer to the house than this one.

Jodi didn't question his order. She ran out of the room, and Gabriel didn't take his attention off the thug. The moment Jodi made it back, he threw open the window and took aim. He waited a couple more seconds, until the man was plenty close enough.

"Stop and put your hands in the air," Gabriel shouted.

Judging from the way the guy snapped back his shoulders, Gabriel had surprised him. What the idiot didn't do was put up his hands. Nor did he stop. He started running, not toward the house but to his right. There were thick woods back there, and Gabriel didn't want him getting away.

"Stay here," he told Jodi.

He didn't figure she would, and she didn't. She was right on his heels and followed him to the door. Gabriel opened it, looking out to make sure he wasn't about to be ambushed. When he didn't see anyone, he hurried to the side of the porch that would give him the best view of the trespasser.

"Stop or I'll shoot," Gabriel called out.

The guy did stop, but he didn't look up at Gabriel. Instead he glanced in the direction of the road in front of the old house. Specifically, he glanced at Jodi's car that was still parked there.

That bad feeling in Gabriel's gut went up a huge notch. His gut was right. Because Jodi's car exploded into a ball of flames.

Chapter 7

Jodi had hoped a long shower would help loosen her tense muscles. No such luck, though. Sleep hadn't helped, either. Too many dreams. Too many nightmarish images. She had the nightmares so often that they were part of what she now considered normal, but sometimes it was next to impossible to deal with her "normal."

Being around Gabriel wasn't helping with those memories, but even with that weighing her down, Jodi had to admit there was something comforting about having him nearby. Which, of course, only put her on edge even more. She'd learned the hard way that when you let down your guard, you got hurt. That's why she needed to make arrangements for a safe place to stay.

Clearly, that wasn't the ranch.

Though Gabriel had disagreed with that. He'd talked her into staying the night mainly because of the bomber still being out there. He had beefed up security by having two reserve deputies patrol the area, and Gabriel had stayed in the guest room with her. Guarding her.

From the floor.

That's where he'd put his makeshift bed, but Jodi doubted he'd gotten much sleep. She certainly hadn't.

She dressed in the loaner clothes Gabriel had left for her in the bathroom. Jeans and a loose gray top. She hoped these were things that Ivy had left behind because she didn't like the idea of wearing something from one of his ex-girlfriends.

Or maybe he even had a current girlfriend.

Gabriel hadn't mentioned one, but it was possible that his "normal" included things like dating and relationships. A life. Something she hadn't quite managed to get since she'd been put in that shallow grave.

After she combed her hair, Jodi made her way to the kitchen, where she'd left Gabriel. He was still there but not alone. Jameson and Cameron were seated with him at the breakfast table. She didn't catch what they were saying, and they hushed when they spotted her.

"What's wrong?" she asked. Because judging from their expressions, there'd been either another murder or a serious hitch in the investigation.

Gabriel got up, poured her a cup of coffee and motioned for her to sit. Jodi took the coffee, but she stood. She'd found that pacing usually worked a lot better than being seated if she was about to have to take another mental punch.

"There's been no sign of the bomber," Gabriel said.

Not good but it was something she'd expected. Gabriel and Jameson had searched for several hours after leaving Cameron at the house to watch her. They'd found nothing and called it a night. Now that the sun had been up for several hours, she'd hoped they would find some evidence that would lead them to him. Apparently not.

"There was a security camera in your car," Gabriel added.

With everything going on, she'd forgotten about that. "It's motion activated, and the feed goes to a storage cloud. Please tell me you saw the guy on there."

Gabriel shook his head. "The bomber managed to jam the feed."

She took a long sip of coffee, her grip too tight on the cup, but at least it stopped her from gasping, trembling or doing something else to make them think she was losing it. But this was critical. Jamming a camera like that would take some expertise and the right equipment. It meant this hadn't been done by some amateur thrill seeker.

"Billy's still locked up and didn't have any computer or phone access," Jameson explained. "That means he's probably not the one who sent this thug."

"His lawyer could have," she quickly pointed out. "Or the person who hired the lawyer for him."

Jameson nodded. "We're looking into it." He didn't sound very hopeful they'd come up with that, but at least it was a lead. Maybe the only one they had right now.

"Why would anyone blow up my car?" she threw out there. "It was obvious I wasn't in it, hadn't been in it for hours. So, if he wasn't trying to kill me, what was the point?"

"To scare you," Gabriel readily answered. "To send you into a panic so that you did something dangerous like run outside so you could be shot."

Jodi heard the disapproval in Gabriel's voice. Disapproval since she had indeed gone outside, but she hadn't panicked. Now, she sat down in the chair next to him and tried to piece her thoughts together.

"If this is a copycat, he'll want to re-create what happened that night," she suggested. "Not just by coming after me but also by killing someone else in the house."

No one at the table disagreed with that. It wasn't exactly a settling thought to have three lawmen admit that someone could want to slice her up again. But there was something in Gabriel's eyes that told her there was more to this than a simple copycat crime.

"We got some of the lab results on the knife," Gabriel continued a moment later. "It's the same one used to murder my parents and attack you. The broken tip was a perfect match to it."

That caused the skin to crawl on the back of her neck. Since she was fighting to tamp down the flashbacks, Jodi was sorry she'd sat down, but she couldn't stand back up. Her legs suddenly felt wobbly.

"And the blood and prints on the knife?" she asked.

"The blood belongs to the guy we found in the pantry." Gabriel looked at her again. "The only prints on it are yours. The lab said they look like defensive prints."

In other words, she had managed to grab the knife that night. That meant she must have seen her attacker's face. Of course, she'd known all along that was possible, but hearing it spelled out made her want to remember even more. If she could just see his face, then it could prove her father hadn't been the one to try to kill her.

Maybe.

And it just might confirm his guilt. But at least she

would know. *Her father* would know, since he'd been too drunk to recall much of what'd gone on that night.

"The obvious question is—where has the knife been this whole time?" Jameson asked. "It didn't show any signs of being out in the elements. Or buried."

Jameson glanced at her, maybe to make sure those two words hadn't been too much for her to handle. After all, she'd been buried. But Jodi was pushing away the memories and the panic so she could concentrate on what this new information might mean.

"The killer—or his accomplice," she quickly amended, "could have had it hidden all this time. Then, when I leaked it to the press that I was remembering details of the attack, maybe he freaked out and decided to try to scare me off."

"Or someone could have found the knife shortly after the attacks, kept it and decided to use it to play a sick game with you," Gabriel commented.

Yes, and that led her right back to August. Even if he hadn't been an accomplice or the killer, August might have found the knife near the scene and kept it, believing that it would incriminate her father. Ironic that it only had her prints and not the person responsible for this nightmarish crime.

Cameron finished his cup of coffee and stood. "I'll head to the sheriff's office and see if I can come up with anything on Billy's lawyer."

Jameson stood as well, and looked at Gabriel. "And I'll drive into San Antonio and find out who I can press to get one of us an interview with Billy."

Gabriel thanked them both. Cameron left, but Jameson lingered behind and aimed some glances at both Jodi and him. "You're both welcome to stay at my place. That way, you won't have to be so close to the old house. I suspect the CSIs will be all over it and the grounds."

They would be, but she had to shake her head. "Thanks for the offer, but I have some places in mind where I can go."

Jodi didn't, not yet anyway, but she would. She'd kept money in her apartment and car, but since she couldn't get to either of those, she would need to go to a bank. Once she had some cash, she could check into a hotel under a fake name and then figure out what her next step was. She didn't want to be tucked away where she couldn't investigate this, but she couldn't allow herself to be an easy target, either.

Jameson made a "suit yourself" sound and walked out. Gabriel got up, too, and followed him. So he could set the security system, Jodi realized. She hadn't needed a reminder of the danger, but that did it. So did Gabriel's expression. It was somehow wired and weary at the same time, and he coupled it with a huff.

"What places?" Gabriel asked, coming back into the kitchen. He went straight to the coffeepot and poured himself another cup.

It took her a moment to realize he was asking her where she had in mind to go. "A friend's house," she lied. "Not Hector's," she quickly added. That wasn't a lie. She had no intention of going there.

Gabriel huffed again, and it was louder than his earlier one. "You have nightmares," he said. "I heard you talking in your sleep, so don't deny it. You've admitted you have panic attacks. Someone tried to kill you, then broke into your apartment and blew up your car.

I'm thinking *a friend's house* isn't the place you should be going."

He was right, of course. Even if she had any close friends, she couldn't bring the danger to their doorstep. Besides, judging from Gabriel's tone, he was thinking *friend* meant *lover*.

"You can't believe it's a good idea for me to stay here." But as soon as she said it, Jodi realized something. Maybe it was a good idea.

If she wanted a final confrontation with this monster. And she did.

Everything happening seemed to be leading back to this place. To the scene of the original crime. Maybe her attacker wanted to finish what he'd started here. Well, she wanted to finish it, too, but with a totally different ending than this sick piece of slime had planned. This time, she wanted to be the one to end his life and put a stop to the danger once and for all.

"Fine," she amended. "I'll stay here."

Gabriel lifted his eyebrow, stared at her. Obviously, he knew what she was doing. But there was no way he could turn her down. Not this time. In fact, after what'd happened ten years ago, he might never turn her down again. Maybe Jodi could use that to bring all of this to a close.

He got in her face. So close that she had no trouble seeing all those flecks of silver in his blue eyes. "You might think you're ready to face down a killer, but it can't go past the thinking stage. Got that?" His jaw was tight. His words spoken through clenched teeth. "I don't want you outside on your own. And I don't want you on the trail that leads between here and my parents' house. I especially don't want you doing anything stupid like making yourself bait."

She shook her head and didn't dodge his intense stare. "You have to admit I'm the ultimate bait. I'm the one he wants."

Gabriel cursed. "You don't know that. Whoever killed that man could be trying to free your father by going after me or my brother. Especially if it's August."

True, and Jodi hated that she didn't know the reason behind all of this. Hated even more that her own kin could be responsible.

And that wasn't all that was causing her nerves to go into overdrive.

There was one more facet to this, especially if she did indeed stay here for another night or two. The attraction. She looked at Gabriel to see if that had occurred to him.

It had.

"It's easy for me to lose focus around you," Gabriel readily admitted, surprising her. Maybe surprising himself, too. "That can't happen. Because it could get one of us killed."

Jodi nodded. With that clarified, she should have looked away, probably should have just excused herself and gone back to the guest room to start making some calls to help with the investigation. But she stayed put.

Gabriel did, as well.

And, mercy, the heat came. She could feel it swirling between them. They'd never kissed, something she regretted simply because it made her want to do that now. Jodi wanted to know the feel of his mouth on hers. His taste. She was betting Gabriel was a good kisser, and there was the problem. With the heat and spent adrenaline already in play, it wouldn't stop with just a single kiss.

No, they'd land in bed.

At least, her body would want them to end up there, but Jodi was betting her mind wouldn't let things get that far. Heck, it was possible the kiss would even trigger a panic attack.

That reminder caused her to step back, though it wasn't necessary. Gabriel's phone rang, the sound slicing through the room—and the heat from the attraction—and he moved back as well to answer it. He didn't put the call on speaker, so she couldn't hear what the caller was saying, but whatever it was caused Gabriel's forehead to bunch up.

"Text them to me," Gabriel insisted, and he clicked the button to end the call. "The person who broke into your apartment left some pictures. Old ones from ten years ago."

Oh, God. "Not pictures of your parents' murders?"

He dragged in a long breath and nodded. "Brace yourself. Because the pictures are of you."

Chapter 8

Gabriel was a thousand percent sure that it wasn't a good idea for Jodi to look at the pictures Jameson had just sent him. He was also equally certain that he wouldn't be able to stop her from seeing them. Not Jodi. She would insist on it.

From a law enforcement viewpoint, it was a good thing for her to study them. It might trigger some memories of the attack that would help them explain what was happening now. But it would also be an emotional nightmare for her. Something he wished he didn't have to put her through. Despite the thick wall Jodi had built around herself, Gabriel still wanted to protect her. Even when she wouldn't want him to do that.

He maximized the size of the first picture on his phone, but it still took Gabriel a few seconds to figure out exactly what he was seeing. It was a grainy shot,

dark, but it soon became clear that it was of his front
porch. The lights were on, and Jodi was in the doorway. She was wearing a familiar outfit—cutoff shorts
and that red top.

Hell.

Someone had clicked a picture of them when Gabriel
was turning her down, and while he didn't remember
the exact words he'd said to her, the gist was for her to
go back to his parents' house, where she was spending
the night with Ivy.

"I didn't notice anyone," she said, her voice barely
a whisper. She moved closer to him, arm to arm, and
had another look.

He hadn't noticed anyone, either, but it could have
been taken with a long-range lens. Still, if Gabriel had
just glanced in that direction, he might have spotted the
person and stopped what was about to happen.

But why would Travis have taken this?

The answer was—he wouldn't have. The man had
been drunk, and it wasn't too likely he'd have been carrying a camera. Even if he'd used his phone for the shot,
there was still no reason to do this. After all, Travis
was well aware that Jodi often visited Ivy, and Gabriel.

Gabriel moved on to the next shot. This one was of
Jodi walking away from his house. She was barely visible in the darkness, but she was already on the trail.
Leaving. He was in the door, watching her go. He'd almost stopped her. Had almost run after her and kissed
her. If he had, they wouldn't be standing here right now.
Of course, his parents would likely still be dead since
Gabriel had gotten the frantic call from Ivy less than
five minutes after Jodi had left.

He cursed when he pulled up the third photo and

tried to move his phone away so that Jodi wouldn't see it. Of course, she snatched it back and saw what had caused his profanity and had twisted his stomach into knots.

Jodi on the ground, bleeding out.

"The SOB took my picture while I was dying," she said.

Yeah, and that told him plenty that he hadn't known before. If Travis had indeed been the one to attack her because he'd thought she had witnessed the murders, he wouldn't have waited around to take a picture of her sliced up and on the ground. That applied to the other pictures, as well.

"You're right. Your father wouldn't have been the one to stab you," Gabriel admitted.

Jodi glanced at him and that's when Gabriel saw the tears in her eyes. She quickly blinked them away and turned her head.

"Yes." And that's all she said for several long seconds. "The person who took these photos was outside your house right about the time your parents were being killed." She paused. "My attack wasn't about them. It was about *me*."

The tears threatened again, and even though Gabriel figured it was a bad idea, he pulled her into his arms. He expected her to fight it or go stiff. But she didn't. Jodi melted against him.

That was what Gabriel wanted to protect her from seeing. Now, those images would stay with her just as they'd stayed with him. Because that's the way he'd seen her after he had found her just off the path.

"It wasn't my father," she whispered. Even through

the emotion, he could hear the relief, and she looked up at him just as he looked down at her.

The air was already thick with emotion, but that eye-to-eye contact made it even worse. The attraction mixed with the old memories and the pain. Everything snowballed together until it felt as if he were being buried in an avalanche of heat. That's probably why he kissed her. Because it wasn't something he'd planned to do.

Definitely not a smart move.

His mouth barely touched hers before she scurried back as if he'd scalded her. "I'm sorry," he said at the exact moment that Jodi said, "I can't."

He nodded and then put even more distance between them. Gabriel was ready to close down the pictures so he could look at them later when Jodi wasn't around, but before he could do that, he heard the sound of a car pulling up in front of his house. Normally, that wouldn't have been a reason for concern, but there was nothing normal about what had been going on.

Gabriel drew his gun and went to the window just in time to see their visitor pull to a stop. It was a black SUV, and since the windows were heavily tinted, he couldn't see who was inside.

"Recognize that vehicle?" he asked Jodi.

"No." She'd drawn her gun as well, and even though she still had to be shaken from those photos, she wasn't showing any traces of being upset now. Like him, she was focused on a possible new threat.

Gabriel could see the front license plate of the SUV, and he was about to phone it in when someone stepped out.

Russell.

That didn't make Gabriel holster his gun, but it was obvious that Jodi and he weren't the only ones on edge. Russell glanced around while staying behind the cover of the SUV door. They were the kinds of glances a person would make if they thought someone was following them.

"Why the heck is he here?" Jodi grumbled.

Gabriel didn't know, but he was about to find out. He disarmed the security system so that it wouldn't go off when he opened the door, opening it about halfway.

"I have to talk to you." Russell ran onto the porch while still firing glances all around him.

Gabriel didn't back up. He certainly didn't invite Russell inside, which earned him a puzzled look. "I'm in danger," the man added.

"Welcome to the club." But Gabriel knew he couldn't be flippant about this. He was a lawman. Danger came with the badge. Ditto for Jodi as a security specialist. But Russell was a businessman, a CPA, and this might be his first brush with some monster with a deadly agenda since he left the army.

Of course, in Gabriel's mind, Russell could be a suspect. Anyone with a personal connection to Jodi could be. Including Hector and August.

"Someone just tried to kill me," Russell spat out. He came closer as if ready to barge in, but Gabriel didn't let him.

Jodi, however, moved to Gabriel's side, which meant she was now in the possible line of fire if their bomber was still in the area. That was a good reason to put a quick end to this conversation so he could get her back inside.

Russell huffed. "Look, I just want you to put a stop to this. My wife and baby could be hurt."

Gabriel wanted to be unaffected by that, but he wasn't. He knew what it was like to have family members in danger. And what it was like to have that danger lead to their deaths.

"What happened?" Gabriel asked.

Russell looked around again and groaned softly. "I leave my car in the driveway overnight outside my house, and when I went to get in it early this morning, there were two rattlesnakes on the seats. Rattlesnakes!" he repeated like profanity. "What if my wife had gone out there with me to kiss me goodbye for work? She could have been killed."

Possibly. But since it was Russell's car, the snakes had been meant for him. "You didn't see anyone suspicious in the area?" Gabriel pressed. "And did you report it to SAPD?"

"Of course I reported it. I called them right away. They came and took my statement. They asked if I saw anyone, too, and I didn't. This has to stop," he repeated after another groan.

While still keeping watch of Russell, Gabriel took out his phone and made a quick call to Cameron to have him request a copy of Russell's incident report from SAPD.

"Maybe you can make a public statement," Russell went on, looking at Jodi now. "Or visit your father and make sure he's not behind this. He could have put his brother up to all this in order to clear his name, but I can't have my family at risk because of you."

Gabriel felt Jodi tense. Probably because those words would have felt like a slap to the face. But it was a strange way of putting it. Yes, Russell was upset, but why had he dumped all of this on Jodi?

"We have reason to believe that Travis wasn't the one who attacked Jodi that night," Gabriel said, and he watched Russell's reaction.

And it was an interesting reaction all right. Russell's eyes widened, and he volleyed glances between Gabriel and her. "Then who the hell did it? Because that's probably the same SOB who put those snakes in my SUV."

Maybe. Probably, Gabriel amended. It was also likely the same person who'd blown up Jodi's car.

"You have to come up with a way to put an end to this," Russell went on, his voice more frantic now. "Maybe set a trap for him or something."

Gabriel had no plans to do that, especially since it would require using Jodi as bait, but he figured Jodi was already thinking of doing just that.

"I'm scared of Hector," Russell added. "If he's the one doing this, then he's got the people and the resources to hurt me and my family."

Gabriel hoped he didn't look too surprised at Russell's comment against Jodi's boss. Hector was indeed a possible suspect, but Russell made it seem as if adding the man to Gabriel's suspect list was a done deal.

"Why would you think Hector's behind this?" Jodi asked, taking the question right out of Gabriel's mouth.

Russell lifted his shoulder. "I thought it was obvious. The guy's crazy in love with you. And he can't be happy that you're staying here with Gabriel. Something like that might send Hector off the deep end. Heck, it might send August off the deep end, too." He settled his attention on Gabriel. "August really hates you, and he wouldn't want his niece spending time with the man who helped put his brother in prison."

August did feel that way, but Gabriel decided not to confirm it. He just waited to see if Russell would say anything else. He didn't.

Russell checked his watch. "I need to be getting to work." He started to leave but then turned back. "I don't want you calling my home or going there. It'd only upset my wife even more." He wasn't talking to Gabriel but rather Jodi.

"No worries. I won't go there." Her voice was tight enough for Gabriel to know that she wasn't pleased with what was essentially a dig. It was long over between Jodi and Russell, and Gabriel doubted she had feelings for the man, but maybe Russell thought she did.

Gabriel stepped back so he could shut the door. He also made another call to Cameron, and the deputy answered on the first ring.

"I need you to bring in Hector and August for questioning again—" Gabriel started.

"August is already here," Cameron interrupted. "And he's demanding to speak to you."

"Put him on the phone." Gabriel still wanted to do a face-to-face interview with both men, but he could possibly clear up some things right now. Well, one thing anyway. "While I'm talking to him, see if you can pull up any financials on Hector, Russell and August. The FBI should have already done that because of the investigation into the email threats and the latest murder."

"Will do. Oh, and brace yourself because August is mad." There was sarcasm dripping from Cameron's voice, probably because August was usually angry about something.

"Where are you?" August snapped the moment he came on the line. "And where's my niece?"

"We're both safe," Gabriel answered. Even though August likely knew Jodi was at the ranch, he didn't want to confirm it. "I just got a visit from Russell. Any chance you put some snakes in his car?"

"What?" August howled. "Is that what he said?" He didn't pause long enough for Gabriel to respond. "Because he's a bald-faced liar. I hope you asked him if he's the one who killed your folks and knifed Jodi."

He hadn't, but Gabriel wasn't planning to accuse Russell of anything yet, especially since he didn't have any evidence.

"Russell had an alibi for the night of the attacks," Gabriel reminded him.

"Yeah, so what? It was a girl he'd met at a bar who admitted she'd been drinking. She could have passed out and not even known he'd gone out and done something like that."

Gabriel hadn't intended for the conversation to swing in this direction, but he went with it. "Okay, I'll bite. What motive would Russell have to kill my folks? He didn't even know them."

Of course, Gabriel had a theory that could work— that Russell could have killed them after going to the house to look for Jodi. Collateral damage.

"Russell didn't have to know them to kill them," August pointed out. "Maybe he was tanked up on drugs. Maybe he just wanted to kill something or somebody, and they were the ones who drew the short straw. I'm just saying, you need to take a hard look at that liar. If there were snakes in his car, he might have put them there himself."

Yes, and that's why Gabriel wanted to read the report from SAPD. There might be something suspicious that stood out. Also, Gabriel could start calling around to the local snake handlers to see if anyone had purchased any recently. Some people collected them for their venom and just because they liked having dangerous "pets." If any of them had recently sold a pair of snakes, it could lead them to Russell.

"Are you going to ask Hector if he put snakes in that idiot's car?" August went on.

"You bet I will. Now, wait there until I can get into the office and we can have a longer chat. For now, give the phone back to Cameron."

"He's on the other line, but I'll put the phone on his desk."

From the sound of it, August practically threw it there. He obviously wasn't happy about having to wait on Gabriel, but people often said more when they were riled, so he'd let August stew a while longer.

Then, he could figure out what to do about Jodi.

"I could go to the sheriff's office with you," she offered while he waited for Cameron. "If you give me access to a computer and a phone, I can start trying to take a better look at the photos that the intruder left at my apartment. I might see something I hadn't noticed before."

That was what Gabriel was afraid of. Still, the killer and she were likely the only ones at that particular time on the part of the trail where she'd been attacked that night. So Jodi might indeed see something new.

Along with having a panic attack.

But that was a bridge he'd cross if they got to it.

"Sorry about the wait," Cameron said when he came back. "I've got something to tell you, but I want to do that in your office. I'm walking there right now."

The deputy probably wanted some privacy because August was right there in his face, but it meant waiting a couple of seconds. "It's about Russell," Cameron said when he finally continued. "The FBI has been monitoring him along with Jodi, you and anyone else who might be connected to the recent threats, and they might have found something."

Jodi moved closer to him, clearly trying to hear what Cameron was saying, so Gabriel put the call on speaker. "Jodi's listening," Gabriel warned the deputy. That way, Cameron could tone down anything that might be disturbing to her.

"Russell recently withdrew a rather large sum of money in cash. Nine grand. It came from an account he had before he got married. His wife's name isn't on the account. She might not even know it exists."

Not telling a spouse about an account wasn't unheard of, but that wasn't what caught Gabriel's attention. It was the amount of money. Just enough not to attract suspicion. At least it wouldn't have been if Russell weren't being monitored. Nine thousand was enough to pay off Billy and hire the guy who'd broken into Jodi's apartment. Maybe even enough to pay the man who'd blown up her car.

When Gabriel's eyes met Jodi's, he realized she'd come to the same conclusion.

"Does the FBI have any idea what Russell used the money for?" Gabriel asked Cameron.

"Not yet. He didn't deposit it into another account,

didn't get a cashier's check with it, either. You want me to get him in here and question him?"

"No. Check with the FBI. It's possible they'll want to monitor him to see if this has anything to do with the murder or anything else."

"Yeah, about that," Cameron continued. "The lab got an ID on the dead guy. It's not good, Gabriel." He paused. "The guy was a cop."

Chapter 9

Jodi's mind was whirling with everything Gabriel and she had learned. Whirling, too, because she'd been on edge the entire drive from his ranch to the sheriff's office. It wasn't far, less than ten miles, but each moment they'd been on the road had felt like an eternity.

Once Cameron had told Gabriel that their dead guy was a cop, Gabriel hadn't asked anything else. He'd just told the deputy that they were on their way there. Not just to read the reports on Russell but also so that Gabriel could reinterview August and Hector.

"I don't want you near the windows," Gabriel told her when he rushed her inside the building.

Cameron was right there to hand him some papers, but Gabriel paused only long enough to take them, and then he led her to his office. He lowered the blinds on the single window behind his desk and waited for Cameron to come in.

"That's a copy of the police report that Russell filed about those snakes," Cameron explained. "We're coming up empty on who might have gotten the snakes, but we'll keep looking. The next paper is about our dead guy. His name was Calvin Lasher, a small-town cop from Louisiana who'd recently been reported missing. I don't know why his prints weren't in the system, but it could have been some kind of computer error."

Jodi repeated the man's name, but it didn't mean anything to her. "Why was he here in Blue River?" She went to Gabriel's side and started reading through the initial report that Cameron had done on the dead man.

"I don't have a clue," Cameron answered. "Lasher's boss and family don't know, either, but his boss said he'd been investigating Hector."

That caused both Gabriel and her to take their attention from the paper and look at Cameron. "Why?" they said in unison.

"An illegal wiretap. Lasher had arrested a pimp who wanted a plea deal. The pimp said Hector had set up an illegal tap on his phone."

Gabriel turned to her. "You know anything about that?"

"No. But we do have out-of-state clients. It's possible Hector knew one of this pimp's girls, and maybe she had complained to him."

"It's not as if Hector hasn't done something like this before," Gabriel grumbled.

She didn't miss the disdain in Gabriel's voice. "True, but it would have been stupid for him to do it when he's on probation. Something like this could land him in jail."

Of course, that might not have stopped Hector. His favorite saying was, never mistake the law for justice, so he was always bending rules to the point of breaking them.

"Hector doesn't live in Blue River, either," she added. "Seems a stretch that he could have lured a cop to the Beckett ranch in order to kill him."

"A stretch but not impossible," Gabriel pointed out. "This way he could eliminate someone who might be able to put him back behind bars."

Maybe. But that seemed extreme for what would have turned out to be a fairly short jail sentence, and it was a sentence that Hector could have perhaps beaten. He had a knack for escaping time behind bars.

"When did this wiretap supposedly happen?" she asked Cameron.

"About two weeks ago."

"Good, that's recent enough that the file won't be archived yet," Jodi explained. "If you let me use your computer, I'll see if I can access the info."

Gabriel motioned for her to use the laptop on his desk, and she was about to log on to the Sentry page when she heard footsteps in the hall. Cameron and Gabriel immediately reacted, both of them putting their hands over their weapons, but she saw them relax just as fast.

"Is my sister here?" someone demanded.

Theo.

Jodi hurried out from behind the desk to see her brother walking up the hall. It was the first time she'd seen him in a year, and she went to him, wanting to hug him but not sure how he would react.

Once Theo and she had been so close. But that had changed the night of her attack. In the aftermath, each of them had been dealing with their own pain. She, because she had nearly died, and Theo, because he'd been a suspect in the murders.

He'd changed a lot since she'd seen him. His hair was long, practically to his shoulders, and he was dressed more like a cowboy-biker than a federal agent. She didn't know if his leather vest and rodeo buckle were his own clothes or if this was something he'd been wearing undercover.

"Jodi," he greeted. He lifted his hand as if he might reach out for her, but he didn't. Maybe because he saw the unease in her eyes. Of course, there was plenty of unease in his eyes, as well. Probably because there was no love lost between Gabriel, Cameron and him.

She didn't ask him where he'd been. Jodi knew as a deep cover DEA agent Theo wouldn't be able to tell her anyway. Plus, she wasn't sure she wanted to know the kind of danger he was in on a daily basis. It was already hard enough to accept that he might never be a real part of her life.

Equally hard to accept that both of them wanted it that way.

"Are you okay?" Theo said to her.

She nodded. "You?"

He lifted his shoulder. "I got a threat just like all of you, but it's been sitting on my old server for days, so I just now got word of it." Theo turned his attention to Gabriel. "I'm guessing Ivy got one, too?"

It wasn't a surprise that Theo had asked about Gabriel's sister, Ivy. Theo and she been a couple of steps past just being close.

"Yeah, Ivy got one all right, but she's not here," Gabriel answered. Cameron and he shared a glance. "In fact, Ivy doesn't stay in touch with us."

Yet another casualty of the aftermath of that horrible night. Gabriel's family had been torn apart as well, and Jodi suspected that Ivy just hadn't been able to stay in Blue River with the god-awful memories of the place.

"I heard about the recent attack," Theo went on. "And the dead cop. I can't stay, but I wanted to let you know that I made some calls to a few criminal informants to see if there's any buzz about this. There isn't," he added a heartbeat later. "But I did turn up something that's been bothering me. It's about Russell."

Of course, Russell was on their suspect radar, but it was still a surprise to hear Theo bring up his name. "You talked to Russell?" she asked, ready to tell him about the rattlesnake incident. But Theo continued before she could do that.

"I didn't talk to him, but a CI happened to know one of his old friends. According to the guy, Russell was binge drinking after Jodi broke up with him. He possibly even used drugs. The friend said Russell kept going on and on about Jodi leaving him for some deputy."

Gabriel.

"I never mentioned Gabriel's name to Russell," she explained, "and I certainly never told Russell I was leaving him for Gabriel."

"The friend said Russell figured it out when he heard you talking with Ivy." Theo paused, rubbed his fingers over his left eyebrow. "From the part of the conversation he listened to, Russell decided that you were going to try to seduce Gabriel."

That had been the plan. No need to verify it because it was part of the statement she'd given the cops after the attack. Of course, Russell wouldn't have had access to the report to confirm his suspicions, but that sort of info tended to get out.

"Russell didn't say anything to you about eavesdropping on your conversation with Ivy?" Gabriel asked her.

"No. And he didn't say anything to the cops about it, either." Unlike Russell, she had managed to get her hands on the report and had read every word of Russell's statement.

"Who are you looking at for these latest attacks?" Theo asked Gabriel.

"We have someone, a schizophrenic teenager, in lockup at a mental hospital." Gabriel made a sound of dismissal that Theo echoed. "That brings us to Hector March, your uncle August and Russell. We already know Russell had a thin alibi for that night. And he came here yesterday to Blue River, maybe hoping to see Jodi." A muscle flickered in Gabriel's jaw. "Jodi put out the word that she was remembering details of her attack."

Theo cursed. "Why the hell would you do that?"

She should have thought before she reacted, but Jodi lifted her T-shirt to remind him of the scars. Even though she only uncovered her stomach, there was plenty enough to see there.

Theo cursed again and glanced away. "Those scars are the very reason you shouldn't have put out a lure like that," he said. But he dismissed it with a shake of his head. "If I'd been in your position, I would have done the same thing. That's not a seal of approval, by the way, since most people think I'm crazy for doing what I do." He snapped toward Gabriel. "You can protect her?"

"I'll try."

"I'm trained to protect myself," she reminded both of them, but she might as well have been talking to the air because Gabriel and Theo stared at each other, some man-bond thing going on between them.

"Whoever attacked you outsized you by a good five inches," Gabriel said. "Outweighed you, too. We know that from the angle of your wounds and placement of your bruises. And all the training in the world won't stop him from trying to put a bullet in you."

Theo seemed pleased with Gabriel's stance. And the truth was—so was she. Even though it felt like this battle was hers and hers alone, it wasn't. In fact, her attacker could use Gabriel, Cameron or even Theo to get to her. That didn't make this easier to accept.

Especially not with this heat swirling between Gabriel and her.

The heat couldn't lead to anything, but her body was having trouble remembering that. And it was getting in the way of what she needed to be focusing on—the person who wanted her dead.

"If Hector's behind this," Theo went on, "things could get uglier than they already are. And as for August, well, he could just hire enough guns to finish whatever the hell he wants finished. Either way, be careful."

She would, but it sickened her to think that it might be any of those men. At various times in her life, she'd trusted each one of them. Of course, it could always be someone else. A nutjob whose name they didn't even know.

Not exactly a thought to ease her churning stomach.

"I have to go," Theo said, not sounding very pleased about that. "If anyone asks, I wasn't here. I can't give you a phone number, and you can't try to contact me," he added to Jodi, "but if I hear anything that'll help catch this piece of dirt, I'll find a way to get the info to you."

Jodi was about to thank Theo, but before she could do that, he brushed a kiss on her cheek, causing her to go board stiff. Theo noticed, too. He pulled back, making eye contact with her, and even though he didn't curse out loud again, she thought that might be what he was doing in his head.

"We'll talk soon," Theo whispered, and just like that she was a little kid again and he was her big brother. All the tension vanished. It wouldn't last, of course. Wounds this deep didn't heal, but for a moment it was good to have Theo back.

She stood there, watching him walk away until he disappeared out the door. Jodi turned to go to Gabriel's computer so she could do the search on the Sentry files, but Gabriel stepped in front of her as soon as she was back in his office. He shot Cameron a glance, and the deputy mumbled something about needing to check on a report.

Uh-oh.

That was not a good look in Gabriel's eyes, especially since his gaze kept drifting toward her stomach. "That's the first time I've seen your scars," he said.

"Sorry."

"Don't be." He put his fingers under her chin, barely

touching her, but lifted it so they were staring at each other. "Please tell me you've let a man kiss you in the past ten years."

She shook her head, moving away from him. Not because his touch had sent her into a panic.

But because it *hadn't* done that.

No way did she want to talk about this with Gabriel, especially with all this energy and attraction zinging between them. While part of her desperately wanted a kiss from Gabriel, it would open wounds she didn't want reopened.

"The Sentry files," Jodi said once she'd gathered enough breath to speak. Somehow, she managed enough energy, too, to move away from him. Definitely not easy.

"You do know that by not answering," he grumbled, "that it was an answer."

Yes. She hadn't let a man kiss her since the attack. Hadn't even wanted a man to do that.

Until now.

Mercy, she was in trouble.

Jodi forced her attention on the laptop. Work had always gotten her mind off things, and she needed that to happen now. It did. The moment she accessed the files, she started going through them, looking for any of Hector's active cases. There were at least a dozen, and none of them had anything to do with their dead guy, Calvin Lasher. In fact, none of them were cases that involved pimps or eavesdropping devices.

She shook her head and was able to move to the archives when she spotted something. Not a case assigned to Hector but to her.

"I didn't work on this," Jodi mumbled, scrolling

through it. "But it did involve a prostitute from the New Orleans area. Her name was Kitty Martin, and she wanted to hire Sentry for bodyguard duty."

"About how much would it have cost for that?" Gabriel asked after a long pause. Obviously, he'd been reading the file from over her shoulder.

"Hundreds at least. There's a start date of a month ago with no completion date. If she'd actually hired me for the full month, the cost would have been in the thousands." She shrugged. "Maybe Hector intended to assign the case to me but took it himself. Or else Ms. Martin changed her mind about wanting our services."

If either of those things had happened, then it should have been in the file and under Hector's name, not hers. Plus, there was the part about the dead cop who'd been investigating Hector's involvement with a pimp from New Orleans. Jodi doubted that was a coincidence.

And apparently Gabriel thought so, too. Mumbling some profanity, he took out his phone. "I'm putting out an APB on Hector. I want him brought in immediately."

Chapter 10

Gabriel didn't like the way this investigation was going. Somehow, he needed to figure out who was behind the recent attack so he could stop another one. Because he doubted the danger was over.

Neither was the fallout.

Jodi was pacing again, something she'd been doing for the past three hours while they waited for SAPD to find Hector and bring him in. While it seemed as if seeing her brother had soothed her a bit, that soothing was long gone now. Probably because she dreaded the idea of Hector being guilty. It would mean the only man she'd completely trusted for the past ten years hadn't been someone she could trust after all.

There was a knock at his office door, causing Jodi to whirl in that direction. Gabriel could see her steeling herself up. But it wasn't necessary because it was only Cameron.

"It'll be another half hour or so before Hector gets here," Cameron told them right off, "but I finally got permission for an interview with Billy Coleman."

That was good news. Or at least it would be if Billy wasn't so drugged up that he couldn't talk to them. Still, it was a start.

"You want me to go see Billy, or should I stay here and do the interview with Hector?" Cameron asked.

If Gabriel could have been in two places, that would be ideal, but he needed to stay put with Jodi. "Since Jameson's already in San Antonio today at the Rangers' office, have him go see Billy," Gabriel instructed. "Jameson can probably be there in a matter of minutes. I also want him to record the interview if he can." Though he seriously doubted Billy's doctors were going to allow that.

Cameron nodded, looked at Jodi. "This probably won't come as a surprise, but Hector's not happy about having to come in."

"No. I wouldn't imagine he would be." Jodi paused. "Did he say anything about me?"

"Words that you probably don't want to hear. The man has a temper."

Great. Not a good combination, and when Hector aimed his temper and venom at Jodi, it would eat away at her.

"Anything else in the Sentry computer files?" Cameron asked, motioning to the computer that was still on Gabriel's desk.

Jodi shook her head. "And I've been through every

one of them for the past year. Those the year of the attack, too."

Cameron's eyebrow lifted, and he shifted his attention back to Gabriel. "You don't think Hector's connected to your mom and dad?"

Gabriel blew out a weary breath. "If he is, he didn't surface as a suspect."

"And I didn't know him back then," Jodi added. She was no doubt thinking about how Hector just showed up out of the blue in her hospital room. "So, unless Hector's somehow linked to the late Hattie Osmond and that money she was seemingly paying out, then he wouldn't have had any part in the murder of Gabriel's parents."

But maybe he had a part now. Hector could have killed the cop and now could be so jealous of Jodi's return to Blue River that he could want her punished. Or worse.

"Would Hector have even been old enough to be swindling money from Hattie?" Cameron, again.

"He would have been in his early twenties," Gabriel supplied. "And he got his money to open Sentry from somewhere." Of course, it was a stretch to believe the money had come from Hattie, but Gabriel had to look at all the angles.

That angle included the most recent ones. The ones that included Jodi's uncle.

"Go ahead and call August and bring him back in for questioning, too. We know that Russell recently withdrew some money from his accounts, but maybe August did, as well."

Cameron nodded, turned to leave but then stopped.

He eyed both Jodi and him. "If you want to take turns guarding Jodi, just let me know."

"What was that about?" Jodi asked the moment Cameron was out of the room.

Gabriel scowled and shut the door.

"Oh," she said, obviously picking up on the emotions behind his scowl. "He thinks we're getting together. Cameron clearly doesn't know me," she added in a mumble.

Gabriel hadn't needed a reminder of his earlier conversation with Jodi, the one about kissing, but her mumble brought it back to the surface anyway. He probably should just let it go, but it was hard to do. Plenty of things were hard when it came to Jodi.

He went to her, knowing it was a mistake but not able to stop himself, either. He cursed this attraction that seemed to be growing by leaps and bounds. The timing for it sucked, and plain and simple, it could be dangerous.

But this wasn't about common sense.

"You're feeling guilty," she said out of the blue. "If you'd kissed me that night, or had sex with me, then I wouldn't be like this."

Since it was true, Gabriel didn't deny it. But there was a flip side to this. "If you'd stayed and we'd had sex, it might not have turned out so well." Of course, almost anything would have been better than what Jodi had endured.

"Yeah. We're back to *sex is a commitment* when both of us know that for you it wasn't."

Gabriel tried to tamp down the slam of emotion that caused inside him. "Sex *with you* would have been a commitment."

As soon as he said the words, he knew it was a mistake. A mistake because it was the truth, and in this case he was pretty sure the truth wasn't going to help.

It didn't.

She looked at him, shook her head as if that couldn't possibly be right and then she cursed. Gabriel knew how she felt. He wanted to curse, too. But instead he made the mistake much, much worse by taking hold of her hand.

He didn't jump into a kiss. Though that's exactly what he wanted to do. Gabriel gave her a moment to adjust to his touching her. Gave her another moment while he eased her closer to him.

"I thought you hated me," she said.

"I wanted to hate you," he admitted. "But mostly I just wanted you. And you were too young. It wouldn't have taken you long to start resenting that you weren't out having those life experiences you should have been having."

The corner of her mouth quivered with a half smile, but it wasn't a smile of humor. "So much for life experiences."

Yeah. The attack had rid her of that chance. And even though it wasn't fair, now wasn't the time to go back and re-create the kiss he'd wanted to give her that night. This was the time to focus on the investigation so he could stop another attack.

But he didn't do that.

While he still had hold of her hand, he leaned in and brushed his mouth over hers. It barely qualified as a kiss, but it slammed into him like a Mack truck. It apparently did some slamming into Jodi, too, because she made a sound that was like a gasp.

Gabriel pulled back to make sure she wasn't on the verge of a panic attack. She wasn't. That wasn't panic he saw in her eyes. It was the fire from this blasted attraction.

She didn't move closer to him. Didn't touch him. Both cues that he should just back away, but again he didn't. Gabriel slid his arm around her waist, pulled her to him and kissed her.

Jodi went stiff. At first. Then, the stiffness vanished when she moved into the kiss. Of course, that meant her moving against him, too. Specifically, her breasts against his chest. Normally, it wouldn't have been a turn-on to be kissing a woman who was plenty unsure about this, but it fired every part of his body.

Especially one part that shouldn't be fired.

She tasted exactly how he thought she would. Like something special—a mixture of fire and innocence. He forced himself to remember that it wasn't a good combination. Of course, there was little about this that was good, other than the kiss itself. And that silky moan of pleasure that purred in her throat.

Kissing Jodi was one thing, but that was as far as it could go. Because that old rule still applied here. Sex with her would still be a commitment, and there was no way either of them was in a place for that to happen. That's why Gabriel moved back from her.

"Any feelings of a panic attack?" he asked.

She hesitated a moment, as if trying to figure that out, and shook her head. "Too bad, huh? Because a panic attack would have kept us away from each other."

Jodi was right about that. "It's still not a good idea for us to be kissing…or anything else."

No hesitation that time. She quickly nodded, but then

ran her tongue on her bottom lip. She probably hadn't meant it to be sexual, but it certainly felt that way to his body, which was primed and ready to go. Gabriel had to remind his body that it wasn't going to get Jodi.

"But at least now I know," she said. She lifted her shoulder when he stared at her. "Before I was attacked, I thought a lot about kissing you. Now, I can tick that experience off my bucket list."

Yeah, but he was betting her bucket list didn't include dealing with the flames that kiss had fanned inside them.

"Sheriff Beckett?" someone called out. Except it was more of a shout. And Gabriel knew that voice belonged to Hector.

Cameron had been right about Hector not being pleased because when Gabriel opened the door and spotted him, he could see Hector's eyes were narrowed to slits. The narrowing didn't ease up when Hector shifted his attention to Jodi.

"Why the hell did you let him do this?" Hector snarled to her.

Gabriel figured he was the *him* in that question. He also guessed that the guy in the suit next to Hector was his lawyer. The two uniformed SAPD officers behind them signed off on some paperwork that Cameron gave them and headed out—fast. No doubt because it had not been a pleasant ride with Hector to the sheriff's office, and they were eager to get away from him.

"We need you here to answer some questions," Jodi explained to her very riled boss.

"You didn't need the cops for that. I would have come. All you had to do was call and ask."

Gabriel was betting Hector wouldn't have been so

cooperative if anyone but Jodi had made that call. And he wouldn't be so cooperative now, either. Clearly, Hector saw this as a betrayal on Jodi's part, and Gabriel hoped that didn't come back to haunt them.

"You have no grounds to hold my client," the suit snapped.

"Yes, I do." Gabriel motioned for them to follow him into an interview room. "He's connected to the man who was murdered. A cop named Calvin Lasher. Want to tell me about him?" he added once Hector, the lawyer and Gabriel were inside. Jodi stayed in the doorway. Maybe because she knew this was an official interview, and she didn't want to do anything to compromise it.

But it was Hector who waved her in. "You honestly believe I had something to do with a dead cop?"

"Lasher was investigating you," Jodi answered.

If looks could have killed, Hector would have finished Jodi off then and there. Yeah, he definitely saw this as a betrayal, so Gabriel tried to put the focus back on himself.

"Lasher thought you'd broken the law," Gabriel told him. "And since we know you've done that in the past—"

"Don't finish that," Hector warned him. "I didn't do anything wrong." He stopped, huffed, and it seemed to Gabriel that he was trying to rein in his temper. "About a month ago, I got a call from a woman, Kitty Martin. She thought maybe her pimp was bringing in underage girls that he was luring in with drugs. She wanted to go to the cops, but her pimp was violent, and she thought he might kill her."

That all meshed with what they'd learned, but

there were still some gaps in the information. "Lasher thought you'd done an illegal wiretap on the pimp."

Hector was shaking his head before Gabriel even finished. "I had him under surveillance, but that was it. Then, I got a call from Kitty, and she told me to back off, that she didn't want to pursue the case. So, I stopped."

Gabriel couldn't tell if Hector was lying about that or not, and judging from the sound Jodi made, she was in the same boat. "Why put the file under my name?" she asked.

Hector's eyes widened for a moment. Either he was surprised or pretending to be. "Must have been a clerical error. I didn't do it," he added when Jodi and Gabriel just stared at him. He cursed. "If I'd wanted to cover up an involvement in this, why would I have left Kitty's file in the Sentry database?"

"Maybe an oversight on your part," Gabriel readily answered. That earned him a glare from both Hector and his attorney.

"I didn't do anything wrong," Hector repeated, turning that glare on Jodi. "I was just trying to help a woman, the same way I tried to help you ten years ago."

Jodi glanced away, and she said some profanity under her breath. "I will always be thankful for what you did for me," she added, "but Gabriel and I need answers."

"You mean you want to send me to jail," Hector snarled.

"No," Jodi readily argued. "I just want the danger to stop." She paused. "Is it possible that Kitty was setting you up in some way?" Jodi looked at Gabriel to finish that. "Maybe someone posing as a prostitute did this, so they could kill a cop and put the blame on Hector?"

It was a theory. Not necessarily a good one, but Gabriel thought about it for a moment. If this was a copycat killing to clear Travis's name, it didn't make sense to frame Hector. Especially since Hector didn't have an obvious connection to those decade-old crimes. A copycat would have stood a better chance of framing Russell or August.

Of course, maybe Russell or August were behind this.

So, perhaps this was as Jodi had suggested and was simply about getting rid of a cop. Someone other than Hector could have had it out for Lasher. Someone who could have seen Hector as an easy target since he had a police record and maybe the wrong enemy who wanted to eliminate both Lasher and Hector. It was certainly something Hector's lawyer would argue.

And a judge would agree.

Now, Gabriel cursed because that meant he couldn't hold Hector. No way would the charges stick unless he had more evidence. Which he didn't.

Hector smiled as if he knew exactly what conclusion Gabriel had just reached.

"Jodi's in danger," Gabriel reminded the man. That caused Hector's smile to vanish. "I need you to go through all your files and figure out if someone is indeed setting you up. Find me anyone connected to Lasher and you."

Hector nodded, but he still looked riled to the core when he stood and faced Jodi. "So, you're helping Gabriel now?" he asked.

She shrugged. "He and I are in the same proverbial boat."

Hector shifted his gaze to Gabriel, and like before, it seemed as if the man could sense what was going on in Gabriel's head. And what was going on was the very recent memory of kissing Jodi.

"Do you know anything about rattlesnakes being put in Russell Laney's car?" Gabriel asked, and he watched the man's expression.

Surprise followed by annoyance went through Hector's eyes. "Trying to pin something else on me?"

"Just asking. And waiting for an answer."

"No, I didn't," Hector insisted. "That sounds like something a coward would do. I'm not a coward."

He probably wasn't, but that didn't mean Hector hadn't resorted to this low level of intimidation.

"Is my client free to go?" the lawyer asked.

Gabriel took his time nodding and wished that it didn't have to be this way. He wanted to get at least one of their suspects off the street, but apparently that wasn't going to happen today.

Jodi stepped back into the hall so that Hector could leave. The man walked out, shooting her a warning glance from over his shoulder, and his lawyer and he finally left the building. The moment they were outside, Cameron came to them.

"I didn't want to say anything with them here," Cameron started, "but I might have something. I called the prison to see who'd visited Jodi's father in the last month, and an interesting name popped up. Russell. He was there the day before we found Lasher's body."

Well, hell. This might be exactly the connection Gabriel had been looking for.

"I've already got approval from the warden if you want to visit Travis," Cameron added.

"I do," Jodi and Gabriel said in unison.

Since Gabriel doubted there was anything he could say or do to stop her from going with him on this visit, he just motioned for Cameron to follow them.

"Pull the cruiser to the front," he instructed Cameron, "so that Jodi won't have to be outside for very long."

Cameron nodded and headed out.

"You don't have to see your father if you don't want to," Gabriel offered her.

"No. I'm going."

That's exactly what he figured she would say. "How long has it been since you've seen him?"

"Shortly after his conviction eight and a half years ago." She paused. "The last visit didn't go well." Another pause. "He broke down, apologizing for nearly killing me."

That got his attention. "I thought he didn't remember anything about the attacks?"

She blew out a long, weary breath. "He didn't. But after sitting through all the court testimony, he had to consider that he could have possibly done it." She dismissed it with the wave of her hand. "My father is a broken man. I think he would have apologized for anything at that point, and he told me then not to come back. He didn't want me to see him behind bars."

Which would make this visit hard on Travis as well as Jodi. Of course, Gabriel didn't care a rat how Travis felt. He only hoped this wasn't a wasted trip.

The moment that Cameron pulled to a stop in front of the building, Gabriel got Jodi moving. He threw open the back door of the cruiser so she could climb inside, and he quickly followed behind her. However, the moment Cameron drove off, Gabriel's phone rang, and when he saw Jameson's name on the screen, he answered it right away. Since this was almost certainly about Billy, he put the call on speaker so that Jodi and Cameron could hear.

"It was no-go on recording the chat with Billy," Jameson said right off. "Our chat, if you can call it that, only lasted a few minutes. And his attorney and two doctors were there the whole time. Added to that, Billy was higher than a kite."

Gabriel didn't bother groaning since he hadn't expected much to come of it anyway. That's why Jameson surprised him with what he said next.

"Billy kept mentioning rattlesnakes," Jameson continued. "In fact, at first that's all he said while he rocked back and forth and asked for his mommy."

Jodi touched her fingers to her mouth, shook her head. They hadn't needed any other proof that they were dealing with a troubled teenager, but there it was.

"And then as I was leaving," Jameson went on, "Billy said a name. Not Russell. But August."

"Did he connect August to the snakes?" Jodi jumped to ask.

"No. But Billy did say I should watch out or that Uncle August would kill me. Then, he said "bye, Jodi.""

Jodi. Maybe he'd said that because August had mentioned her to Billy. Or it could simply be something Billy had overheard while he was at the sheriff's office.

"Please tell me you found some kind of link between Billy and August," Gabriel said while he kept watch around them. He didn't breathe easier until they were clear of all the buildings on Main Street.

"Not yet. But someone must have told Billy about those rattlesnakes because he was locked up when it happened."

Maybe he'd heard it from the person who'd killed, or who'd put him up to killing, Lasher. But that didn't mean the person was August. As much as it pained Gabriel to admit it, someone could have planted that name in Billy's sick mind. Heck, planted the idea of rattlesnakes, too.

"Jodi and I are going to the jail now to see Travis," Gabriel told his brother, "but when I get back, I'll question August again."

"I can do it. I'm heading back to Blue River right now, and I can call him on the way and have him meet me."

"Thanks." As much as Gabriel wanted to hear what Jodi's uncle had to say, he was already bone tired, and he had to face Travis. Besides, any confrontation with August would include Jodi as well, and Gabriel doubted that she wanted to deal with him, either.

Gabriel ended the call and was putting his phone in his pocket when he glanced at the road ahead. They were still several miles from the interstate and were on a two-lane country road where there was usually little traffic. If this had been normal circumstances, the car ahead of them wouldn't have caught his eye. But since things lately had been far from normal, Gabriel had a closer look.

It was a dark blue four-door, and the driver turned on the right blinker before he pulled onto the shoulder.

Such that it was. It was really just a narrow strip of gravel that divided the farm road from a ditch.

"You think that could be trouble?" Cameron asked.

"Maybe." And just in case it was, Gabriel added to Jodi, "Get down on the seat." Thankfully, she didn't argue, but she did draw her sidearm. So did Gabriel. "Don't stop or slow down," he added to Cameron.

Cameron didn't, but as soon as they got closer to the car, Gabriel saw that the driver's-side window was down.

And that the driver was wearing a ski mask.

Before Gabriel could even react, the ski-masked thug fired a shot directly into the cruiser.

Chapter 11

Jodi didn't see the gunman, but she instantly knew that someone had fired a shot. The sound of it blasted through the air and slammed into the window on the front passenger's side of the cruiser. The glass cracked, but it held, thank God.

She lifted her head to see what was going on, but Gabriel pushed her right back down. However, she did get a glimpse of a man behind the wheel of the car. Since he had a gun in his hand, he was almost certainly the one who'd shot at them.

When he fired two more rounds at them, Jodi had her answer.

"Get us out of here," Gabriel told Cameron.

Cameron did, but Jodi also heard another sound. The squeal of tires from the car that was now behind them. It was coming after them.

Gabriel cursed. "There are at least two of them." One to drive and one to shoot, and that's exactly what was happening.

The bullets continued to slam into the cruiser. So far, the metal and glass were holding, but eventually the shots could make it through. Worse, Cameron couldn't get away from the bullets by going on the interstate. Because there'd be plenty of other vehicles, and an innocent bystander could be killed. Of course, the same could happen if one of the ranchers who lived out this way was on the road at the wrong time.

Gabriel took out his phone, and while she couldn't hear the other end of the conversation, he asked for backup and gave them their location. It wouldn't be long before one of the deputies arrived, and maybe another cruiser could come up behind the car, and they could sandwich in the shooters.

"I want at least one of these clowns alive," Gabriel said under his breath.

Jodi wanted the same thing. Because then they might find out who was behind this. Heck, they might even be able to confront the person directly since it could be any one of their three suspects in that car.

"Hell," Cameron said. He didn't hit the brakes, but he did slow down.

That caused Jodi to peer over the seat again. One look and Jodi was doing some cursing, too. Because straight ahead, sideways on the road, was another car.

Jodi doubted it was a coincidence. And it wasn't. Because almost immediately someone from inside that vehicle started shooting at them.

"I can't get around the car," Cameron said, slowing down even more.

Again, that wasn't a coincidence. So, they'd either have to stop and be sitting ducks caught in cross fire or crash into the car with the hopes of taking out that set of gunmen while not disabling the cruiser.

Not exactly stellar options.

Gabriel glanced at her. "There's not a ranch trail we can use," he let her know.

The gunmen probably knew that, too. And that meant Cameron, Gabriel and she were going to have to fight their way out of this. It wasn't the first time Jodi had been caught in gunfire. There'd been two cases where someone had tried to kill people she'd been assigned to protect. Like those other times, there was no feeling of panic. Strange, but in some ways this felt more comfortable than having someone touch her.

"I'll keep an eye on the guys behind us," she offered, and Gabriel didn't decline. Probably because he knew it would no longer do any good for her to stay down. The closer they got to the second car, the more bullets riddled the cruiser.

Cameron cursed when one of the shots tore through the front windshield. It was just a matter of time before more made it into the interior, and that meant they had to do something fast.

"Slow down enough to minimize the impact for us," Gabriel instructed. "But ram the cruiser right into the shooter."

The shooter wasn't hard to see because he was leaning out of the passenger's side of the second car. "I might be able to take him out," Jodi said. "I'm a good shot."

For a moment she thought Gabriel was about to

agree to that, but two more shots tore through the glass, one in the front and one in the rear.

"Hit the second car!" Gabriel told Cameron. He pushed Jodi back down, but both knew she couldn't stay on the seat. Once they collided, all three of them would have to start firing.

"Hold on," Cameron warned them.

Jodi braced herself for the impact, and she didn't have to wait long. It was only a couple of seconds before she jolted forward, and she heard the slam of metal crashing into metal. Someone yelled out in pain. Probably the gunman in the second car. But that didn't stop the shots. They continued to come at them, shredding what was left of the front and back and windshields.

"Cameron, get down," Gabriel warned him.

Gabriel took aim at whoever was continuing to shoot at them from the second car. That made him an easy target for whoever was behind them. Jodi unbuckled her seat belt, came up on her knees and pivoted in that direction.

And fired.

She took out the shooter who was on the passenger's side. That didn't stop the driver, though.

"He's about to hit us," Jodi shouted, but the words had barely left her mouth when the first car slammed into them.

The jolt sent her flying into both Gabriel and the back of the seat. Her shoulder was hit so hard that it nearly knocked the breath out of her. Gabriel didn't fare much better. He landed partially over the front seat with his head just a few inches from Cameron. That wasn't good. Because the other shooter in the first car was clearly trying to kill him.

Gabriel fixed that.

Cursing, he emptied his clip into the driver of the second car.

The shots stopped then.

From that direction anyway. They continued behind them, and while Gabriel reloaded, both Cameron and she returned fire. She wasn't sure which of them managed to hit the driver, but she finally saw him slump forward onto the steering wheel.

Not dead, though.

He was groaning in pain.

Gabriel finished reloading and threw open the cruiser door. "Cover me," he said, the urgency not just in his voice but in his movements, as well. "I need to get to him before he dies."

Gabriel cursed himself for being too late. He couldn't go back and undo the attack, but in hindsight he should have never agreed to take Jodi to the jail. At least not without more backup. Now, they had four dead men on their hands, and he still didn't have any answers. Because the fourth one had died before Gabriel could question him.

"Anything?" Jodi asked when his phone dinged with a text.

He glanced at the text from Jameson and shook his head. "No ID on the gunmen, but they're running the prints now. Jameson is rescheduling our visit to see your father. We'll go in the morning."

With plenty of extra security. No way did Gabriel want a repeat of today. Judging from Jodi's shell-shocked expression, neither did she.

She was no longer pacing. Probably because the

spent adrenaline had left her too tired to do much of anything. Still, she was searching through Sentry's archived files, trying to find anything that could help them with their investigation. She almost certainly didn't feel like doing that, but it was better than focusing on the fact that they'd come damn close to dying again.

"I nearly got Cameron and you killed," she said, glancing up at him. "I'm sorry."

So that was the reason for the look on her face. Not because she'd been in danger but because Cameron and he had been. Both of them were fine, literally not a scratch on them, but Jodi wasn't seeing that, only the possibility that it could have been much, much worse.

Gabriel sighed and sank down on the sofa beside her. His own legs were feeling the effects of the adrenaline, too, but he was afraid if he stopped moving, he'd crash. Still, he wanted to make something crystal clear, and it was best if he looked her straight in the eyes when he said it.

"Those men could have been after me," he reminded her. "We don't know why we're being attacked, but when the dust settles, I could be the one who owes you an apology."

She shook her head. "I'm the one who made myself bait, and in doing so, I put targets on all of us."

That theory only worked if their attacker was someone trying to cover up nearly killing Jodi ten years ago. But this might not have anything to do with that.

"Maybe your dad can give us some answers tomorrow," Gabriel added. Then, he paused. "Will it do me any good to ask you to stay at the sheriff's office while I go to the jail?"

"No," she immediately answered. "I'm going. Plus, if my father does know anything, he's far more likely to tell me than you. He still considers you the enemy."

No way could he argue with that. Because Gabriel considered Travis the enemy, as well.

"If anyone stays behind, it should be you," Jodi went on. "I can't imagine it'll be easy for you to see the man convicted of murdering your parents."

"It won't be. But I'd visit Travis a thousand times if it meant stopping another attack. Besides, it'll be just as hard for you since he was also convicted of attempting to kill you."

She made a sound of agreement and took a deep breath. "Being here brings it all back." Another deep breath. "But it's not all bad. I'd forgotten that."

Yeah. Easy to forget the good stuff after being knifed and left for dead on the very land where she'd played as a child.

"For as long as I can remember, I've had a crush on you," she said. She winced a little, probably because she hadn't meant to say that out loud.

"I know," he admitted, since she had been so honest. "You used to follow me around and talk to Ivy about me. Once you turned eighteen, she started trying to play matchmaker."

Jodi nodded. "But she didn't get to play it for long. Ivy and I left for college, and when I came back, you were dating that lawyer from over in Appaloosa Pass. When I finally caught you in between women, it was too late."

Because the attack had happened.

The timing had certainly sucked.

"I'm the one who found you," Gabriel admitted. "You didn't remember?"

"No." She stayed quiet a moment and repeated it.

Hell. He shouldn't have brought that up because she got that haunted look again, the one that was deep in her eyes.

"You did CPR on me," she whispered.

Gabriel wanted to drop this, but Jodi was staring at him, waiting for him to say something. "Do you remember that or did someone tell you?"

She moved the laptop to the table, motioned toward her head. "I get little flashes of memories. Pieces. Most of them I push away because of, well, just because. But I remember a little of the CPR. You saved my life."

Believing that had helped him get through some god-awful nightmares, but Gabriel wasn't sure it was true.

She smiled a little. "I thought you were kissing me, but you were giving me mouth-to-mouth. You were giving me your breath."

He was, all the while cursing himself and praying that the ambulance would get there in time. Now, Gabriel cursed himself again because he leaned in and kissed her. Much, much better than mouth-to-mouth and the memories of that.

Well, better for him anyway.

But as he'd done in his office, he pulled away to make sure Jodi was okay with this. Apparently, she was because she slipped her hand around the back of his neck and drew him to her.

No.

That was the thought that went through his mind. Jodi's hand slide was the same as a green light. One that could lead straight to sex. And that couldn't happen. This went back to the bad-timing thing again, but he certainly didn't push her away when she kissed him.

It was Jodi who deepened the kiss. Jodi who pulled him so close to her that they were touching in plenty of the wrong places. Or the right places, he amended, if they were going to have sex.

But they weren't.

She moved, angling herself so that her leg was on the outside of his thigh. Not fully in his lap but close. The kiss, which was already too hot, turned even hotter, and the heat slid right through him. Hard to think with that kind of fire going on inside him. And his body reacted all right.

He went rock hard.

Unlike Jodi. She seemed to be softening. Her silky skin, against his. Her moving in for the taking. Gabriel had to do something to stop this or at least cool it down to give her time to think. Because once she thought about it, Jodi would probably decide this just wasn't a good idea.

"You're a virgin, aren't you?" he said when she broke for air. She also stopped her hand, which was in the process of going to his stomach.

She didn't have to confirm it because he saw in her expression that the answer was yes. Of course, she was. This was a woman who had panic attacks when a man touched her. Well, most men anyway. She didn't seem to be having trouble with the touching now.

She studied his eyes as if trying to figure out what was going on in his head, and she cursed. "I missed my window of opportunity for sex. Because I wanted you to be my first. And then…afterward, because I didn't want to be with anyone."

He got that. "But if we have sex now, it's going to complicate things." That was not only stating the obvious but putting it mildly.

She nodded. "Plus, there's that whole commitment thing you don't want. But what if we take commitment off the table? What if this is only about sex for us?"

Gabriel gave her a flat look to let her know that wasn't possible. She must have believed it, too, because Jodi cursed again and moved off him.

"It would have been a bad idea anyway," she said, but it didn't sound as if she believed it.

Because he still had an erection, Gabriel didn't believe it, either.

Thankfully, his phone buzzed again, giving them a much-needed interruption, and since it was Jameson's name on the screen, it could turn out to be important.

"It didn't take long for us to get IDs on the dead guys," Jameson said the moment Gabriel answered. He put the call on speaker so Jodi could hear. "That's because all four had prints in the system. Kevin McKee, Scott Hartman, Walter Bronson and Barry Hiller."

She repeated the names and shook her head. "I don't recognize any of them."

"Neither do I," Gabriel agreed. "What do you know about them?"

"That they're not from here. McKee and Hiller are from Houston. The other two are from Laredo. There's something not quite right about this," Jameson added. "These guys were thugs. Long police records. Drug users. In and out of jail. Not the sort to hire out for an attack on two lawmen and a security specialist."

Gabriel thought about that for a moment. "You believe they were hired because they'd work cheap?"

"That's exactly what I'm thinking. I'm betting these clowns came after you for just a couple of thousand dollars."

Which would make it next to impossible to find a money trail. Any of their three suspects could have that kind of cash on hand. Still, it had to be a risk to hire someone who was underqualified and maybe even high.

And Gabriel thought that might point to Hector. Because Jodi's boss dealt with criminals like this.

"Did these thugs have cell phones?" Gabriel asked.

"No. No IDs on them, either. Nothing in their pockets and nothing in the cars. We might be able to get something on those, but they're late models, so it's possible the person behind this bought them used through someone online."

Again, hard to trace that.

"I'll keep looking," Jameson said. "We can't keep having this string of bad luck."

You'd think they would get a break. Gabriel just hoped it was sooner than later.

He was about to thank his brother, but Jameson spoke before Gabriel could say anything. "Hold on a second. I'm getting another call from Cameron."

Cameron was supposed to be home, having some downtime after the attack, but Gabriel suspected the deputy was already back at work. He certainly would be, but he didn't want to have to take Jodi out in the open. They'd already had one attack too many today.

The seconds crawled by with Jodi making uneasy glances at him and the phone. It seemed to take an eternity for Jameson to come back on the line, and when he did Gabriel knew it was bad because Jameson cursed.

"It's Billy," Jameson said. "Someone murdered him."

Chapter 12

Every muscle in Jodi's body seemed to be aching, and her head was throbbing. That probably had a lot to do with the fact that she hadn't slept and was using caffeine to help her stay alert.

It wasn't a good idea to go into a visit with her father when she couldn't think straight, but she had no choice. Now more than ever, they needed answers.

Because someone had murdered Billy.

The one person who could have possibly cleared all of this up.

It was hard to grieve for him. After all, Billy had likely murdered a cop, but he'd no doubt been manipulated into it. It was a sick, dangerous person who would do something like that to a mentally disturbed teenager.

A smart person, too.

According to the preliminary report, someone had

injected Billy with a lethal dose of barbiturates. And the suspect? His high-priced lawyer, Mara Rayburn. The problem, though, was that Mara was missing.

"Are you okay?" Gabriel asked, pulling Jodi out of her thoughts. He was seated next to her in the prison visiting area where they were expecting her father to arrive at any minute. He wouldn't actually be in the room with them but rather on the other side of some thick Plexiglas.

"I'm okay about this visit," she said, choosing her words. The rest of her was pretty much spent. She was tired and confused. Confused not just about who wanted to kill them but also her feelings for Gabriel.

Until she'd come back to Blue River, Jodi had been so certain that what she'd once felt for him was long gone. She had also been sure that she would never again want a man to touch her.

Well, she'd been wrong about that.

She had certainly wanted Gabriel to touch her after the latest attack. Even after "sleeping" on it, she should have realized that would be a mistake. But it didn't feel as if it'd be one. And that was a problem. Because the last thing they needed right now was to have their thoughts straying in the wrong direction. She had a strong suspicion that handing Gabriel her virginity would drop them smack-dab in the "wrong direction" category.

"It'd be so much easier if I hated you," she admitted. That caused him to smile. Which, in turn, caused her to go all warm.

She so didn't have time for this.

"Part of you probably does hate me," he answered. He was talking about the attack now, but somehow even it had changed in her mind. Not the attack itself but rather her blaming Gabriel. He'd saved her, and no part of her body or mind was going to let her forget that.

The side door finally opened, and Jodi felt herself go stiff when she spotted her father. The past eight years had obviously been hard on him, and he looked several decades older than he actually was. But his eyes seemed to be clearer than ever. Probably because he wasn't drinking.

Her father glanced at Gabriel, and she didn't see a trace of the bitterness that she'd expected. In fact, Travis nodded a friendly greeting to him, then to her as the guard ushered him to the chair behind the glass. He didn't move fast because both his hands and feet were chained, and those chains rattled as he sank down across from them.

"Thank you for coming," he said. His voice had aged, too. It cracked from the hoarseness. "It's good to see you, finally." He stopped, and it seemed as if he was trying to rein in his emotions. "God, I've missed you."

"I miss you, too. And it's good to see you, but it's not a social visit," Jodi clarified.

She hated that she had practically snapped it because it put some sadness in her father's eyes. Since he was a convicted killer, he didn't need anyone, especially her, to add sadness to the obvious miserable life he already had behind bars.

Travis nodded. "I suspected as much. Still, I'm glad you're here. I think about you all the time."

Jodi could say the same about him. In fact, she gave him too much thought, considering that remembering him only brought back the images of the night she'd nearly died.

Well, mostly that's what it brought back.

There were other memories of those times when he hadn't been so drunk that he had been a father to her. That didn't make this visit easier. Because part of her—the girl who hadn't been stabbed yet—wanted to hang on to those rare good times, and she couldn't. She didn't want that coming into play as she tried to get to the truth.

Travis shifted his attention to Gabriel. "This is about the attacks?"

"Yeah. How did you know about them?" Gabriel asked.

"August." A weary sigh left his mouth. Maybe his brother was wearing on his nerves the way he was wearing on everyone else's. "He visits me at least once a week. He thinks all this mess that's going on will help clear my name, but the only thing I want is for them to stop." He paused. "Were either of you hurt?"

Jodi shook her head. "But some gunmen were killed. Thugs. So was a teenage boy who got caught in the middle of this. Did August happen to mention that? Better yet, did he say anything about hiring them?"

Her father didn't seem surprised by the questions, and he certainly didn't jump to defend his brother. However, his mouth did tighten, the way it would when a person was going to have to talk about something unsettling.

"I told August that he'd better not do a single thing to harm you. Or you," he added to Gabriel. "You've both been through enough hell."

Yes, they had, but Jodi suspected the trip through Hades was far from being over. Until they had a name, the attacks would continue and wouldn't stop until someone else was dead.

"Did August say anything to implicate himself in these attacks?" Gabriel asked.

"No. He's too smart for that. Too loyal to me, as well." Travis groaned, shook his head. "God knows I don't deserve it."

Her father had definitely changed. This wasn't the defiant drunk who'd made so many people's lives miserable. Including hers. He'd never been physically abusive, but he'd had a razor-sharp tongue and an awful temper when the booze was in him. And the booze was often in him.

"I'm sorry," her father continued, still talking to Gabriel. "I'm scared for Jodi and you. Equally scared for your brother and sisters. For Theo. But I honestly don't know who's behind what's going on. If it's August, he hasn't given me any hint of it. And he won't. First, because he knows I absolutely wouldn't approve. Plus, he also knows our conversations are being recorded."

"What about Russell?" she asked. "He visited you. Did he mention anything about what's been going on?"

Travis nodded. "He did, but he didn't bring up the attacks. It's the second time he's come. He was here a few years back, not long after I was convicted."

This was the first she was hearing of that original visit. But then she hadn't exactly stayed in touch with either Russell or her father. Still, she had to wonder why Russell would have done that. It wasn't as if Russell and she had ever had a real relationship.

"What did Russell want?" Gabriel pressed.

"The first time he came, it was because he was mad about being a suspect in the murders and in Jodi's attack. He said it'd messed up his life, and he blamed me. Russell thought if I'd just confessed right off, that he wouldn't have been brought into it. But I couldn't confess to something I didn't remember."

Since Gabriel's arm was touching hers, she felt him tense. Probably because this was bringing back the mother lode of memories for him.

"I still don't remember," Travis added, "but I'm not whining about being innocent. Because I'm probably not. There was enough evidence to convict me, and I'll live with that. Die with it, too," he said under his breath.

She wasn't immune to hearing him spell everything out so clearly. No matter what he'd done, he was still her father, and she felt that biological connection tug at her. It was probably doing a lot more than just tugging at Gabriel, though. It was likely twisting him inside, and that's why she slid her hand over his.

Gabriel glanced at her, their gazes connecting for just a second. Since his mouth tensed, he was probably questioning what she was doing, but it didn't take long before he gripped her hand in his.

"Russell said you two were back together," Travis commented.

That caused both Jodi and Gabriel to snap toward him. "We're not," she assured him. "In fact, Gabriel and I have never been together."

Best not to mention that kiss and near-sex from the night before. Especially since there was something much more pressing to ask.

Jodi looked straight in her father's eyes. "Why did Russell come to visit you this second time?"

"He said it was because of an email threat he got. He thought maybe I was behind it, and he was worried about his wife and baby. Can't say I blame him, especially considering somebody murdered that cop and keeps trying to murder you."

Those emails definitely hadn't been empty threats, so Travis was right about Russell's concern. Two people were dead, along with some gunmen, and Gabriel, Cameron and she had come close to dying. No way did Jodi want an innocent baby to be caught up in another round of gunfire.

"I told Russell I had no idea who was doing all of this," her father went on. "I mean, I get *fan* letters, if you can call 'em that, but I don't answer them. Those people who write those letters are sick. And none of them have ever said anything about copycatting the crimes to set me free. The guards can verify that because they read everything before it comes to me." He paused again. "But I got the feeling Russell was here for more than just concerns about that email."

"What do you mean?" Gabriel snapped, taking the question right out of Jodi's mouth.

"Russell asked if I remember seeing anything that night. Specifically, he wanted to know if I remembered seeing Hector March around the Beckett ranch before or after the murders. I didn't know Hector, so Russell showed me a picture of him."

Maybe Russell was doing what Gabriel and she were—following the leads. But that wasn't a safe thing to be doing if he truly wanted to keep his wife and baby out of this. If Gabriel and she had found out Russell had visited the prison, then Hector or August could have learned it, too.

"And had you seen Hector?" Jodi pressed when her father didn't continue.

"He sort of looked familiar, but I couldn't be sure. Remember, I was drinking a lot in those days, and it's hard to sort it all out in my mind. It's possible, though, that I saw him at my trial."

Gabriel looked at her, no doubt wondering if that could have happened, and she had to nod. Hector had indeed come to the courthouse on the day she'd had to testify. He hadn't come into the courtroom itself, but he'd been in the hall, so there was a chance that her father had gotten a glimpse of him.

"August said you might be remembering more of what happened to you ten years ago," Travis said.

This was tricky territory. If she told the truth and admitted there were no new memories, it wouldn't stop the danger because her attacker might think she was lying. Besides, she wasn't sure she wanted to share any info like that with her father because he might just pass it along to August.

Plus, she *was* remembering.

When Gabriel had kissed her, her mind had slipped into a dreamy haze. Maybe it was because the kiss had caused her to relax, and she'd gotten some bit of the memories of him trying to revive her on that blood-spattered trail. If that had come back, maybe some of the other pieces would, too.

"I recalled the sound of his footsteps," she said. It was the truth. But that was a memory she'd had right from the start. "And grabbing the knife." That was a lie, but the prints proved she'd touched it.

"But you don't remember seeing his face?" her father pressed.

She studied his eyes, looking for any sign that he was worried about her recovering that particular memory, and she did see some concern. However, she didn't think it was for him but, rather, for her.

Jodi shook her head. "What about you? Have you remembered anything? Maybe dropping the knife? If you had done that, then someone else could have picked it up and used it on me."

Now, it was her father's turn to shake his head. "There are gaps in what went on that night, and some of that is just blank space. I remember arguing with Gabriel's dad about our cows that were breaking through his fences. After that, I got drunk, and I recall seeing Cameron. He took my truck keys 'cause I was trying to drive off from the bar, and he had somebody take me home. I kept drinking when I got there."

And she hadn't been at the house to stop him because she'd been at the Becketts. Of course, Cameron blamed himself, too, since he hadn't just arrested Travis and locked him up for the night. Jodi had given up on wondering "what might have been," but it was as if the fates had worked to bring about the murders and her attack.

"Other than the memories of drinking once I got home," her father went on, "there's nothing after that until the deputies found me by the river. I don't have a clue how I got there."

It was the same story her father had told after he'd been taken into custody, and it hadn't changed a bit over the years. She didn't know if that meant it was the truth or if he had made sure there were no variations to prove he was lying. Too bad she might never know which it was.

"Tell me about Hattie Osmond," Gabriel said, surprising her. Surprising her father, too, judging by the way his forehead bunched up. "Did you ever see her with August?"

"Probably. I mean, she lived not far from us. Why?"

Gabriel lifted his shoulder. "It might be nothing, but it's possible someone was milking money from her."

Travis stayed quiet a moment. "And you believe it could have been August?" He didn't wait for Gabriel to confirm that. "If it was him, then that would give him motive for murdering your father?"

Bingo. But she could tell from her dad's expression that it was a connection he wasn't going to make. Or else he didn't want to make.

Travis dragged in a weary breath. "August has been good to me, and I talk to him a lot. Never once has he hinted that I'm here because of something he did."

That didn't mean it wasn't true. And it could explain why August was so hell-bent on clearing her father's name. What was missing, though, was any kind of proof. However, if they could connect August to the recent attacks, they might be able to get him to confess to things that happened a decade ago.

"Visiting time's up," one of the guards said to them. Both guards then went to Travis and helped him stand.

Travis made eye contact with her. "Thanks for coming." Then, he shifted his attention to Gabriel. "Don't let this SOB get to her again."

Gabriel nodded, but Jodi knew this was out of Gabriel's hands. He had already tied up three of his deputies just so they could make this trip to the prison. But he couldn't keep that kind of protection detail on her forever. That meant she either had to go into hiding or bring this monster out into the open.

She preferred doing the latter.

She'd lived enough of her life in the shadows, fearing another attack. Maybe it was time to face this head-on and, one way or another, bring it to an end.

Gabriel and she walked out after they ushered her father away. The moment they were back in the entry, Gabriel got back his weapon and phone, and he immediately called Cameron. Probably so the deputy could bring the cruiser to the front of the building.

"There's a problem," she heard Cameron say from the other end of the line.

Gabriel cursed and moved her to the side away from the door. "What happened?" he snapped.

"We found Billy's lawyer. And it's not good news."

Chapter 13

Dead.

Gabriel wondered just how high this body count was going to go before he could finally arrest someone and put a stop to it. The latest casualty was Mara Rayburn, Billy's high-priced attorney, but in the end she hadn't fared any better than her client. Because now both of them had been murdered.

The moment Gabriel had Jodi in the back seat of the police cruiser, Cameron handed him his phone so that Gabriel could see what the SAPD officer had sent him about Mara. While Gabriel did that, Cameron started driving away from the prison. Fast. He was following Gabriel's orders since he didn't want Jodi on the roads any longer than necessary.

There was another cruiser directly behind them with two deputies inside. Jace Morrelli and Edwin Clary. All of them were prepared for a possible attack, but Gabriel hadn't braced himself nearly enough for the picture that was on Cameron's phone. One obviously taken from the most recent crime scene at the lawyer's condo.

The woman had been stabbed multiple times and had died in a pool of her own blood.

Jodi cursed, glanced away from the phone, and Gabriel cursed himself for not screening her from seeing the images. She already had enough nightmares without adding this.

"While you were inside talking to Travis, I've been getting a lot of updates," Cameron went on after he mumbled an apology to Jodi. An apology that she waved off, and she probably would have gone back for a second look at Mara if Gabriel hadn't handed Cameron the phone. "The ME doesn't have an exact time of death yet, but it appears she died shortly after Billy was killed."

So, if they went with their theory that Mara had murdered Billy, then someone had probably done this to make sure she stayed silent. That someone was no doubt the person behind the attacks.

"Mara's coworkers believe she was having an affair," Cameron went on, "and they said she seemed upset lately, like maybe the affair wasn't going so well. Of course, she could have been upset because she was plotting to murder her teenage client. That means if we can find her alleged lover, then perhaps we find the person who really did this."

"Her coworkers didn't know who her lover is… was?" Jodi corrected.

"No. They said she kept it secret. Who knows if that was her choice, or her lover's."

Yes, because if the killer's plan all along was to manipulate Billy and then have Mara off him, then no way would this snake want people to know who he was. It might not have started out that way, though. The affair could have started first, and then both Mara and, therefore, Billy could have been roped into committing murder. Then again, Mara could have agreed to all of this to please the man she "loved," and when the man was through with her, he killed her.

"There's more," Cameron continued. "Mara had a connection to our four dead thugs."

"I'm listening," Gabriel assured him. And so was Jodi. She'd moved to the edge of her seat.

"She once defended one of them, Walter Bronson, when she was doing pro bono work, and her coworkers said he recently showed up at her office. The thugs were friends, so it's possible she only had to convince Bronson to go after us yesterday, and he brought his buddies along to help."

That made sense, but Gabriel was betting that Mara hadn't been pleased about the gunman going to her office. "Is there a money trail that leads to Mara?" Gabriel asked.

"She withdrew about three grand yesterday morning. That could have been a partial payment or payment in full. I'm guessing the thugs worked cheap."

Jodi made a soft groan. "They were willing to kill us for what was probably pocket change to Mara."

Gabriel heard the disgust in her voice. The pain, too. All of this had to be clawing away at her, and there was nothing he could do to stop it.

Not yet anyway.

"SAPD thinks Mara knew her killer," Cameron explained. "There were no signs of forced entry into her condo, no signs of a struggle. Her attacker had simply gone in and started stabbing her. Her phone was in her pocket, and she hadn't even taken it out."

As she'd done to him, Gabriel slipped his hand over Jodi's. Yeah, definitely clawing away at her.

"The CSIs are still going through her condo," Cameron said a moment later. He, too, was checking Jodi's response in the rearview mirror. "Maybe they'll find something there to connect her to this secret lover. I told them to specifically look and see if there's anything to indicate if that lover could be Hector, Russell or August."

Jodi nodded. "That would be nice if it were all tied in a neat little package. But I doubt she left anything behind, and even if she had, the killer would have taken it." She paused. "What about surveillance cameras at her condo?"

"There weren't any, but SAPD said they'd check traffic cameras. If we have video proof that either Hector, August or Russell was near her condo, that might be enough to get an arrest warrant."

Coupled with the other circumstantial evidence they'd found, it should be, but they were still a long way from putting someone behind bars. Plus, SAPD would have jurisdiction in this, so Gabriel might not be able to interrogate a suspect even if the San Antonio cops did manage to take someone into custody.

"You want me to take you two back to the office or to your place?" Cameron asked.

One look at Jodi, and Gabriel knew the answer. She was exhausted and probably hungry. "To my house." Other than interviewing suspects, he could do pretty much everything else from his home office.

Jodi moved back, resting her head against the seat, and she closed her eyes. Gabriel doubted she was actually sleeping. More like trying to get rid of the images of seeing a butchered woman. No way for him to get rid of it. Because it had triggered the memories of how he'd found Jodi.

Since there was nothing he could say to her to help, Gabriel decided to get some work done. He texted Jameson to find out if he'd learned anything new on any of the legs of the investigation. No updates with the exception that his brother had managed to get access to Hector's bank account. Since Hector was a security expert, Gabriel doubted he'd left a money trail, but if someone had used such a trail to try to set the man up, then that part of it might be traceable.

The miles and minutes crawled by with Gabriel checking his phone while he continued to keep watch around him. Cameron and the other deputies were no doubt doing the same, but there wasn't even a hint of trouble.

Not until Cameron arrived at the ranch. That's when Gabriel spotted someone he didn't want to see on the front porch of the old house, the one where his parents had been murdered.

August was waiting for them on the steps.

His car was parked on the side by some shrubs.

Jodi groaned, and that's when Gabriel realized her eyes were not only open but that she, too, had spotted her uncle. "What's he doing here?" she muttered.

Gabriel didn't know, but he intended to find out fast and then get rid of him. No way did he want one of their suspects hanging around Jodi or anywhere near the ranch.

Cameron pulled to a stop, and Gabriel threw open the door. "Wait in the cruiser," he told both of them. Cameron would, but he figured Jodi had no intention of doing that.

August stood, staggering a little, and that's when Gabriel noticed he had a bottle of whiskey on the steps where he'd been sitting. "You had Jameson haul me in like a common criminal," August snarled.

"Not common," Gabriel corrected. "You're a suspect in a murder investigation. That makes you far from common."

"Well, I didn't do it." His words were slurred, so he was clearly past the "having a drink or two" stage. He certainly wasn't in any shape to drive, so that meant two deputies would have to take him home. Gabriel didn't like to split his security detail like that, but he hadn't planned on them staying once he had Jodi inside his house.

"I didn't have anything to do with those snakes," August went on, "or with trying to hurt Jodi. I wouldn't do that. Do you know how pissed off Travis would be with me if he thought for one minute that I'd tried to hurt his little girl?"

"He wouldn't be happy," Jodi said, stepping from the car. "Now, what do you want?"

"I want you to tell everyone that I'm not guilty of all this bad stuff I'm getting accused of. I'm just doing what you should be doing—busting your butt to clear your daddy's name so he won't end up dying behind bars."

"You sound like a man with a guilty conscience," Gabriel remarked. He moved away from August so he could stand near Jodi. He also motioned for Cameron and the other deputies to keep watch. He didn't want Jodi gunned down while trying to get info from a drunk man.

August shot him a glare. It didn't last because August staggered again and had to catch on to the step railing to stop himself from falling.

"Russell's wife came to see me this morning," August went on. "Tracy. She's a pretty little thing, but she was boo-hooing about her husband. She's scared he's going to be hurt or killed because of Jodi."

"Was Russell with her?" Gabriel asked.

"No. And she said I wasn't to tell him, that he wouldn't like it if she stuck her nose in his business."

Interesting choice of words, but of course, Gabriel was hearing it secondhand, so there was no telling what she'd actually said. Still, it wouldn't hurt for someone to question the woman. While he was at it, he could arrange for Hector's employees to be interviewed, as well.

"Take August home," Gabriel instructed Cameron.

August didn't put up an argument. He started for the cruiser just as Gabriel went with Jodi to the second one.

"I told Hector about you and Jodi," August said, stopping in his tracks. Jodi quit walking, too.

"Told him what?" she asked.

"That you two were sleeping together." August smiled, and it wasn't a pleasant one. "Want to know what Hector said?" he continued before Gabriel or Jodi could say anything. "He called you an ungrateful bitch and said you'd be sorry."

Jodi had certainly been called worse than the *B*-word. But never by Hector.

"August could be lying," Gabriel reminded her.

He could be. In fact, he probably was. But there was some truth in what he was saying. If Hector did indeed believe that Gabriel and she were lovers, then he wouldn't be happy about that. Jodi had seen how he'd behaved in the past couple of days, and plain and simple, he was jealous.

"I need to find a new job," she said as they made their way into Gabriel's house.

He immediately set the security system and moved her away from the windows. She was already heading away from them anyway since she wanted to sit down on the sofa. Her legs no longer felt steady.

"I could hire you as a deputy," Gabriel offered.

She looked at him and saw that he was already regretting that. "I doubt it would work out. Since you'd be my boss."

No need to say more, because it was clear that this attraction wasn't going away. Best not to bring that into the workplace. And if she worked for him, that would put them in constant contact each day. He wanted that contact but didn't especially want her to have a job where she could be required to put her life on the line.

Gabriel glanced out the window and gave a thumbs-up to Deputy Jace Morrelli, who'd be patrolling the grounds. There was a lot of ground to cover, which meant all of them were far from safe, but they couldn't keep everything fully guarded.

"Besides," she went on a moment later. "I have that badge-phobia thing." She was only half kidding, but the thought kept coming back to her—badges hadn't done a darn thing to keep his folks from dying or her from being attacked. "I need to find something that doesn't involve Hector."

Jodi cursed when her voice cracked. Cursed even more when the tears burned her eyes. "I'm not crying about Hector," she insisted. "I just hate knowing that I dragged you into this."

There was suddenly a lot of cursing going on, and it was coming from Gabriel. He sank down next to her. "Whatever you're thinking, the answer is no. You're not going to make yourself bait to protect me, and you're not going on the run to try to distance me from the danger."

Since those were the exact things she'd been thinking about doing, she just gave him a flat look. Well, as flat as she could manage, considering she was very close to tears again.

"I'm so tired of being afraid," she admitted. Of course, that wasn't the right thing to say to help with the tears or to steady her nerves. But Gabriel had something that worked.

He kissed her.

Even though he was already right there next to her, she hadn't seen the kiss coming, and despite the sizzle of heat she instantly felt, it didn't seem to be one generated by passion on his part. She figured that out when he pulled back, and she saw his eyes.

"You're distracting me," she said.

He certainly didn't deny it. "Did it work?"

It did. And there was no need for her to confirm that with words because the corner of his mouth kicked up. The smile didn't last, but he did brush his fingers on her cheek. Then, groaned.

"Eventually we're going to land in bed." His voice was a husky whisper. "I'm just trying for it not to be now. I don't think you could handle *now*."

Jodi wanted to assure him that she could, but that was attraction nudging her in his direction. The truth was, she could have a panic attack when they were only a few kisses in. She'd had attacks triggered by far less contact.

He didn't say anything for several moments, but she could see the debate he was having with himself. A debate he apparently lost.

Because he kissed her again.

This time she didn't feel the doubt or hesitation. And it didn't seem to be a distraction, either. Gabriel kissed her, sliding his hand around the back of her neck and pulling her to him.

Her stomach fluttered. Her heart began to race. It took her a moment to realize that it wasn't the beginnings of panic, but rather, it was pleasure.

Mercy, was it ever.

The heat from his kiss warmed her from head to toe, and she let that silky feeling wash over her. It both calmed and excited her, and it didn't take long before Jodi put her arms around him.

"You can stop this at any time," he assured her.

His voice only made her hotter. Of course, the kiss that followed his "stop" reminder probably had plenty to do with that increase in heat. The old feelings returned. Those days when she'd daydreamed about being with Gabriel just like this. Her, in his arms. Him, kissing her.

He lowered his hand from her neck to her back, all the while nudging her closer. Definitely no feelings of panic from this kind of contact. It felt natural.

Necessary.

As if she'd been starved for a very long time and

was finally getting what she needed. And apparently what she needed was Gabriel.

He lowered the kisses to her neck, pausing between each one, no doubt to give her a chance to tell him to stop. But Jodi couldn't see herself saying that anytime soon.

She moved her hand, too. To his chest, and she slid her fingers over the muscles there. All toned and perfect, Gabriel had always had a great body. She got to see some of that body when she undid the buttons on his shirt. Then, she touched bare skin and got a nice reward when he grunted with pleasure.

So, she touched him again. While he took those wildfire kisses lower, to the tops of her breasts, she pushed open his shirt. He was still wearing a shoulder holster, so she couldn't get it all the way off, but she saw enough of him to kick up her pulse another notch.

"Remember, we don't have to keep doing this," he repeated. He slipped his hand under her shirt and did some touching of his own. Each stroke of his fingers created new fires and sent her soaring.

Jodi forgot how to breathe.

And didn't care if she ever remembered.

He didn't take off her top. Maybe because he knew it would bother her for him to see the scars, but Gabriel did lower his head, and he kissed them, one by one. But he didn't stop there. He kept kissing, going lower to the front of her jeans.

Oh, man.

That was what she wanted, and it didn't take much of that before Jodi was searching for his zipper. He stopped her by unzipping her first. The touches on her stomach were mild compared to what she felt when he slid his hand into her jeans. And then her panties. He pushed his fingers through the slick heat he found and nearly caused her to scream.

In a good way.

The pleasure soared, so intense that Jodi wasn't sure she could take it. But she did. And Gabriel clearly had plans to do more than touch.

"Should we stop?" he asked.

"No." She didn't have to think about that, either.

She wasn't sure if he was relieved, but he did start to shimmy her jeans off her. Jodi helped, though she was trembling now. Not from fear or panic but because Gabriel kept adding some of those slick strokes in between the undressing.

By the time he had finally removed her jeans and panties, Jodi was more than ready to have him haul her off to bed. But he didn't do that. He hauled her onto his lap instead. She was about to protest, but then he kissed her again, and that rid her of any doubts that this was the right way to go.

She reached between them, finally locating his zipper, and she freed him from his boxers while he fumbled in his pocket. Then, his wallet. To take out a condom, she realized. Jodi had been so caught up in the heat of the moment that she'd forgotten all about safe sex. At least Gabriel had remembered.

There was just a jolt of panic when she saw him put on the condom, but again, that vanished when he kissed her. He also reminded her once again that they could stop. That's when Jodi took matters into her own hands. Literally. The moment Gabriel had gotten the condom on, she took hold of him and guided his erection inside her.

She got another jolt. Just a quick pinch of pain—that she ignored. Because there were much, much better feelings to focus on. Like this heat that was burning her from the inside out.

Gabriel didn't move. He gave her a moment, probably to adjust, but it wasn't a moment she wanted. Jodi started to move, and even though she didn't have a clue what she was doing, she went with what felt right.

He helped. Gabriel caught on to her hips with one hand, and he slid the other one between her legs. At first she had no idea why he'd done that. But she soon found out. He used those maddening touches in just the right place while the strokes inside her continued.

It didn't take long for her body to respond to that. In fact, it was too short. She wanted to hang on to this moment for a long, long time. But there was no way she could last. Gabriel made sure of that. He kept touching. Kept moving inside her. Until everything pinpointed to just him.

He pushed her right to the point where she could take no more. And then with one last touch, Gabriel sent her flying.

Chapter 14

Gabriel hadn't remembered a mistake ever being this good. But despite the slack feeling he had from the great sex, he still had enough common sense to know that he shouldn't have done this.

This was a complication neither of them needed.

And it would be a complication all right. Not just because here he was holding her in bed but because he wanted to keep holding her.

He couldn't, and that's why Gabriel forced himself from the bed so he could pull on his jeans and go back into the living room to check his laptop. Even though it was already after regular duty hours, there could still be reports coming in. Updates. Hell, the world could have ended in the past couple of hours, and he wouldn't have even noticed it.

That's because he'd made another mistake by taking Jodi a second time.

She definitely hadn't said no, and he'd been counting on her doing just that. Because he certainly hadn't had the willpower to turn her away—as he'd done ten years ago.

He put on his shoulder holster—old habits—and grabbed a slice of leftover pizza from the fridge before he sat down to boot up his computer. Six emails from Jameson and all of them were about the dead lawyer. The first two weren't good news, either.

SAPD hadn't been able to find a security or traffic camera yet that had been at the right angle to see who'd gone into Mara's condo complex and knifed her to death. Jameson had managed a phone conversation with Russell's wife, Tracy, but it'd been a bust because Russell had told his wife to hang up—and she had. Russell might have just wanted to protect her, and he might not know that Tracy had paid August a visit.

Gabriel went to the next message. Photos of both Billy's and Mara's crime scenes. Photos that Jodi wouldn't be seeing. The next email was a lab report on the drugs Billy had been given, and which caused him to overdose.

And then Gabriel got to the last email.

Hell.

It was yet another picture, and according to Jameson, it was a note that the cops had found beneath Mara's body. It was just two words, scrawled on a piece of paper.

For Jodi.

If Gabriel had had any doubts that Billy's and Mara's deaths weren't connected to what'd happened a decade ago, that would have cleared them up. Because it was linked even if it was solely due to someone trying to cover their tracks.

He heard Jodi stirring in the bedroom and immediately closed the email. A moment later, she came in. She yawned, pushed her hair from her face and smiled at him.

She'd gotten dressed, but she still looked rumpled. Damn attractive, too. The woman certainly knew how to make his body notice her. He also noticed her weapons. She had put them on, as well. Apparently, he wasn't the only one with some old habits. But despite the fact that they were behind locked doors and the security system was on, it still didn't feel safe.

Maybe no place would.

"Apparently, sex is the cure for panic attacks," she said. "Or maybe you're the cure. Either way, I'm hungry." She started toward the kitchen but then stopped. Probably because she'd noticed the worried expression on his face.

"What happened?" she asked.

It was a cheap, dirty trick, but he went to her and kissed her. He thought maybe she still had enough post-sex haze for it to work at distracting her. It didn't.

"Is someone else dead?" she pressed.

Since her mind was already leaping to a worst-case scenario, Gabriel knew he had to tell her the truth. Or rather, show her. He reopened the email and turned the laptop so she could see the message and Jameson's remark.

"Oh." That's all she said for several seconds, and then Jodi sat on the sofa. "I guess whoever's after me wants to rub salt in the wound."

It seemed that way to Gabriel, as well. And he was afraid the salt-rubbing would continue with another attack. That was probably why he went on full alert when he heard the movement in front of his house. Gabriel jumped to his feet, and in the same motion he drew his gun. Jodi drew her weapon as well, but he made sure he was in front of her when they went to the window to look out.

And he cursed.

"Hector," he said under his breath.

Jodi's boss was in the front yard. And he wasn't alone. Deputy Jace Morrelli was with him, and judging from Jace's expression, he wasn't any more pleased about this visit than Gabriel was. Not only was Hector a suspect, his car wasn't anywhere in sight, which meant he might have been trying to sneak up on them and that Jace had caught him.

Hector looked up at the window, making eye contact with Gabriel, and while the man didn't have a gun in his hand, Gabriel figured he was heavily armed. That's why Gabriel told Jodi to stay back. He disarmed the security system and opened the door just a fraction.

"What the hell are you doing here?" Gabriel demanded.

Hector spared him a glance. "Protecting Jodi. Something that I've been doing quite well for the past ten years. She comes back here, to you, and twice someone's tried to kill her."

"Because her attacker is afraid she's remembered his face. You think it's your face she'll remember?"

Now, Hector did more than glance at him. He turned, his hard stare drilling into Gabriel. Even though the sun was already setting, and there wasn't a lot of light,

Gabriel had no trouble seeing the hatred in the man's eyes. Or the fact that Hector was armed to the hilt, along with wearing a bulletproof vest.

"I told him to leave," Jace said.

Good. Because it saved Gabriel from telling Hector that himself.

"I was just going back to my car," Hector insisted. "There's no law against a man sitting in his own car on the road." He made an uneasy glance around. "Someone's trying to set me up. Maybe August or Russell."

"They claim someone's trying to set them up, too," Jodi said. "And they believe you might be doing that."

She stepped to Gabriel's side. Well, as much of his side as she could manage since he was taking up most of the doorway, and he didn't intend to go out on the porch with Hector where the man could maybe try to gun him down.

Hector nodded, readily admitting that. "One of us is probably guilty, and it isn't me. That means someone is making himself look bad to get the limelight off him."

That was Gabriel's theory, too.

Hector shifted his gaze back to Jodi, and while she was fully clothed, Gabriel figured the man knew what had gone on tonight. What Gabriel couldn't tell was if Hector's tight expression was because he was jealous or just concerned about Jodi. Either way, he couldn't take the chance that it was the jealousy.

"Leave," Gabriel warned Hector.

For a couple of long moments, Gabriel thought he was going to have to arrest the man, but Hector finally turned and started walking away.

"Follow him to his car," Gabriel told Jace, and Gabriel intended to stand there and watch. If Hector was guilty and desperate, he might decide to try to shoot the deputy.

"Any chance Hector would have brought some of his security guys with him?" Gabriel asked while he glanced around the grounds.

"No. Hector works alone." She paused. "But if he's truly innocent, he could have come here with the hopes of trying to draw out the killer. Of course, that would only work if the killer was watching us."

Gabriel had the sickening feeling that he was. And no, he wasn't ruling out Hector. In fact, the man could have come here to set up cameras or listening devices, which meant Gabriel needed to get some backup out here.

While continuing to keep watch, he took out his phone to do that, but something flashed in the corner of his eye. It wasn't Jace or Hector because this came from the opposite direction.

From his parents' old house.

The electricity was off, but there was definitely a light in the window. Maybe either a candle or a flash-light.

"Someone's inside," Jodi said under her breath. "Could it be Jameson?"

"No. He wouldn't go there." They had had trouble over the years with thrill-seeking teens, but Gabriel figured with everything going on, this was much more serious.

"You see that?" Jace called out, tipping his head to the house.

"Yeah. Don't go there just yet." And Gabriel called the sheriff's office to round up every available deputy.

However, before he could even press the number, a shot cracked through the air.

* * *

The sound of the bullet had barely registered in Jodi's mind when she felt herself being shoved back. That was Gabriel's doing. He rammed his shoulder into her and sent her flying backward.

She caught on to him to keep from falling, but Jodi also did that to pull him back, too. He immediately shut the door but then went straight to the window. No doubt to check on Jace.

Jodi hurried to the side window in the living room, which would give her the best view of his parents' house. She didn't stand directly in front of the glass, though, since it would make her an easy target. She stayed to the side so she would not only have a view of the old house but also that stretch of the road. What she didn't have a good view of, however, was the trail in between the two houses. Too many shrubs and trees.

Too many places for someone to hide.

Just as they'd done the night she was attacked.

She tried not to think of that now because it wouldn't help. The only thing she could do was keep watch to make sure someone didn't get close enough to fire another shot.

The light was still on upstairs in the old house, and it was flickering. Maybe because someone was moving it, but if it was a candle, it was possible the wind was blowing it since the window seemed to be open a couple of inches. It definitely hadn't been open when she'd visited the place two days ago.

From the other side of the room, she heard Gabriel call the sheriff's office and ask for backup. It wouldn't take the deputies long to get out here, but she prayed they wouldn't be driving into the middle of a gunfight.

But there were no other shots.

In fact, there were no other sounds, period. The place had suddenly gotten so quiet that the only thing she could hear was her own heartbeat drumming in her ears. And she wasn't sure that silence was a good thing. At least if she could have heard footsteps or spotted movement of some kind, she would have known where the shooter was.

"Is Jace okay?" she asked Gabriel.

"Can't tell, but he doesn't appear to have been hit. Hector and he are behind some trees."

Not ideal, because if Hector was the one responsible for the attacks, he could kill Jace. The deputy had to know that, of course, so maybe he was watching carefully to make sure that didn't happen.

"The shot couldn't have come from anywhere near my parents' house," she heard Gabriel say.

No, the angle was all wrong. Whoever had fired that shot was closer to where Hector's car was parked. Did that mean there were two attackers out there—one in the house and the other on the road?

Jodi glanced back at Gabriel, but he had his attention pinned to his side of the house. "Do you see anyone?"

"No. Maybe the person ran off after he fired." But Gabriel didn't sound very hopeful about that.

Part of Jodi didn't want this snake to run. She wanted to go ahead and have a showdown, one that would put an end to the danger once and for all, but with Jace out there, and the other deputies on their way, that wasn't a good idea. There had already been too many murders, and she didn't want anyone else dying tonight.

A sound shot through the room, causing her to gasp, but it was only Gabriel's phone. Without taking his attention off their surroundings, he hit the answer button and put the call on speaker.

"Sorry that I didn't see the guy before he took a shot at us," she heard Jace say from the other end of the line.

"I didn't see him, either," Gabriel answered. "He must have come on foot from up the road."

"Yeah, that's what I figured, too. But I did get a glimpse of him. Male, wearing a ski mask like the other guys who attacked us. He ran into the woods across from your folks' house. That was just a couple of seconds after Hector and me got behind these trees, and I haven't seen the guy since."

So, maybe he had run after getting off that single shot, but the knot in her stomach told her that there was another reason he wasn't firing. Like because maybe he was getting in a better position to do more damage. This way, too, Gabriel was separated from his deputy, so not only didn't he have immediate police backup in the house, Jace was out there without backup, as well.

"I'm going after him," someone said. Hector. She had no trouble hearing him, either. "I'm not just going to cower here while he picks us off one by one."

"You're staying put," Gabriel told him.

But neither Jace nor Hector answered. Jace did curse, though, and there seemed to be some kind of scuffle going on. Mercy, no. Hector couldn't be doing this.

However, he was.

"The SOB punched me," Jace said, "and then he started running. You want me to go after him?"

Before Gabriel could answer, there was another shot, then another. Both came from the same area where the first one had been fired.

"Stay put and take cover," Gabriel told Jace. There

was a franticness in his voice. In his movements, too, because he threw open the door, took aim and fired.

Jodi couldn't see the person Gabriel had shot at, and she didn't want to leave the window in case someone came in or out of the old house.

"Get back!" she shouted to Gabriel when a bullet smacked into the door frame right where he was standing.

He did get back, but cursing, he hurried to the front window and threw it open. Like her, he stayed to the side, and he fired out through the screen.

"I think I might have hit him," Gabriel relayed to her.

Good. She hoped he'd killed him because this was probably a hired thug. Yes, they could possibly get answers from him, but the only way for that to happen was to get to him and arrest him. No way did she want Gabriel going out there.

"When Jameson gets here, I'll have him stay with you," Gabriel added. "Jace and I can go after this clown who shot at us. Hector, too."

Jodi shook her head. "The attacker will come to us, and when he gets close enough, we can kill him."

"Hector was right. This guy will try to pick us off, and he can sit out there and shoot at us until he gets us. We need to stop him."

She couldn't argue with that, but she didn't want Gabriel out there. He glanced at her, their eyes connecting, and even though he didn't say anything, the glance was a reminder that catching bad guys was his job. No way would he want to stay inside where it was safe while his deputies and heaven knew who else was in danger. But "safe" was where she wanted him to be.

This was about the sex.

It had indeed changed everything. And while even

before tonight Jodi certainly hadn't wanted Gabriel hurt, now it cut her to the core to think of him being shot. Or worse.

Two more shots came at them, both of them smacking into the side of Gabriel's house. She doubted the bullets would be able to get through the walls, so maybe the gunman was doing this as a way of pinning them down.

But why?

She didn't like any of the answers that came to mind, but it was possible the shots were a distraction, meant to keep them occupied while someone sneaked closer to them. Jodi had already been keeping a close watch around them, but she tried even harder to pick through the near darkness and see someone.

And she did.

"Gabriel," she managed to say despite her breath having gone thin.

"Hell," Jace said only a few seconds later. Probably because the deputy had seen the same thing Jodi had.

Hector, coming out of the trees near the old house, and he wasn't alone.

The ski-masked thug was behind him and had a gun pointed right at Hector's head.

Gabriel felt a punch of dread and adrenaline. This was not what he wanted to happen, especially not without plenty of backup in place.

His first thought was this could be a ruse, one concocted by Hector to draw them out into the open. After all, Hector was a trained security specialist. But Gabriel knew firsthand that sometimes all the training and experience wasn't enough to keep thugs from getting to you.

Jodi moved away from the window, coming toward him. "You're not going out there," she said to him.

He was about to tell her the same thing, but if Hector was innocent, Gabriel didn't just want to stand by and watch an innocent man get killed. Especially since it appeared that the ski-masked guy had disarmed Hector.

"Call Hector right now," Gabriel instructed. "I need to see what this thug wants." And he also wanted to hear Hector's voice, to try to figure out what was really going on here.

Jodi nodded, and while she took out her phone and made the call, she also returned to the window to keep watch. Good. He hated having her near the glass where she could be shot, but Gabriel needed someone to keep an eye on that side of the house since it was essentially a blind spot for him.

Gabriel opened the front door, and while he didn't go onto the porch, he angled himself in the doorway so he could better see Hector. And also get a look at the guy in the ski mask. No way did Gabriel have a clean shot, but he wanted to be ready just in case.

Since he was watching Hector so closely, he saw when the man glanced down at Hector's pocket. Probably because his phone was ringing with the call from Jodi. His captor must have told him to answer it because a couple of seconds later, Hector reached in his pocket. Using just two fingers, he took out his phone, pressing the button on it and then lifting it in the air.

"Jodi," Hector answered. She put the call on speaker, so Gabriel had no trouble hearing the man.

Or the guy who had Hector at gunpoint.

"Do you want him dead?" the thug asked.

That was still to be determined, but for the moment Gabriel wanted both of these guys alive.

"I don't want Jodi coming out here," Hector said before Gabriel or she could answer.

"Neither do I," Gabriel assured him. "And it's not going to happen. She's staying inside, where she's safe." Hopefully.

"Then you're going to have to watch a man die," the gunman said.

Maybe it was a bluff, but every one of his lawman's instincts were yelling for him to stop this. If for no other reason than he didn't want Jodi to have to witness her boss and mentor being murdered in front of her.

"I might have a shot," Jodi mouthed, and she hit the mute button on her phone after she laid it on the window ledge. By doing that, she freed up both her hands. Probably to take that shot she'd just mentioned.

But Gabriel shook his head. "I don't want you that far out of cover. Besides, if you miss, you'll hit Hector."

Her mouth went flat, and she looked a little insulted that he'd even suggested she wouldn't be able to hit her intended target. "I'll aim for the goon's left leg. With the way he's standing, I can hit it, and when goes he down, Hector can get the gun away from him. Hector's probably already planning to elbow this guy in the gut or something."

Gabriel had figured that out. He just hoped it didn't get Hector killed. Because it was possible this guy wasn't alone. In fact, it was probable that he wasn't. Heaven knew how many *friends* he'd brought along with him. And if he wasn't holding his boss at fake gunpoint, then he could be out there, as well.

In the distance, Gabriel heard the sirens from the

police cruisers, and that meant he had to make a decision now. He definitely didn't want his brother and deputies driving into a hostage situation.

"On the count of three, I'll fire over their heads," Gabriel finally told her. "You go ahead and try to hit the guy in the leg. If Hector moves out of the way, then one of us can take the kill shot."

She nodded, turned and didn't waste any time taking aim.

Gabriel wanted to count as fast as possible, so he could get her out of the line of fire. "One, two, three." And he pulled the trigger.

So did Jodi.

She didn't miss, either.

Her shot slammed into the thug's leg, and he howled in pain. The guy staggered back, and Hector went after him. If this was Hector's hired muscle, then Jodi's boss made the punch that he delivered look very convincing. Hector ripped the gun from the man's hand and took aim.

Just as another shot cracked through the air.

This one went right into Hector.

He fell, clutching his chest, but he didn't stay on the ground. Even though he was clearly struggling, Hector was trying to crawl toward the ditch.

"Oh, God." Jodi automatically turned as if ready to run out and help him.

"He's wearing a Kevlar vest," Gabriel reminded her.

But Kevlar wasn't going to help him if the wounded gunman shot him in the head. And that's what Gabriel thought he had in mind when the gunman whipped out another weapon from an ankle holster. When he took aim at Hector, Gabriel took aim at him.

And fired.

He went for the kill shot, two bullets to the head, since an injured hired gun could still do plenty of damage. The man fell back, his head smacking onto the ground. It gave Hector time to get into the ditch before the next shot came.

The second gunman was somewhere in the trees near the road. The very road where the cruiser would be arriving soon, so Gabriel fired off a quick text to let Jameson know to stay back until Jodi and he could figure a way to draw him out. Then, they could get an ambulance for Hector in case he was hurt.

"Watch out!" Gabriel heard Jace yell.

That's when Gabriel also heard something else. A car engine.

Gabriel pivoted, whipping around in Jace's direction, and saw a black car driving up the road. It was coming from the opposite direction of the cruiser, and the driver was speeding. He considered shooting into it, but it's possible this was someone who was merely in the wrong place at the wrong time.

It wasn't.

When the car reached the treed area where Jameson was, it veered off the road, and the driver, who was wearing a ski mask, jumped out. The car, however, continued to come right toward Gabriel.

"Run!" Gabriel shouted to Jodi. He hurried to her, caught on to her arm and got them moving toward the back of the house.

Not a second too soon.

The car rammed into the porch, and it wasn't just a simple crash. No.

The car exploded into a fireball.

Chapter 15

Because of where she'd been standing, Jodi hadn't seen the car until she glanced back over her shoulder while Gabriel and she were running. It was an older model vehicle and obviously loaded with some kind of explosives for it to go up in flames like that.

Those flames could easily make it into the house.

Gabriel led her to the kitchen. No sign of any trouble here, but the smoke was already starting to make its way through the house. It reeked of gasoline, so maybe it hadn't actually been a real bomb. The person could have just filled the car with open containers of gas, and the impact could have triggered a spark.

"Who did this?" she asked, keeping her voice at a whisper.

What she wasn't able to do was tamp down all the fear and panic that was starting to roar through her.

Gabriel's front porch was on fire. A fire that would no doubt spread—fast. And his brother, Jace and Hector were out there, maybe under attack right now. Since Gabriel and she could no longer see them, they couldn't help them. Not from the back of the house anyway.

"I don't know," Gabriel said, answering her question. He hooked his arm around her waist and moved her to the side of the fridge while he hurried to the back door to look out. "He was wearing a ski mask and jumped from the car."

Mercy. That meant the guy was still out there, and he had at least one hired gun to help him because there'd been the shot fired at Hector from the other end of the road. If Hector was innocent, she hoped he had managed to find some cover, because it was obvious things had gone from bad to worse.

"Keep watch behind us," Gabriel instructed. He opened the back door several inches.

Jodi did as he said, but she wouldn't be able to keep watch for long because of the smoke. It was getting thicker with every passing second, and soon they wouldn't be able to stay put. That meant going outside.

Where gunmen could be waiting for them.

What they needed was to get a better look at what was going on. Unfortunately, a better look came with risks. Because the moment they left the house, it could put them right in the line of fire.

"Call Jace," he said, passing her his phone. "Ask if he's got eyes on the driver of that car."

While she volleyed glances all around them, Jodi found his number and pressed it. She wasn't sure if the deputy would even be in a position to answer, but he did.

"Gabriel," Jace said. His voice was barely audible. "It's me, Jodi. Are you okay?"

"For now." Jace whispered, as well. "The guy who was driving that car has to be nearby."

"Any idea where the other shooter or Hector is?" she asked.

"No. But you and Gabriel should get out of the house right now. The fire's spreading, and the fire department won't be able to get out here until we've rounded up these two thugs."

Jace was being optimistic that there were only two of them. There could be a dozen. She cursed the person who'd put all of this together.

"If Gabriel and you run out the back, I'll try to cover you," Jace said, ending the call.

There was no need for her to relay that to Gabriel since he'd been standing close enough to hear. He looked back at her, making eye contact, and he seemed to be saying he was sorry about all of this. Well, she was sorry, too, but only because she was probably the reason so many people were in danger right now.

Gabriel tipped his head to his truck that was parked out back. "That's where we're heading." And he pressed the remote on his keys to unlock the doors.

He didn't remind her to keep watch or be careful because he knew that she would be. As careful as she could be anyway.

Gabriel used his shoulder to open the door wider, and he stepped out onto the porch. He took a quick look around before he motioned for them to get moving. She did. Gabriel barreled down the porch steps, and Jodi was right behind him. They made a beeline for the truck.

But didn't get far.

Jace fired, his bullets going well over their heads. But one shot slammed into his truck, right into the engine. Judging from the angle, this bullet had almost certainly come from the driver of the car that was up in flames. She doubted that a single shot had disabled it, but the gunman fired again.

And again.

These didn't go into the truck, though.

They came right at Gabriel and her.

They immediately dropped to the ground, both of them rolling to the side of the porch. It wasn't much protection, especially considering this new position possibly put them in the direct sight of Hector and the other gunman, but at least the driver's shots were no longer an immediate threat. Not to them anyway. The goon could turn that gun on Jace.

"We can't stay here," Gabriel said, but it sounded as if he were talking more to himself than to her.

But Jodi agreed. Eventually, the fire would make it back here, and the flames and smoke could kill them. Running to the truck was out, too, since it was obvious the shooter had a good angle on that.

"The barn," Gabriel added.

It was to the side of the truck, and while it would indeed provide some cover, they still had to get to it. There were some trees and shrubs dotting the way, but it was possible Gabriel and she could get caught in the cross fire.

Gabriel's phone dinged with a text message, and since she still had his cell, she read Jameson's text aloud. "Approaching on foot. Don't fire in our direction."

However, the words had no sooner left her mouth

when someone did fire. Not the driver or Jace this time. The shot had come from the area where she'd last spotted Hector. Of course, that was the same general direction as Jameson and the other shooter, so it could be one of them. She prayed that Jameson was all right.

She put Gabriel's phone back in her pocket, so her hands would be free when they ran. Which she didn't have to wait long for. Almost immediately, Gabriel got them moving, but they didn't make it far before the shots came. Not a single bullet, either. But a hail of them. They had no choice but to get back on the ground behind one of the trees.

Jodi automatically maneuvered into a position that would allow her to keep watch behind them, and she hated that her pulse kicked up when she realized her area to watch was the very trail where she'd nearly died.

The sun had fully set now, but there was enough illumination coming from the fire that she could see it. At least she could see the trail itself. However, it was impossible to tell if anyone was hiding in those tall shrubs. The very ones her attacker had used ten years ago.

"See anything?" Gabriel whispered.

Before she could answer, the phone dinged, but this time, it wasn't Gabriel's. It was hers. Keeping watch, Jodi took it from her pocket. Not a text but rather a call, and it wasn't from Jace.

It was from Hector.

Gabriel mumbled some profanity under his breath when she showed him the name on the screen. Jodi pressed the answer button, but she didn't say anything. That's because this might not be Hector. The gunman could have finished him off, taken Hector's phone and could be using this call to pinpoint her location by listening for the sound of her voice.

"Jodi?" someone said from the other end of the line. She couldn't tell if it was Hector or not because the voice was a hoarse whisper. "Please," he said. "I need your help."

It was Hector all right.

"What's wrong?" she asked as softly as she could manage.

"I've been shot, and I'm bleeding out fast." Hector cursed. "I'm pinned down."

And then Jodi heard something she didn't want to hear. Another gunshot. Followed by Hector's sharp sound of pain.

Gabriel heard the sound that Hector made. And he got a glimpse of the stark expression on Jodi's face, too. She was no doubt torn between getting to her boss but balancing that with the real possibility that this could be a trap that could get her killed.

Especially since it would mean going on that trail between his and his parents' houses.

"I can't go out there," she whispered. Maybe to herself. Maybe to Hector.

She then hit the End Call button so she could text for an ambulance. One was almost certainly on the way. Jameson would have called for it, but the medics wouldn't come closer as long as there was gunfire.

And there was plenty of that.

Shots came from Jace's direction. From Hector's, too, and Gabriel couldn't tell who was doing the shooting. It was possible that Jameson was in on this by now, since he would have had a chance to at least reach the area where Hector was. Maybe his brother had managed to take out the gunman. Gabriel didn't have to remind Jameson to be mindful of Hector, too, since his brother already knew Hector was a suspect.

Perhaps a dead one, though.

"Should we try to make it to the barn or truck again?" she asked.

It was tempting—especially the truck since they could possibly use it to escape. But Gabriel shook his head, and he tried to pick through the sounds to make sure no one was sneaking up on them. He could hear... something, but it was hard to tell what it was exactly, thanks to the fire now snapping and eating through his house.

His *home*, he mentally corrected.

It twisted at his gut to see it being damaged like this, but there was nothing he could do to save it. Right now, his priority had to be keeping everyone alive.

"I'm sorry," someone called out.

Jace.

Gabriel pivoted in that direction and saw something he didn't want to see. Jace being held at gunpoint. It was almost identical to what had happened to Hector just minutes earlier with a ski-masked thug behind him. The guy had jammed a gun to Jace's head.

"I didn't see him before it was too late," Jace added.

Gabriel hated that Jace felt the need to apologize for something like that, but it did put them in a really bad position. Because Gabriel figured he knew what was coming next, and he didn't have to wait long for it.

"Start running down the trail," the gunman said. "Or I'll shoot him where he stands."

Gabriel had obviously figured wrong. He'd expected

the thug to tell Jodi and him to put down their guns. What kind of sick plan was this?

A bad answer immediately came to mind.

The same person who'd attacked Jodi ten years ago wanted a chance to finish her off in the same spot.

"And if we don't run?" Gabriel challenged.

The gunman fired a shot. Not into Jace's head. But rather his shoulder. At the same time, there was another shot—it came from Hector's direction—and Gabriel heard what was another loud groan of pain. Maybe Hector had been shot again. Maybe it was a ruse, but the ruse definitely didn't apply to Jace.

Jace dropped to his knees, the pain etched all over his face, and the gunman dropped with him, staying behind him so he could continue to use Jace as cover. Gabriel didn't have a clean shot, and he figured Jodi didn't, either.

"Run or I'll shoot him in his other shoulder," the gunman warned them. "The third shot will go in his gut. I'm thinking if you hadn't obeyed by the fourth shot, then your deputy will be a goner."

Hell, Jace might not survive the second, much less a third and fourth, shot. With the angle the clown was holding that gun, the bullet could go down Jace's shoulder and straight into his heart.

"Run!" the gunman shouted to them.

"We have no choice," Jodi said. Her voice was trembling a little, but that didn't stop her from turning in the direction of the trail.

Where someone was no doubt waiting to kill her.

"I can't let Jace die because of me," she added.

Gabriel couldn't let that happen, either, but he could take some precautions. "Stay low. I don't want this idiot gunning us down, and he might do that if we stand up. Crawl. And stay close to me."

Of course, that wouldn't stop anyone on that trail from shooting at them, too, but Gabriel figured the monster who was waiting there wanted to use a knife.

On Jodi.

Maybe that's why she pulled her own knife from her boot and clamped it between her teeth. The moment she did that, they started moving. Of course, there was no guarantee that the gunman holding Jace wouldn't just go ahead and shoot him, but at least this way, the deputy had a fighting chance. Plus, there was the possibility that Jameson would be able to help since the gunman was out in the open with Jace.

"I need to listen for footsteps," Jodi said under her breath. "I'll recognize the sound of his steps."

Maybe. But he wasn't sure how she would manage that. Her heart had to be beating a mile a minute right now, and added to that, there was still the occasional gunshot near Hector.

The very direction where they were going.

They crawled, stopping every few feet, and when they reached the first curve in the trail, Gabriel and she got to crouching positions. It still wasn't ideal, but it might give them a fighting chance.

Just ahead were the thickest shrubs. It was also the place where Jodi had been attacked. She knew that, of course, and it was probably why he heard her breath hitch in her throat. Yes, she was a trained security specialist, but she was also the woman who'd nearly died here. No way to erase that from her mind.

"If he gets his hands on me," she said, "kill him."

That was the plan, but Gabriel preferred to do the killing before this monster touched her.

They inched their way up the trail, and Gabriel heard another sound. One that caused him to curse. Not footsteps. Not gunshots. But it was something he instantly recognized.

A rattler.

Hell. They didn't need this now.

It wasn't unusual for rattlesnakes to be out among all the underbrush, but Gabriel figured it could be something that their attacker had planted. Something to get them moving so fast that it'd be easier to kill them.

"Freeze," Gabriel whispered to her.

In the darkness it was going to be pretty much impossible to see the snake, so he followed the sound of it. It was definitely agitated because the rattler was going practically nonstop. A warning to get them to back off. Gabriel wished they could do just that, but instead they had to crouch there and wait it out. That was the plan anyway.

But it didn't happen.

There was some movement to their left. Definitely footsteps this time, and Gabriel got just a glimpse of a hand that reached out from the shrub. The moonlight was just at the right angle for it to glint off the shiny blade.

As the knife plunged right into Jodi.

Chapter 16

The pain shot through Jodi's shoulder. Familiar pain. It brought all the memories crashing back. The nightmare.

He was killing her again.

And she felt the warm blood start to slip down her back.

She took her own knife from her mouth and slashed it at him. Jodi thought maybe she connected with some part of him, but she couldn't tell for sure. That's because he was in the bushes, and she couldn't see him. However, she could see his knife, and he sliced it at her again. She ducked out of the way, barely in time.

If the rattler was still there, it had stopped making that god-awful sound. That was something at least, but it was also possible that it had been a recording. Her attacker probably wouldn't have wanted to risk being bitten by one of his "pets."

From the corner of her eye, she could see Gabriel. He lunged toward her, taking aim at her attacker, but he didn't get a chance to shoot. That's because the man latched onto her hair and dragged her into the shrubs with him. Gabriel wouldn't have risked shooting because he could have hit her.

She felt another cut from the knife. This time on her arm, and he knocked her blade from her hand. More pain came. Not just from her physical wounds but because once again she was that nineteen-year-old girl. The one who this monster—or maybe the monster who'd hired him—had put in a shallow grave.

For a moment the fear froze her, but then she heard the shot. Heard Gabriel curse, too. And Jace shouted for him to watch out. The gunman who had Jace was no doubt on the trail, too, and he was trying to gun down Gabriel. Or else just keep him occupied while this goon stabbed her. Either way, that got her unfrozen, and Jodi remembered her training.

He still had hold of her hair. The knife, too, but she got to her feet, bashing her head into his chin. That stopped the next blow, but he made a feral sound and took another swing at her.

"Jodi!" Gabriel called out, and she heard him scramble toward her. Heard another shot fired, too. She only prayed they'd get out of this alive, but that might not happen if she didn't stop the knife.

Gabriel pushed through the shrubs, and she got just a glimpse of him before her attacker dragged her to her feet with her back against his chest. Like Jace, she was now a human shield. And she was bleeding. She could feel at least two stab wounds, but it was as if he'd cut her many more times.

Just like that night.

Her attacker motioned for Gabriel to drop his gun, and he put the tip of her knife right at her carotid artery. One jab of the blade, and she'd bleed out in no time at all.

"Let her go," Gabriel tried. "No way can you get out of here alive."

The man's silence let them know he didn't agree with that. For a good reason. He had at least one healthy gunman and two hostages, Jace and her. That would get not only Gabriel but the deputies and Jameson to back off.

He started backing up, dragging her with him. The brushes scraped at her hands. Probably at him, too, but he didn't react. He was solely focused on getting her away from Gabriel. No doubt so he could finish her off.

This wasn't a hired thug. That feral sound he'd made had dripped with emotion. And she doubted it was a coincidence that he'd yet to say anything to them. This wasn't some hired gun. This was the *one*.

She heard it then. The sound that had been in her head for nearly ten years. His footsteps. Yes. They were identical to the ones that night. When he'd been dragging her nearly lifeless body into these very shrubs.

But who was it?

He was wearing a ski mask, so she couldn't see his face even if he would have allowed her to turn around. All of their suspects had similar builds, and she couldn't assume that Hector had truly been hurt. No. All of that could have been faked to bring them to this point.

Jodi let everything inside her go still. Just as Hector had taught her to do, and she gathered her energy.

Her focus. And she pinpointed into the only weapon she had readily available to her.

Her own body.

It was a risk, but everything, and nothing, would be at this point. So, she made eye contact with Gabriel to try to give him some kind of heads-up that she was about to make her move. Whether he noticed her look or not she didn't know because he was volleying glances between her attacker and the approaching gunman.

Jodi dropped, her weight dragging her attacker down with her, and in the same motion she rammed her elbow into his ribs. He staggered back, letting go of her and dropping the knife, but she soon realized the only reason he did that was so he could draw a gun and take aim.

He fired at Gabriel.

Thankfully, Gabriel must have realized what was happening because he was already moving to the side before the man pulled the trigger. The shot blasted into the ground.

Jodi fumbled around, looking for a knife or gun, but the man latched onto her again. He bashed the gun against her wounded shoulder, causing the pain to shoot through her. It was blinding and robbed her of her breath for a few precious seconds. Seconds that he used to drag her in front of him again. But Jodi did some grabbing of her own.

She caught on to the ski mask, dragging it from his face.

And she finally knew who wanted her dead.

Russell.

Even with only the watery moonlight, she saw him

smile. A sickening smile that revealed the monster beneath. He'd been the bogeyman all this time.

"Why?" she managed to asked.

"You were a mistake," he said, surprising her with his answer. "I was mad, high and thinking like an idiot when I came here and saw you leave Gabriel's house. I lost my temper."

"You did all of that because you lost your temper?" she repeated, and Jodi didn't bother to take out the sarcasm. Nor the rage that was bubbling up inside her. "You stabbed me and tried to bury me."

"Like I said, it was a mistake. But your mistake was remembering after all this time. I couldn't risk my wife finding out. I'd lose everything."

It twisted at her to hear that. It notched up the anger inside her, too. This sick excuse for a man was ready to murder heaven knew how many people to cover up his crimes.

Gabriel didn't move, but she could tell he was trying to figure out what to do. Once again, he couldn't risk shooting the man, so, like Jodi, he just had to wait and hope for some kind of opportunity.

"A lot of people are dead because of you," Gabriel said, his voice low and dangerous. "Why did you kill my parents?"

"I didn't," he said without hesitation. "They were already dead when I went to their house looking for Jodi. The blood was fresh, as if they'd just been killed. I figured the person who did that to them could still be around, so I ran out. I saw the knife in the yard, picked it up and then spotted Jodi at your house. I waited for her on the trail."

She wasn't sure about the timing of that. Jodi had

always assumed that the Becketts had been murdered during a twenty minute or so window when she'd been at Gabriel's. But she'd thought that because of when Ivy had called Gabriel after discovering the bodies. Maybe, though, Ivy hadn't found her parents until minutes after they'd been killed. That would have given Russell time to find the knife, come after her and put her in that grave before Gabriel even started running up the trail to his parents' house.

Of course, Russell might be lying, too.

"That's when I lost my temper," Russell went on. "When I saw her on the trail. I figured she'd just left your bed."

It wouldn't do any good to say that she hadn't done it, that Gabriel had rejected her that night. Even if Russell believed her, it wouldn't change anything that'd happened.

"Is Hector dead?" she asked.

"Maybe. If he's not, he should stay away from me because I'd have to kill him, too."

So, Hector hadn't been a part of this. That was something at least, though it might be too late for Jace and Hector.

"I'm tired of talking now," Russell said, dragging her even deeper into the shrubs just as he'd done ten years ago. "Jodi, I'm thinking you aren't going to cheat death this time—"

"Your wife is suspicious of you," Gabriel interrupted.

That stopped Russell in his tracks. Not Gabriel, though. He moved slightly to the right, and since he still had his gun in his hand, maybe he'd get in a position to shoot. Since the original attack, everything in her life had centered on killing the man who'd done those horrible things to her. But now, she just wanted him dead or at least locked up.

"What are you talking about?" Russell snapped.

"Your wife went to see August earlier today."

Judging from the way Russell's arm tightened, he hadn't known that. "What did that SOB tell her?"

"That he thought you were the one trying to kill Jodi and me."

Russell made another of those vicious sounds. "I'll kill him for doing that. He had no right. That fool has been interfering from day one, always digging, always sticking his nose where it doesn't belong."

"Ironic that you'd mention *rights* when you had a cop murdered so you could set up Hector. Billy and Mara, too. Plus, you might have let an innocent man spend a decade in jail for murders that he didn't commit. I'm guessing you and Mara were having an affair, and that's why she was so willing to help you." Gabriel paused, moved again. "By the way, your wife talked to August about your affair with Mara."

That was a lie, of course, but she understood why Gabriel had said it. It was to make Russell believe that this was all for nothing, that his marriage was going to fall apart after all. That way, he might let them go, so they could get an ambulance out for Jace, Hector and her.

"I'll fix things with Tracy when I'm finished here," Russell mumbled. He was getting more agitated with each passing second. "She's not like Jodi. She's loyal to me."

Jodi could have told him that she hadn't been loyal because they'd dated only a short period of time. It certainly hadn't been serious. Couldn't have been. Because she'd been in love with Gabriel.

Still was.

Too bad it was a tough time to remember that. Because it was also a reminder at how much she had at stake. She couldn't lose him.

She braced herself for Russell to shoot her. And there was a shot. It just hadn't come from him. It had come from the direction of Gabriel's house.

"It's me," Jameson called out. "We've got both gunmen in custody and an ambulance on the way for Hector and Jace. Where's Russell?"

Apparently, one or both the gunmen had decided to rat out their boss. So much for loyalty. Of course, if they were like the others Russell had hired, they were common thugs.

Thugs who could have easily killed them.

"Russell's here," Gabriel answered. "He's holding Jodi at gunpoint."

Before Gabriel had even finished what he was saying, Russell fired, the shot so loud that it blasted through her head. She couldn't hear, but Jodi could certainly feel, and she knew Russell was getting ready to run.

She dropped down before he could do that and grabbed the knife.

Jodi didn't have time to get back up and stab him in the heart, so she just slashed the blade at him, the knife gouging into his stomach.

Russell cursed at her, calling her a vile name, and he backhanded her with the gun. Again, the pain came and put her right back on her knees. Russell took advantage of that. He shoved her at Gabriel.

Gabriel and she collided, both of them falling to the ground.

Russell fired another shot and took off running. Jodi got up to go after him. But she stopped.

Because she saw the blood on Gabriel's chest.

Chapter 17

Gabriel wished he had something to punch—hard. Preferably Russell. That might rid him of some of this lethal energy that was bubbling up inside him.

The pain didn't help with that energy, either. This was his first gunshot wound, and it thankfully hadn't been life-threatening. Russell's bullet had been a through and through into Gabriel's shoulder, but even after some meds, it was throbbing like an abscessed tooth. However, his pain was nothing compared to what he was feeling about Jodi.

Gabriel had refused to leave her side not only for the ambulance ride but while they were both getting examined and stitched up at the hospital. His staying close to her was partially because he was just plain worried about her.

But it was also because her would-be killer was still at large.

Somehow, Russell had managed to escape. Probably because he had a car stashed near the ranch, and he'd no doubt fled while Jameson was concerned with keeping Jace alive. The deputy and Hector were both going to be okay, but their injuries were more serious than Jodi's and his.

Of course, nothing was more serious to Gabriel than seeing the blood all over her. Hell. It was like that night all over again. He'd saved her then, but the cost of that attack had been sky-high, and he wasn't sure how long it would take Jodi to recover a second time. The images of this attack would now be piled on top of the nightmarish memories she already had.

Despite all the blood, Jodi had gotten lucky, too. There was a cut on her upper arm. Another near her left wrist. The doctor had taken off her T-shirt while he'd examined her, so Gabriel had no trouble seeing each wound. The camisole she'd had on beneath her shirt had blood on it, as well.

He wanted to punch something again, and that feeling got worse with every new bruise, cut and scrape he saw on her silky skin.

Jameson stepped into the treatment room, glancing at both of them and shaking his head. "I hope you know how to get bloodstains out of clothes."

It was a really bad joke, and Gabriel scowled at him. Jameson, however, went to Jodi and brushed a kiss on her forehead. She flinched a little, but that was possibly because she was reacting to the stitches that the nurse was just finishing applying to her wounds.

"Please tell me you caught Russell," she said.

"Not yet. But SAPD has officers at his house to protect his wife and baby. I had a Ranger go to August's place just in case, too."

Good idea. Russell had been pretty riled about his wife going to see August, and he might want to find out what the woman had told him. Of course, that was all water under the bridge now. They knew Russell was a killer, and soon his wife would know that, as well.

"I put two deputies at the hospital doors," Jameson went on, and he looked at Jodi's empty hip holster. Gabriel had managed to hold on to his own gun, but Jodi had lost hers in the scuffle. Jameson took out his backup from the slide holster in his jeans and gave it to her. "Just in case."

That put some alarm back in Jodi's eyes. Not that she'd exactly looked calm and serene before his comment, but this was a reminder that Russell could come charging in there and try to kill them. According to the hired guns Jameson had rounded up, there wasn't anybody else on Russell's dirty payroll, but Gabriel had seen the sick hatred in Russell's eyes.

If there was any humanly way he could get to Jodi, he would.

That's why Gabriel was thankful his brother had given her the gun. Now, he had to pray she didn't need it.

Gabriel stood from the table and reached for his shirt to put it back on. Before he could do that, though, Jameson snatched it away.

"No," Jameson said, "you're not going after Russell."

Since that's exactly what Gabriel had been planning to do, he couldn't deny it, but he could pull rank on a younger brother. He wasn't so sure, though, that he could do that with Jodi.

"You're not going after Russell," she echoed. "Not without me anyway." She stood, too, reaching for her shirt. Wincing and grunting in pain, she started to put it on.

"You're not leaving this hospital," Gabriel warned her.

"And neither are you." Jodi's chin came up, and he could have sworn she was fighting back a smile. Maybe because she'd just one-upped him. He didn't want her out there, so that meant he was staying put, too.

Gabriel went to her with the hopes of convincing her to stay seated. She did but only because he hovered over her and kissed her. He had intended for it to be just a peck, but it felt so good that he lingered a few seconds.

God, he could have lost her.

"I'll see if your rooms are ready," the nurse said, standing. She was fighting back a smile, as well. "And no, it won't do any good to tell Dr. Holliwell that you don't want to stay. He's already said he's keeping both of you for the night."

Yeah, that was an argument he didn't even want to try to win with the doc. Dr. Holliwell wanted Jodi in the hospital in case her injuries were worse than the original diagnosis, and Gabriel didn't want her alone. That meant both Gabriel and she were staying.

"I'll see if there are any updates," Jameson said. "You two look like you could use some alone time."

Gabriel gave him another scowl, but he did want some time with Jodi. There were things he had to tell her.

"I'm so sorry," he started. "I should have stopped this—"

She caught on to his neck, pulling him down to her, and kissed him. It hurt. Mainly because it tweaked the muscles in his throbbing shoulder. But he didn't care. Kissing her was worth the pain.

"I'm the one who should be saying I'm sorry," she insisted. "Russell was on the trail because he thought I would remember that he was the one who'd attacked me."

This called for another kiss to shut her up, but Gabriel got in something else he wanted to say first. "Neither one of us made Russell a killer. He did that all by himself."

And they'd both be cleaning up Russell's mess for a long, long time.

Now, he kissed her, and it wasn't to hush her. It was because he needed it. Judging from the sound she made in her throat, she needed it, as well. The kiss might have gone on a lot longer if his phone hadn't buzzed. Since it could be about Russell, he stepped back to take the call.

"It's August," he told her after seeing the name on the screen.

He considered letting it go to voice mail, but since August was in possible danger, he hit Answer and put it on speaker.

"Is it true?" August practically yelled. "Is that idiot Russell after me?"

"He could be. I told him that his wife had visited you."

August cursed him. And Gabriel let him go on for a while. In hindsight he probably should have figured out a different way to get Russell to confess to using Mara and then murdering her, but considering everything else that had been going on, it was the best he could do.

"I want you to stay in your house with the Rangers," Gabriel told him. "If Russell shows up, have the Rangers call me."

"Hell, no, I won't. I'll kill him on sight. And in the meantime, you'll get my brother out of jail. This proves he didn't—"

"Russell said he didn't kill my parents."

"And you believed him?" August howled.

"Yeah, I did. Because he didn't deny murdering Mara. Didn't deny attacking Jodi, either." Gabriel had to pause and gather his breath. It was hard to think of just how close Russell had come to ending her life— again. "If he had killed them, I believe Russell would have taken great pleasure in letting me know."

Jodi nodded in agreement. "It would have made things easier, for me anyway, if Russell had committed all the murders."

Yes, because it would mean her father was innocent. And with Russell's confession, Travis was clear of Jodi's attack. But clearing his name didn't extend to the deaths of Gabriel's parents. No. There wasn't enough evidence to overturn his conviction. However, it was something Gabriel would take a closer look at. Jodi would no doubt do the same.

Jodi took hold of his hand, gave it a gentle squeeze. Considering it was such a small gesture, it had a big effect. It didn't rid him of the ache in his heart, but it sure as heck helped.

"Don't think I'm just going to drop this," August went on. "As soon as you catch Russell, I'm finding a judge who'll set Travis free." With that, he ended the call.

"That won't happen," Gabriel assured Jodi.

She nodded. "I agree. If Russell had killed them, he would have said so." She paused. "But at least now I know my father wasn't the one who attacked me."

In all the chaos, Gabriel had forgotten just how important that was to her. Good. It might help with the nightmares and panic attacks. But she certainly wasn't panicking now.

She slipped right into his arms.

"I'm in love with you, you know," she said.

No. He hadn't known. And it left him speechless. Not the best time for that because she was clearly waiting for him to respond. Before he could get his mouth working, though, the nurse stepped in.

"Are you up to seeing Hector March?" The nurse directed her question to Jodi. "He's asking for you."

Gabriel wasn't sure it was a good idea, especially since Hector might verbally blast Jodi again for not sticking up for him, but he didn't stop her when she started to follow the nurse. Gabriel did go with her, though. For one thing, because she didn't look steady on her feet. For another, he didn't want her alone.

The hospital wasn't that large by anyone's standards, and it took them less than a minute to make it to the room where Hector was recovering. Unlike Jodi and him, Hector had required some surgery. Ditto for Jace, but both had come out of it just fine. Physically fine anyway.

The moment Jodi and Gabriel stepped into the room, Hector tried to sit up, but the nurse motioned for him to lie back down. He didn't listen. Instead, he winced and grunted until he got into the position he wanted. Probably so he'd be able to face them head-on.

Hector's mouth tightened when he looked at Jodi.

"I would ask if you're okay, but I can see you're not." His attention lingered on the bloodstains on her shirt. "He knifed you?"

She nodded. "This time, though, he didn't hit any vital organs, and I did manage to cut him." Jodi tipped her head to the fresh bandage on his leg and chest. "How about you? Are you okay?"

"I'll be fine in no time. Just a few broken ribs."

"And two gunshot wounds," Jodi added. "The doctor mentioned it when he was examining Gabriel and me."

"Flesh wounds. I'll be back at work tomorrow."

"In a week if you're lucky," the nurse corrected, and she stepped out.

Gabriel was betting Hector wasn't going to stay in that bed for a week. A night maybe, until the effects of the anesthesia wore off.

"It can't be easy for you to be here," Hector went on, and it surprised Gabriel that the man wasn't speaking to Jodi but to him. "You're probably blaming yourself for what happened to Jodi. I know I sure as hell am."

Jodi frowned. "It wasn't your fault." She looked at Gabriel and repeated it before she went to Hector and slid her hand over his.

Hector stared at her, clearly surprised. Maybe because Jodi wasn't the touching type. Ironic that she could manage to do it now when she'd just weathered another attack.

"Thank you for everything you did for me," she said.

Hector's stare continued. "But?"

Jodi drew in a long breath. "But I can't work for you any longer. And no, it doesn't have anything to do with what went on tonight."

"It has to do with Gabriel." Hector huffed, groaned

softly and then scrubbed his hand over his face. "I'm guessing he's the reason I no longer see the panic in your eyes?"

She nodded. "He's the reason for a lot of things."

That got him a quick glare from Hector. Then, a nod. Hector and he would probably never be friendly to each other, but they could agree on one thing. They wanted what was best for Jodi. Because they both cared deeply for her.

"You're not going to become a cop, are you?" Hector asked, and it sounded as if he was only partially joking. Partially disgusted with the thought of that, too.

"No, but maybe a PI. That way, I can put all the training you gave me to good use. I can still help people. Protect them, maybe. I could even set up an office right here in Blue River."

So, she was staying. Or least thinking of staying. Even though it wasn't a sure thing, it felt as if someone had lifted a weight off his shoulders.

Hector stayed quiet a moment while he continued to study Jodi's face. "Is this goodbye then?"

"Yes," she answered after a long pause. "Thanks again, Hector." She leaned down, dropped a kiss on his forehead.

Gabriel hated the punch of jealousy that went through him. Especially since it was obvious that Jodi didn't have any romantic feelings for her former boss, but Gabriel was just feeling possessive at the moment. That probably had something to do with what she'd said to him.

I'm in love with you, you know.

He was definitely still reeling from that. Because, no, he hadn't known.

The moment they were back in the hall, Gabriel eased her into his arms. He'd intended it to be just a hug since he figured she needed a little TLC after that chat. Of course, nothing ever stayed just a simple hug with them, so when she looked up at him, Gabriel kissed her. He would have also brought up that "I'm in love with you" if he hadn't heard the footsteps heading their way. He automatically stepped in front of Jodi and drew his gun.

But again, it was only Jameson.

However, unlike earlier when Jameson had come into the treatment room, his brother was now smiling. "The Rangers found Russell."

Gabriel still had his arm around Jodi, and he felt her practically sag against him in relief. "Where was he?" she asked.

"Not far from the ranch. He was on one of the old trails. He's dead," Jameson added a heartbeat later.

Gabriel's mind started to whirl with all sorts of bad scenarios—like a shoot-out where more law enforcement officers had been hurt, or worse. "Did Russell kill anyone else?"

Jameson shook his head. "He didn't get the chance. He bled out while sitting in his car. A knife wound to the stomach. Your doing?" he asked Gabriel.

"No. Jodi's."

So, she'd killed Russell after all.

Gabriel looked down at her to see how she was handling that. No tears. And she seemed a little stronger than she had been a couple of seconds earlier. Relieved, too.

"Good," she whispered.

Yeah, it was. Not only because they didn't have to worry about Russell coming after them, but because he also couldn't try to kill his wife or August. Of course, his wife's troubles were just beginning, because she'd have to live with the aftermath of what her husband had done.

"Are you okay?" Jameson asked her, but he waved it off. "Of course, you are. You're in good hands." He smiled, no doubt noticing that Gabriel and she were practically wrapped around each other, and he strolled off.

"Are you really okay?" Gabriel repeated to her.

She took a moment, as if trying to figure out how to answer him, and then nodded. "For years, I've dreamed about this happening. About getting back at my attacker. But now that I've managed it, it no longer seems important. *This* is what's important."

Gabriel hoped that she was talking about him. "Earlier you said you were in love with me."

She stared at him, maybe trying to figure out how he felt about that and how he felt about her. But Gabriel didn't want there to be any question in her mind.

"Right back at you," he said. He even managed a smile before he kissed her. And because he figured she needed the words as well, Gabriel added, "I'm in love with you, too."

Now, she smiled. Kissed him and slid as close to him as their injuries would allow.

She'd been right. This was what was important. And Gabriel now had everything he wanted right in his arms.

* * * * *

Nicole Helm grew up with her nose in a book and the dream of one day becoming a writer. Luckily, after a few failed career choices, she gets to follow that dream—writing down-to-earth contemporary romance and romantic suspense. From farmers to cowboys, Midwest to *the* West, Nicole writes stories about people finding themselves and finding love in the process. She lives in Missouri with her husband and two sons and dreams of someday owning a barn.

Books by Nicole Helm

Harlequin Intrigue

Carsons & Delaneys: Battle Tested

Wyoming Cowboy Marine
Wyoming Cowboy Sniper
Wyoming Cowboy Ranger
Wyoming Cowboy Bodyguard

Carsons & Delaneys

Wyoming Cowboy Justice
Wyoming Cowboy Protection
Wyoming Christmas Ransom

Stone Cold Texas Ranger
Stone Cold Undercover Agent
Stone Cold Christmas Ranger

Harlequin Superromance

Falling for the New Guy
Too Friendly to Date
Too Close to Resist

Visit the Author Profile page at
Harlequin.com for more titles.

WYOMING
COWBOY
PROTECTION

Nicole Helm

To my husband, who always asks,
"Do you need time to write?"

Chapter 1

August

Addie Foster watched from the car's passenger seat as a whole new world passed by her window. If she'd thought Jackson Hole was like nothing she'd ever known, Bent, Wyoming, was an alien planet.

She'd grown up in the heart of Boston, a city dweller always. Occasionally her family had traveled up to Maine for quaint weekends or vacations in little villages, enjoying beaches and ice-cream shops.

This was not that. This wasn't even like those dusty old Westerns her grandpa had loved to watch as he'd reminisced about his childhood being a Delaney in Bent, Wyoming—as if that had ever meant anything to Addie.

It meant something now. Seth fussed in his carrier in the back seat and Addie swallowed at the lump in her throat. Her sister had died trying to protect this sweet little man, and Addie had spent the past nine months struggling to protect him.

The baby's father hadn't made it easy. Addie had been able to hide Seth for three months before Peter Monaghan the 5th had discovered her sister's deception, and *no one* deceived Peter Monaghan the 5th.

For six months, Addie had crisscrossed her way around the country, running out of false identities and money. Until she'd had to call upon the only person she could think to call upon.

Laurel Delaney.

Addie had met Laurel at Addie's grandpa's funeral some twenty years ago. They'd taken an instant liking to each other and become pen pals for a while.

They'd drifted apart, as pen pals always did, once the girls got into high school, and Addie never would have dreamed of calling Laurel out of the blue until desperation led her to think of the most faraway, safe place she could imagine. Someplace Peter would have no reach. Someplace she and Seth would be safe from his evil crime boss of a father.

"Don't worry," Laurel said pleasantly from the driver's seat as Seth began to cry in earnest. "We're only about five minutes away. I'm sorry I can't have you stay with me, but my place is pretty cramped as it is, and Noah needs the help."

Noah Carson. Addie didn't know anything about him except he was some relative of Laurel's boyfriend, and he needed a housekeeper. Addie didn't have experience keeping anyone's house, let alone a ranch, but she needed a job and someplace to stay, and Laurel had provided her with both. In the kind of town Peter would never dream of finding on a map, let alone stepping foot into.

She hoped.

"I'm going to have to apologize about Noah, though," Laurel said, maneuvering her car onto a gravel road off the main highway. "This is kind of a surprise for him."

"A surprise?" Addie repeated, reaching into the back and stroking her finger over Seth's leg in an effort to soothe.

"It's just, Noah *needs* the help, but doesn't want to *admit* he needs the help, so we're forcing his hand a bit."

Addie's horror must have shown on her face, because Laurel reached over and gave Addie's arm a squeeze, her gaze quickly returning to the road.

"It's fine. I promise."

"I don't want to be in anyone's way or a burden, Laurel. That isn't why I called you."

"I know, and in an ideal world Noah would hire you of his own volition, but we don't live in an ideal world. Noah's cousin, who used to do most of the housekeeping, moved out. Grady—that's Noah's other cousin—tried running an ad but Noah refused to see anyone. This, he can't refuse."

"Why?"

Laurel flicked a glance Addie's way as she pulled in front of a ramshackle, if roomy-looking, ranch house.

"Addie, I know you're in trouble."

Addie sucked in a breath. "You do?"

"I could be reading things wrong, but I'm guessing Seth's father isn't a very good man, and you need to get away from him."

Addie swallowed. It was the truth. It wouldn't be a lie to tell Laurel she was right. Seth's father was a terrible man, and Addie desperately needed to get away from him.

"I'm a cop, Addie. I've dealt with a lot of domestics. This is the perfect place to get away from a guy who can't control himself. You're safe here. In Bent. At the Carson Ranch, and with me looking out for you." Laurel smiled reassuringly.

"I just…" Addie inhaled and exhaled, looking at the house in front of her. It looked downright historical. "I need a fresh start. I'd hate to think it's built on someone who doesn't want me around."

"Noah might not want you around, but he needs you around. The way I see it, you two need each other. Noah might be quiet or gruff, but he's not a jerk. He'll treat you right no matter how much he doesn't want you to be here. I can promise you that."

"And the baby?"

"I've never seen Noah hurt anyone, and I've known him all my life and worked in law enforcement here for almost ten years. But most especially, I've never seen him be cruel to anyone, even Delaneys. He's not an easy man to read, but he's a good man. I'd bet my life on that."

The door to the house opened and a big, broad, bearded man stepped out. He wore jeans and a T-shirt, the lines of a tattoo visible at the sleeve. His grin was like sin, and all for Laurel. So this couldn't be the quiet, reserved Noah she was apparently ambushing.

"That's your man?" Addie asked, watching him saunter toward where they were parked. She'd never seen two people just look at each other and flash sparks.

Laurel grinned. "Yes, it is. Come on. Let's get you introduced."

* * *

Noah glowered out the window. Damn Grady. More, damn Laurel Delaney getting her Delaney nose all up in his Carson business. Since he wasn't the one sleeping with her, Noah didn't know why he had to be the one saddled with her relative.

But saddled he was.

The young woman who got out of the passenger seat looked nothing like a housekeeper, not that a housekeeper had ever graced the uneven halls of the Carson Ranch. He came from hardscrabble stock who'd never seen much luxury in life. Never seen much purpose for it, either.

Noah *still* didn't, but all his help had moved out. Grady was off living with a Delaney. Vanessa, who'd once taken on much of the cleaning and cooking responsibilities—no matter how poorly—had moved into town. His brother, Ty, came and went as he pleased, spending much of his time in town. Any time he spent at the ranch was with the horses or pushing Noah's buttons. Noah's teenage stepcousin was as helpful as a skunk.

Noah was running a small cattle ranch on his own, and yes, cleaning and cooking definitely fell by the wayside.

Didn't mean he needed an outsider lurking in the corners dusting or whatnot. Especially some wispy, timid blonde.

The blonde pulled a baby out of the back seat of the car. And she had a baby no less. Not even a very big-looking baby. The kind of tiny, drooly thing that would only serve to make him feel big and clumsy.

Noah's scowl deepened. He didn't know what to do

with babies. Or wispy blondes. Or people in general. If only the horses could housekeep. He'd be set.

The door opened, Laurel striding in first. Noah didn't bother to soften his scowl and she rolled her eyes at him.

Noah was a firm believer in history, and the history of Bent, Wyoming, was that Carsons and Delaneys hated each other, and anytime they didn't, only bad things came of it. Noah didn't know what Laurel had done to Grady to change Grady's mind on the importance of the feud, but here they were, ruining his life. As a couple.

It was a shame he liked Laurel. Made all his scowling and disapproval hard to hang on to.

The blonde carrying the baby stepped in behind Laurel, followed by Grady.

"Noah," Laurel said with one of those smiles that were a clear and sad attempt to get him to smile back.

He didn't.

"Noah Carson, this is your new housekeeper, Addie Foster, and her son, Seth. Addie, this is Noah. Ignore the gruff Wyoming cowboy exterior. He's a teddy bear underneath."

Noah grunted and Grady laughed. "Ease up there, princess. No one's going to believe that."

Laurel shot Grady a disapproving look. "The point is, Noah will be a fair and, if not pleasant, a *kind* employer. Won't you, Noah?"

He grunted again. Then looked at the blonde. "Thought you were a Delaney."

"Oh, well." Addie smiled, or tried to. "Sort of. My grandfather was one." She waved a nervous hand, her eyes darting all around and not settling on any one thing.

"I'll show you to your room, and Noah and Grady can bring in the baby stuff," Laurel said cheerfully, already leading Addie and baby down the hall like she owned the place.

"Come on, let's get the stuff," Grady said once the women were gone.

"Remember when this was my house because I was the only one willing to work the ranch full time?" Noah glanced back at where the two women had disappeared. "Your woman's going to get baby ideas," he muttered.

Grady scoffed, but Noah noted that he didn't argue.

Which was to be expected, Noah supposed, but Noah hated change. Especially uncomfortable change. People change.

"You don't have to be prickly about it. You're going to have a clean house and a few home-cooked meals. Try a thank-you."

"You know me a lot better than that," Noah returned as they opened the trunk to Laurel's car.

Grady sighed, grabbing a stroller. "Laurel thinks Addie's in a bit of trouble."

"What kind of trouble?"

"Laurel's theory? Abusive husband."

"Hell," Noah grumbled. He didn't know what to do with babies, and he definitely didn't know what to do with a fragile woman who'd been the victim of abuse.

"She just needs a fresh start is all. Somewhere she feels safe. I'll keep an eye out for any other jobs that'll work while she's got the baby, but this is important. And it isn't like you don't need the help."

"It isn't that bad."

Grady looked at him dolefully as they hefted a menagerie of baby things out of Laurel's trunk and headed toward the house. "Pretty sure you were wearing that shirt yesterday, cousin."

Noah looked down at the faded flannel work shirt. "No, I wasn't." Maybe. He didn't mind doing laundry, but he hated folding laundry, and then the clean and dirty sometimes got a little mixed up if they weren't muck clothes.

Grady stepped inside, but Noah paused on the stairs. He looked back over his shoulder at the mountains in the distance. Clouds were beginning to form and roll, and there'd be a hell of a storm coming for them soon enough.

On a sigh, Noah stepped inside. This was his idea of a nightmare, but he wasn't a jerk who couldn't put his own wants and preferences on the back burner for someone in trouble. If the woman and the baby were really running from some no-good piece-of-trash ex...

He'd suck it up. He might be growly and taciturn, but he wasn't a bad guy. Not when it came to things like this. She might be related to a Delaney, but he knew what violence could do to a family. Carsons couldn't help but know that, and he'd promised himself he wouldn't be like them.

Somehow it had worked out. This generation of Carsons wasn't half as bad as the last, if a little wild, but he and Grady and Ty stood up for people who couldn't stand up for themselves. He wouldn't stop now.

Even if the woman and her baby did have Delaney in their blood.

Noah walked down the hall and into the room where Grady was already setting up all the baby gear for

Addie while Laurel cooed over the baby in her arms. Noah gave Grady a pointed look but Grady ignored it.

"Well, we better get going and let you have some settle-in time," Laurel said, looking around the room as if inspecting it. "You can call me day or night. Whatever you need, or Seth needs."

"Thanks," Addie said, and Noah tried not to frown over the tears shimmering in the woman's eyes. Hell, female tears were the worst thing. Laurel and Addie hugged, the baby between them, before Grady and Laurel left. Laurel paused in front of Noah.

"Thank you," she mouthed, holding a hand over her heart.

Noah merely scowled, but the annoying thing about Laurel was she was never fooled by things like that. She seemed to be under the impression he was the nicest one of the lot.

Noah hated that she was right.

"So, I'll leave you to settle in," Noah offered, not expressly making eye contact considering this was a bedroom. "Need anything, let me know."

"Oh, but… Shouldn't I be saying that to you? I mean, shouldn't we go over duties? Since Laurel and Grady set this up, I… I'm not sure what you expect of me." She bounced the baby on her hip, but Noah figured it was more nerves than trying to keep the boy from fussing.

He tried to smile, though even if he'd accomplished it he knew it was hard to see beyond the beard. "We can do it in the morning."

She blinked at him, all wide blue-eyed innocence. "I'd like to do it now. This is a job, and I should be working it."

"It's Sunday. Rule number one, you don't work on Sunday."

"What do I do then?"

"I don't care, but I'll cook my own meals and clean up after myself on Sundays. Understood?"

She nodded. "What's rule number two?"

Timid. He did not know what to do with timid, but he was being forced. Well, maybe he needed to treat her like a skittish horse. Horse training wasn't his expertise, but he understood enough about the animals to know they needed a clear leader, routine and the opportunity to build their confidence.

Noah glanced at the hopeful young woman and tried not to grimace.

"I have a checklist," she blurted.

"A checklist?"

"Yes, of duties. Of things I do for people. When I'm housekeeping. I… You…"

The sinking feeling that had been plaguing him since Grady announced his and Laurel's little plan that morning sank deeper. "You haven't done this before, have you?"

"Oh." She looked everywhere around the room except him. "Um. Well. Sort of."

"Sort of?"

"I… I can cook, and clean. I just haven't ever been on a ranch, or lived in someone else's house as their employee. So that's, um, well, it's super weird." She glanced at the kid in her arms. "And I have a baby. Which is weird."

"Super weird," he intoned.

She blinked up at him, some of that anxiety softening in her features. "If you tell me what you want me to do, I promise I can do it. I'm just not sure what you expect. Or want."

"I'll make you up a checklist."

She opened her mouth, then closed it, then opened it again. "I'm sorry, was that a joke? I can't exactly tell."

Noah's mouth twitched of its own accord. "Settle in. Get the baby settled in. Tomorrow morning, six a.m., kitchen table. We'll discuss your duties then."

"Okay."

He turned to go, but she stopped him with a hesitant "um."

He looked over his shoulder at her.

"It's just, could you give us something of a tour? A map? Smoke signals to the bathroom?"

Noah was very bad at controlling his facial features, half of why he kept a beard, so the distaste must have been clear all over his face.

"I'm sorry, I make jokes when I'm nervous."

"Funny, I just shut up."

Those big blue eyes blinked at him, not quite in horror, but not necessarily in understanding, either.

"Sorry," he muttered. "That was a joke. I joke when I'm nervous, too."

"Really?"

"No. Never," he replied, chastising himself for being prickly, and then ignoring his own chastisement. "Follow me. I'll show you around."

Chapter 2

September

Addie liked to use Seth's afternoon nap for laundry folding and listening to an audiobook, then dinner prep. She'd been at the Carson Ranch for a full month now, and while she couldn't claim comfort or the belief she was truly safe and settled, she'd developed a routine, and that was nice.

She found she liked housekeeping, much to her surprise. As an administrative assistant in the family business—a franchise of furniture stores Grandpa had moved to Boston to run when his father-in-law had died suddenly back in the fifties—she'd hated waiting on people, keeping things and meetings organized. She'd taken the job because it had been expected of her, and she hadn't known what else to do with her life.

So, the fact keeping everything neat and organized at Noah's house, making meals and helping the ranch run smoothly felt good was a surprise. Maybe it was the six months of being on the run and not having a house or anything to care for except Seth's safety.

Maybe it was simply that she felt, if not safe here, like she *fit* here.

Addie worked on chopping vegetables for a salad, the baby monitor she'd bought with her first overly generous paycheck sitting on the sill of the window overlooking the vast Carson Ranch. She hadn't needed a monitor in any of the previous places she'd been. They were all hotel rooms or little one-room apartments where she could hear Seth no matter where she went.

Now she had a whole house to roam, and so did Seth. They had these beautiful views to take in. For as long as it lasted, this life was *good*.

Some little voice in the back of her head warned her not to get too attached or settle in too deeply. Peter could always find her here, although it was unlikely. She hadn't shared anything with her father since he'd cut off Kelly long before Seth, and she'd been on shaky ground for *not* cutting Kelly off as well.

As for the rest of her friends and family, she'd sent a cheery email to them saying she'd gotten an amazing job teaching English in China and she'd send them contact information when she was settled.

If anyone had been suspicious, she'd been long gone before she could see evidence of it.

Addie didn't miss Boston or her cold father or even the furniture store that was supposed to be her legacy. That was also a surprise. Boston and her family had always been home, though not exactly a warm one after

Mom had died when Addie'd been a kid. Still, striking out and starting over as a faux single mom had been surprisingly fulfilling. If she discounted the terror and constant running.

But she wasn't running right now. More and more, she was thinking of the Carson Ranch as *home*.

"You are a hopeless idiot, Addie Foster," she muttered to herself.

She startled as the door swung open, the knife she'd been using clattering to the cutting board from nerveless fingers.

But it was only Noah who swept in, looking as he always did, like some mythical man from a Wild West time machine. Dirty old cowboy hat, scuffed and beaten-up cowboy boots. The jeans and heavy coat were modern enough, but Noah's beard wasn't like all the fashionable hipster ones she was used to. No, Noah's beard was something of an old-fashioned shield.

She found herself pondering a little too deeply what he might be shielding himself from. Snapping herself out of that wonder, she picked up the knife. "You're early," she offered, trying to sound cheerful. "Dinner isn't ready yet."

It was another thing she'd surprisingly settled into with ease. They all three ate dinner together. Noah wasn't exactly a talkative guy, but he listened. Sometimes he even entertained Seth while she cleaned up dinner.

He grunted, as he was so often wont to do, and slid his coat and hat off before hanging them on the pegs. She watched it all through her peripheral vision, forcing herself not to linger on the outline of his muscles in the thermal shirt he wore.

Yes, Noah had muscles, and they were not for her to ogle. Though she did on occasion. She was *human*, after all.

"Just need to call the vet," he said.

"Is something wrong?"

"Horses aren't right. Will there be enough for dinner if Ty comes over?"

"Of course." Addie had gotten used to random Carsons showing up at the house at any time of day or night, or for any meal. She always made a little extra for dinner, as leftovers could easily be made into a lunch the next day.

Gotten used to. She smiled to herself as Noah grabbed the phone and punched in a number. It was almost unfathomable to have gotten used to a new life and think she might be able to stay in it.

Noah spoke in low tones to the vet and Addie worked on adding more lettuce to the salad so there would be enough for Ty. She watched out the window at the fading twilight. The days were getting shorter and colder. It was early fall yet, but the threat of snow seemed to be in the air.

She loved it here. She couldn't deny it. The mountains in the distance, the ramshackle stables and barns. The animals she didn't trust to approach but loved to watch. The way the sun gilded everything gold in the mornings and fiery red in the evenings. The air, so clear and different from anything she'd ever known before.

She felt at *home* here. More so than any point in her life. Maybe it was the circumstances, everything she was running from, how much she'd taken for granted before her sister had gotten mixed up with a mob boss. But she felt it, no matter how hard she tried to fight it.

She could easily see Seth growing up in this amazing place with Noah as something like a role model. Oh, it almost hurt to think of. It was a pipe dream. She couldn't allow herself to believe Peter could never find them here. Could she?

Noah stopped talking and set the phone back in its cradle, looking far too grim. Addie's stomach clenched. "Is everything okay?"

"Vet said it sounded like horses got into something chemical. Poison even," Noah said gruffly with no preamble.

Any warmth or comfort or *love* of this place drained out of Addie in an instant. "Poison," she repeated in a whisper.

Noah frowned at her, then softened that imperceptible amount she was beginning to recognize. "Carsons have some enemies in Bent. It isn't unheard of."

It was certainly possible. The Carsons were a rough-and-tumble bunch. Noah's brother, Ty, could be gruff and abrasive when he was irritated. Grady was certainly charming, but he ran a bar and though she'd never spent any time there since the ranch and Seth took up most of her time, Laurel often spoke disparagingly of the clientele there.

Then there was Noah's cousin Vanessa. Sharp, antagonistic Vanessa would likely have some enemies. Or Grady's troublemaking stepbrother.

The problem was none of them lived at the ranch full-time. They came and went. Noah could be grumpy, but she truly couldn't imagine him having enemies.

She, on the other hand, had a very real enemy.

"Are you sure?" she asked tentatively.

"Look, I know you've had some trouble in your past, but who would poison my horses to get at you?"

He had a point. A good point, even if he didn't know the whole story. Peter would want her and Seth, not Noah or his horses. He'd never do something so small and piddly that wouldn't hurt *her* directly.

"Trust me," Noah said, dialing a new number into the phone. "This doesn't have a thing to do with you, and the vet said if he gets over here soon and Ty helps out, we'll be able to save them." Noah turned away from her and started talking into the phone, presumably to his brother, without even a hi.

Addie stared hard at her salad preparations, willing her heart to steady, willing herself to believe Noah's words. What *would* poisoned horses have to do with her?

Nothing. Absolutely nothing. She had to believe that, but everything that had felt like settling in and comfort and routine earlier now curdled in her gut.

Don't ever get too used to this place. It's not yours, and it never will be.

She'd do well to remember it.

October

Noah frowned at the fence. Someone had hacked it to pieces, and now half his herd was wandering the damn mountains as a winter storm threatened in the west.

He immediately thought of last month and the surprise poison a few of his horses had ingested. The vet had saved the horses, but Noah and Ty had never found the culprits. Noah liked to blame Laurel and her precious sheriff's department for the crime still being un-solved, even though it wasn't fair.

Whoever had poisoned the horses had done a well enough job being sneaky, but not in creating much damage. For all he knew it was some kids playing a dumb prank, or even an accident.

This right here was no accident. It was strange. Maybe it could be chalked up to a teenage prank, but something about all this felt wrong, like an itch he couldn't reach.

But he had to fix the fence and get the cows be-fore he could worry about wrong gut feelings. Noah mounted his horse and headed for the cabin. He'd have to start carrying his cell to call for help if these little problems kept cropping up.

What would Addie be up to? She'd been his house-keeper for two months now, and he had to admit in the quiet of his own mind, he'd gotten used to her presence. So used to it, he relied on it. She kept the cabin neat and clean, her cooking was better and better, and she and the boy… Well, he didn't mind them underfoot as much as he'd thought he was going to.

Maybe, just maybe, he'd been a little lonely in that house by himself earlier in the summer, and maybe, just maybe, he appreciated some company. Because Addie didn't intrude on his silence or poke at him for more. The boy was loud, and getting increasingly mo-bile, which sometimes meant he was crawling all over Noah if he tried to sit down, but that wasn't the kind of intrusion that bothered him. He found he rather en-joyed the child's drooly smiles and screeches of delight.

"What has happened to you?" he muttered to him-self. He looked at the gray sky. A winter storm had been threatening for days, but it hadn't let down its wrath yet. Noah had no doubt it would choose the most inopportune time possible. As in, right now with his cows scattered this way and that.

He urged his horse to go a little faster. He'd need Grady and Ty, or Vanessa and Ty if Grady couldn't get away from the bar. Maybe even Clint could come over after school, assuming he'd gone today. This was an all-hands-on-deck situation.

But as he approached the cabin, he frowned at a set of footprints in the faint dusting of snow that had fallen this morning. The footprints didn't go from where visitors usually parked to the door, but instead followed the fence line before clearly hopping the fence, then went up to the front window.

A hot bolt of rage went through Noah. Someone had been at that window watching Addie. He jumped from the horse and rushed into the house. Only when he flung open the door and stormed inside did he realize how stupid he looked.

Addie jumped a foot at her seat on the couch, where she was folding clothes. "What's wrong? What happened?" she asked, clutching one of his shirts to her chest. It was an odd thing to see, her delicate hands holding the fabric of something he wore on his body.

He shook that thought away and focused on thinking clearly. On being calm. He didn't want to scare her. "Somebody broke the fence and the cows got out."

Addie stared at him, blue eyes wide, the color draining from her dainty face as it had the day of the poisoning. He'd assured her *that* had nothing to do with her, and he believed it. He believed this had nothing to do with her, too, but those footsteps and her reaction to anything wrong or sudden...

He wondered about that. She never spoke of Seth's father or what she might be fleeing, and her actions always seemed to back up Laurel's theory about being on the run from an abusive husband. Especially as she now glanced worriedly at Seth's baby monitor, as if she could see him napping in his room through it.

Noah shook his head. He was being paranoid. Letting her fear outweigh his rational mind. He might have a bit of a soft spot for Addie and her boy, which he'd admit to no one ever, but he couldn't let her fears become his own.

She was his employee. If he sometimes caught himself watching her work in his kitchen... A housekeeper was all he needed. Less complicated than some of the other things his mind drifted to when he wasn't careful.

Luckily, Noah was exceedingly careful.

"Going to call in some backup to help me round them up."

"Shouldn't you call Laurel?" She paused when he scowled, but then continued. "Or anyone at the sheriff's department?"

She had a point, but he didn't want to draw attention to repeated issues at his ranch. Didn't want to draw the town's attention to Addie and that something might be going on, if it did in fact connect to her.

Maybe the smarter thing to do would be keep it all under wraps and then be more diligent, more watchful, and find whoever was pulling these little pranks himself. Mete out some Carson justice.

Yeah, he liked that idea a lot better.

"I'll handle it. Don't worry."

"Does this have to do with the poisoning? Do you think—"

Noah sent her a silencing look, trying not to feel guilty when she shrank back into the couch. "I'll handle it. Don't worry," he repeated.

She muttered something that sounded surprisingly sarcastic though he didn't catch the words, but she went back to folding the laundry and Noah crossed to the phone.

He called Ty first, then let Ty handle rounding up whatever Carsons could be of help. He didn't tell Ty about the footsteps, but a bit later when Ty, Grady and Clint showed up and Noah left the cabin with them, he held Grady back while Ty and Clint went to saddle their horses.

"What's up?" Grady asked. "You think this is connected to the poison?"

"I think I can't rule it out. I don't have a clue who's doing it, but part of me thinks it's some dumb kid trying to poke at a Carson to see what he'll do."

Grady laughed. "He'd have to be pretty dumb."

"Yeah. I don't want Addie to know, but..." He sighed. He needed someone besides him to know. Someone besides him on the watch, and Grady ran the one bar in town. He saw and heard things few other people in Bent did. "There were footprints at the window, as if someone had been watching her."

Grady's jaw tightened. "You think it's the ex?"

"I don't know what it is, but we need to keep an eye out."

Grady nodded. "I'll tell Laurel."

"No. She'll tell Addie. She's just calmed down from the poisoning—now this. I don't want to rile her more."

"Laurel will only do what's best. You know that."

Noah puffed out a breath. "Addie's settled from that skittish thing she was before. Hate to see her go back."

"She's not a horse, Noah." Grady grinned. "But maybe you know that all too well."

Noah scowled. "I want to know who poisoned my horses. I want to know who ran off my cattle, and I damn well want to know who's peeping in my window."

Grady nodded. "We'll get to the bottom of it. No one touches what's ours. Cow, mine or woman." Grady grinned at the old family joke.

Noah didn't. "No woman issues here," he grumbled. But Grady was right in one respect. No one messed with the Carsons of Bent, Wyoming, and walked away happy or satisfied about it. For over a century, the Carsons had been pitted on the wrong side of the law. The outlaws of Bent. The rich, law-abiding Delaneys had made sure that legend perpetuated, no matter what good came out of the Carson clan.

It was a good thing bad reputations could serve a purpose now and again. He'd do anything to protect what was his.

Addie wasn't his, though. No matter how he sometimes imagined she was.

He shook those thoughts away. "Will you stay here and watch out?"

"You could," Grady suggested.

"Addie'd think that's weird. I don't want her suspicious."

"That's an awful lot of concern for a Delaney, cousin," Grady said with one of his broad grins that were meant to irritate. Grady had perfected that kind of smile.

Noah knew arguing with Grady about the cause of his concern would only egg Grady on, so Noah grunted and headed for the stables.

Addie Foster was not his to protect personally. Grady'd do just as good a job, and Noah had cows to find and bring back home.

When that weird edge of guilt plagued him the rest of the night, as if his mission was to protect Addie and asking for help was some kind of failure, Noah had the uncomfortable feeling of not knowing what the hell to do about it.

When Noah didn't know how to fix a problem, he did the next best thing. He ignored it.

Chapter 3

November

Addie hummed along with the song playing over the speaker at the general store. Seth happily slammed his sippy cup against the sides of the cart as she unloaded the groceries onto the checkout counter.

"I swear he grows every week," Jen Delaney said with a smile as she began to ring up Addie's items.

"It's crazy. He's already in eighteen-month clothes." Addie bagged the groceries as Jen handed them to her.

It was true. Seth was growing like a weed, thriving in this life she'd built for them. Addie smiled to herself. After the horse poison and the fence debacle, things had settled down. She'd been here three months now. She had a routine down, knew many of the people in town and mostly had stopped looking over her shoulder at every stray noise. Sometimes nights were still hard, but for the most part, life was good. Really good.

Noah had assured her time and time again those two incidents were feud-related, nothing to do with her, and she was finally starting to believe him. She trusted Noah. Implicitly. With her safety, with Seth. Laurel had been right on that first car ride. Noah wasn't always easy to read or the warmest human being, but he was a *good* man.

Which had created something of a Noah situation. Well, more a weirdness than a situation. And a weirdness she was quite sure only she felt, because she doubted Noah felt much of anything for her. On the off chance he did, it was so buried she'd likely not live long enough to see it.

"Addie?"

Addie glanced up at Jen. The young woman must have finished ringing everything up while Addie was lost in Noah thoughts. Something that happened far too often as of late.

Addie paid for the groceries, smiling at Jen while she inwardly chastised herself.

Noah Carson was her boss. No matter that she liked the way he looked or that she got fluttery over his gentle way with the horses and cows. And Seth.

She sighed inwardly. He was so sweet with Seth. Never got frustrated with the boy's increasing mobility or fascination with Noah's hat or beard.

But no matter that Noah was sweet with Seth, or so kind with her, he was off-limits for her ever-growing fantasies of good, handsome men and happily-ever-afters.

She glanced down at the happy boy kicking in the

cart. Sometimes Seth gave her that smile with big blue eyes and she missed her sister so much it hurt. But it always steadied her, renewed any resolve that needed renewing.

She would do anything to keep him safe.

She pushed the cart out of the general store to where her truck was parallel parked, but before she reached it, a man blocked her way.

She looked at him expectantly, waiting for him to move or say something, but he just stood there. Staring at her.

She didn't recognize him. Everything about him was nondescript and plain, and still he didn't move or speak.

"Excuse me," she finally said, pulling Seth out of the cart and balancing him on her hip. "This is my truck."

The man moved only enough to glance at the truck. Also a new skill for her, driving a truck, but Noah had fixed up one of the old ones he used on the ranch for her to use when she had errands.

The strange man turned his gaze back to her and still said nothing. He still didn't move.

Addie's heart started beating too hard in her chest, fear seizing her limbs. This wasn't normal. This wasn't…

She turned quickly, her hand going over Seth's head with the idea of protecting him somehow. This man was here to get her. Peter had finally caught up with them. She had to run.

She could go back in the store and…and…

"Oof." Instead of her intended dash to the store, she slammed into a hard wall of man.

"Addie."

She looked up at Noah, whose hand curled around

her arm. He looked down at her, something like concern or confusion hidden underneath all that hair and stoicism.

"Everything okay?" he asked in that gruff voice that suggested no actual interest in the answer, but that was the thing about Noah. He gave the impression he didn't care about anything beyond his horses and cows, but he'd fixed up that truck for her even though she hadn't asked. He played with Seth as if people who hired housekeepers usually had relationships with the housekeeper's kid. He made sure there was food for Ty, room for Vanessa and Clint, and work if any of them wanted it.

He was a man who cared about a lot of people and hid it well.

"I just…" She looked back at where the strange, unspeaking man had been. There was no one there. No one. She didn't know how to explain it to Noah. She didn't know how to explain it to anyone.

The man hadn't said anything threatening. Hadn't done anything threatening, but that hadn't been normal. "I thought I saw someone…" She looked around again, but there was no sign of anyone in the sunshine-laden morning.

"As in *someone* someone?" Noah asked in that same stoic voice, and yet Addie had no doubt if she gave any hint of fear, Noah would jump into action.

So she forced herself to smile. "I'm being silly. It was just a man." She shook her head and gestured with her free hand. "I'm sure it was nothing." Which was a flat-out lie. As much as she'd love to tell herself it was nothing, she knew Peter too well to think this wasn't *something*.

She blew out a breath, scanning the road again. There was just no other explanation. He knew where she was. He knew.

"Addie."

She looked back at Noah, realizing his hand was still on her arm. Big and rough. Strong. Working for Noah had made her feel safe. Protected.

But this wasn't his fight, and she'd brought it to his door.

"I'm sorry," she whispered, closing her eyes.

"For what?" he asked in that gruff, irritable way.

Seth lunged for Noah, happily babbling his favorite word over and over again. "No, no, no." Addie tried to hold on to the wiggling child, but Noah took him out of her arms with ease.

"Aren't you supposed to be back at the ranch? You know I get groceries on Wednesdays. I could have picked up whatever for you."

"It's feed," Noah said. "Couldn't have loaded it up yourself with the baby." He glanced at the grocery cart behind her. "We'll put the groceries in my truck."

"Oh, I can handle…"

"He always falls asleep on the way home, doesn't he?" Noah asked as if it wasn't *something* that he knew Seth's routine. Or that he was letting Seth pull the cowboy hat off his head, and then smash it back on.

Noah moved for the cart, because you didn't argue with Noah. He made a decision and you followed it whether you wanted to or not. Partly because he was her boss, but she also thought it was partly just him.

"Let's get home and you can tell me what really happened." Noah's dark gaze scanned the street as if he could figure everything out simply by looking around.

She knew it was foolish, but she was a little afraid he could. "I swear, nothing happened. I'm being silly."

"Well, you can tell me about that, too. At home." He handed her Seth and then took the cart.

Home. She'd wanted to build a *home*. For Seth. For herself. But if Peter had found her…

She couldn't let herself get worked up. For Seth's sake, she had to think clearly. She had to formulate a plan. And she couldn't possibly let Noah know the truth.

Noah didn't think running away was the answer, that she knew after listening to his lectures to Clint.

Beyond that, regardless of his personal feelings for her—whether they existed deep down or not—he had a very clear personal code. That personal code would never let a woman and a baby run away without protection.

Which would put him in danger. Very much because of her personal feelings, she couldn't let that happen.

"Okay. I'll meet you back at the ranch." She smiled pleasantly and even let him take the cart of groceries and wheel it down to where his truck was parked on the corner. She frowned at that. "If you were in town to pick up feed, why are you here?"

Noah didn't glance at her, but he did shrug. "Saw the truck. Thought you might need some help loading." Then he was hidden behind his truck door, loading the groceries into the back seat.

Addie glanced down at Seth. "I really don't know what to do with that man," she murmured, opening her own truck door and getting Seth situated in his car seat. She supposed in the end it didn't matter she didn't know what to do with him. If someone was here…

Well, Seth was her priority. She couldn't be a sitting duck, and she couldn't bring Noah into harm's way. This wasn't like the poison or the fence. This was directed at *her*. That man had stared at *her*. Whether or not those first two things were related didn't matter, because *this* was about *her*.

Which meant it was time to leave again. She slid into the driver's seat, glancing in her rearview mirror, where she watched Noah start walking back toward the store to return the now-empty cart.

Addie had become adept at lying in the past year. She'd *had* to, but mainly she only had to lie to strangers or people she didn't know very well. Even that initial lie to Laurel, and the past three months of upholding it with everyone, hadn't been hard. Pretending to be Seth's biological mother was as easy as pie since he was hers and hers alone these days.

But finding a new lie, and telling it to Noah's face— that was going to be a challenge. She changed her gaze from Noah's reflection to Seth in the car seat. She smiled at him in the mirror.

"It's okay, baby. I'll take care of it." Somehow. Someway.

Noah had unloaded the groceries at the front door, and Addie had taken them inside, the baby monitor sitting on the kitchen table as they quietly worked.

He should have insisted they talk about what had transpired at the general store, but instead he'd gone back out to his truck and driven over to the barn to unload the feed.

Then he'd dawdled. He was not a man accustomed to dawdling. He was also not a man accustomed to *this*.

Every time something bad had happened in the first two months, he'd been the one to find it. Little attacks that had been aimed at the ranch.

Whatever had shaken Addie today was about her. What she'd seen. He could attribute her shakiness to being "silly" as she said, or even her previous "situation" with her ex, but he didn't know what that was. Not really. He certainly hadn't poked into it. He was not a poker, and Addie was not a babbler. It was why this whole thing worked.

But she'd eased into life at the Carson Ranch. So much so that Noah, on occasion, considered thanking Laurel and Grady for forcing his hand on the whole housekeeper thing. She'd made his life easier.

Except where she hadn't. Those uncomfortable truths he'd had to learn about himself—he was lonely, he liked having someone under his roof and to talk to for as little as he did it. He liked having her and Seth in particular.

Which was his own fault. She didn't carry any responsibility for his stupid feelings. Even if he'd had a sense of triumph over the fact Addie didn't jump at random noises anymore, and she didn't get scared for no reason. Both with the poison and the fence, she'd walked on eggshells for a few days, then gotten back to her old quietly cheerful self.

He'd never told her about the footprints and they'd never returned. So maybe he'd overreacted then. Maybe *he'd* been silly, but whatever had rattled her at the store was something real. Which meant they needed to talk about it.

But he wasn't the *talker*. He was the doer. Grady or Ty went in and did all the figuring out, and Noah brought up the rear, so to speak. He was there. He did what needed to be done, but he was no great determiner of what that thing was. He left that to people who liked to jack their jaw.

Which was when he realized what he really needed. He pulled his cell phone out of his pocket and typed a text. When he got the response he'd hoped for, he put his phone away and got back to his real work. Not protecting Addie Foster and whatever her issue was, but running a ranch.

He worked hard, thinking as little about Addie as possible, and didn't reappear at the main house until supper. He stepped up onto the porch, scraping the mud off his boots before entering.

The blast of warmth that hit him was an Addie thing. She opened the west-facing curtains so the sun set golden through the windows and into the kitchen and entryway every day. Whenever he stepped in, she had supper ready or almost.

Seth slammed his sippy cup against his high-chair tray and yelled, "No!" Noah was never sure if it was a greeting or an admonition.

Noah grunted at the boy, his favorite mode of greeting. He sneaked a glance at Addie to make sure she still had her back to him, then made a ridiculous face that made Seth squeal out a laugh.

Noah advanced closer, but he noted Addie was slamming things around in the kitchen and didn't turn to face him with her usual greeting and announcement of what was for dinner.

It all felt a little too domestic, which was becoming more and more of a problem. He couldn't complain about being fed nightly by a pretty woman, but sitting down with her and her kid for a meal every day was getting to feel normal.

Integral.

Noah hovered there, not quite sure what to do. Laurel had assured him via text she'd come in and figure out whatever was up with Addie after he'd contacted her, but Addie did not seem calmed.

He cleared his throat. "Uh. Um, need help?" he offered awkwardly.

She turned to face him, tongs in one hand and an anger he'd never seen simmering in her blue eyes.

She pointed the tongs at him. "You, Noah Carson, are a coward. And a bit of a high-handed jerk."

He raised an eyebrow at her, but Addie didn't wilt. Not even a hint of backing down. She crossed her arms over her chest and stared right back at him. In another situation he might have been impressed at the way she'd blossomed into something fierce.

"Because?"

She huffed out a breath. "You went and told Laurel I was having a problem when I told you I was not."

"But you were."

"No. I wasn't." She pointed angrily at the table with the tongs. "Sit down and eat."

He'd never seen much of Addie's temper. Usually if she got irritated with him she went to some other room in the house and cleaned something. Or went into her room and played with Seth. She never actually directed any of her ire at him.

He didn't know what to do with it. But he *was* hungry, so he took his seat next to Seth's high chair, where the kid happily smacked his hands into the tiny pieces of food Addie had put on his tray before Noah walked in.

She slammed a plate in front of Noah. Chicken legs and mashed potatoes and some froufrou-looking salad thing. Usually she didn't *serve* him, but he wasn't one to argue with anyone, let alone an angry female.

She stomped back to the kitchen counter, then to the table again. She sat in a chair opposite him with an audible *thump*.

Her huffiness and sternness were starting to irritate him. He didn't have much of a temper beyond general curmudgeon, but when someone started poking at him, things tended to… Well, he tended to avoid people who made him lose his temper. Addie'd never even remotely tested that before.

But she sure was now.

"I can handle this," she said, leveling him with her sternest look. She shook out a paper towel and placed it on her lap like it was an expensive cloth napkin and they were in some upscale restaurant.

"What? What is this thing you can handle?" he returned evenly.

She stared right back at him like he was slow. "It's nothing. That's why I can handle it."

Noah wanted to beat his head against the table. "You were *visibly* shaken this morning, and it wasn't like it used to be."

Her sharp expression softened slightly. "What do you mean?"

Noah shrugged and turned his attention to his food. "When you first got here you were all jumpy-like. This was not the same thing."

She was quiet for a few seconds, so he took the opportunity to eat.

"I didn't know you noticed," she said softly.

He shrugged, shoveling mashed potatoes into his mouth and hoping this conversation was over.

He should have known better. Addie didn't poke at him, but she also didn't leave things unfinished. "I need you to promise you won't call Laurel like that again. The last thing I need is well-meaning people…" She trailed off for a few seconds until he looked up from his plate.

Her eyebrows were drawn together and she was frowning at her own plate, and Noah had the sinking, horrifying suspicion those were tears making her blue eyes look particularly shiny.

She cleared her throat. "I'll handle things. Don't bring Laurel into this again." She looked up, as if that was that.

"No."

"What did you say?" she asked incredulously.

"I said no."

She sputtered, something like a squeak emanating from her mouth. "You can't just…you can't just say no!"

"But I did."

Another squeaking sound, which Seth joined in as if it was a game.

Addie took a deep breath as if trying to calm herself. "A man stood in my way and wouldn't move. He said nothing, and he did nothing threatening. It was nothing. Calling Laurel, on the other hand, was something. And I did not appreciate it."

"If what happened this morning were nothing, it wouldn't have freaked you out. What did Laurel say?"

"She said you're an idiot and I should quit and move far away."

"No, she didn't." He didn't believe Laurel *would* say

something like that, but there was a panicked feeling tightening his chest.

"Noah, this isn't your problem," Addie said, and if he wasn't crazy, there was a hint of desperation in her tone, which only served to assure him this *was* his problem.

"You live under my roof, Addie Foster. You are my problem."

She frowned at him as if that made no sense to her, but it didn't need to. It made sense to *him*. The people in his family and under his roof were under his protection. End of story.

Chapter 4

Addie ate the rest of her dinner in their normal quiet companionship. Quite honestly, she was rendered speechless by Noah's gruff, certain proclamation.

You are my problem.

He had no idea what kind of problem she could be if she stayed, and yet no matter how many times she'd chastised herself to pack up and leave *immediately*, here she was. Cleaning up dinner dishes while Seth crawled in and out of the play tent she'd placed on the floor for him.

You are my problem.

She glanced at the door. Noah had stridden back outside right after dinner, which he did sometimes. Chores to finish up or horses or cows to check on, though sometimes she thought he did it just to escape her.

She sighed heavily. Noah made no sense to her, but

she didn't want to be his *problem*. He'd been nothing but kind, in fact proving to her that her sister's determination after Peter that all men were scum wasn't true in the least.

Noah might be hard to read and far too gruff, but he was the furthest thing from scum she'd ever met.

She glanced at Seth, who popped his smiling face out of the tent opening and screeched.

"Except for you, of course, baby," Addie said, grinning at Seth. Growing like a weed. It hurt to look at him sometimes, some mix of sorrow and joy causing an unbearable pain in her heart.

He'd settled in so well here. Their routine worked, and what would she do when she left? Where else would she find this kind of job where he got to be with her? Even if she could find a job that would allow her to afford day care, they wouldn't have the kind of security she needed. Seth always needed to be with her in case they needed to escape.

Like now.

She squeezed her eyes shut. She was in an impossible situation. She didn't want to put Noah—or any of the Carsons—at risk of Peter, but if she ran away without thinking things through, she risked Seth's well-being.

"No! No! No!" Seth yelled happily, making a quick crawling beeline for the door.

Addie took a few steps before scooping Seth up into her arms, a wriggling mass of complaint.

"He's not back yet," Addie said gently, settling Seth on her hip as she moved to the windows to close the curtains for the night. Sometimes, though, she and Seth stood here and watched the stars wink and shimmer in the distance while they waited for Noah's last return of the evening.

It felt like home, this place. Even with a man whose life she didn't share and was her boss living under the same roof. It was all so *right*. How could she leave?

And how can you stay?

She shook her head against the thought and closed the curtains. As she stepped back toward the kitchen to gather Seth's tent, she noticed something on the floor.

An envelope. Odd. Dread skittered through her. Noah always brought the mail in when he came to grab lunch. He always put it in the same place. Which was most definitely not the floor.

Maybe it had fallen. Maybe someone had managed to shoehorn the envelope through the bottom of the door; most of the weather stripping was in desperate need of being replaced.

Her name was written in dark block letters. With no address. She swallowed, her body shaking against her will.

Seth wiggled in her arms and it was a good anchor to reality. She had a precious life to keep safe. Somehow. Someway. She was the only one who could.

She forced herself to bend down and place Seth gently on the floor. He crawled off for the tent, and with a shaking hand Addie picked up the envelope.

Slowly, she walked over to the table and sat down. She stared at it, willing her breathing to even and her hands to stop shaking. She'd open it, and then she'd know what her next move would have to be.

She forced one more breath in and out and then broke the seal of the envelope and pulled out the sheet of paper. Feeling sick to her stomach, Addie unfolded the paper until she could see text.

I see you, Addie.

She pressed her fingers to her mouth, willing herself not to break down. She'd come this far. She couldn't break down every time he found her. She just had to keep going, over and over again, until he didn't.

She wanted to drop the paper. Forget it existed. But she didn't have that option. She folded it back up and slid it inside the envelope, then pushed it into her pocket. She'd keep it. A reminder.

He wanted her scared. She didn't know why that seemed to be his priority when he could have her killed and take Seth far away.

There was no point trying to rationalize a sociopath's behavior. She knew one thing and one thing only: Peter wouldn't stop. So neither could she.

If she'd been alone, she might have risked staying in one spot. Just to see what he would do. But she wasn't alone. Now she had to protect Noah and the Carsons and Delaneys who'd been so kind to her.

She stood carefully, walking stiffly over to Seth. She pulled him out of the tent, much to his screaming dismay.

She patted his back. "Come on, baby. We don't have much time." She glanced at the windows where the curtains were now pulled. Was he out there? Waiting for her? Was it all a lure to get her to come out?

Were his men out there? Oh, God, had they hurt Noah? True panic beat through her. She could escape. She'd had enough close calls—a landlord letting her know a man had broken into her apartment, noticing a broken motel window before she'd stepped inside—to know she could find her way out of this one.

But what if they'd hurt Noah? She couldn't leave him. She couldn't let them...

Seth was bucking and crying now, and Addie closed her eyes and tried to think. She couldn't rush out without thinking. She couldn't escape without making sure Noah was okay, which was not part of any of the escape plans she always had mapped out in the back of her mind.

She should call Laurel. She hated to call Laurel after yelling at Noah for doing so, but this wasn't about her pride or her secrets. It was about Noah's safety.

Seth was still screaming in her ear, kicking his little legs against her. Addie retraced her steps, perilously close to tears.

She made it to the kitchen and fumbled with the phone. She was halfway through dialing Laurel's number when the front door squeaked open. Addie dropped the phone, scanning the kitchen for a weapon, any weapon.

If she could make it two feet, there was a butcher knife. Not much of a weapon against a gun, but—

Noah stepped inside, alone, his dark cowboy hat covering most of his face as he stomped his boots on the mat. When he glanced up at her, her relief was short lived, because there was a trickle of blood down his temple and cheek.

Addie rushed over to him, Seth's tantrum finally over. "Oh, my God, Noah." He was okay. Bleeding, but okay. She flung herself at him, relief so palpable it nearly toppled her. "You're okay," she said, hugging Seth between them.

"What the hell is wrong with you?" Noah grumbled, a hard wall against her cheek.

Which was when she realized she'd miscalculated deeply. Because he would know everything was wrong now, and she had no way of brushing this off as being silly.

He felt Addie stiffen against him and then slowly pull away. She did not meet his gaze, and she did not answer his question.

He was a little too disappointed she wasn't holding on to him anymore. "Addie," he warned, too sharp and gruff. But the woman affected him and he didn't know how to be soft about it. "What is it?"

"You're...bleeding," she offered weakly, still not looking at him.

"Yeah, one of my idiot cousins left a shovel in the middle of the yard and I tripped right into the barn door. What's going on? And don't lie to me. Just be honest. I'm not in the mood to play detective."

"Are you ever in the mood for anything?" she muttered while walking away from him, clearly not expecting him to catch her words.

"You'd be surprised," he returned, somewhat gratified when she winced and blushed. Still expressly not looking at him. It grated. That she was lying to him. That today was one big old ball of screwy.

That when she'd thrown herself at him he'd wanted to wrap his arms around her and hold her there. Worst of all, her *and* the kid.

"So, I just thought... I thought I heard something and—"

"Bull." Did she have any idea what a terrible liar

she was? It was all darting eyes and nervous hand-wringing.

"Well, I mean, maybe I didn't hear anything, but when I was closing the windows there was a bird and—"

"Bull."

She stomped her foot impatiently. "Stop it, Noah."

"Stop feeding me bull and I'll stop interrupting."

She frowned at him and shook her head and heaved an unsteady exhale. She looked frazzled and haunted, really. Haunted like she'd been when she'd first gotten here, but he'd never seen her look panicked.

She walked over to the tiny kitchen, where Seth's tent was on the floor. She crouched down and let the boy crawl inside. She watched the kid for a second before walking over to a drawer and pulling out a washcloth. She wet it at the sink, then moved to the cabinet above the oven where they kept a few first aid things and medicine. She grabbed a bandage before returning to him.

She stood in front of him, gaze unreadable on his. She stepped close—too close, because he could smell dinner and Seth's wipes on her. That shouldn't be somehow enticing. He wasn't desperate for some domestic side of his life.

But she got up on her tiptoes and placed the warm cloth to where he'd scraped his forehead on the edge of the door. She wiped at the cut, her gaze not leaving his until she had to open the bandage.

Her eyebrows drew together as she peeled it from its plastic and then smoothed it over his forehead, her fingertips cool and soft against his brow. She met his gaze again then, sadness infusing her features.

"Noah, I have to leave."

He studied her, so imploringly serious, and, yeah, he didn't think that was bull. "Why?"

She glanced back at Seth, who was slapping his hands happily against the floor. "I just do. I can't give any kind of notice or time to find a new housekeeper. I have to go now." She glanced at the window, vulnerability written into every inch of her face that usually would have made Noah take a big old step back. He didn't do fragile, not a big, rough man like him.

But this wasn't about smoothing things over. This was about protecting someone who was very clearly in trouble.

"You're not going anywhere. You just need to tell me what's going on and we'll figure it out."

She looked back at him, expression bleak and confused. "Why?"

"Why?" He wanted to swear, but he thought better of it as Seth crawled over to his feet and used Noah's leg to pull himself into a standing position. Addie needed some reassuring, some soft and kind words, and he was so not the man for that.

But he was the only man here, and from everything Laurel and Grady had told him, and from Addie's own actions, Noah could only assume she'd been knocked around by Seth's father and feared him even now.

Softness might not be in him, but neither was turning away from something a little wounded.

"You're a part of the house. You've made yourself indispensable," he continued, trying to wipe that confused bleakness off her face.

"No. No. No," Seth babbled, hitting Noah's leg with his pudgy baby fingers.

Noah scooped the kid up into his arms, irritated that Addie was still standing there staring at him all big-eyed and beautiful and hell if he knew what to do with any of this.

"You didn't just take a job when you came here— you joined a family," he said harshly. "We protect our own. That wasn't bull I was feeding you earlier. That is how things work here. You're under Carson protection."

"I've never known anyone like you," she whispered. Before that bloomed too big and warm and stupid in his chest, she kept going. "Any of you. Laurel, Grady. Jen, Ty. The whole lot of you, and it's so funny the town is always going on about some feud and Grady and Laurel cursing everything, but you're all the same, all of you Carsons and Delaneys. So good and wanting to help people who shouldn't mean anything to you."

"You've been here too long for that to be true. Of course you mean something to us." He cleared his throat. "Besides, you're a Delaney yourself by blood."

She looked away for a second, and he couldn't read her expression but Seth made a lunge for her. One of his favorite games to play, lunging back and forth between them. Over and over again.

Addie took Seth, but she met Noah's gaze with a soft, resigned sadness. "I'm not safe here. More importantly, Seth isn't safe here. We have to go."

"Where?"

"What?"

"Where will you go that you'll be safe?"

"I…" She blew out a breath, that sheen of tears filling her eyes, and if this hadn't been so serious, he would have up and walked away. He didn't do tears.

But this was too big. Too important.

"I don't know," she whispered, one of the tears falling over her cheek. "I'm not sure anywhere will ever be safe."

Noah had the oddest urge to reach out and brush it away. He tamped that urge down and focused on what needed to be done. "Then you'll stay."

"Noah."

"If you don't know where to be safe, then you'll stay here where a whole group of people are ready and willing to protect you and Seth."

"I can't put any of you in this, Noah. It's dangerous."

"Not if you tell us what we're up against." Not that it'd change *his* mind. He'd fight a whole damn army to keep her here.

Because she was useful. Like he'd said before. Integral. To his house. To the ranch. That was all.

"Promise me you'll stay put." They were too close, standing here like this. Even as Seth bounced in her arms and reached for his hat, their eyes didn't leave each other.

But she shook her head. "I can't, Noah. I can't promise you that."

Chapter 5

Addie knew the next step was to walk away. Run away, but Noah's gaze held her stuck. She was afraid to break it, that doing so might break her.

She'd been strong for so long, alone for so long. She had to keep being that, but the allure of someone helping... It physically hurt to know she couldn't allow herself that luxury.

"Here are your choices," Noah said in that low, steady voice that somehow eased the jangling nerves in her gut. "You can try to run away, and I can call every Carson, hell, *and* Delaney, in a fifty-mile radius and you won't get two feet past the town limits."

Irritation spiked through her. "Noah, you—"

"Or you can sit down and tell me what's going on and we can fight it. Together."

Together.

She couldn't wrap her mind around this. Protection and together. Because she was his employee? Because she lived under his roof? It didn't make any kind of sense.

Her father had cut off Kelly when she'd dropped out of school and refused to work at the furniture store. Then when she'd asked him for help in Kelly's final trimester when the depth of her trouble with Peter was really sinking in, he'd refused to help.

He'd told Addie to never come home again if she was going to help Kelly.

If a father had so little love for his daughters, why was a friend, at best, so willing to risk himself to protect her?

"Telling me would be much easier," Noah said drily.

It sparked a lick of irritation through her. She didn't care for this man of such few words ordering her around. "You don't get to tell me what to do. You aren't my keeper. You aren't even…" She trailed off, because it wasn't true. No matter how quiet and stoic he could be, he *had* become her friend. Someone she relied on. Someone she worked *with* to keep the Carson Ranch running. It had given her so much in three short months, and she'd pictured Seth growing up here, right here. A good man.

Just like Noah.

Noah *was* her friend. Something like a partner, and wouldn't that be nice? Wouldn't that make all this seem possible? Which was why she couldn't. She just couldn't. She'd made a promise to herself. No one else got hurt in this.

"Noah, the truth is, I care about you." Far more than she should. "I care about all of you—Laurel and Grady and Jen and…the lot of you who've made me feel like this was home." She glanced toward the window, but she'd closed the curtains. Was someone out there? Waiting? Would they attack? "But the kind of danger I'm in is the kind I can't bring on all your heads. I couldn't live with myself."

"I don't think that's true," he said, still standing so close and so immovable. Like he could take on the evil that was after her. "I think you'd do anything, risk anything, to keep Seth safe."

Her chest felt like it was caving in. Because he was right. She would do anything. She didn't want to bring the people who'd been so good to her into the middle of it, but what if it was the best bet to keep Seth safe?

"And so would I," he continued. "No little kid deserves to live in the shadow of the threat of violence, so we don't run. *You* don't run. We fight it. But I need to know what I'm fighting."

What was there to do in the face of Noah's mountain wall of certainty and strength? She didn't have any power against it. Not when she could all but feel the determination coming off him in waves. Not when he let Seth gleefully fall into his arms, and there was so much danger outside these walls.

"Seth's father is a dangerous man," she whispered. She knew *that* was obvious and yet saying it out loud…

"He knocked you around."

He said it like a statement, and maybe she should treat it like a question and refute it. But what was the point? "He's a mobster." She laughed bitterly. "I didn't believe it the first time someone told me. As if mobsters are real."

"But he is."

Noah's voice was serious. Not a hint of mocking or disbelief. Which hurt, because when Kelly had told her about Peter's criminal ties, over a year ago, Addie had laughed it off. Then, she'd figured they'd call the cops. It had taken Kelly's death for Addie to finally get it through her head.

Kelly had been talking about going to the cops, telling them what little she knew. The very day after she'd told Addie that, she'd been shot and killed on her way home from the drugstore.

A mugging gone wrong, the police had told Addie.

But Kelly had been certain she was in danger and in that moment Addie had finally gotten it through her thick skull that Peter was not the kind of man who was ever going to pay for his crimes or listen to reason.

He was a murderer and she couldn't stop him.

Kelly had kept Seth a secret, or so Addie had thought. But she'd gotten Peter's first note ten minutes after the police had left her apartment informing her of Kelly's murder.

Too bad.

She hadn't understood at first. Then she'd gotten the next a month later.

We're watching.

She'd taken it to the police, but they'd decided it was a prank.

The next month's letter arrived and had prompted Addie's flight reflex.

We're coming for my son. And you.

Peter was dangerous, and there was nothing...*nothing* she could do to stop him. Laws didn't matter—the police had never helped her, and once he'd involved

Seth she couldn't trust law enforcement not to take Seth away from her.

Right or good certainly didn't matter when it came to Peter *or* the law.

"He could have me killed and Seth taken away with the snap of a finger. But he doesn't. I don't know what game he's playing. I only know I have to keep Seth safe. I thought we'd be safe here. Too isolated for even him to find, but I was an idiot. And now we have to leave."

"You won't be leaving."

She looked up at him, wondering what combination of words it would take, because he didn't understand. Maybe he wasn't scoffing at the idea of the mob, but he didn't truly get it if he thought he could keep her protected. "Noah, the cops couldn't help…" She almost mentioned Kelly, but she couldn't tell him about Kelly. Couldn't tell him she couldn't go to the police regarding Seth because she technically had no rights over her sister's child. "…me. I tried. Who are you to stop him? I realize you and the Carsons fancy yourselves tough, Wild West outlaws, but you cannot fight the *mob*."

"I don't see why not."

She blinked at him. "You have a screw loose."

His mouth quirked, that tiny hint of a smile she so rarely got out of him, and usually only aided by Seth. All hopes of more of Noah's smiles were gone. Dead. She had to accept it. She couldn't let him change her mind.

"I don't want you hurt," she whispered, all the fear welling up inside her. "I don't want anyone getting hurt."

"Same goes, Addie." He had started to lean back and forth on his heels as Seth dozed on his shoulder.

It was such a sight, this big, bearded, painfully tough man cradling a small child to his chest. They were both in so much danger and she didn't know how to fix any of it.

"It's late. Let's get some sleep tonight. I'll call up Grady and Ty in the morning and we'll plan."

"Plan what?"

"How to keep you and Seth safe." He rubbed his big, scarred hand up and down Seth's back.

"They're here, Noah." Her voice broke, and she'd worry about embarrassment later. "They left me a note. They're *here*. We don't have time for plans."

She hadn't realized a tear escaped her tightly and barely held control until Noah reached out, his rough hand a featherlight brush against her cheek, wiping the tear away.

"Then we'll have to fight."

Truth be told, Noah didn't know what a man was supposed to do when a woman told him the mob was after her, but he'd learned a long time ago that in the face of a threat, you always pretended you knew what you were doing.

"Show me the note."

She backed away then, though not far. He didn't think even at her most scared she'd back away from the baby sleeping in his arms. Seth was a nice weight. Warm and important.

"Show me the note," he repeated, in the same quiet but certain tone. The kind of tone he'd employ with a skittish horse and not, say, how he'd speak to his teen-age cousin who annoyed the piss out of him.

She inhaled sharply, but he watched the way she let

it out. Carefully. Purposefully. She was scared witless, but she was handling it. Though he'd grown to know her, respect her even, the way she was handling this without falling apart was surprising him.

She reached behind her and pulled out an envelope. "It was…" She paused and cleared her throat. She'd cried a few moments ago, just a few tears, and it cracked something inside him. But she was handling it now. Holding her own. Against the threat of a *mobster*.

"It was on the floor. I assume slipped under the door." Her face paled. "God, I hope that's how it got in here."

Noah kept his expression stoic and his gaze on her, though now he wanted to search the house from top to bottom. Too many nooks and crannies. Too many…

One thing at a time. That's how things got built and solved. One thing at a time.

Her hand was shaking as she held out the envelope. He could see her name written there. Addie Foster. Yet it didn't matter what was in the letter. It mattered that Addie get it through her head he was going to protect her.

He put his hand over her shaking one. "Let's go to your room. We'll put Seth down, and then I'll make sure the house is secure." He'd call Laurel, and she could decide how involved the police needed to be. "You know Laurel's a cop, right? A good one." He nudged her toward the hall.

"I'm sure she is," Addie replied, gaze darting everywhere as they walked back toward the bedrooms. "But the law can't touch him."

"That might be true back where you're from, but it ain't true here."

She looked at him bleakly as they stepped into her room. "It's true everywhere."

Noah was not a demonstrative person by any stretch of the imagination, but he had the oddest urge to pull her to his chest. Let her nestle right there where the baby was sleeping.

Instead, he turned to the crib and transferred Seth onto the mattress. The baby screwed up his mouth, then brought his thumb into it and relaxed. Within moments his eyes drooped shut and his breathing evened.

Noah glanced around the room. Nothing was amiss, and he knew for a fact the window didn't open. It'd accidentally been painted shut two years ago, and they'd left it that way so they had a room to put Clint in he couldn't escape without going through one of the main thoroughfares.

The joy of teenagers.

So, one room checked out and safe. Addie stood next to her bed, arms wrapped around herself, envelope clutched in one hand. She shook from head to toe. And why wouldn't she? She'd been running from a mobster for how long?

Noah'd be damned if she ran another mile.

He eased the note from her grasp and then pulled the letter from the envelope.

I see you, Addie.

He muttered something particularly foul since the baby was too fast asleep to hear him. "I'm going to call Laurel." She opened her mouth to argue, no doubt, but he kept going. "I'm going to check out the house. I want you to stay put, door locked, until I'm sure everything is secure." She wanted to argue, he could see it all over her, so he played dirty. "You're in charge of Seth. Stay put."

"I know you want to help," she said, her voice raspy with emotion. "I also know you think you *can* help." She shook her head. "You don't know what you're up against."

It poked at the Carson pride he didn't like to put too much stock in, but Carsons had survived centuries of being the poor-as-dirt underdog in the fight. Carsons always found a way to make it work, and even a mobster wouldn't make that different. "And you don't know what or *who* you've got in your corner."

She visibly swallowed. "I'm afraid, Noah, and I don't know how not to be. He killed my sister. Seth's father had her *killed*. I've taken his son from him. I'll be lucky if all he does is kill me, too."

He couldn't stomach the thought, and it was that horrible, clutching panic that moved him, that had him acting with uncharacteristic emotion. He touched her, too-rough hands curling around her shoulders. His grip was too tight. She was too fragile, and yet she didn't wince or back away.

Because she wasn't actually fragile. He thought of that first moment he'd seen her, when he'd been so sure. He'd been wrong. She was brave and bone-deep strong.

She looked up at him, all fear and hope.

"He will not lay a hand on you," Noah growled. "Not a finger. This is Bent, Wyoming, and we make some of our own rules out here. Especially when Carsons and Delaneys are involved. Now, you sit. Maybe make a list of all the players so Laurel knows who she's looking for, and try to remember in detail everything that's happened with Seth's father so far. I'm going to search the house and once I know we're safe in here, we'll come up with a plan to stop him where he stands."

"If we escalate, he escalates," Addie said miserably.

"Then we'll escalate until it's finished. You're done running, Addie Foster. You belong right here." He'd do whatever it took to make that true.

Chapter 6

Addie's eyes were gritty from lack of sleep and her throat ached from talking. Far as she could tell, she'd told her story—well, a version of it—four times. Noah first, then once to Laurel and Grady, once to Noah's brother, Ty—who apparently had been an Army Ranger. Then she'd spouted the story all over again to a youngish-looking deputy in uniform.

She left out the fact Seth wasn't hers. If Peter being in the mob didn't matter here, maybe Seth's parentage didn't, either.

After the whole endless rehashing of it, Laurel and the other deputy, followed by Noah, Grady and Ty, had gone out to search the property. Noah's cousin Vanessa had arrived to watch after Addie.

"You're babysitting me," Addie said, watching the woman move around the kitchen.

"Babysitting happens when you've got a mobster after you, I think."

Fair enough.

Addie imagined Vanessa Carson was the kind of woman who'd know how to handle this on her own. She looked as infinitely tough as her brother, Grady, and male cousins. She had the same sharpness to her features, and there was the way she held herself. Like she knew she was right and she'd fight to the death to prove it.

Addie wanted so badly to believe the Carsons could take on Peter and his thugs.

But *why*? No matter how often Noah told her he'd protect her, she couldn't figure out *why*.

"This is an awful lot of manpower for the maid," Addie said, a comment she might have swallowed if she hadn't been exhausted, nerves strung taut. She stared miserably at Seth's monitor. He'd wake up soon, and how was she going to take care of him without falling apart?

The same way you've been doing for the past year. You're strong, too, whether you feel that way or not.

She liked to think of that as her sister's voice urging her on, but she knew it was just herself. Kelly had always had more of a glass-is-half-empty outlook on life.

"But you aren't just a maid," Vanessa said, as if it wasn't even a question. "Noah runs the ranch, you run the house. That's a partnership, at least—Noah'd see it that way. Noah doesn't just *employ* people. He collects them."

When Addie only stared at Vanessa, trying to work that out, Vanessa sighed and walked over to the table, taking the seat across from Addie.

"Noah's got a soft heart. I think that's why he hides it all with beard and grunts. I think some people were just born that way. Protectors. He doesn't see it as a debt to be paid, or an inconvenience. Once you're in his orbit, you're his. Even if he doesn't like you much."

"That doesn't make any sense."

Vanessa laughed, low and rumbly, just like the rest of the Carsons. "I've never thought Noah made much sense, so I agree. But it doesn't have to. It's who he is. It's what he does. You know, Noah's a firm believer in this feud business between the Carsons and the Delaneys. Delaneys are always out to get us, and messing with that is a historical recipe for disaster."

"But—"

Vanessa held up a hand. "When Laurel was in some trouble before you moved here, Noah jumped right in to help. When Grady announced he and Laurel were shacking up…" Vanessa shuddered. "He was the only one who didn't make a loud, raucous argument against it."

"I think they're sweet," Addie whispered, staring at the table. Even though it wasn't the point. Even though her heart beat painfully in her chest. Noah was unlike any man she'd ever known.

How differently things would have turned out for her and her sister if they'd had more honorable men in their lives.

"Of course you do," Vanessa returned. "You're a Delaney."

Addie looked up at Vanessa's sharp face, because she didn't particularly consider herself family. "I guess, along the line, but—"

"Here? Along the line counts."

"So Noah thinks I'm cursed, but he'll protect me anyway?"

"He will."

"But he'll never see beyond the fact I'm a Delaney?" Another thing she shouldn't have said. What did it matter what he saw her as? She was just his maid, even if that meant she'd fallen into the path of his protection.

"Now, that is an interesting question," Vanessa drawled. "If we weren't worried about mobsters and such, I'd probably—"

A faint sound staticked through the monitor. Both Vanessa and Addie looked at it. Then another sound.

"It sounds like someone's—"

"Breathing," Vanessa finished for her, and then they were both on their feet, scrambling toward the room.

It could have been Seth, having a bad dream, puffing out those audible gasps of air. But she knew what her baby sounded like. Knew what odd noises the monitor picked up. This was not that.

Vanessa reached the door first, pulling a small gun out of the inside pocket of her jacket. "If someone's there, you let me deal. You get the baby and get out."

Addie nodded as an icy, bitter calm settled over her. She didn't have time to be afraid. She could only focus on saving Seth.

Vanessa quietly and carefully turned the knob, then flung open the door in a quick, loud movement.

There was a figure in the window. Addie didn't have time to scream or panic. She rushed to Seth's crib and pulled him into her arms. She couldn't hear anything except the beating of her heart as she held Seth close, too close. He wiggled and whimpered sleepily.

It was only with him safely held to her chest that

Addie realized there was shouting coming from outside. Vanessa was standing on the rocking chair, peering out what appeared to be a hole cut in the glass of the window.

"What happened?" Addie asked, her voice no more than a croak. Safe. Safe. Seth was safe. It was paramount.

Vanessa glanced back at her. "They got him. Laurel's arresting him."

"Who—"

Noah barreled in through the door, all gasping breath and wild eyes. Addie had never seen him in such a state, and she didn't even get a word out before he grabbed her. *Grabbed* her, by the arms, searching her face as Seth wriggled between them. It was the most emotion she'd ever seen on the man.

"You're both all right?"

Addie nodded wordlessly. She didn't know what to say to him when he was touching her like this, looking at her like this. It was more than just that stoic certainty that he'd protect her. So much more.

"I'm good, too," Vanessa quipped.

"Shut up," Noah snapped, seeming to remember himself. He dropped Addie's shoulders as though they were hot coals. He stepped back, raking a hand through his hair, his face returning to its normal impassive state.

It was as if that simple motion locked all that *feeling* that had been clear as day on his face back down where it normally went.

If there weren't a million other things to worry about, she might have been thrilled to see that much emotion geared toward her.

"Who was it? What happened?" Addie asked, cradling Seth's small head with her hand.

"As to who, we're not sure. He's not talking. No ID. We'd canvassed the buildings. Ranch is too big in the dark to find anyone. We were coming back when I caught the figure at your window. We all ran over, pulled him out, Laurel cuffed him. She'll take him down to the station now. She wanted you to come out and see if you could ID him first."

It was all so much, and she knew they wouldn't understand it was only the beginning. This was only the first wave. Peter would keep coming, wave after wave, until she had no strength or sanity left. That's when he'd take Seth. When she was at her weakest.

She swallowed against the fear, the futility. She wouldn't let it happen.

She was a Delaney, apparently, and she had a Carson—or four—in her corner. Noah—all that worry and fear and determination and vengeance flashing in his eyes for that brief minute—was in her corner.

They would keep Seth safe. *They* could.

He didn't walk Addie outside to ID the guy. Couldn't manage it. Not with all the awful things roiling in his gut. If he went out there, he wasn't certain he'd control himself around the man who'd been breaking into his house.

So he sent her with Vanessa. He held Seth, the boy back asleep again despite the commotion. Noah studied the room he'd thought was safe, glared at the window where a carefully cut circle gave adequate access for a small man to try to crawl through.

She couldn't sleep here tonight. It wasn't safe. No

room with windows was safe, it seemed, and *all* the rooms had windows. Nothing was safe.

He ran his free hand over his face. What a mess.

But it wasn't an insurmountable mess. They'd caught this guy, and Noah was under no illusions it was the mobster after Addie and Seth, but he worked for him. He had to have information, and with information, they could keep Addie safe.

She had two families ready to take up arms and keep her and the kid safe. He had to let that settle him.

Addie returned, clearly beaten down. "It wasn't the same man from the store. So Peter has two men here. Usually he only sends one." She looked exhausted and all too resigned to a negative fate.

Not on his watch.

"You can't stay here," he said when she didn't offer anything.

Her entire face blanched in a second. "But you said…" She looked around the room desperately, then straightened her shoulders and firmed her mouth. "Well, fine, then, better to have a running start."

"Running?" He stepped toward her, lowering his voice when Seth whimpered into his shoulder. "Where the hell do you think you're going?"

She fisted her hands on her hips, that flash of temper from before at dinner. He was glad to see it now. Better than resigned.

"You just told me I can't stay here!"

"*Here.* In this room."

She blinked. "Oh." She cleared her throat. "Be more specific next time."

That she could even think he was kicking her out…

Everything in him ached, demanded he touch her,

but he kept the impulse in check. "Nothing that happens is going to change the fact that we're in this together."

"Noah..." She bit her lip and took a few steps closer to him. She seemed to be studying him. His eyes. His mouth.

My damn soul.

"You were so worried," she said, her voice hushed and nearly awed. "When you came in here. About me. About Seth."

"Of course I was. A man was climbing in your window. You were being threatened in *my* house. What man wouldn't be worried?"

"Because it's your house?"

She was fishing, he realized with a start. Fishing for more. It was his turn to swallow, and he was man enough to admit he backed away. Sometimes a man had to tactically retreat.

She didn't let him. She took those steps he'd backed off, closing the necessary distance between them. He thought for a blinding second she was going to reach out to touch him.

Instead, her fingertips brushed Seth's cheek. "I wish I understood you." She looked up, dark blue eyes too darn perceptive for any man's good. "I wish I understood what makes a man think people are his possessions to control, to warp, to let live and die at will, and what makes a man protect what isn't even his."

You are *mine.*

It was a stupid thought to have and he needed to get rid of it.

"We need to figure out what we're going to do. We need to formulate a plan. This house isn't safe, but I don't know where else would be safe."

Addie turned away from him then. He wished he could erase her fear. But he knew even when you were afraid and had someone protecting you, someone helping you, it couldn't eradicate fear. Fear was a poison.

But it could also be the foundation. He'd lived in fear and learned to protect out of it. So he would figure out a way to protect her.

"There's a cabin," he continued. "It's well-known Carson property and it's entirely possible that since someone tracked you here, they could track you there. But it's smaller. We could protect it better."

"We?" She turned around again. "Noah, what about the ranch?"

"Grady and Ty can take care of the ranch. And Vanessa, if necessary. I have plenty of help to carry out the day-to-day, and to keep an eye out in case any other uninvited guests show up."

She shook her head vigorously. "You can't leave your ranch. It's your work. It's your home."

It was. His heart and soul. But he could hardly send her off alone, and he'd be damned if he sent her with anyone else.

"We'll go. Until we get some information from Laurel about who this guy is and what he's doing. We'll go. You'll be safe there. Seth will be safe there, and we'll figure something out. A plan."

"Now?"

Noah nodded firmly. "Pack up whatever you need for yourself and for Seth. I'll make arrangements."

"Noah."

He told himself one of these days he would get that wary bafflement off her face. But for now, there was too much work to do.

"I don't know how to thank you. I don't know how to…" Her gaze moved from his face to the little boy in his arms. "You've been so good to us."

"It sounds like you deserve a little of people being good to you."

She nodded. "Deserve." She blew out a breath and he could see the exhaustion and stress piling on top of her, but she was still standing. He remembered that first moment, when he'd been irritated Grady and Laurel had thrust someone fragile on him.

But Addie had turned out to be something else entirely, and he would do whatever it took to ease some of that exhaustion from her. Get her out of here now, and then once they got to the cabin she could sleep. Rest. He'd take care of everything.

"I will keep you safe. I promise you." She didn't believe him yet. He didn't need her to, but he'd keep saying it until she did.

She stared up at him and reached out. He thought she was going to take Seth, or gently brush the baby's cheek again, but this time she touched *him*. Her fingertips brushed his bearded jaw. "I know you want to."

"I will. I don't make promises I can't keep."

Her mouth curved the slightest bit, but Noah couldn't catch a breath because she was still touching him. She traced the line of his jaw to his chin, then back up the other side, and no amount of stoicism he'd adopted over the years could keep the slight hitch out of his breathing.

Her smile grew. "I believe that," she said, watching her own hand as it traveled down to rest on his chest, just above his heart.

She looked up at him from underneath her lashes,

and it wasn't the first time in three months he'd wanted to kiss her, but it was the first time in three months it seemed right. Possible. Infinitely necessary.

He shifted Seth easily, carefully, and if he leaned toward Addie's pretty, lush mouth, well, he was a man, damn it. Who could deny this attraction when they were both exhausted and scared to their boots?

The door swung open and Addie jumped back. Noah had some presence of mind. He simply glared at their intruder.

"Hey, you guys ever com…" Ty trailed off, looking from Noah to Addie, and then back again with a considering glance. "Sorry to interrupt."

"Weren't," Noah returned, that one word all he could manage out of his constricted throat at first. "I'm going to take Addie to the cabin."

Ty nodded. "Good idea. Safer. Less room to watch. Grady, Vanessa and I will handle things here."

Noah jerked his head in assent. "Let's move fast."

Chapter 7

Addie slept like the dead. No matter how many fears or worries occupied her brain, she'd been up for nearly twenty-four hours by the time they reached the isolated Carson cabin.

And, she supposed, as she awoke slowly in an unfamiliar bed in an unfamiliar house, knowing Noah was nearby keeping her safe had made sleep easy.

She stretched in the surprisingly comfy bed. Surprising because everything about the Carson cabin was rustic and sparse, but the bed was nice.

She had to get out of it, though, because Noah would need some sleep. He'd probably been up before her yesterday, and now he'd spent who knew how long taking care of Seth and keeping them safe.

She pressed her hand against her chest. It simply ached at how much that meant. How much she'd wanted to kiss him last night. Or this morning. Whatever moment in time. He'd been about to. She'd almost been sure of it.

Almost.

She pushed out of the bed. She hadn't even changed out of her jeans and T-shirt last night. She'd fallen into that bed, making noises about when Seth would wake up and need a diaper change, and Noah had hushed her, and that was the last thing she remembered.

She ran a hand through her hair. It'd be good to tidy up, but she had no idea how long she'd slept. There was no clock in here, the window was boarded up and she had no idea where she'd left her phone.

She opened the bedroom door and stepped into basically the rest of the cabin. A small living room, an even smaller kitchen that attached, and a bathroom on the other side. There was another door she had to assume was another bedroom.

The diminutive size of the place made it far more secure than the ranch. Just as isolated, of course, but there wasn't much in Bent by way of bustling cosmopolitans.

She frowned at the empty room. The front door was locked shut. Multiple times. A door lock, a dead bolt, a padlock on some latch-looking thing. It was dark because all the windows were boarded up. Surely Noah couldn't have done all that while she was sleeping.

And where *was* he?

It was then she heard the faint snore. She pivoted so she could see the front of the couch, and there was all six-foot-who-knew of Noah Carson, stretched out on a tiny couch, a cowboy hat over his face, while Seth slept just as soundlessly in the little mobile crib, Noah's arm draped over the side—his fingertips touching Seth's leg.

It was too much, the way this big, gruff cowboy had

taken to a small child who wasn't even his. But Addie understood that. Seth was her nephew, not her own, but he was hers now. All hers.

Noah wanted to protect her and Seth, but he was putting himself in danger to do so. He was even changing his life, for however brief a time, to do so.

So she would protect him right back. Take care of him as much as he'd allow.

She tiptoed to the kitchen and started poking around the cabinets seeing what kind of provisions they had. She knew Noah had packed a lot of things before they'd loaded up Vanessa's small car—an attempt at throwing anyone who might be watching off the scent—and drove up the mountains in the starry dark to this place. Vanessa had driven off so no evidence would be left that the cabin was occupied, and then it'd just been her and Noah and Seth.

She blew out a breath. *Breakfast.* She needed to focus on the here and now, not what came before and not what would come after. She looked around for her phone, found it on the small kitchen counter.

She flipped it open, searching for the time, only to see the text message from a Boston-area number.

Her stomach turned. She'd gotten a new burner phone in every city she'd stayed in for a while, but Peter somehow always found out what her number was.

She wanted to delete the message before looking at it, because she knew it would say something awful. Something that would haunt her. She remembered each and every one of his previous messages, and how many had made her run again.

All the words of the terrible things he was going to do to her once he found her that she'd read months and months ago swirled around in her head. She couldn't erase them.

But she could erase this message.

"What's wrong?"

Addie jumped a foot, not having realized Noah had woken up and was peering at her over the back of the couch.

"Nothing," she said automatically.

"Addie, I know you're scared, but you have to be honest with me if we are going to do this. There can't be any lies between us anymore."

She glanced at the crib where Seth was still sleeping. Was the fact that Seth wasn't her child a lie? How could it be? He was hers now. One way or another.

Then she glanced at the phone in her hand.

"It might be nothing," she said hopefully. She didn't believe it was nothing. There wasn't anything *nothing* about a Boston area code texting a number she'd given no one except Carsons and Delaneys.

Noah stood. He skirted the couch and raked fingers through his hair. It was sleep tousled and all too appealing. Even with the awful fear and panic fluttering in her breast, she looked at him and there was this soothing to all those awful jitters. They still existed, fear and worry, but it was like they were wrapped up in the warm blanket of Noah's certainty.

Noah's certainty, which existed around him like his handsomeness. Funny in all of this mess, she could finally admit to herself that she wanted him. Not just a little attracted, not just a silly little crush because he'd given her a home.

No, she *wanted*. Maybe it had to do with that moment last night where she'd thought he was about to kiss her, because he'd never given any inclination of interest before. So surely his reciprocating feelings was her silly fantasy life taking over because a man like Noah… Well, he knew what he wanted. In all things. If he wanted her, he would've said something.

Probably. Unless there was some noble reason in his head he thought he shouldn't. There was no reason to wish for that. Except, she *wanted*.

She had to push all these thoughts and feelings away, though, because right now Noah was standing there, frowning at her. And she was going to protect him and take care of him right back, so that meant not irritating him.

Which apparently meant the truth.

"There's a text message," she managed to say, reluctantly holding her phone out to him. "From a Boston area code."

"That's where this bastard is?" Noah demanded, his voice hard as he took the phone out of her hands.

Addie nodded. "I don't want to open it. It's always some vile thing." At the spark of Noah's temper moving over his face, she quickly continued. "Whenever he finds me, he texts me threats. This is the first one I've had here. I think he likes making me scared."

Something in him closed up. That anger vanished off his expression, but she could still feel it vibrating under that stoic demeanor. "Some people like knowing they're in your head. That you're running scared. Gives them a thrill."

"Yes," Addie agreed, feeling sick to her stomach. "He could have had Seth by now. So, what he's doing isn't just about getting him back. I mean, I think he wants him back, but he wants me to suffer for as long as possible. I think. I don't know. He doesn't make any sense. That's why I have to run." She wanted to sink to the floor, but she leaned against the wall and it held her up.

"You're done running," Noah said forcefully, as if it was his decision to make. "Now we go after him."

Noah angrily pushed a button on the phone. Though he heard Addie's intake of breath, his anger was too close to a boiling point to worry about comforting her. Besides, he wasn't any good at comforting. He had learned how to protect, and that's what he would keep doing.

He read the text message grimly.

Hello, Addie. Wyoming. Really? Going to ride a few cowboys? Are you about to get lassoed? Maybe we'll have ourselves a little standoff. You, me and the baby. Who will live? Only time will tell.

He hit a few buttons, finding a way to forward the text message to Laurel with the number on it. Then he deleted it from Addie's phone, since he didn't want her looking at it.

"Has *he* ever come after you? Or is it always his goons?"

"Uh, goons, as far as I know. Usually only one per town."

Noah nodded. "We'll need to get him here, then."

"Noah, he *killed* my sister. Well, he had her killed. If he comes here, he will have more people killed. Not just me or Seth, but you and your family. He's capable, if he wants to be."

"You don't know how deeply sorry I am about that, Addie. Sorry you had to go through it, sorry someone lost their life. But if you run away, it doesn't end. As long as he has something to come after, he's coming after you. Stopping him is the only answer."

"What if we can't?" There wasn't just a bleak fatality in her tone, there was genuine question.

"I have stopped bad men before. I am not afraid to do it again. We have good and right on our side."

"Good doesn't always win."

"It will here." Because he'd made a promise to himself, growing up in the midst of all that *bad*, that he would make sure good prevailed once he had the power. "Now, instead of arguing, let's discuss our plan."

Addie pushed her fingers to her temples and he took stock of how much sleep had helped her. She wasn't shaking and didn't look as pale. While there were still faint smudges under her eyes, they weren't that deep, concerning black they had been early this morning when they'd arrived at the cabin.

She was more mussed than usual, but that didn't detract from how pretty she looked in the middle of the dim cabin. Like a source of light all herself.

Get yourself together.

She dropped her hands from her temples. "Before we plan, you need to sleep. I don't know what time it is, but I—"

"I caught a few hours once Seth settled," he said, nodding toward the portable crib they'd brought. "I'm fine."

She stared up at him, much the way she'd been doing since he'd told her she was under his protection. Not as if she didn't believe him, but as if he were some mythical creature.

He wanted to be able to be that. Someone she could

trust and believe in. Someone who could save her from this. He only prayed he could be.

"Are you hungry? Let me make breakfast. Or dinner. Or whatever meal. I'll make something. That'll be the first step."

"Addie." He gently closed his fingers around her arm as she passed. "You're not the housekeeper here, okay? You don't have to cook or clean."

She looked at his fingers on her arm, then slowly up at him. "If I'm not the housekeeper here, what am I?"

Mine. That stupid word that kept popping unbidden into his head. She stepped closer to him then, like last night, when he'd thought he could kiss her and it would be okay. When he'd been driven by relief instead of reason.

She reached up with her arm not in his grasp. He should let her go. He didn't. She touched his jaw as she had last night, her fingertips lightly brushing across his beard.

Her tongue darted out, licking her bottom lip, and oh, hell.

"You *were* going to kiss me last night before Ty came in," she said on a whisper. A certain, declaratory whisper. "Right?" she added, and if he wasn't totally mistaken, there was *hope* in that "right?"

He might have been able to put her off if not for the hint of vulnerability. Because what was hope but a soft spot people could hurt and break? He cleared his throat, uncomfortable with the directness of the question. "I was thinking about it."

"So, you could do it now."

His gaze dropped to her mouth, no matter how much his conscience told him not to give in to this. Protecting was not taking advantage of. Fighting evil with good was not giving in to something he didn't have any right to want.

But she was close, the darker ring of blue around her pupils visible. The hope in her eyes too tempting. Her lips full and wet from where she'd licked them.

It didn't have to be a distraction. It didn't *have* to be wrong. It could be the start of something.

What? What are you going to start on this *founda-tion? What do* you *have to offer?*

Since the last question sounded a little bit too much like his father, he pushed it away. He wouldn't be driven by his father's voice.

He leaned closer, watching in fascination as her breath caught, and then she, too, leaned forward.

His phone trilled, which startled him back to real-ity. They were in a serious, dangerous situation with her child sleeping a few feet away. She was scared and out of sorts.

Now was not the time for nonsense. He glanced at the caller ID, frowned when it was Laurel's number. "It's Laurel."

Addie nodded.

"What?" Noah greeted.

"Bad news," Laurel said in her no-nonsense cop tone. "He's gone."

Before Noah could demand to know what that meant, Laurel continued.

"We did some questioning, but two armed men broke into the station. We're small and understaffed and... Well, three deputies were injured. Badly. They're..." She paused, and though she kept talking in that same efficient cop tone, Noah could tell she was shaken.

"Are you okay?"

"I'd gone to get dinner for everyone," Laurel said bitterly. "Hart got the worst of it. He's in surgery. The other two should be okay, but it'll be... Well, anyway, I need you to be on guard. Three men, at least, are now on the loose and likely after Addie and Seth. I've called in more men, but we don't have an endless supply of deputies."

"We're boarded up. Armed. You keep your men."

"There could be more of them."

Noah tried not to swear. "I'll be ready."

"Everyone in Bent has been told to be on the lookout for out-of-towners and immediately report it to us. Aside from Carsons and Delaneys, no one has the full story—I didn't want anyone doing anything stupid. So you'll have warning if someone's coming your way, but I'm stretched so thin now here and—"

"I'll handle it."

"We'll all work together to handle it." She paused again. "You know, my brother—"

"No Delaneys."

She sighed heavily. "Addie *is* a Delaney, moron. We're all in this together. If you dare bring up the feud right now, I swear to God..." Then she laughed. "Oh, you did that on purpose to get me riled up about something else."

"I don't know what you're talking about," he muttered. Except she'd sounded *sad*, and sad wasn't going to do anyone any good. "I gotta go."

"Keep your phone on you, and be careful."

"Uh-huh. Keep me updated."

"Will do."

Noah hit End and looked at Addie, who'd moved into the kitchen, her back to him, as she hugged herself. He wasn't sure how much she'd heard, but clearly enough to be concerned. He could try to put it lightly, but he thought after the whole almost-kiss thing, they needed the straightforward truth. "He escaped."

Addie leaned against the tiny slab of countertop in the minimalist kitchen. "How?" she asked, her voice strangled.

Noah didn't want to tell her. He even toyed with the idea of lying to her. But in the end, he couldn't. If they were going to win this, they needed to be open and honest with each other.

"Someone helped him. A few deputies were hurt in the process."

She whirled on him then, all anger and frustration. "I can't have this, Noah. I cannot have people's lives on my head."

"They're on the mob's head. Beginning and end of that story."

She shook her head and marched over to the living room, purposefully keeping as much room between them as possible in the tiny cabin. "I'm packing Seth up and we're running. You can't stop me."

She paused over Seth's crib, clearly warring over the idea of picking him up when he was sleeping.

Noah parked himself in front of the door, picking up the rifle he'd rested there. "You're not going anywhere."

She glanced back at him, her expression going mutinous. "You can't keep me prisoner here."

"Watch me."

Chapter 8

Addie was so furious she considered walking right up to him and punching him in the gut.

Except Noah was so big and hard her little fist couldn't do much damage, if any. And that was the thing that had dogged her for a year.

She had no strength and no power. She couldn't win this fight. She could only put it off a little while.

And everyone trying to help her was going to die.

Her knees gave out and she fell with an audible *thump* onto the couch, guilt and uselessness washing over her.

"Don't… Don't cry. Please." Noah grumbled.

Which was the first time she realized she *was* crying. Not little slipped-out tears. Huge, fat tears. She sobbed once, tired and overwhelmed. It was easier when it was her and Seth against the world. She didn't have to deal in hope or guilt. All she had was *run*.

"Addie, honey, come on." She felt the couch depress and Noah's arm go around her shaking shoulders. "Please. Please stop crying. You're not a prisoner. You're just… We're just lying low, that's all. Together. Hell, you have to stop crying. It just about kills me."

He sounded so desperate, she wished she could stop. But she was just so *tired*, and the truth was she wanted to let Noah handle it. Believe him. But the man who'd tried to steal Seth away had escaped, and people had been hurt, and all those people would have been fine if she'd never come here.

"Those men are hurt because of me. You're in this cabin because of me. You should have let me run. I'm only trouble."

His strong arm pulled her tighter. "You're not trouble. You've been a victim, and you've been brave and strong for a long time. Let someone take the reins."

"I'm hardly brave. I'm sitting here crying like a baby."

"You escaped a madman for how long?"

She blew out a breath. "But I can't beat him."

"Maybe not alone. Together we will, and I don't just mean me. You've got Laurel and Grady and everyone. The whole town is with us. That doesn't make what you've managed to do less. Addie, look at him," he said, gesturing toward the crib and Seth. "He's perfect."

"He is."

"You did that."

"No, I didn't." *He's not mine.* The words were on the tip of her tongue, but Noah's rough hand cupped her cheek.

"Promise me you won't try to run off. Promise me you'll trust me on this. We are in this together, until you're both safe."

He was touching her so gently, looking at her so earnestly, asking for a promise she didn't want to give. She even opened her mouth to refuse the promise, but something in the moment reminded her of before.

Noah believed her. From the beginning. Without hesitation. If she had done that with Kelly, maybe everything would be different.

Grief threatened to swamp her, but she couldn't change the past. What she could do was change her future.

Trusting him to help was what she had to do. And maybe anyone who got hurt along the way... She hated to even think it, but it was true.

She would sacrifice a clean conscience for Seth, so if people got hurt, as long as Seth was safe, she couldn't let it matter.

"Okay. Okay." She nodded, even as his hands stayed on her cheek. "I promise we're in this together." No matter what guilt she had to endure. It was for Seth. If she could remember that...

It was hard to remember anything with Noah's big, rough hand on her face. She'd long since stopped crying, but he was still touching her. And he was not a man given to casual touches.

Yet it didn't feel like the other two moments. Those moments that had been interrupted, where everything in her had stilled and yearned. There was some lack of softness on his face.

But unlike those other two moments, this time he did close the distance between them. His mouth touched hers, and for all the ways Noah had *clearly* resisted this moment, there was nothing tentative about it.

He kissed like a man who knew what he was doing. His lips finding hers unerringly, no matter how much beard separated them. There was nothing she could have done to prepare herself for that wave of feeling. Something so warm and sweet and bright she thought she couldn't name it.

But the word *hope* whispered across the edges of her consciousness as she reached out for him, wanting to hold on to something. Wanting it to be him.

When he pulled away, all too quickly in her estimation, he searched her face, relaxing a millimeter, and somehow she understood.

It wasn't a real kiss. It wasn't loss of control because passion so consumed him. "You did that to distract me," she accused. She should be angrier, more hurt, but all she could really be was bone-deep glad he'd done it.

Now she knew how much *more* was worth.

He pressed his mouth together, though she thought maybe under the beard was some kind of amused smile. "Maybe," he rumbled.

She crossed her arms over her chest huffily. "It didn't work."

His mouth quirked that tiny bit. "Yes, it did."

Her heart fluttered at his easy confidence. She didn't understand this man. Gruff and sweet, with so many walls, and yet he could kiss like he'd been born to do it and *knew* what kind of effect he had on her.

She was torn between kissing him again—much deeper and much longer this time—and eliciting more of this almost-smiling, certainly half-teasing man out of him.

But a loud *bang*, something like an explosion outside, had them both jumping. Addie was afraid she'd screamed, but in the end it didn't matter. Noah was on his feet, rifle in his hands, and she had already swept Seth up against her chest.

Noah's mouth was a firm line under his beard. Without a word he took her by the arm and propelled her around the couch. He shoved a narrow table against the wall out of the way, and then as if by magic, pulled up a door in the middle of the floor. An actual door.

"It's a cellar. Cramped and dark, but it can keep you safe if you're quiet. Go down there."

"But what about you?"

"I'll handle it. I promise."

"There could be—"

He slapped his phone into her palm. "Call or text everyone. You stay here and safe and let them come to my rescue, got it?"

Remembering her earlier promise to herself—*anything for Seth*—she swallowed and nodded. She turned to the dark space the pulled-up door allowed and did her best to ignore fear of dark or cramped or not knowing as she felt her way down a shaking length of stairs.

Seth wiggled and fussed against her, but was mostly content when she held him hard and close.

"Good?" Noah asked.

"Peachy," she muttered, and then she was plunged into darkness.

Noah's heart beat too hard and too fast, but he focused on keeping his breathing even. He kept his mind on the facts he had.

Someone was outside and trying to get in. Addie

and Seth were safe in the cellar if he kept them so. The boarded-up windows made no entrance into the cabin undetectable. *He* had the tactical advantage.

Except he couldn't see who was out there or how many, and though he knew the general vicinity that loud bang had come from, he didn't know exactly what had caused it or what kind of weaponry the undetermined number of men had.

He knew how to fight bad men, but he'd never had to fight off a possible group of them. He'd have to figure it out. Seth and Addie were counting on him.

The door shook in time with another large bang. And then another. He realized grimly there was also a banging coming from the back of the cabin, so there were at least two of them. Trying to get into the cabin from two different directions.

He needed to create some kind of barrier and he needed to make sure he kept both men—if it was only two—far away from Addie and Seth. He didn't want to leave them alone to draw the men away, but if she called Laurel, there would be help on the way.

Because the cabin had been used as a hideout for the Carson clan for over a century, it had all sorts of hidden places and secret exits. Maybe he could sneak out and pick off whoever was out there. Based on the banging, he had a better idea of where they were than they had of where he was.

It was a chance he'd have to take. He couldn't let them get inside. There would be too many ways he could be cornered, too many ways Seth making noise might give Addie away. And he had to know more about what he was dealing with so he wouldn't be caught unaware.

He strode to the kitchen, gripped the rifle under his arm and gave the refrigerator a jerk. He didn't push it all the way out, in case he needed to hide this little secret passageway quickly. Instead, he yanked the wallboard open and shoved his body through the narrow opening.

There was a crawl space that would lead him outside—one of the sides he hadn't heard banging against. And if he miscalculated, well, he pulled his rifle in front of him. He'd use that to nudge the door open, shoot first and ask questions later. Whatever would keep Addie and Seth safe.

On his hands and knees, pushing the rifle in front of him, he squeezed his too-big body through the too-small space. He nudged the door with the gun, then frowned when it didn't budge.

After a few more nudges—harder and harder each time—he finally got the small door to move, but just enough to see what was blocking it.

Snow. Far too many inches of snow. He pushed the rifle behind him, army-crawled up to the slight opening he'd made and got as close to the crack as possible so he could look out.

The world was white. He couldn't even see trees. Just snow, snow and more snow. On the ground, still falling from the sky, accumulating fast.

The chance of help coming was about as remote as it'd ever be. Even if Addie got through to Laurel or a Carson, it'd take extra time.

Which meant he had to get back inside the cabin. There'd be no trying to lure the men away when he didn't have much hope for quick backup.

He turned and pushed himself through the crawl

space after pulling the door to the outside closed. He twisted his body this way and that, getting out behind the refrigerator, trying to come up with a new plan.

He was breathing heavily, but he heard the distinct sound of something. Not pounding anymore.

Footsteps.

He didn't have time to push the refrigerator back in place, because a man dressed in black stepped out from the room Addie had been sleeping in just hours before.

Noah raised his rifle and pulled the trigger without even thinking about where the bullet would hit. The most important thing was stopping him.

The man went down with a loud yowl of pain, but another gunshot rang out in the very next moment. Noah only had the split second to realize it wasn't his own gun before a pain so bright and fierce knocked him to his back. His vision dimmed, and damnation, the pain threatened to swallow him whole.

He stared up at the ceiling, a blackness creeping over him, but he fought it off, clinging to consciousness with everything he had in him.

He had to keep Addie safe.

He tried to move, to do anything, but he felt paralyzed. Nothing in his body worked or moved. It only throbbed with fire and ice. How was it both? Searing licks of heat, needling lances of cold.

When a man stood over him, hooded and dim himself, it gave Noah something external to focus on. The man's black coat, not fit for a Wyoming winter, was covered in melted snow droplets. He had his face covered by a bandanna or hat. His eyes were a flat brown.

Evil eyes that were familiar—not because he knew

this man, but because Noah had stared evil in the face before.

"Where's the baby?" the man rasped, pointing his small handgun at Noah's head.

Noah groaned, more for show, though the pain in his side was a blinding, searing fire. He'd heard Addie scream, but apparently the man hadn't, or just couldn't figure out where they were.

Noah thought of Addie and Seth and pretended to roll his eyes back in his head. He could hear Seth crying now, which distracted the man's attention. Noah took that brief moment to gather all his strength and kick as hard and groin-targeted as he could.

Chapter 9

Addie listened to the persistent thumping. She knew it was people trying to get in. People trying to get her and Seth.

She knew Noah would fight them with all he had, but would it be enough? The horrifying worry that he was only one man and there were at least two men out there curdled her stomach.

She reminded herself she'd texted every last Carson and Delaney Noah had in his phone. Even though she hadn't had a response, the messages showed as sent, which meant she only needed one person to see it.

She could not think about what it might mean if no one was looking at their phone. If no one came to help them. So she paced the cellar, trying to work off all her nerves while at the same time keeping Seth happy. She needed to feed him. Even if Noah had fed him while she'd been asleep, he'd be getting hungry again.

She glanced above at the light footsteps. She knew Noah was moving around carefully and quietly on purpose and *God* she just could not think about what he was doing up there.

She used the weak light from Noah's tiny phone screen to illuminate her surroundings until she found a large flashlight sitting at the base of the stairs. She clicked it on, relief coursing through her when a strong beam popped out.

Clearly the Carsons used this cabin at least somewhat frequently, because there were a few shelves lined with provisions. Mainly canned foods, but if she could find one with a pop-top, she could at least give Seth a little something to keep him happy.

No matter that her arms shook and she felt sick to her stomach, she forced herself to read through all the labels. She found a can of pears, one of Seth's favorites.

"Okay, little man, let's get you a snack." She looked around the cellar again with Noah's flashlight. She needed a blanket or something she could put Seth on.

She poked around a pile of old furniture in the corner. Broken chairs, a bent mattress frame. Tools of some sort. A conglomeration of rusty, broken crap.

And a crib. She blinked at it. The legs had been broken off of it, and there was no mattress, but it had once been a crib.

"Something is going our way, Seth," she murmured, glancing warily above her as things got eerily quiet.

Quiet was good. Quiet had to be good.

Balancing Seth on her hip, she carefully picked through the debris of nonsense and pulled the crib out.

She studied it, then the room around her. If it was even, and she could push the broken side up against a wall, it could act as an effective playpen if she wanted to go check on Noah.

She heard footsteps again, tried not to think too hard about what that silence might have meant.

She shrugged out of her sweater and placed it in the bottom of the crib. Quickly she ran her fingers around the wood and didn't find any exposed nails or sharp edges. She set Seth down and searched around for other soft things.

She found a stack of folded dish towels and sniffed them gingerly. A little musty, but not terrible. She started placing them over the corners of the crib. A little softening to—

The gunshot was so loud, so close, she screamed. Seth began to wail and she grabbed him to her chest, trying to muffle both their cries as another gunshot almost immediately rang out.

Two gunshots was not good. She didn't have a weapon, but she did have this pile of tools. She bounced Seth until he stopped crying, and she tried to keep her own tears at bay as she heard another thump, then more thumps. Grunts.

No gunshots.

She scrambled to the pile of debris and grabbed the heaviest, sharpest-looking tool she could find. She'd pushed the crib against the wall sort of behind the stairs, and that would work in her favor if she could keep Seth quiet.

The food. The food. She set the tool down by the crib and grabbed the can she'd dropped. She transferred

Seth to the little crib and made silly faces to keep him distracted and quiet as she opened the can.

Seth gurgled out a laugh at one of her faces, but it didn't assuage any of her shaking fear, because something scraped against the floor right above her. She could hear someone fiddling with the floorboard. Oh, God, it wasn't Noah. Noah knew how to open it.

On a strangled sob she popped the can of pears open and grabbed one without thinking twice. She handed it to Seth. Usually she didn't give him such big pieces, but she needed time. She needed to keep them both safe.

She clicked off the flashlight just as the door opened and light shone in. Addie grabbed the tool and gripped it in both hands as she stepped back into the shadows.

The tool was sharp. It would cause serious damage even with her limited strength. Her stomach threatened to revolt, but she refused to let it.

She was done running, cowering and giving in. She'd made that choice to stand and fight up there with Noah. So she would do whatever it took. Whatever it took to fight for him. Fight for Seth.

She was done being a victim.

She swallowed the bile that threatened to escape her throat as some man who was most definitely not Noah took the stairs. He didn't have a flashlight, which put her at an advantage. Seth was liable to make a noise any second, so she had to be ready.

She quietly lifted the tool above her head and just as Seth murmured happily over a piece of pear, the man turned.

She brought the tool down onto his skull as hard as she could, and he strangled out a scream and fell in a heap. Her stomach lurched as she realized the tool was lodged in his skull as it fell with him.

But she couldn't worry about her stomach. She needed to get to Noah, and if no one was coming at the sound of the man's scream, he had to be acting alone.

Or someone else is hurting Noah.

She picked Seth up, much to his screaming dismay, and scurried around the motionless body on the floor.

Oh, God, had she killed him?

Had *he* killed Noah?

She climbed the stairs, Seth screaming in her ear. She stumbled up into the living room, desperately searching for Noah.

Then she saw him lying on the floor. And blood. Too much blood.

"Noah. Noah." She dropped to her knees next to him, not even worried she was getting bloody herself as long as she kept Seth out of it. "Noah. You have to be alive, Noah."

"No! No!" Seth said gleefully, clearly not understanding the scene around them.

Addie had to focus. Focus on what was in front of her. He'd clearly been shot. Blood pooled on one side of his body, but not the other. His face was ashen. But, oh, *God*, his chest was moving. Up and down.

"Noah." She wasn't sure what to do with a gunshot wound. Pressure. That's what they did in the movies, right? Apply pressure.

"Not dead," he muttered, though his eyes stayed closed.

"Oh, thank God you're awake." She pressed a kiss to his forehead and his eyelids fluttered, but they didn't fully open.

"No!" Seth squealed again.

"Where's he?" Noah demanded.

She assumed he meant the man she'd... "I... Well, he came down and I think I killed him." She'd still need to close up the door, cover it with something really heavy to keep him down there just in case. But for now she had to focus on Noah.

"Good," Noah replied, his voice firm for the first time, though his eyes remained closed. "I killed the other one. Must be it or they'd be in here."

"For now."

Noah grunted.

"I have to... I have to get you help." She pawed at her pocket for the phone Noah had given her earlier. She had a text from Laurel and as she clicked to read it, Noah said almost the exact thing.

Blizzard. Can't get up. Grady and Ty trying with horses. Will be a while.

"Blizzard. No help."

Addie closed her eyes in an effort to try to think. "We need to focus on you right now." She stood and crossed to the travel crib. It was upended, but she righted it and set Seth inside, cooing sweet reassurances at him as she gave him a toy.

She went through the next few steps as though it were a to-do list. Get as many blankets, towels and washcloths she could. Put a pillow under Noah's head. Peel the bloodied shirt away from his side. Try not to throw up. Gently wash out the terrible wound.

Noah hissed out a breath, but that just reassured her he was *alive*. "Is there a first aid kit anywhere?"

"Bathroom maybe," he muttered.

She was on her feet in an instant. Seth fussed but not a full-blown cry...yet. She had to get Noah some semblance of patched up. She wished she could move him to a bed, but who would lift him? Her and what army?

She jerked open the cabinet under the sink and rummaged. Soap, extra toilet paper, a box of condoms. Her cheeks warmed, but she kept looking until she found a flimsy canvas pouch with the red first aid cross on it.

She hastened back to Noah's side. His eyes were open so she tried to smile down at him. "Well, we survived."

His mouth didn't move and he looked so pale even under all his hair and beard. "For now," he managed in the same tone of voice she'd used earlier.

Wasn't that the truth?

She studied the wound again, and it was bleeding once more. She tried not to let despair wash over her. The only way Noah survived this was her somehow making it so.

So that's what she'd have to do.

It was a strange thing to be shot. Noah would have thought just the bleeding part of his body would hurt, but everything hurt. He kept losing consciousness, awakening who knew how long later on the cold, uncomfortable floor.

He tried not to groan as he forced his eyes open. He looked around the quiet room. The only sound he recognized was Seth sucking on a bottle.

It was a little bit of a relief to know things were business as usual for the baby.

Addie appeared in his wavering vision, and she knelt

next to him, a tremulous smile on her face. "Oh, good, you're really awake this time."

"Was I kind of awake before?"

She nodded down at his chest and he realized that under the blanket draped over him he was shirtless and bandaged. "You came to a few times when I was bandaging you up best as I could. Well, I called Laurel and she patched me through to a paramedic. You're lucky because it didn't seem to make any kind of…hole."

No, the bullet seemed to have grazed him. Badly, but no holes and no bullets floundering around in his body. It was good and it was lucky.

He was having trouble feeling it.

"I need to get up," he said. Lying there was making things worse. If he got up and moved around he could hold on to consciousness. He tried to push himself into a sitting position. His head swam, his stomach roiled and the pain in his side *burned.* Addie's arms came around him, though, surprisingly sturdy, and she held him up.

He was so damn dizzy, even if he had the strength he wasn't sure he could get to his feet. It was unacceptable. This was all unacceptable. Because he did need stitches, and there was no way to get them. Which meant he was going to halfway bleed to death and be a weak, useless liability to Addie and Seth.

No, he wouldn't be that.

"We need to secure the place. They got in through your room—"

"I dragged the man you shot outside," Addie said flatly. "I boarded up the bedroom window again best as I could. I've locked the room from the outside— since we won't be spending any more time in separate rooms, we don't need it. I also barricaded the cellar just in case the man I…hurt isn't dead."

He stared. "You did *all* that while I was out?"

"It's much better than sitting here fretting that you're dead. Or waiting. Grady and Ty are still trying to get to us with the horses, but the blizzard set them back quite a bit. Apparently Ty knows some battlefield medicine or *something* and can stitch you up when he gets here." Addie shuddered.

"I don't know what to say." Or feel. Or do. She'd handled it all. He was a burden now, but somehow she'd handled it all.

"Let's get you to bed and then you're going to lie down and stay put. You need to rest and not aggravate the bleeding until someone can get up here to help." She glanced over at Seth's travel crib. "Let's do it now before he finishes that bottle and starts yelling."

He wasn't sure he could get to his feet, but he wasn't about to admit that to her. There had to be *something* he could handle. Something he could do.

He rolled to the side that wasn't injured and tried desperately not to groan or moan as he struggled onto his feet. The world tipped, swayed, but he closed his eyes and with Addie's arms around him, he managed to stay upright.

Because slight little Addie—the woman he'd deemed fragile the first time he'd met her—held him up as he swayed.

She pulled the blankets that had been around him over his shoulders, then held tight, leaning her body against his tipping one as he took a step.

He walked, and noted she moved slower than he might have tried to. She was holding him back. Making him take it easy. He should have worked up some irritation, but mostly he could only concentrate on getting the interminable distance from the kitchen floor to his bed.

But they inched their way there, no matter how awful he felt. Somehow he got his feet to keep moving forward. Managed to ease himself onto his bed, with Addie's help.

Once he was prone again, he managed a full, painful breath. She was already tucking blankets around him, though she paused to inspect the bandage, the strands of her hair drifting across his chest. Somewhere deep down there was the slightest flutter of enjoyment and he figured he had a chance of surviving this yet.

"You need to rest. No getting up without help. No pushing yourself. Do you understand me?"

He grunted irritably. He hoped she considered it assent, even though it wasn't. Not a promise, because why would he promise that?

"You need to try to get something to eat. Keep up your strength. I'm going to—"

He grabbed her, unmanned at the fact there was a beat of panic at the thought of her leaving him. It was the aftereffect of shock. Had to be.

She patted his hand reassuringly, and it was that something like *pity* in her gaze that had him withdrawing his hand. He wasn't to be pitied. Yeah, he'd been shot trying to save *her*.

And she saved herself, didn't she?

"I'm just going to get Seth. Grab you some soup I already warmed up. Trust me, Noah, the three of us are plastered to one another's sides until this is all over."

She slid off the bed, and still that panic inside him

didn't disappear. "How'd you kill him without a gun?" he asked. Anything to keep her here. Here where he could see her. Where he could assure himself they'd come out this on the other side.

For now. What about the next other side?

Addie fiddled with the collar of her T-shirt, eyes darting this way and that. "Well." She cleared her throat. "Th-there were a bunch of tools down there so I just picked up the sharpest, biggest one and when he came down the stairs I hid in the shadows, then bashed him over the head." She let out a shaky breath. "I've never…hurt someone. I've never had to. I don't know how to feel."

"You feel relieved you were able to defend yourself," he said, hoping even though he felt weak and shaky and a million other unacceptable things she could feel that in her bones. "You took the relief of saving yourself or someone else—it was all you could do." He should know.

She cocked her head, those blue eyes studying him. He might have fidgeted if he'd had the energy. "You've hurt people? I mean, besides today?" she asked on a whisper.

Part of him wanted to lie or hedge, but he was too tired, too beat down to do either. "When I've had to."

"Like when?"

"It isn't important now. What's important is surviving until Grady and Ty get here. What's important is coming up with the next step of our plan."

"What on earth is the next step going to be?"

The trouble was, he didn't know.

Chapter 10

Watching Noah search for an answer to that question hurt almost as much as watching him suffer through what must be unbearable pain. Even though the paramedic she'd talked to who'd walked her through sterilizing and bandaging Noah's wound had assured her that Noah would survive for days as long as he rested and kept hydrated, Noah looked terrible. From his ashen complexion to the way he winced at every move.

Seth began to fuss in the main room and she forced herself to smile at Noah. "Be right back."

She wasn't sure if it was fear or something else written all over his face. He clearly didn't want her to leave, but she had to get Seth and try to feed Noah.

It was strange, and maybe a little warped, but knowing Noah was hurt calmed her somehow. Much like protecting Seth, it gave her a purpose. She couldn't cry. She couldn't fall apart. She had to be strong for her men.

Noah is not your man.

Well, she could pretend he was. It might get her through this whole nightmare, and that was the goal. Coming out on the other side.

She moved into the living room and smiled at Seth. He made angry noises, though hadn't gone into full-blown tantrum yet. He'd been up for a solid eight hours now, and was fighting a nap like a champ. But he was otherwise unaffected by everything that had happened, and she could only be grateful for that. It soothed.

She picked up the toy he'd thrown out of his travel crib and handed it to him. He took it, though he didn't smile. When she picked him up, he sighed a little and nuzzled into her shoulder.

Oh, he was getting so big. And somehow she had to make sure he grew up. When she stepped into the room, she laid Seth in the middle of the bed next to Noah.

He fussed, then rolled to his side, cuddling up with Noah's not-shot side.

Noah looked slightly alarmed, but Addie didn't have time to assure him Seth would be okay for a few minutes. She went back and folded the travel crib, then set it back up in the room before heading to the kitchen.

She ladled out some soup she'd been keeping warm for when Noah woke up. She went through the very normal motions of making Noah dinner, then went through the not-so-normal motions of taking it to him.

In bed.

With a sleeping baby between you and a gaping wound from a bullet in his side and who knows how many psychopaths after you.

She darted a look at the door, the many locks, then the windows and all the boarding up they'd done. She'd found a heavy metal cabinet in a back mudroom and moved it over the door to the cellar. None of these things would permanently keep bad people out, but it would slow them down and give her and Noah warning.

Besides, she had the snow in her favor now. Unless there'd been other men with the two they'd killed who were lying in wait, any more of Peter's men would have to contend with the same weather Grady and Ty were facing.

She straightened her shoulders and breezed back into Noah's room, hoping she looked far more calm and capable than she felt.

She lost some of that facade, though, when she caught sight of the big, bearded cowboy with his arm delicately placed around the fast-asleep baby. Something very nearly *panged* inside her, but she couldn't allow herself to dwell on any pangs.

"You need to try to eat as much of this as you can," she said quietly. She placed the bowl of soup on the sturdy, no-nonsense nightstand. "I'll go get a chair," she said, searching the room. "Then I can feed you."

"No."

"Noah—"

"Just need to sit up, and I can do it myself," he said through clenched teeth as he worked to move himself into a sitting position, pain etched all over his face.

She stood over him, fisting her hands on her hips. "You shouldn't. Don't make me stop you from moving."

He winged up an eyebrow at her, and something in that dark expression had her faltering a little bit. Because it made her think of other things she shouldn't be thinking of with Seth asleep next to him and the gaping wound in Noah's side.

"You're not feeding me," he said resolutely as he struggled to get into a sitting position in the bed.

She wanted to push him back down, but she was afraid she'd only hurt him more, so she tried to take a different approach. "It wouldn't be any problem to do it. You're injured. Let me take care of—"

"You're not feeding me," he repeated.

Maybe she was reaching, but his complexion didn't seem quite as gray, even as he managed to lean against the wall…because in this sparse, no-nonsense room there was no headboard.

She frowned at him, then at the soup, then back at him. "Fine. You've worn me down. Let it cool while I move Seth to—"

"He's fine. Give me the soup."

"Noah."

"Addie, you killed a man. Saved us. Boarded up windows and talked to paramedics. Give me the soup and take a sit."

You killed a man. She was trying so very hard not to contemplate that. So she handed him his soup.

"What part of take a sit did you not understand?" Noah asked, and though his tone was mild she didn't miss the harsh thread of steel in his tone.

"What part of *I killed a man* don't you understand? I might snap and kill you, too, if you keep bossing me around."

Noah smiled then. Actually smiled. "I'll take my chances."

"I want to be relieved you're feeling good enough to smile, except you so rarely smile, I'm just prone to think you have a fever or some kind of horrible brain sickness."

"If I do, you should probably sit down because your fluttering around is stressing me out."

Addie frowned. "I'm not… I don't *flutter.*" This time he didn't smile, but his lips *did* quirk upward. She slid onto the bed, Seth's sleeping body between them. She sighed heavily. "If I sit still, all I think about is all the ways things can go wrong."

He reached over and touched her arm, just a gentle brush of fingertips. "We'll get through this."

Addie blew out a breath. "We're stuck in a room in a tiny cabin that people have already infiltrated in the middle of a blizzard with no medical help or backup."

"But we fought off two armed men."

She frowned. "You've been *shot*, that's not exactly a victory."

"Not dead, though." He gave her arm a little squeeze, and though he tried to hide it, she noticed the wince. "Why don't you try to sleep while I eat? We need to take the opportunities to rest while we can."

"Noah…" Only she didn't know what to say or ask. She glanced down at Seth, who was sprawled out between them, blissfully unaware of everything going on around him.

She had to make sure he stayed that way, and this ended. "Noah, when you said you'd hurt people before this because you'd had to, what did you mean?"

He opened his mouth, most definitely to change the subject, but she needed to know. Needed to know how to go on from here. How to deal with the fact she'd hurt someone. "Tell me."

Noah brought the spoon to his mouth, slowly, carefully. Not because his body hurt, though it did, but because every part of him recoiled at the idea of telling her that. It would likely change her opinion of him, and more than that, he didn't want to tear down all those walls that kept it firmly in the past.

But maybe she needed to hear it. She needed to understand how to justify it so she could accept the things a person had to do to keep the people she loved safe.

She was so tense, sitting there on the opposite side of his bed. Eyes darting everywhere, hands clasping and unclasping. It was an interesting dichotomy: the woman who'd managed to do *everything* while he'd been unconscious, and this nervous, afraid-to-sit-and-think woman sharing a bed with him.

With a baby between you, idiot.

"My father wasn't a particularly kind man." Understatement of the year. "Ty and I were capable of withstanding that, but sometimes his targets weren't quite as fair or equal to the task."

"I'm not sure a son should ever have to be equal to the task of an unkind father."

"It was fine. We were fine, but Vanessa came to live with us for a bit when she was in high school. Her dad had died, and she'd gotten kicked out of her mother's house when her mother's new husband hadn't treated her so well. It was the only place to go, and we figured we'd keep her safe."

"From what? Unkindness? Because *safe* sounds like more than an unkind father."

"I suppose it was. It most certainly was when it came to Vanessa. Dad drank, more once Mom was gone, and she was by this point. Once Dad decided someone had the devil in them…"

"What does that even mean?"

Noah shrugged, trying not to think too deeply on it. Trying not to remember it as viscerally as he usually did, but it was a bit too much. Seth and Addie. This cabin. The pain throbbing at his side.

He took another spoonful of the soup, trying to will all this old ugliness away with the slide of warm soup down his throat. It didn't work. Instead the black cloud swirled around him like its own thick, heavy being.

But Addie slid her hand over his forearm. Gentle and sweet, and the black cloud didn't depart, but that heaviness lifted.

"He was a hard man. A vicious man. Made worse when he was drinking. He decided Vanessa had the devil in her and it was his job to get it out. I never quite understood it. He was not a religious man. No paragon of virtue. A Carson villain as much as any that came before."

"So you hurt him to protect Vanessa?"

Noah shouldn't have been surprised Addie could put it together, though it shamed him some. It must be obvious, the mark his father had made on him no matter how many years he'd striven to do good, *be* good.

"I guess."

"You *guess*?"

"I mean, that's the general gist."

"Then what's the actual story? I don't just want the gist."

He glanced at her then, the frown on her face, the line dug across her forehead. He didn't quite understand this woman, though he supposed he'd very purposefully tried *not* to understand her. To keep his distance. To keep everyone safely at arm's length.

But she'd slid under that at some point, and he didn't

think she'd even really tried. She'd shown up at his door looking fragile and terrified, and he'd been certain it would be easy or she'd disappear or something.

She'd killed a man. In self-defense. Of herself, her son, of *him*. And her hand rested on his arm, a feather-light touch, soft and sweet.

But she was stronger than all that. It was probably the blood loss, but he wanted to tell her now.

"Sometimes he'd whale on us," Noah offered, lifting a shoulder. "We were big enough to take it. Vanessa wasn't. I couldn't let him hurt her. Not just because she was my cousin and family, but because she hadn't done anything wrong. She didn't deserve it."

"Then neither did you or Ty."

But they'd weathered their father's many storms and Noah had never felt… It had felt like his lot in life. The way things were. He wasn't a philosophical man. He'd always played the cards he'd been dealt. Bitterness didn't save anyone.

But violence could. "He went after her one day. Really went after her." Noah tried to block it out. The sound of Vanessa sobbing, how close his father had come to hurting her. In every way possible.

"I wanted to kill him. To end it. Part of me wanted that." Still, even years after Dad had died in a cell somewhere. He wished he'd killed him himself.

"And that weighs on you," Addie said, as if she couldn't understand why even though it was obvious.

"He was my father. Everything he was weighs on me."

"But you're you." Her hand slid up his arm to cup his cheek. She even smiled. How could she possibly smile at *that*? "A good man. A noble one. I didn't think they existed, Noah. Not outside of fairy tales."

"I'm no fairy tale."

Sheer amusement flashed in her eyes, and it sent a pang of longing through him he wasn't sure he'd ever understand.

"No. You're no fairy tale, but you remind me good exists in the real world when I most need to remember that." She leaned across the sleeping baby and gently brushed her mouth across his bearded cheek. "Thank you," she whispered.

Maybe if they weren't on the run, if she hadn't killed a man, if he wasn't bleeding profusely where a man had shot him, he might have known what to do with all that. As it was, all he could do was stare.

"You should rest," he managed to say, his voice rusty and pained.

She sighed, dropping her hand from his cheek and settling into the pillows underneath her head. She stared at the ceiling rather than him. "So should you."

"Food first for me, which means you rest first. Just take a little nap while Seth does, huh?"

She yawned, snuggling deeper into the pillows. "Mmm. Maybe." She turned her gaze to him, so solemn and serious. "Noah…"

"We're going to make it out of here. I promise." If he of all people could make her believe in good, he could get her out of here. He would.

"No, it isn't that. It's just… Seth's not—"

A loud pounding reverberated through the cabin. Noah bit back a curse as he tried to jump into action and the move caused a screaming burn in his side. He put a hand on Addie's arm as he glanced at her pale face.

Three short raps later and Noah let out a sigh of relief. "It's Ty."

Chapter 11

Addie scurried out of the bed and toward the front door, hoping Seth would stay asleep and Noah would stay put.

Even though Noah had seemed so abundantly sure it was Ty at the door, Addie hesitated. What if it was a trick? What if Noah was hallucinating? She frantically searched the living room and kitchen for a weapon. For anything.

Before she could grab a knife from the kitchen, she heard Noah's footsteps and labored breathing. She turned and glared at him.

"You should have stayed in bed."

He didn't say anything, just carefully maneuvered himself to the door. He pounded on it, and it was only then she realized he knew it was Ty because they were pounding in some secret code.

"You could have explained."

Noah merely grunted.

"Move this?"

Addie hurried to move the couch away from the door, Noah reaching out to open the locks on the door as she did.

Irritably, she slapped his hand away and undid the last lock herself before yanking the door open.

Ty stood there, his hat pulled low and the brim dusted with snow. He had to step up and over to get through the snowdrift that had piled up outside the door.

"What the hell are you doing on your feet, idiot?" Ty demanded the moment he stepped inside and his eyes landed on Noah. He quickly started pushing Noah back toward the room he'd only just come from.

"Where's Grady?" Noah said.

"Shoveling out some room for the horses in the barn. We'll search the area once I've got you patched up," Ty returned. With absolutely no preamble he turned to Addie. "Boil water, find me all the bandages or make-shift bandages you can, and a few towels. Bring them to the bed."

"Seth's asleep in the bed," Noah muttered as Ty kept pushing him toward the bedroom.

Without even stopping, Ty barked out another order Addie's way. "Move the kid out of the bed."

"You'll be respectful," Noah said in that stern, no-nonsense tone.

Ty rolled his eyes. "Leave it to you with a bullet hole in your side to worry about respectful."

"It's fine. The most important thing is patching Noah up," Addie said resolutely, passing them both into the room and carefully maneuvering Seth from the bed to the mobile crib.

She stood there for a second looking at her baby as he squirmed, scowled, then fell back to sleep. She'd been so close to telling Noah he wasn't hers, which had been so silly. What did it matter? In every important way, Seth was hers.

No one needed to know that she had no legal claim over him. That would complicate everything.

On a deep breath, she turned to Ty, who was disapprovingly helping Noah into a prone position on the bed.

"Boiling water, bandages, towels. Anything else?"

"That'll do," Ty returned, lifting Noah's makeshift bandages she'd put on him herself. "You're one lucky son of a gun," Ty muttered to his brother, and it was in that moment Addie realized Ty's gruffness and irritation all stemmed from worry and fear.

It softened her some, and steadied her more. This family was like nothing she'd ever known, and she'd do whatever she could to help them, protect them. She just had to remind herself every now and again she didn't really belong to them, no matter what it might feel like when Noah touched her so gently, kissed her to distract her or smiled at her despite the bullet wound in his side.

As Addie marched to the kitchen, Grady came inside. He stomped his snowy boots on the mat as he latched the front door with the variety of locks. He looked pissed and dangerous, and yet it didn't make her nervous or even guilty. It made her glad this man was on her side.

"I saw the dead one outside. Nothing of any interest

on him," Grady said roughly as Addie prepared a pot to boil water in. "Laurel said there were two."

"I... There's one in the cellar," Addie said, nodding toward the metal cabinet she'd dragged across the door. "I think... I think he's dead." Dead. She'd killed a man and kept *telling* people about it and she wasn't sure how to feel about it...except Noah had said she should be relieved. Glad she'd protected herself and Seth. *And him.*

"If he's not dead now, he will be," Grady said, so cool and matter-of-fact it sent a shiver of fear through Addie.

Grady pulled a small gun from beneath the jacket he still wore. Whatever stabs of guilt from before the attack were gone now, because she could only be relieved she had people to help her.

Grady moved the cabinet off from the cellar door and eased his way down. Addie grabbed a knife from a drawer and eased her way close to the cellar. While she thought the man was dead, she'd absolutely jump to Grady's defense on the off chance the man was alive and got the better of him.

But Grady returned, grim-faced and serious. "Dead," he said stoically, and yet she could tell he was searching her face for signs of distress.

Addie straightened her shoulders. "Good." She wanted it to be good. She headed back for the kitchen and the boiling water.

"Laurel's beating herself up over this."

"She shouldn't," Addie said resolutely. "They're mobsters. Escaping police custody and doing the most damage possible is part of their job."

She grabbed some towels out of the drawer, trying

to force her face to look calm and serious. Like Laurel herself. In charge and ready for anything.

Grady smiled ruefully. "And just think, you and Noah managed to stop a few. I wish I could convince Laurel she's not to blame, but what we feel and what's the truth isn't always the same. Not much we can do about it. Though Laurel will try, till she's blue in the face and keeling over. We're all going to try to put an end to this."

"Noah thinks we need to lure Peter here. I think he'll just keep sending men. After all, we know at least one more is out there. I can only imagine more are coming to do more damage."

"We'll handle it."

"Are all you Carsons so sure of yourselves?"

Grady grinned. "Damn right we are. You don't survive centuries of being on the wrong side of history without knowing how to face the bad guy."

But Peter was so much more than a *bad* guy. Addie thought he was evil incarnate. Even a rational man would have taken Seth long ago. Instead, he wanted her in a constant state of fear. She had no doubt Peter would take away everything she loved before he was done.

She had to find some Carson bravery and surety. She had to believe in her own power, and theirs.

Peter couldn't win this, if she had to sacrifice herself to make sure he didn't.

"Grady, I have a plan." The scariest plan she'd ever considered. Dangerous. Possibly deadly. But if she had to face that to keep everyone she loved safe, well, then so be it.

Noah would not admit to anyone, even his own brother, he was feeling a little woozy. Part the loss of blood, and part the fact that someone stitching him up while he was unmedicated wasn't really that great of a time.

"That should do it," Ty said, and because Noah had spent his childhood shoulder-to-shoulder with his brother and knew all the inflections of his voice, he knew Ty was struggling with all this.

He also knew the last thing Ty would want was to talk about it.

"How often you have to do that in the army?"

"Don't worry about it."

So Ty didn't want to talk about that, either. Well, lucky for Ty Noah didn't have the energy to push. "When am I going to feel normal?"

Ty raised an eyebrow as he cleaned up the mess he'd made. "You got shot and patched up by passable emergency stitches at best. You need a whole hell of a lot of rest. Worry about that, not when."

"I have to keep her safe. *Them* safe."

"You have to rest first."

"I don't have time to rest."

Ty sighed heavily and Seth began to move around. A few little whimpers escaped his mouth, but he was still half-asleep.

"There is too much at stake," Noah said in a whisper. "Don't you see that?"

"Of course I see that. I also see that you've been shot. You're going to have to let some people step up and do the protecting here. We're all on it. Carsons. Delaneys."

"What good has that ever done?"

"You're still alive, aren't you?" Ty returned.

"Thanks to Addie."

"Well, she's a Delaney herself."

Noah scowled, well, much as he could with this terrible exhaustion dogging him. "You're not hearing me."

"I'm hearing you just fine. Enough to know you're getting mixed up with her."

"I'm protecting her," Noah replied resolutely. He was not mixed up in anything, because Addie was... well, whatever she was. *Strong. Vibrant. Everything.*

"Whatever you want to call it," Ty said with a shrug, having cleaned up all the stitching debris. "You need to rest before you can do more of it."

Seth began to whimper in earnest and Ty looked at the baby with something like trepidation in his gaze. "I'll get Addie."

"He won't bite you, you know," Noah offered irritably.

"I'll get Addie," Ty repeated, hurrying out of the room.

"Coward," Noah muttered, smiling over at Seth. "I'd pick you up, but I think I'd get in a little bit of trouble, kid." He painfully adjusted so Seth would be able to see him over the edge of his crib.

"No!" the boy demanded, pounding his little stuffed animal against the sides of the crib.

"I'd be in a whole heap of trouble."

"No," he repeated forcefully, and Noah had to smile. A year old and he already had Addie's spirit. A no-nonsense certainty, but with it a certain headstrong quality that wasn't Addie at all, and still Noah admired it. Because it would serve the boy well as he grew up.

Seth was damn well going to grow up somewhere where Noah could protect him.

"Awake already, baby?" Addie swept in, smiling at

Seth as she scooped him into her arms. She turned to Noah. "You okay?"

"I'll live."

"Well, that is encouraging," she returned. Her voice was…odd. A little high. Not exactly panic, but nerves threaded through it. He watched as she moved around the room, collecting Seth's diaper change supplies.

Something was wrong. He'd learned in the past few months that poking at it would only make her insist everything was fine. He had to be sneakier in getting the information out of her.

Too bad he didn't have any idea how to be sneaky.

"Everything okay out there?"

"Oh, you know." Addie's hand fluttered in the air as she laid Seth down on the bed, preparing to change his diaper. "The guy in the cellar is definitely dead. Laurel is blaming herself." She hesitated a second, only a second, before she said the next part. "Grady and I devised a plan."

Noah could tell by hesitation he wouldn't like the plan at all. Besides, why was she devising plans with Grady?

"What kind of plan?" he asked, hoping his voice sounded calm and not accusatory.

She smiled sweetly at him. Too sweetly as she expertly pulled the used diaper off Seth's wriggling body and wiped him up before replacing it with a new diaper.

"You need to rest. We'll catch you all up when you're feeling a little more up to things." She finished changing Seth's diaper and pulled the boy to his feet, tugging his pants back up.

"Catch me up now."

"Everything is fi—"

When he started to get up, she hurried to his side of the bed, Seth bouncing happily on her hip. She slid onto the bed next to him, pressing him back into the pillow. Not forcefully enough that he *had* to lie back down, but he didn't like the idea of fighting her. Not when she was touching him and looking at him with such concern in her expression.

"Don't get up." She didn't say it forcefully like Ty had, but plaintively, worry and hurt swirling in her blue eyes. He didn't want to admit it might come from the same place—care.

"No!" Seth grabbed Noah's nose. Hard. And squealed for effect.

Addie gently pried Seth's fingers off his face. "You need to rest."

"Now is not the time to rest. I can rest when this is over."

"Ty's worried. I can tell he's worried. Can't you be a good patient? For your brother?"

Noah grunted.

"I'll take that as a yes." Addie smiled. "I'm going to go get Seth something to eat. Why don't you try to rest?"

"No! No! No!" Seth lunged at him, smacking his pudgy hands against Noah's cheek.

"Gentle," Addie said soothingly.

It was all too much, these two people who'd come to mean so much to him no matter how hard he'd tried to keep them out. He'd told Addie the worst parts of himself, and she was still here, wanting to protect him and get him better. That little boy *knew* him and *liked* him for whatever darn reason.

He had to protect them, not just because it was the

right thing to do, but because he cared. He needed them, much to his own dismay and fear.

But dismay and fear were no match for determination. He took Addie's free hand, gave it a squeeze as her blue gaze whipped to his, looking surprised by the initiation of physical contact.

Which was a little much. He had kissed her before everything had blown up. Maybe he'd used the distraction excuse, but that didn't mean…

Well, none of it meant anything until she and Seth were safe. "Tell me what the plan is, Addie. I care too much about you to pretend I'm not worried about this."

She blinked, clearly taken aback by the mention of care, and maybe he should have been embarrassed or taken the words back, but he was too tired. Too tired to pretend, to keep it all locked down.

"You won't like it, Noah. I'm sorry. But you have to understand, it's what I have to do. For Seth. Once and for all."

"Explain," he growled.

"I'm going to be bait."

"Over my dead—"

"It'll get Peter here, and if we plan it out right, Laurel will have grounds to arrest him and transfer him to the FBI, which means he won't be able to escape this time."

"You don't know that."

He could tell that doubt hurt her, scared her, but she clearly needed both so she'd start thinking clearly.

"Or maybe I kill him, Noah. Maybe I do that. I don't know. What I do know is I can't keep running. You said so yourself. He has to come here. He doesn't want Seth, not really. He wants to cause me pain. So, I give him the chance."

"We can make that happen without you being bait."

"Yes, it's gone so well so far," she said drily, pointing to his bandaged side.

Which poked at his pride as much as the fear settling in his gut. That she would put herself in a situation where she could be hurt, or worse.

"I won't allow it."

She scoffed, shoving to her feet. Seth complained in his baby gibberish but Addie only paced. "I don't know why you insist on acting as though you have any say, any right. You don't get to tell me how to live my life, Noah Carson. You don't get to boss me around. This is my problem. Mine."

"And I don't know why you insist on acting as though that's true when I have told you time and time again it's mine, too. I'm here. I'm injured. I've killed to protect you and Seth. It is *our* problem."

She closed her eyes briefly before sitting back down on the bed. "I know. I know. I just… We have to work together but that doesn't mean… You're hurt, Noah. We have to play to our strengths. You have to watch over Seth for me. You'll have to protect him and keep him safe. That's what I need from you. What *we* need from you."

"Addie," he all but seethed.

"I'm counting on you, so you have to do it."

"I'll be damned if I let that madman touch you. If I have to fight you *and* Grady to make sure that's the case."

"It's the only way. You're the only one who can keep Seth safe. I need you to do that for me, Noah. You're the only one I can trust with him."

"I can't let you do this, Addie."

"I know you must think I'm weak or stupid to have gotten mixed up in this thing—"

"I don't think that at all."

"Then you have to *trust* me." She took his hand in hers, Seth still happily slapping at his face while tears filled Addie's eyes. "Noah, I need you to protect him. He is the most important thing in the world to me. You're the only one who can do it. I know this kills you, but I wouldn't ask if it wasn't the only way. I can handle Peter as long as you can keep Seth safe."

He couldn't do this anymore. He was too tired. His head was pounding. Everything hurt, throbbed and ached. He couldn't fight her like this. He needed to build up his strength first. "We'll discuss it more tomorrow."

She sat there for a few seconds looking imperiously enraged before she let out a slow breath. "Fine." She seemed to really think over tomorrow. "We can talk more tomorrow. You need to rest."

"Yeah."

She started to move, but she still had her hand on his, so he grabbed it. Squeezed it. He needed her to understand that plans where she went off and put herself in danger just weren't an option. Not because she was weak. Not because of anything other than a selfish need to keep her close and safe.

Addie's and Seth's blue eyes peered at him, and he looked at them both, some brand-new pain in his chest. Not so much physical, this one.

"You're both important to me," he said resolutely. As much as he'd wanted to keep care and importance to himself, it was getting too dangerous to keep it bottled up. Too dangerous to try to keep her at arm's length. She had to know. "So important."

Some ghost of a smile flittered across her mouth before it was gone. Then she pressed her lips to his forehead, warm and smooth and somehow reassuring. "You're important to us," she whispered. "Now get some rest."

He wanted to fight it, but exhaustion won as Addie slipped out of the room, and Noah fell into a heavy sleep.

Chapter 12

Seth's schedule was so off it was nearly two in the morning before he was down for the night. Ty was asleep in the other bed in the cabin, having fixed up all the broken-in areas from earlier. Grady was asleep on the couch, snoring faintly.

Addie slipped into Noah's room and carefully laid Seth in his crib, watching him intently.

She would sacrifice anything for this boy. Including herself. It hadn't been an option before, but now she had people she could trust. People she could *entrust*.

Noah would protect him. The Carsons and Delaneys would give him love. Stability. Family.

She turned to Noah, asleep on the bed.

Knowing what she was going to do tomorrow she had to accept this might be the last time she spoke with him. She wouldn't allow herself to consider she might not survive, but she had to consider the fact that Noah might be so angry at her he'd never speak with her again.

She had to do what she had to do. For Seth, and for the only opportunity for a future that didn't involve running, losing or fighting for her life.

She slid onto the empty side of the bed, her heart beating a little too fast no matter that she was sure. Sure what she was going to do tonight, and sure what she was going to do tomorrow.

Noah stirred next to her and instead of staying on her own side, she scooted closer to him. The warmth of him, the strength of him. It was such an amazing thing that time and luck had brought her this man who wanted to protect her.

"Morning?" he murmured sleepily.

"No. Middle of the night." She should let him sleep. She should insist he rest. But she only had this one moment. She couldn't waste it. She pressed her mouth to his bearded cheek. "Would you do something for me?"

"In the middle of the night?"

"Well, it's a naked kind of something. Night seems appropriate."

She felt his whole body go rigid, and she was almost certain she could feel his gaze on her in the darkened room.

"Am I dreaming?" he asked suspiciously.

She allowed herself a quiet laugh and slid her hand under the covers and it drifted down his chest, his abdomen and then to the hard length of him. "Feels pretty real to me."

"That's a terrible line," he muttered, but he didn't shift away. Which might have been because of the injury on his opposite side, except he didn't shrink from her intimate touch. If anything he pushed into it.

"Noah, I want to be with you." She kissed his cheek, his jaw. "I've been pretending I don't, but it seems so silly to pretend with all of these horrible things going on. I don't want to pretend anymore, but if you don't want me—"

His mouth was on hers, fierce and powerful, before she could even finish the sentence. He carefully rolled onto his good side and his arms wound around her, drawing her tight against his body, trapping her own hand between them.

"I shouldn't," he said against her mouth. "God knows I shouldn't." But he didn't let her go, and his mouth brushed her lips, her cheeks, her jaw.

"Why not?" she asked, if only because he hadn't stopped touching her, holding her, kissing her.

"You're too..." He trailed off.

When he never finished his sentence, she cupped his face, holding him there, a tiny inch away from her mouth. "I'm just me," she whispered before kissing him, something soft and sweet instead of intense and desperate.

That softness lingered, all those furtive glances they'd hidden over months of being under the same roof. All the hesitant touches immediately jerked away from. Longing glances behind each other's backs.

It had seemed so necessary then, and now it was stupid to have wasted all that time. Time they could have been together—getting to know each other, touching each other. And they hadn't only because she'd been certain he was too good and honorable to even look

at her twice, and he'd been convinced she was too…
something.

But they were just them, and for a little while they
could be together. She tugged at his T-shirt, trying to
pull it off him without hurting him. Carefully, she rid
him of the fabric and discarded it on the other side of
the bed.

His calloused hands slid under her shirt, the rough
texture of his palms scraping against her sides and
sending a bolt of anticipation through her. He lifted
her shirt off her and dropped it.

"I closed the door, but Seth's asleep in his crib. We
have to be quiet," she whispered.

He exhaled, something close to a laugh. "You
think?" His breath fluttered across her cheek, his hands
tracing every curve and dip of her body, cupping her
breasts.

She groaned, trying to arch against him, bring him
closer.

"Shh," he murmured into her ear, something like
laughter in his voice.

Her heart squeezed painfully, because she wanted
all of Noah's smiles and all of Noah's laughter and she
was putting all of that in jeopardy. He was too noble,
too sure to ever forgive her for going out on her own.

But that didn't change the fact that it needed to be
done.

She trailed her hands across the firm muscles of his
abdomen, sighing happily as she reached the waistband
of his shorts. She moved to pull them down and off,
give her full access to him, but he hissed out a breath
and Addie winced, pulling away from him.

"I don't want to hurt you." No matter how much she wanted this, the thought of him in pain—

"I'll live. Keep touching me, I'll live."

She might have argued with him if his hands weren't on her. Tracing, stroking, pulling responses out of her body she didn't know were possible. She felt as though her skin were humming with vibrations, as though the room were filled with sparkling light instead of pitch-black.

They managed to remove the rest of each other's clothes without causing Noah any more pain—at least that he showed. Addie straddled his big, broad body, her heart beating in overtime, her core pulsing with need and something deeper in her soul knowing this was something meant. Elemental.

Noah was hers, and maybe she even loved him. She'd probably never get to explore that, but at least she got to explore this. Something she'd never felt, certainly not with this bone-deep certainty it was right. *They* were right.

She kissed him as he entered her, a long, slow slide of perfect belonging. His arms held her close and tight, and when he moved inside her, she sighed against his mouth and he sighed against hers.

He took her as though he was studying every exhale, every sigh, and making sure she did it again. And again, and again, with a kind of concentration and care no one had ever shown her. Until she was nothing but shaking pleasure, dying for that fall over into release.

"Noah."

"Addie."

It was the way he said her name, low and dark, full of awe, that propelled her over that sparkling edge of wonder. Noah pushed deep and held her tight and they lay there for who knew how long.

It didn't matter, because she wanted time to stop. Here. Right here.

But life didn't work that way. She slid off him, curling up into his good side. He murmured something, but she couldn't make it out.

"Sleep," she whispered, brushing a kiss below his ear.

"You, too," he murmured, holding her close.

She should. Sleep and rest, because tomorrow she would have to face a million hard things she'd been running from for too long.

So she gave herself this comfort. Noah's arms around her, his heart beating against hers. The fact that he'd been as desperate for her as she'd been for him, and out of something horrible that may change her life forever, at least she'd gotten this little slice of rightness.

It would give her strength, and it would give her purpose, and tomorrow she would find a way to end this all.

Noah awoke to the sound of a woman's voice. But it was all wrong. It wasn't Addie.

He opened his eyes, glancing at the woman sitting next to him on his bed.

"What the hell are you doing here?" he grumbled, his voice sleep-rusted and scathing against his dry throat. His body ached, just *ached*, and yet there was something underneath all that ache. A bone-deep satisfaction.

Except Addie wasn't here, and his cousin was.

"Good morning to you, too, sunshine," Vanessa

offered cheerfully, bouncing Seth in her lap. "I don't know what the hell you do with these things, but he's a pretty cute kid."

"Where's Addie?"

"Can you hold him, or will that hurt your stitches?"

"Where the hell is Addie?"

Vanessa sighed gustily. "I know you've been shot and all, but there's no need to be so grumpy and demanding."

"Don't make me ask again, or you will regret ever stepping foot in this cabin."

Vanessa raised an eyebrow, and it was the kind of warning he should probably heed, but panic thrummed through his body, making it impossible to heed anyone's warning.

"You're hurt, so I'll give you a pass on that, Noah, but don't ever speak to me that way."

He struggled to get himself into a sitting position.

"Geez, you really are hurt." She wrinkled her nose. "Please tell me you're not naked under there."

He glared at her as Seth made a nosedive for him. With a wince, Noah caught the boy. Poor kid was too cooped up. He needed to crawl around and move, but the cabin wasn't the place for it.

And where the hell is Addie?

"I am not naked." At some point he'd pulled his boxers back on last night.

Vanessa clucked her tongue and shook her head. "First Grady. Now you."

"Now me what?"

"A Delaney, Noah. Really?"

"She's not a… Not…really. Where is she?"

"Well, she and Grady went somewhere."

"Where?" he growled.

"Sworn to secrecy, sorry."

The only thing that kept Noah's temper on a leash was the fact that if he started yelling at Vanessa, he'd likely scare Seth. And then Vanessa would make him pay for the yelling later. He took a deep breath, doing everything in his power to keep his anger from bubbling out of control.

"I know you don't like this, but you're hurt, and Addie had an idea and… Look, Grady promised he and Laurel would keep her safe. Ty's out seeing if he can get a truck up here to take you to the doctor. We're on baby patrol. It isn't so bad."

She'd done it anyway. After last night, after saying they'd talk about it, she'd gone and done some stupid, dangerous thing anyway. "She's going to put herself in harm's way. How is that not bad?"

"She's the one who brought this mob mess to your doorstep, Noah. You'd be at your ranch, unharmed, if it weren't for her."

"She's not responsible for that. The man who's after her is."

"A man she had a kid with, Noah."

Slowly, because he couldn't believe Vanessa of all people would say that, he turned his head to face her. "You didn't just say that."

Vanessa shrugged, crossing her arms over her chest, adopting that pissed-off-at-the-world posture that seemed to propel her through life. "Well, it's true. You're paying because of the choices she made to get involved with someone awful. And yeah, the awful guy is at fault, but that…" She looked away, and Noah noticed a flicker of vulnerability he understood only because he'd once saved her from the abuses of his father.

"You're hurt," she said forcefully. "I get to be a little put out about my cousin being hurt."

He softened, only a fraction. "She's been hurt, too. You should be able to find some sympathy. You of all people."

Whatever vulnerability that had been evident in the cast of her mouth disappeared into hard-edged anger. "Then you need to understand that sometimes, not always but sometimes, people need to fight their own battles. Without you."

Which hit far too many insecurities of his own. He looked down at Seth, who was happily pulling at his chest hair. It might sting when he gave a strand a good tug, but it had nothing on knowing Addie was out there trying to fight her own battles.

She'd done that enough and he'd promised her no more, they were in this together, and she'd just ignored it. "I should have known what that was," he muttered.

"What *what* was?"

"Nothing. Never mind." But it had been a goodbye, plain and simple. And worse, so much worse, she'd chained him here under a responsibility he couldn't ignore. He scooted out of bed, hefting Seth onto his good side. "He needs to eat."

"No!" Seth tugged at his hair, making a sound Noah had a sneaking suspicion was his attempt at the word *hat*.

Noah strode out into the living room, Vanessa at his heels. Ty pushed in the door at the same moment, grim-faced and blank-eyed.

"We can't get out quite yet."

"How'd you stab me in the back and get Addie out of here?"

"They took the horses," Ty said with a shrug, clearly not worried about the backstabbing.

Figured.

"Give me your hat," he demanded, holding out his hand to Ty.

Ty cocked his head, but handed the Stetson over after shaking some of the snow off it. Noah handed it to Seth, who squealed happily.

"If anything happens to her," Noah said, deadly calm, because he didn't have any other choice of what to be—he had to protect Seth—"God help all of you." With that he strode into the kitchen to get Seth some food.

Chapter 13

Addie sat in the Carson ranch house for the third boring, alone day in a row and tried not to cry. None of
this was going like it was supposed to.

The plan had been to install her at the Carson Ranch,
making it look like she had Seth with her, and wait
for the next ambush. They'd moved her, faked Seth's
presence and acted as though they were trying to be
sneaky while laying all sorts of clues that this is where
they were.

But it had been three days. No matter how often she
talked to Laurel on the phone about how sure Addie
was that having Grady or one of the sheriff's deputies
be a lookout was clearly keeping Peter away, Laurel
insisted they keep going without Addie attempting to
make personal contact with Peter.

Better to wait him out, Laurel insisted. Let him feel like he was the one making the moves, not being lured.

Addie was learning that arguing with Laurel was absolutely pointless. The woman would do whatever she wanted, whatever she thought was best. Noah was like that. Grady, too. All the Carsons and all the Delaneys so sure they knew what was best and right.

Her included. She smiled a little at the thought. She was here because she'd been certain her being bait was the *only* way. She hadn't let Noah stop her.

But thinking about Noah only hurt. She missed him. She missed Seth like an open, aching wound. All there was to do in the silence of the Carson ranch house was miss them and worry about them and think about how mad Noah must be at her. If she managed to get over that she could only fret over the way it kept snowing and snowing and snowing.

She stared at her phone, trying to talk herself out of the inevitable panic call to Laurel. But she couldn't do it. This couldn't keep going. How long would she survive this endless, crazy-making waiting?

What awful things was Peter planning? He'd already proved he could wait as long as he pleased. He'd let her get settled here, hadn't he? Oh, she was now certain he was behind the poison and the fence-breaking. Little hints he was on the way, but enough doubt to cause her to wonder and worry, then talk herself out of it and settle in. Something like psychological warfare, and Peter was a pro.

She hit Call on Laurel's number in her phone, determined to talk Laurel out of the lookouts. She had to do this alone, without help or watchdogs. Maybe if she was persistent enough with Laurel—

"Addie, if you're calling me to tell me you can't do this—"

"I can't do this."

Laurel sighed. "Look, we've got some stuff brewing."

Addie straightened in her seat at the kitchen table. Noah and Seth missing like limbs she didn't know what to do without. "What does that mean?"

"Give me a sec."

Addie waited, trying not to think too hard about what *brewing* might mean.

"There. Some privacy. Listen, we've had five brand-new visitors to Bent in the past three days. That never happens. Now, none of them match the FBI's description of Peter, but that doesn't mean they don't work for him."

"I can't wait around for Peter if he's just going to send people. Maybe I should go to Bost—"

"You're not going anywhere." Laurel said it with the same kind of finality Noah had said it with days before. Addie hadn't listened to him. Why should she listen to Laurel?

"But Peter hasn't left Boston." If she went there. If she confronted him… She might die, sure, but maybe…

"According to the FBI, but who knows what they know."

"Laurel, they're the FBI. Maybe if I worked with them—"

"They clearly don't care enough. When I spoke with an agent all he could talk about was some other organized crime group they're infiltrating as part of the Monaghan case. They want a case. We want you safe. It's personal for us. Look, there was this guy at Grady's bar last night. He didn't match any of the descriptions we have on file as Peter's men, but maybe that's good. Maybe he sent someone new. He disappeared somewhere out of town last night, but if he comes back we'll be ready to tail him."

"What did he look like? Peter isn't big on hiring new men. His goons are all either friends from childhood or people his father used."

"Red-haired guy, about six foot maybe. Green eyes. Little scar next to his eye."

Addie's heart stopped, or at least it felt as though it did. "Laurel," she managed to whisper.

"You recognize him?"

"Laurel, that's Peter."

"What?"

"You just described Peter," Addie repeated, something like panic and relief swelling inside her chest. Thank God they could move forward. Peter was here.

And what would he do to her? She couldn't think about that. She had to think about the future. About ending this.

"No. The description we have of Peter is six-four, two forty, dark hair, blue eyes, with a tattoo on his wrist."

"No. No, that's not Peter. That's not Peter at all. He's shorter. Wiry. Red hair. Green eyes. The scar. I would know, Laurel. I would know."

Laurel swore. "So much for the damn FBI. Okay, I've got to radio this new description out to my men. Because he's here, Addie, and things are going to go down soon. Be smart. Be safe. Keep everything on you. Phone. Gun. Everything. Got it?"

Addie nodded before remembering she was on the

phone. "Yeah, yeah, I got it." She didn't like carrying the gun around, so she'd started keeping a sheathed awful-looking knife in her pocket and the gun hidden in the kitchen. But she'd go get the gun. She'd be safe. She'd end this.

"I'll call again soon. Be safe." And with that the line went dead.

Addie took a deep breath. This was what she'd left Noah for. This was what she needed to do to keep Seth safe once and for all. She got to her feet, shaky with nerves, but filled with righteous determination.

Peter was here. Which meant he'd be *here* soon enough. They'd made it look like they were trying to keep her safe, but the locks were paltry and the windows weren't boarded. It'd be easy for anyone to sneak in.

When someone did, she'd have a deputy at her door, or Grady, or someone to save her and arrest Peter. If she could keep calm. If she could think clearly and make sure Peter made his intent known.

He would. She was sure he would.

"God, please, please, let that all be true," she whispered.

A loud smacking sound startled a scream out of her. She whirled at the sound of clapping, and her knees nearly buckled when Peter stepped around the corner, applauding as he smiled that horrible dead-eyed, evil-infused smile.

"Impressive performance, Addie."

She stood straighter, reminding herself to be strong. Reminding herself what she was doing. Saving Seth. Saving herself.

"Really, that was impressive," Peter said, gesturing

at the phone clutched in her hand. "You should thank me for such a compliment."

"Go to hell."

Peter sighed heavily. "Always so rude. Your sister at least had some manners."

"Don't talk about her."

Peter rolled his eyes. "Well, this has gone on quite long enough, hasn't it? Though your fear and running has kept me quite entertained, and this darling little *family* you think you've created here. I can't decide if I want to kill them all and let you live with the guilt of *that* or something else entirely."

Addie smiled, some inner sense of calm and rightness stealing over her. Any second now, she'd be rescued and Peter would be put in jail. "Good luck, Peter," she offered faux-sweetly.

Any fake smiles or pretended enjoyment on his face died into flat, murderous fury. "I don't need your luck. I wonder if my son is old enough to remember watching me kill you."

Addie lifted her chin. "You'll never touch him."

There was a commotion somewhere in the back and Addie let out a shaky breath. They'd gotten his murder threat, which meant the deputy was coming to arrest Peter.

Except Peter's mouth twisted into a smile that sent ice down her spine. "Oh, you think that's your savior? You think your sad little plan was going to work on me? You're even dumber than your sister, Addie."

"She wasn't so dumb. She got Seth far away from you, didn't she?"

Peter lunged, grabbing her around the throat. She fought him off, and he didn't squeeze her hard enough to cut off her oxygen. He simply held her there, glaring at her with soulless green eyes no matter how she punched and kicked at him.

"It was fun while it lasted. Watching you run. Watching you settle in and convince yourself you were safe, bursting that bubble over and over again, but you stopped running. That really ruins my fun, Addie."

"Good," she choked out.

"Good indeed. I suppose it's time to find my son. I'm going to kill whoever has him in front of you. No one's going to save you, Addie, because right now in the back of this property a man who looks an awful lot like me is forcing a woman who looks quite a bit like you at gunpoint toward the mountains. And while your friends follow *him*, we'll be going in the opposite direction." He stuck his mouth right up against her ear. "No one's going to find you, Addie, and Seth will be all mine."

In a low, violent voice she cursed him. In the next second she felt a blinding pain, and the world went dark.

The continuous rage that had begun to exist like a tumor in Noah's gut never, ever let up in the three days of being stuck in the Carson cabin knowing Addie was somewhere out there without him to keep her safe. The only thing that kept him from exploding was the boy. Not just Noah's job to keep him safe, but watching Seth take hesitant steps from couch to wall and back again was…something. It eased a part of the horrible anger inside him, and he thanked God for it.

"No," the boy said, grinning happily up at him. Noah held out his hand and Seth slapped it with enthusiasm.

Noah had taught a kid to high-five, and even amid the worry and anger, there was some joy in that. Some pride. Silly, maybe, but it was good. This was good.

This he would protect. "Gonna be a bruiser, aren't you, kid?" Noah murmured.

"Ma?"

Noah didn't let that rage show on his face. He kept his smile placid. "Mama will be home soon." Which was a promise he wasn't about to take lightly. Three days had healed his stitches well enough. He wasn't dizzy anymore, and he felt much stronger. Everything still hurt like hell, but it was bearable.

He was going to get out of here soon. Whether Ty and Vanessa wanted him to or not. He just had to formulate his plan and make sure Ty and Vanessa had the ability to protect Seth. So he could protect Addie.

Noah glanced over at Ty. Every morning and afternoon he went tracking out down the road in the vain hopes it was clear enough to get them all down the mountain.

They still had Vanessa's horse, but it couldn't carry them all, and Seth was too little to be traveling in this kind of weather, anyway.

Laurel checked in with Ty every evening, but no one would ever talk to Noah. The minute he grabbed the phone or tried to use his own, they hung up. Everyone refused to communicate with him, and it made the rage bigger, hotter. Rage was so much better than fear.

Every person in his life was a coward, and what was worse, he *felt* like one. No matter that watching Seth and protecting him was a noble pursuit. It felt like a failure not to be protecting Addie, too.

Vanessa was in the kitchen complaining about mak-

ing dinner even though she was by far the best cook out
of the three of them, and had insisted they stop trying
as it all tasted like "poison."

Noah wasn't convinced his reheating a can of soup
could poison someone, but Vanessa was happiest when
she was complaining so he just let it go. Let her pound
around and pretend she didn't like taking care of all
three of them.

"No. Ha." Seth smashed Noah's hat onto his head.
Noah tried to pay attention to their little game and not
the fact that Ty's phone was trilling about two hours
earlier than Laurel's usual check-in.

"Yeah?" Ty asked gruffly into his phone.

Seth continued to play his favorite game of taking
the hat on and off, though he'd now added putting the
hat on his own head to the mix.

"I see," Ty said, his voice devoid of any inflection.

Noah looked over at him, a heavy pit of dread in
his stomach. He tried to reason it away, but it stuck
like a weight, because Ty's expression was as blank
as his voice.

In anyone else, Noah might have said he couldn't
read that practiced blankness. Ty hadn't had it growing up, but he'd come home from the Army Rangers with the ability to completely blank all expression
from his face.

It was just in this situation Noah knew the only reason he'd have to do that was if Addie'd been hurt.

"What happened?"

Ty didn't speak for a moment as he slowly placed
his phone back in his pocket. But his gaze held Noah's.
"The guy's in Bent."

The guy. Noah got to his feet, carefully maneuvering around Seth. "The guy's in Bent. Where's Addie?"

Ty stayed where he was. Still and blank. "It's all part of the plan."

Which did absolutely nothing with the way the dread was turning to fear, which he'd channel into fury. "Where is Addie?"

Ty blew out a breath. "If you can calm yourself, I'll explain it to you."

Calm? How was anyone *calm* knowing that a person he'd vowed to protect was just wandering around out there? A target. Aided by his family. He didn't know what was worse, that she'd made love to him and left to face evil alone, or that his family had helped her.

"They put Addie up at the ranch. Alone, but under the watch of either a deputy or Grady or even Laurel, depending on the time of day."

"Let me guess. It went so well. The bad guy's caught and Addie is one hundred percent safe."

Ty scowled. "The guy created a bit of a diversion. Instead of just trying to take Addie, he had another guy with him who made it look like *he'd* taken Addie. So, two guys with a woman apiece went in opposite directions. Since only one deputy was watching, he had to make his best guess on which one was actually Addie."

Noah laughed bitterly. Idiots. All of them. He strode for his rifle, which was hung up on the wall out of reach of Seth. He started gathering what he'd need. His coat, a saddlebag, a first aid kit.

"Noah, you can't just leave," Vanessa said.

"Like hell I can't."

"What about Seth?" Vanessa demanded.

"You'll keep him safe."

"Addie asked *you* to do that."

"And I asked you all to keep Addie safe. She's not. She's with a mobster who's been chasing her for a year, who will very likely kill her once he finds out where Seth is. Who in this damn town is a better tracker than I am?" he demanded, glancing back and forth from Ty to Vanessa and back again.

"I'm not half-bad," Ty said. "Army Ranger and all. Besides, the deputy is tracking one of them. It could be Addie."

"And it could not be. Regardless, a mobster and his buddy have two women. Both are likely going to end up dead if someone doesn't do something."

"Let me do it," Ty said. "I can track as well as you. And I don't have a gunshot wound."

"You can't track as well as I can *here*. *I'm* the one who knows Bent and those mountains better than anyone. *I* helped track Laurel down when she was kidnapped. No one, and I mean *no one*, is better equipped to do this thing than I am. Not Laurel's idiot deputies, and not you or Grady. So I am taking that horse. You are arming yourself to the teeth. You die before you let anyone harm that child. And I will die before I let anyone harm Addie."

"You're hurt, Noah."

"I'll damn well live." Because he didn't think he could if something happened to Addie. So he couldn't let that happen.

Chapter 14

Addie woke up groggy, her head pounding. It felt like a hangover, but in painful detail she remembered all too well what it was.

Peter had hit her with something and knocked her out. Nausea rolled in her gut, and she wished she knew more about head trauma or concussions. Was she seriously hurt? Was she going to die?

You will not die. Not until Seth is safe. Seth. Noah. She had to hold on to the belief that she could end this for them.

She took a deep breath in and slowly let it out. She took stock of her body as she looked around her surroundings.

She was cold. So cold. She smelled hay and horse. The walls were slats of wood and… She was in the stable. In one of the horses' individual pens. Tied to the wooden slats and sitting in the hay. Cold without a coat on in the middle of winter, head throbbing from who knew what kind of head trauma.

But she was not far from the Carson Ranch. At least, she didn't think. This didn't look exactly like the stables close to the house. Everything out here was a little dilapidated, and the hay certainly wasn't new. It was gray and icy. She knew for a fact someone had been doing Noah's chores around the ranch to keep the horses and cows alive.

So maybe she wasn't at the Carson Ranch at all.

She couldn't panic. Even as it beat in her chest like its own being, she couldn't let it win. She had to be smart. She had to *think*.

She was tied to the wooden slats of the stables with a rope. The wooden slats didn't look particularly sturdy, but the rope on her wrists was tight and rough.

She gave her arms a yank and the wooden slat moved. She paused and listened, but there were no sounds except the howling wind. Was Peter around?

She gave her arms another yank. Again the wooden slat moved, even creaked a little as though she'd managed to splinter it. She tried not to let the hope of it all fill her with too much glee. She had to focus. Listen for Peter. Be smart. She had to be smart.

Still there was nothing but silence. No footsteps. None of Peter's nasty comments. She didn't feel the oppressive fear of his presence. So she kept yanking. Harder and harder with fewer pauses between times. Each time Peter didn't appear, she felt emboldened to move faster.

She lost track of how many yanks, of the burning in her wrists from the way the rope rubbed, because all she could think about was escape. She could outrun Peter in the snow. While he fancied himself a hunter and an outdoorsman, she knew from her sister he did it in upscale lodges with guides doing most of the work.

She'd been living in Wyoming for months now, doing somewhat physical labor by keeping house. She wasn't soft like Peter. She could outrun him. She knew at least some of the area. She could win.

She had to believe she could win.

She gave another hard yank and it was followed by the sound of wood splintering. Her momentum sent her forward, and since she didn't have the arms to reach out and catch herself as her wrists were tied together, she maneuvered to her side and fell that way.

She blew out a breath, not moving for a few seconds as she lay on the icy hay. Peter still didn't come running.

She laughed out a breath. She'd done it. She'd actually done it. But she had to focus and be careful and smart. Peter could be anywhere, and with her hands tied behind her back and a piece of wood dangling from the rope, she couldn't fight him off. Her only option right now was to escape.

And go where?

It was winter in Wyoming and she had no coat. She had some kind of head injury and her hands were tied behind her back.

Taking her chances with the elements was a much better option than taking her chances with Peter. Someone would find her. They knew she'd been taken, diversion or not. Someone would find her. She had to believe that.

She got to her feet, leaning against the wall as dizziness washed over her. She was definitely not 100 percent, but she could do this. Her legs were fine.

Once the dizziness settled, she took a step away from the wall. She wasn't completely steady on her feet, but it would have to do. Maybe Peter had tied her up and left her to die from exposure, but she had a bad feeling he wasn't done with her yet.

If she escaped now she could press charges. She could tell the FBI everything she knew and they'd have to arrest him for all the other things as well. She'd never had any evidence he'd killed Kelly, but she had proof that he'd tried to kill *her* in the here and now.

It had to be enough.

Carefully, she poked her head out of the stall she'd been in. The entire stable was empty. Ramshackle. She had no idea where she was. She'd never seen this building before. All of the buildings she'd seen on Carson property were certainly old and a little saggy, but cared for. No holes in the sides or roofs caving in like this building had.

So, not on Carson property, but people were looking for her. So all she had to do was run.

And hope she didn't end up in the mountains. Alone. Overnight.

There was a giant door on one side of the stable, but she wasn't stupid enough to go out that way. If Peter was still around, he'd see that. So she needed a window or a loose board or something. It was still dangerous, but she'd cut down as much chance of detection as she could.

She searched the stable and found two long-ago-broken windows. There wasn't an easy way to leverage herself up and out with the jagged edges of glass, the height, or her hands tied behind her back. So she went to the holes in the walls, poking and prodding at the wood around them as best she could without the full use of her arms.

It wasn't easy going and frustration was threatening, but she couldn't let it overwhelm her. Couldn't let—

She frowned as the faint smell of gasoline started to filter through the air. She hadn't seen any machinery in the stables that might be leaking old fuel. Panic tickled the back of her throat, but she swallowed it away. Maybe it was a side effect of the head injury.

Except then she heard laughter and everything inside of her roiled with futility as Peter's face appeared in the hole she'd been working on.

"Here's Johnny!" he offered all too happily before kicking at the loose boards around the hole—creating an even bigger one. The debris flew at her and she tried to move back so it wouldn't hit her, but she lost her balance and fell back on her butt, unable to stop from falling all the way onto her back since she couldn't use her hands to hold her up.

Peter stepped through the large hole he'd kicked and loomed over her. "Did you think you'd escape?" Peter laughed as if this was all just fun for him, to torture someone. To hurt someone. What had been warped in him to feel good at another's misfortune?

The smell of gasoline got even stronger, and Addie tried not to let fear destroy all the courage she had inside her.

But Peter calmly pulled a lighter out of his pocket, flicking the small flame to life in the frigid air between them, and the smell of gas was only making her feel even more dizzy than she already had.

"Actions have consequences, Addie. Your sister learned that. The hard way. I thought you might have more sense, but I see I was wrong. You stopped running. You tried to fight. No one fights me and wins."

"I've been doing an okay job. You don't have Seth."

"But I will. The question is whether I let you die here, or in front of him."

The smell of gas was making her sick to her stomach. The flick of the lighter. He was going to kill her.

She breathed through that fear, because he would want to save himself. He'd want to be far enough away before he set this place on fire. It would give her a chance. It had to give her a chance.

"If you tell me where he is, I might just let you out. Let you run again. If not…" He shrugged and flicked the lighter again.

"You'll never find him. Ever."

"I guess you're dead, then." And he dropped the lighter.

Horseback took too damn long. Especially with the snow and the isolation of the cabin. Carson Ranch was too far away. Everything was stacked against Noah, including the pain ricocheting through his side where he might have already busted his stitches.

He wouldn't let any of that stop him.

Besides, if he'd been in a vehicle he would have to go down through Bent. On horseback—slower or not—he could cut up through the valleys where there weren't any roads and enter the property through the northeast pastures. It'd be more of a surprise approach, and maybe he'd even catch Peter with Addie trying to get out.

The closer he got to Carson property, the less he let his brain move in circles. He was focused. He was determined. For Seth and for Addie, he'd do whatever it took.

"Stop!"

The order seemed to have come out of nowhere, and Noah would have ignored it if not for the glint of a gun from behind the tree line next to him. He brought his horse to a stop, surreptitiously eyeing his surroundings, what options he had.

"Carson?"

Noah stared at the glint of gun. He couldn't see the person and he didn't recognize the voice, but whoever it was continued on.

"Get behind the trees. Now."

He followed the harsh order if only because if it was someone out to hurt him, they would have done it by now. He nudged his horse back into the trees and eyed the man.

Crouched behind a rock was one of the Bent County deputies. He looked more like a boy to Noah, but Noah dismounted and looped the reins of the horse to the closest tree. He crouched next to the *kid*, ignoring the throbbing pain in his side.

"I've got one of the fugitives in my sights," the deputy offered. He held out a hand. "Deputy Mosely. Laurel made sure we knew what all the Carsons looked like so we didn't actually hurt the wrong person." He frowned. "She didn't tell me you'd be coming as backup, though."

Noah shook the man's hand and said nothing. He was more interested in scanning the valley below the rocks. There were two lone figures standing next to a ramshackle building that had been an outhouse long before Noah's lifetime.

He couldn't make out faces or even heights, but his stomach sank. "That's not Addie," Noah said flatly. Even from this distance he knew that wasn't the shade of her hair. It was too white blond, not honeyed enough.

"What? How... You don't know that." The man shifted in his crouch and brought a pair of binoculars to his eyes.

"I know that," Noah replied, striding back to his horse. He didn't even need to take a look through the binoculars. "Which way did the other couple go?"

"I don't... The opposite. You can't just..." The kid straightened his shoulders, adopting what Noah supposed was meant to be an intimidating look. "Mr. Carson, I would kindly suggest you don't try to get in the way of the Bent County Sheriff's Department's actions."

Noah snorted and didn't stop moving. "The Bent County Sheriff's Department can go to hell."

Deputy Mosely sputtered. Hell, was this kid just out of the academy or something?

"What are you going to do?" Noah demanded, gesturing toward the couple in the valley.

"Not that it's your business, but I'm going to radio Deputy Delaney and follow her orders to—"

Noah rolled his eyes. No damn way was he letting this go even more wrong. He lifted his rifle and pointed it toward the couple below.

"Sir, put the weapon down immediately..."

Noah looked through the sight, saw his target—the man's arm, because he wasn't an idiot or scared of doing the wrong thing while in uniform—and shot, ignoring the fact that the deputy had pulled his gun. The kid wasn't going to shoot a fly, let alone Noah himself.

"You…" The man gaped at him, like a damn grounded fish.

"Well, go arrest him," Noah ordered, putting his gun back in its soft case. "Get her back wherever she came from. Send everyone you've got available in the *opposite direction of…*" He trailed off as he noticed something not quite right in the horizon. Weirdly hazy.

He whirled around and there was a billow of smoke off to the west. "There," he said, already moving for Vanessa's horse. "Send everyone there. North point of Carson property. Follow the smoke."

"You can't just—" the deputy called after him.

Noah urged his horse into a run. "I just did." Vanessa's horse sped through the snow, agile and perfect, and Noah thanked God they had the kind of animals who could handle this.

Now he just had to make it across the entire north pasture to whatever was on fire and hope he could get there quick enough to save Addie, because he had no doubt she was somewhere in the middle of it.

God help the man who hurt her.

Chapter 15

It turned out Addie had learned something in school. Stay low during a fire. Cover your mouth. Use your hands to feel out a possible escape route.

It was difficult to nudge her shirt over her nose with only the use of her chin and neck, but she managed after a while. Crawling was even more difficult with her hands tied behind her back, but she forced herself through an awkward, careful crab walk.

It didn't matter, though. There was no escape. There was only smoke and heat. Everything around her was burning. *Burning.*

She held on to the insane hope Peter had set himself on fire in the blaze instead of only trapping her inside. Even as the roaring of the fire creaked and crackled. Even as she had no idea where she was in the stables, let alone if she was close to some escape.

But she kept moving. Kept blinking against the sting of the smoke, kept thinking past the horrible sounds around her. She could lie down and die, but where would that leave Seth?

And Noah? What would happen to Noah?

She had to keep fighting.

So she scooted around, even as it got harder and harder to breathe. Even as she was almost convinced she was crawling in endless circles she'd never escape. But anything was better than stopping, because stopping would be *certain* death instead of just maybe death.

She thought she heard her name, and she was more than sure it was in her head, but she moved toward it anyway. It was either death or some guardian angel.

"Addie."

Some unknown voice above the din of the fire, and still she crawled toward it. She paused in her crawling. She tried to call back, but nothing came out of her scorchingly painful throat except a rusty groan muffled by her shirt.

Useless. She resumed crawling. Toward that faint sound.

"Addie."

"Noah." It came out scratchy and sounding nothing like his name and really she had to be hallucinating, because how would *Noah* be here? He was watching Seth.

Oh, God, he had to be watching Seth. She crawled faster, ignoring the way she couldn't see, the way her whole body felt as if it were swaying. She moved toward Noah's voice. Whether it was a hallucination or not, it had to be her escape.

She tried to keep her breathing even, but it was so

hard. Tears stung her eyes, a mix of emotion and stinging from the flames around her. It was a searing, nauseating heat and she kept crawling toward it. Toward salvation.

Or is it your death?

Out of nowhere, arms were grabbing her, and there was somehow something cool in all the ravaging heat. Then it was too bright, and she had to squeeze her eyes shut against all that light.

For a moment she lay there in the foreign icy cold, eyes squeezed shut, almost certain she'd died.

But hands were pulling her to her feet, and then to take steps, and she let whoever it was lead her. Wherever they were going, it was away from that horrible fire.

"Just a ways farther."

She opened her eyes even though they burned like all the rest. "Noah." She could hear the fire raging behind them, even as he pulled her forward in the drifts of snow.

"Come on, sweetheart, a little ways farther."

"Am I dreaming?"

He glanced back at her, but continued to pull her forward. "Feels pretty unfortunately real to me," he said. There was no hint of a smile, and yet she wanted to laugh. Those were her words.

This was real. The misty gray twilight that hurt her eyes after the dark smoke of the stable. Noah, *Noah*, leading her to safety.

"Where's Seth?" Her voice sounded foreign to her own ears, scraped raw and awful, but she only barely felt the seething pain beyond the numbness. Still, the words were audible somehow.

"He's safe. That I promise you. Where's Peter?"

"I don't…" They reached the tree line and finally Noah allowed her to stop walking, but she was pulled into the hard press of his chest. He swore ripely, over and over again even as his hands methodically moved over her body.

"I don't think we have time for sex," she said, attempting a joke.

"I'm checking you for injuries," he replied, clearly not amused.

Her arms fell to her sides as Noah cut the rope holding her hands together.

"No broken bones," he muttered. "I imagine you have some kind of smoke inhalation." He pulled her back, studying her face intently. "What hurts?"

"I don't…" She couldn't think. All she could see was the blazing fury in his gaze. "How are you here?"

"I wasn't going to let him take you, and apparently I'm the only one in this whole world with any sense. You running off. Laurel having *children* watch you who follow the wrong damn people." His hands gripped her arms, his eyes boring into her. "I swear to God if you ever do anything like this again, I'll lock you up myself."

He was so furious, so violently angry, and yet his grip was gentle, and he kept all that violence deep within him. This man who'd been shot trying to keep her safe, and was now pulling her out of burning buildings.

"Noah…" She didn't know what to say, so she leaned into him and pressed her mouth to his. Everything hurt except that.

His hand smoothed over her hair and he kissed her

back, the gentleness in the kiss the complete antithesis of everything she could tell he was feeling.

She'd believed she could take Peter on alone—well, with the help of Laurel and Grady and the deputies, but mostly on her own. And she knew, even now with a bullet hole in his side to tell him otherwise, Noah thought he could take Peter down bare-handed.

But in this moment, and in his kiss, Addie realized something very important. They could only survive this *together*.

"You don't have a coat," he murmured, immediately shrugging out of his and putting it around her. She didn't even know how her body reacted to it. She felt numb all over, but somehow she was standing.

"You'll be cold now."

"I have more layers on," he returned, scanning the horizon around him. "Where'd he go?"

"I don't know." She pulled away and looked back at the burning stable, feeling an unaccountable stab of grief even with her renewed sense of purpose. "I was hoping he'd burned himself up."

Noah squinted down at the building. "Not likely. There." He pointed at something. Addie squinted, too, but she saw nothing.

"Tracks," Noah said flatly. "Coming and going."

"How can you see that? It's been snowing and—"

"I can see it." His gaze returned to her. "You need a doctor."

"Over my dead body are we separating ever again, Noah Carson. It's you and me against Peter, or you're going back to Seth right this instant."

He opened his mouth and she could tell, just *tell*, he was going to argue, so she gave his chest a little push until he released her. "We don't have time to argue, and if you can't see that the only way we survive this, the only way we *win* this, is together, I don't have time to convince you."

"You're right we don't have time to argue," he muttered, taking her hand. "But you better keep up until we get to Annabelle."

"Who's Annabelle?"

"Our ride."

Noah wasn't seriously worried about Peter being on the run.

At first.

After all, Addie was safe with Noah, and Ty and Vanessa together could take care of any lone psychopath who clearly wasn't as good of a criminal as he fancied himself. So far Peter'd had ample opportunity to really hurt Addie and he hadn't done it. He kept giving her opportunities to escape. Maybe he expected her to die in the fire, but he certainly hadn't made sure.

Maybe he didn't want to hurt Addie. Maybe he just wanted his son back. Noah would never let that happen, but it soothed him some to think maybe this could all be settled without Addie getting hurt.

He glanced back at where she sat behind him on Annabelle's back. Her face was sooty and her breathing sounded awful. She was clearly struggling, and still she watched the ground and the trail of Peter's footprints they were following on horseback.

Any magnanimous thoughts he'd had toward Peter Monaghan obliterated to ash. He had left Addie to die in that fire. A painful, horrible death. No, he was no kindhearted criminal who couldn't bring himself to end her life on purpose. He wanted her tortured. He was evil.

He needed to be stopped. Ended. So Seth never had to grow up and truly know what it was like to have that kind of soullessness in a father.

Noah would make sure of it.

He led Annabelle next to Peter's footprints, shaking his head at how easy this all was. Scoffing at the FBI and everyone else who hadn't caught this moron.

Until he realized that the footprints doubled back and followed Noah's original ones. Back to where he'd stopped with Deputy Mosely. Then carefully going along the trail of his horse's prints.

It had snowed, but lightly. There'd been no major wind. Since the snow had been a crusty, hard ice, the horse's stuck out.

With a sinking nausea, Noah realized Peter was going to use Noah's own damn trail to lead Peter to Seth.

"How did Peter get a horse?" Addie wondered aloud, her voice still low and scratchy.

Noah tensed and tried to think of a way to explain it that wouldn't lead her to the conclusion he'd drawn. Not that Peter had gotten a horse, but that he was following Noah's horse's tracks. Noah tried to think of how to hurry without drawing attention to the fact that they needed to hurry.

Vanessa and Ty could handle Peter, but Noah was slowly realizing Peter had more in his arsenal than Noah had given him credit for.

"Noah," she rasped in his ear. "Tell me what you're thinking."

He swore as the footprints stopped and suddenly vehicle tracks snaked out across the snow. Peter clearly wasn't alone anymore. He had what Noah assumed was some kind of snowmobile, and at least one man helping him.

A vehicle that could traverse the snow better and faster than his horse. Following his tracks back to the cabin. The only hindrance would be trees, but that wouldn't make the tracks unfollowable on foot.

"Noah... Noah, please tell me this isn't what I think it is," Addie said, her voice shaky from cold or nerves, he didn't know.

He couldn't tell her, so he kicked Annabelle into a run. He didn't want to push the horse this hard, but they had to get to Seth. "What do you think it is?" he asked through gritted teeth as wind rushed over them, icy and fierce. If he was cold without his jacket, fear and determination kept him from feeling it.

Addie didn't answer him. She held on to him, though, the warmth of her chest pressing into his back. She was careful to hold him above his wound, but sometimes her arm slipped and hit him right where it already ached and throbbed.

But the pain didn't matter. What Addie thought didn't matter. All that mattered was getting to Seth before Peter did.

Addie held on tight as they rode hard toward the Carson cabin. Much like his desperate ride in the opposite direction, the land seemed to stretch out in never-ending white, and there was no promise in the beautiful mountains of his home. There was only danger and failure.

Still, Noah urged Annabelle on, and the horse, bless her, seemed to understand the hurry. As they got closer to the cabin, Noah eased Annabelle into a slower trot. The snowmobile tracks veered one way, but if Noah went the opposite they could sneak up on the back of the cabin through the wooded area.

"Why are we slowing down? He's got so much time on us if he was in a vehicle. We can't let him get to Seth."

"Vanessa and Ty will fight him off."

"He isn't alone," Addie said flatly. "Someone had to bring him that snowmobile."

Noah ducked and instructed her to do so as well as they began to weave their way through the trees, bobbing around snow-heavy limbs. He didn't need the snowmobile's tracks anymore. "They couldn't cut through the trees with the vehicle. It looks like someone walked this way and instructed them how to get around this heavily wooded part. So they didn't approach the cabin this way as a group. That's good."

"Is it?"

"Ideally, it gives us the element of surprise, but that can't be all. We need to slow down, think and plan. We need to end this."

She laughed bitterly. "I keep thinking that and we keep running this way and that."

"You said we needed to work together. Well, here we go. Peter must think you're dead. He has to." Which got Noah thinking… "Addie, if he thinks you and Seth are dead…"

"How could we possibly do that? What would it solve? We'd always be in danger if he found out."

"Not if he's in jail, which is the least of where he belongs. Convincing him you're dead would just be insurance. A layer of safety on top of all the other layers."

"I… I guess, but do we have time to figure out how to do that? We have to make sure Seth is safe."

"All you have to do is make sure Peter doesn't see you."

"I don't give a… We just need to get Seth. That's all I care about."

Noah understood that, whether he wanted to or not. But he couldn't let fear or panic drive him. That's what had led him to the Carson Ranch, and yes, he'd saved Addie in the process, but he'd also led Peter straight to Seth.

"You're going too slow," Addie insisted, desperation tingeing her voice.

"I can't imagine what it must be like, the fear and the panic, but we can't let it win. You know I wouldn't let anything…" He trailed off, because he *had* let things happen to her and Seth. "We have to end this, which means we have to be smart. Leading with emotion, with fear, with letting someone else call the shots, is what got us here, Addie. If we'd fought straight off, if you'd stayed in the cabin, if I hadn't flown after you half-cocked… We're mucking things up right and left, and we can't keep doing it. Because Seth *is* at stake."

He felt as much as heard Addie's sharp intake of breath, feeling bad for speaking so harshly to her, but it was all true. They couldn't keep *reacting*, they had to plant their feet and act.

"Maybe you're right," she said softly into his ear as he brought Annabelle to a stop. They were deep in the woods, but he knew exactly where the cabin was though he couldn't see it though the snow and thick trees. About a hundred yards straight ahead.

"So, let's figure out a plan. A real plan. A *final* plan. One that brings you both home safe."

"Home?" she echoed.

"Bent is your home, Addie. Yours and Seth's. From here on out, it'll always be your home." He'd fight a million battles and risk life and limb to make it so.

Chapter 16

Addie let Noah help her off the horse. The horse was panting heavily, and Addie couldn't help but breathe in time with her. Too shallow. Too fast.

But Noah was right. No matter that she wanted to tear through the woods screaming, shooting at anyone who got in her way with Noah's rifle, until Seth was safely in her arms. It wouldn't do the thing that needed to be done.

Seth. She needed Seth's *permanent* safety at the top of her list. Not just these snatches of time with it-didn't-matter-how-many people protecting him. She needed to give him safety, stability, a *home*.

Bent is your home. She hadn't realized how desperately she wanted that to be true until Noah had said it, had held her gaze steady and sure. Underneath all that surety, she'd seen…she was sure she'd seen the kind of bone-numbing fear and fury she felt in her soul at Seth being in direct line of danger.

"If we're going to convince him Seth's dead, we have to get Seth away first."

Noah nodded, his jaw set. She could see the way he thought the problem through. She could see the same thing she felt.

How? How? How?

"I'm not usually the one with the plan. I'm the one who acts," he muttered.

"Well, the other plans haven't worked. Maybe you need to be."

He flicked a glance at her, eyebrows drawing together. "We don't know how many men he has."

"There were only tracks to one vehicle, right? So it can't be more than a couple. Maybe four of them altogether. And there's four of us. It's a fair fight."

"Really," Noah replied drily.

"It's close, anyway."

"We'll go with four men," Noah said, staring through the trees. "Armed, probably better than us." Noah glanced at her again. "Do you think he meant to kill you?"

"I don't think he cares either way. He wants me hurt and scared, but what he really wants is Seth."

"You don't think he has some kind of feeling for the mother of his child?"

Addie had to look away. She should tell him. Explain the whole thing. Except they didn't have time for that right now. "It's complicated."

Noah rubbed a hand over his beard. "There's a secret passageway into the cabin. The guy who shot me saw me come out of it, but surely he couldn't relay that information back to Peter considering you killed him."

Killed him. She'd killed a man. And she was prepared to kill another. If the opportunity arose, she needed to be willing to kill Peter. Seth's father.

She steeled herself against that soft spot. Yes, Peter was Seth's father, and maybe Seth would never fully understand the threat his father posed. She prayed he didn't. That he'd never fully understand. Even if it meant he grew to hate her.

Seth was the most important thing. His life. His future. His happiness.

"So, we'll create a diversion," Noah said, steel threaded through his voice. He might not be used to being the one making the plans, but he was certainly used to being in charge. "I'll be careful and try to sneak in the cabin, but the most important thing is getting you into the secret passage. If I can get to Ty and Vanessa, we can work out how to get Seth to you through the passage. If we can, we'll get Vanessa, too, and you two can figure out how to make it look like something happened to Seth while Ty and I fight them off."

"That leaves you vulnerable. Four against two."

"We don't know they have four, and I'd bet on me and Ty anyhow."

"You said yourself they probably have better weapons."

"You can't beat the bad guy without taking some risks, Addie. I think we can both agree Seth is the most important thing, right? It's why you left. It's why you let yourself be bait. I lost sight of that, took Seth's safety for granted in the face of a danger to yours, and look where it led. Right here. It's my fault Peter figured out how to get to Seth, because I lost sight of that one thing. Well, not again. I'd die before I let anything happen to him."

Addie blinked back the tears that stung her eyes. She'd come to that same conclusion, too, and as much as the idea of losing Noah physically hurt, Seth... Seth was the priority.

"All right," Addie managed, though her voice was scratchy from the fire, from the cold, from emotion. "We'll go up to the cabin, scope it out. You'll show me the secret passageway. We'll get me in, then I'll wait."

"I'll see if I can get to Ty or Vanessa without detection. You stay in that secret passageway until we get you Seth, or we can get Vanessa and Seth in. We'll keep the rest occupied."

"What if—"

"That's the plan. We focus on the plan. If we get there and we can't get to the secret passageway, we'll come back here and reevaluate. Now we move. We have to be silent. They can't know we're there yet, but most especially they can't catch sight of you."

"Most important after Seth, that is."

Noah nodded. "We'll promise each other, here and now, everything we do is to protect that boy." He held out his gloved hand.

Dwarfed and warmed by his coat, she slid her hand out of the sleeve and shook Noah's. "Agreed."

Noah turned to the horse, pulled some things out of the bags that hung off the saddle. Feed and water. A blanket. He took those few minutes to make the horse comfortable. "If you and Vanessa get out, you need to be able to make your way back to Annabelle. We're going to cover our tracks, so you have to be able to get back here blind."

Addie swallowed. She didn't know the area at all, especially out here. "How?"

Noah considered the question, then pulled a small Swiss Army knife out of his pocket. "We'll mark the trees." He gave her a once-over. "I don't have a gun to give you, so you'll have to take this once we're done. You need some kind of protection."

Protection. She pulled out the knife she'd managed to stick into the back of her pants back at the ranch. It hadn't helped her against Peter because she'd been trying to lure him, not hurt him, and then he'd knocked her out.

She wouldn't be so stupid next time.

"I have this."

Noah raised his eyebrows, since it was a pretty impressive knife she'd found with a bunch of hunting supplies in one of the supply closets at the ranch. It had been the easiest-to-conceal weapon she'd been able to find that had a kind of sheath that would keep her safe from the blade.

"That'll do. Let's get started." With that, Noah began a path toward the cabin, carefully marking a network of trees with little *x*'s a person would have to know were there to find, while Addie carefully covered their tracks in the snow.

When they could start to see the cabin through the trees, their pace slowed, but they didn't stop. As silently as they could, they crept forward, still working, always watching.

Addie could make out the snowmobile, empty and parked to the side of the cabin. But as her gaze searched the space around the cabin, the woods around her, she saw no sign of any men. Only their footprints around the snowmobile.

Noah nodded toward the cabin and she followed him, wordlessly stepping into the bigger prints he left. They didn't have time to cover these. Not yet.

With one last look around the yard and tree line, Noah stuck his fingers into some crevice Addie hadn't even seen and seemingly magically pulled, amassing snow in a large hill behind it, until a very small door opened.

He gestured her forward, and even though it was dark and who knew what all lay inside, Addie knew she had to crawl in there. So on a deep breath, she did. Squeezing through the opening and contorting her body into the dark space that was some hidden part of the cabin. She re-sheathed her knife and shoved it where it had been down the back of her pants.

"Stay inside," Noah said, worry reflecting in his dark eyes even if it didn't tremble in his voice. "On the opposite side is another door, but it's covered by the fridge. If we can get Seth, or Vanessa and Seth, to you, it'll be through there. There's a peephole here." He pointed to a hole in the wall that allowed her to see out into the backyard. "But there's no way to see inside."

"Okay." She tried to keep her mind on those instructions. On the plan they'd created together.

"Stay put until one of us gets you. Promise?"

She didn't want to promise that. There were so many what-ifs in her mind.

"The only exception to that promise is if you know Seth is in immediate danger. Okay? Deal?"

She still didn't love that deal, because she wanted to

protect him, too, but… Well, they'd seen how well that worked out when Noah had rushed to protect her. She was glad to be alive, and Peter probably would have found Seth eventually, anyway, but…

But Seth had to come first. "Deal."

Noah nodded and started to push the door closed, then he swore roughly. Addie jumped, thinking they'd been caught, but he only reached forward and pulled her to him.

"Do you want your coa—"

Then his mouth was on hers, rough and fierce. A kiss of desperation, anger and, strangely, hope.

"I love you, Addie," he murmured against her mouth.

And before she could even think of what to say to *that*, Noah pushed the door closed with an audible *click*.

She was in the dark and alone, and she had to sit with *that* and wait.

I love you.

What kind of man said I love you before he closed you into a secret passageway while mobsters were after you and the baby in your care?

But neither anger nor bafflement took hold quite like she intellectually thought they would. Instead, she felt only the warm glow of *love*. Love. Noah—taciturn, grumpy, sweet, good Noah—had said he *loved* her.

After she'd spent so much of the time before Peter had come being afraid to even think he might look at her with more than blind disinterest, Noah *loved* her.

She couldn't possibly predict what would happen with all this, if they'd all survive unscathed or not, but Noah loved her, and Seth needed her.

For Seth, she could endure anything. With love, she could face any challenge.

* * *

Noah made quick work of covering up the snow around the door and his tracks to and from the secret passageway. He searched his surroundings, listening for any faint hint at where everyone was. It left a terrible feeling in his gut. Everything was too quiet.

He moved soundlessly through the trees to make a circle around the cabin, checking the perimeter. Once he was satisfied there was no lookout on this side, he focused on the tracks around the cabin.

There were quite a few sets of footprints, though he could assume the shallow ones were old and filled with new snow. The heavy ones… He counted, tried to make out different footwear, tried to decide who was who based on where they'd come from.

Three men, it looked like, though looks could be deceiving. There was the pair of tracks that had followed Noah's original ones. They came out of the woods, then went down the road. Then the vehicle tracks.

Only one set of footprints went toward the cabin. The other two fanned out down the road.

So they had two men watching the road for intruders, and one man—probably Peter, though he couldn't be sure—on the inside.

His odds were good, because if he only had men looking out from the road, the Carsons could kill Peter before he could make a peep.

But Noah wouldn't be that cocky this time around. He'd still be careful. Cautious. He glanced at the snowmobile. No one was getting away on that thing. He didn't want Addie to be seen, and Seth wouldn't be safe on it. So it was useless to him.

He needed to make it useless to them as well. Moving as quickly but as quietly as he could, he lifted the panel to the engine and then used his Swiss Army knife to snap any wires or tubes he could find. He paused, waiting for someone to fly out of the trees or a bullet to come whizzing by, but nothing happened.

He crept closer to the cabin. The windows were boarded up, so there was no way to see in. He frowned at the door, because it appeared to be cracked open.

Noah moved toward it, gaze still darting behind him and at the road. The closer he got, the more he realized he could hear someone talking in there.

"You lot seem to think you're awfully tough."

Noah reached for the rifle on his back. Still, no matter how he maneuvered himself, he couldn't see inside the crack of the door. He could only hear.

He was tempted to bust in and start shooting, but he couldn't do it without knowing what was on the other side. He couldn't risk his brother or his cousin any more than he could risk Seth.

"Tougher than some pissant who has to hide behind a mob to make himself feel like a big strong man. What are you compensating for, buddy?" Ty's voice drawled the question lazily and Noah shook his head. You'd think a former Army Ranger would have more sense than to poke at the enemy with people's lives on the line, but Ty had never been what Noah would consider predictable.

"The only reason I haven't shot you in the head, you miserable sack of nothing, is that I'm waiting on one of your loved ones to show up so they can watch the life drain out of you. That might be avoidable if you tell me where the boy is."

Ty laughed and Noah nearly sagged with relief.

They'd hidden Seth somehow. In the cellar maybe? It'd be impossible to get him out of there without Peter seeing him and Vanessa, if she was down there with him.

Noah winced as a flash of light hit his peripheral vision. He did a quick scan of the tree line, but he didn't see anyone or any sign of a gun. He turned his attention back to the cracked door of the cabin, but the flash of light persisted. *Flash. Flash. Flash.*

Noah studied the tree line, over and over again, seeing no sign of anyone. Another flash, and he finally got it.

It was coming from the barn, and since it seemed purposeful rather than the precursor to being picked off, Noah moved toward it.

He wouldn't lead Peter to Seth again, so he took a long circuitous way that involved using some of the other men's tracks to hopefully throw anyone off the scent, then his own back into the woods. Once hidden in the trees, he took off on a dead run.

When he reached the back of the barn, he gave three short raps against it. When they were returned in double time, he rounded the corner. He kept his body close to the barn, dragging his feet hoping to make the trail simply look like melted snow runoff causing a rut in the snow.

When he reached the barn opening, which had no closure anymore as the barn was almost never used and falling apart, he slid inside.

Vanessa was holding a very frightened-and-bundled-up-looking Seth. She had a quilt around them that had hay stuck all over it, and he assumed Vanessa had hidden them in a pile of old hay.

Noah winced, but he didn't have time to worry about whether Seth was comfortable. He had to keep the boy alive. "What's going on?"

"We heard them coming. Ty sent me to the barn. I have no idea what's going on aside from that. I've been trying to stay hidden, but Ty's been in there so long…" She bit her lip, sending an uncharacteristic worried look toward the cabin.

"I heard him. He's holding his own, it appears. They've got men watching the road, but none watching the cabin. I don't think they expected to be followed, but maybe they're expecting police to show up. They think Addie's dead. She's in the secret passageway. I need you to go get her. She'll lead you to Annabelle, then you take the quickest route to Bent."

He started pulling Vanessa toward the opening, glancing every which way before he nodded toward the back of the cabin.

"What about you?" Vanessa asked as she ran.

"Ty and I will take care of it." He did his best to hurriedly cover the tracks they were making. "Get Addie and go. Now."

"If either of you die, I swear to God I'll find a way to make you pay," Vanessa said angrily, eyes suspiciously shiny.

"Love you, too, Van," Noah muttered, pulling the rifle off his back. "Now get him and her the hell out of here."

With one last angry look, she gave a nod and pulled the door open. Noah kept watch, ready to shoot anyone who might appear and try to intercept.

Addie scooted out, wide-eyed, and then immediately held out her arms and Seth fell into them, crying faintly. Addie soothed him, and Vanessa encouraged her into a run toward the trees.

She never even looked his way.

Chapter 17

Addie wished she could go faster, but following the small marks on the tree back to Annabelle wasn't as easy as it had sounded an hour or so ago. Though she could somewhat follow the disturbance in the snow that was her and Noah's covered tracks from earlier, the wind and fading daylight had made that difficult as well.

Vanessa had a thin, weak flashlight out and Addie was using her fingers to feel the bark of the trees for the heavy slash of a cut. But Seth clung to her, whimpering unhappily, and that kept her going regardless of the frustration.

"It's okay, baby," she murmured, searching the trees, every pain and ache in her body fading to a dull numbness.

"Here's the next," Vanessa announced. They'd been

trying to cover their tracks, at the very least obscure how many people had run away from the cabin. It was all getting so tiring, and she needed to get Seth somewhere warm, even if he was bundled to the hilt.

"Man, you guys sure made a trek," Vanessa mumbled as they searched the next grouping of trees.

"Noah wants them to think I'm dead."

In the dim twilight Vanessa looked back at her. "Dead? Well, that's smart. I'd prefer *him* dead, but that'd do, too."

"And Seth."

Vanessa's eyebrow winged up as she went back to searching the trees. "How's that going to work?"

"I don't know. I'm taking ideas." Addie sighed and stood to her full height. "Here's the next."

A huffing sound caught both women's attention and they looked toward it. Addie nearly cried from relief as Vanessa ran the few yards to Annabelle.

"There you are, sweetheart," Vanessa offered to the horse, running a hand over her mane. "I bet you're cold. Let's get you home, yeah?"

Addie approached as Vanessa pulled some feed out of the saddlebag and fed it to Annabelle by hand. Vanessa looked at her and Seth and then pressed her lips together.

"This is going to be tough and slow going. We're going to have to do this bareback so we all fit, and go slow so Seth is safe."

Addie swallowed at the lump in her throat. "Do you think we'll make it?"

"We won't know until we try. Once we get somewhere warm, we'll figure out a way to make it look like Seth's… Well."

Addie didn't like to say it, either, even if it was just a ruse they were planning. It felt too possible, too real, especially on the run from Peter.

"The dark is going to be a problem," Vanessa said flatly. "I could maneuver Bent blindfolded and turned around, but these forests and mountains? It's another story."

"Can't we make our way to the road?" Addie asked as Vanessa unbuckled the saddle and dropped it to the ground.

"Noah thinks Peter has men on the road. Any ideas on where to hide the saddle? If we're trying to hide the fact more than just me and Seth escaped, we can't leave this lying around."

"We'll bury it," Addie said resolutely.

"It'll take time."

"I think it's time we have." She had to hope it was time they had. As long as Peter wasn't after them, they had to do everything they could to hide the fact that she was still alive. "We could use it maybe. Make it look like the horse threw you and Seth and the saddle. A horrible, bloody accident. Then we see if Laurel can get someone at the hospital to forge records or something."

"Far-fetched. A horse couldn't throw a saddle, and that's only for starters."

"Peter wouldn't know that. He'd see a saddle and blood and then we'll leave the horse's prints and go straight for town. Get someone, anyone, to drive us to the hospital and see what we can fabricate from there."

Vanessa considered. "We'll need blood."

Addie shifted Seth onto her hip, then pulled the sheathed knife out of the back of her pants.

Vanessa swore under her breath. "You aren't really going to cut yourself open for this, are you?"

"Better me doing the cutting than Peter." Addie grimaced at the thought. "Well, you might have to do the cutting."

Vanessa swore again. "I don't know how you got into this mess, Addie, but boy do you owe me once we're through it."

"Then let's get through it." With that, Addie set about to create quite the fictional scene.

Noah wanted to give Addie and Vanessa as much time as possible to get a head start before he engaged with Peter and his men, but the longer Ty stayed in there at the mercy of a mobster, the less chance his mouthy brother had of escaping unscathed.

When Noah had returned to the door after watching Vanessa, Addie and Seth disappear into the woods, it had been closed so there was no hope of overhearing more. Maybe he could sneak down the road and try to pick off Peter's men? Then there'd be no one to come running if he and Ty overpowered Peter.

But the problem remained: he couldn't see inside the cabin. He had no idea what weapons Peter had or what he might have already done to Ty.

And how much longer did he give Addie and Seth and Vanessa before he stepped in and helped his brother?

He frowned at a faint noise. Something like horse hooves off in the far distance. Couldn't be Addie and Vanessa, because the sound was more than one horse. Could they have reached help already?

Noah stayed where he was, scrunched into a little

crevice in the outside logs of the cabin that gave him some cover. A horse came into view, but it wasn't anyone Noah recognized, which meant it had to be one of Peter's men.

How the hell did he get a horse? Noah seriously considered shooting the stranger, but he stopped himself. He didn't know what Peter was doing to Ty in that cabin, and he couldn't risk his brother's life.

The man dismounted stiffly if adeptly. Almost as though he'd been given rote instruction on horseback riding but hadn't had much practice. He went straight for the snowmobile, far too close to Noah for any kind of comfort.

But the man didn't look his direction. He tried to start the vehicle and was met with silence. He swore ripely, then pulled a walkie-talkie out of his coat pocket.

"Snowmobile's been tampered with," the man said flatly into the radio.

Static echoed through the yard and Noah tried to think of some way to incapacitate the man without making sound.

"Leave it. Search the woods on horseback. Someone has my kid and is trying to get to Bent. We can't let them." It was Peter's voice, Noah was fairly sure.

Noah didn't have time to worry anymore. He had to act. As silently as he could, he pulled his rifle out of the back case. He couldn't risk shooting the man and having anyone hear the gunshot, so he'd have to use it as a different kind of weapon.

He took a step out of his little alcove, and the man was too busy fiddling with the snowmobile to notice. Another step, holding his breath, slowly raising the rifle to be used as a bludgeon.

Without warning, the man whirled, his hand immediately going for the gun he wore on his side. Noah had been prepared for the sudden movement, though, and used the rifle to smack the gun out of the man's hand before he could raise it to shoot. Noah leaped forward and hit the butt of the weapon against the man's skull as hard as he could.

The man fell to his feet, groaning and grasping the ground—either for his own weapon or to push himself up, but Noah pressed his boot to the back of the man's neck. The man gurgled in pain.

Before Noah could think what to do next, the front door was flung open and Noah raised his rifle, finger on the trigger, a second away from shooting.

But Ty was the one who emerged, and immediately hit the deck upon seeing Noah's rifle.

"Help me out here," Noah ordered.

"Thought I was going to die at my own brother's hand," Ty muttered, and it was only as he struggled to get to his feet that Noah realized he was tied up.

"What the hell is going on?"

"Oh, that idiot burst in and I let him think he had the upper hand so Van could get the kid away. He tied me up. Yapped at me till I thought I was going to die of boredom, but he was searching the house the entire time."

"Where's he now?" Noah asked, pushing his boot harder against the squirming man's neck.

"He found the passageway," Ty muttered disgustedly. "Smarter than he seems. He's got radio contact with his men. Somehow they got horses. Can't imagine they know how to ride them, but the idea was to start searching the tree perimeter. He's got some fancy

GPS and all sorts of crap. They're out there, looking for them."

"Get over here."

Ty complied. When the gasping man on the ground grasped for his leg, Ty kicked him in the side.

Noah retrieved his Swiss Army knife, then used it to cut the zip ties that were keeping Ty's hands together and behind his back.

"Managed to get out of the ones around my feet, but the hands were a bit harder."

"Thought Army Rangers could escape anything."

"I'd have done it eventually. But I heard a commotion. Figured I didn't have much time. Luckily it was just you."

"And Peter is out there."

"Van'll keep Addie safe."

Noah glanced down at the man, who was still struggling weakly against his boot. "Addie's dead," Noah said flatly.

"What?" Ty demanded on an exhale.

Noah brought a finger to his lips, mimed being quiet, and his brother seemed to catch on. "Peter set a fire on the property. She died in it."

"Then he'll pay," Ty said, his voice nothing but acid, which Noah wasn't even sure was all for show.

"Yes, he will. Get me something to tie this garbage up with."

Ty nodded and disappeared back inside. He returned with some cords. "These will have to do."

They worked together to tie the man's hands and legs together around an old flagpole in the front yard. He fought them, but weakly, and in just a few minutes he was tightly secured to the pole.

Noah moved to the back of the cabin, searching the perimeter for any signs of Peter or his men. Peter had left tracks from the back of the cabin to the trees, so that was something.

"We're outnumbered," Ty said from behind Noah. He slid the other man's gun into his coat pocket. "We've got one horse and no vehicle. How are we going to catch this guy?"

Noah looked around at the trees and the mountains as shadowy sentries in the dark. The moon shone above, bright and promising. The night was frigid, but he and Ty had survived worse. "Wyoming is how we're going to catch this guy."

Chapter 18

Addie's arm burned where she'd had Vanessa cut it. Without warning or discussion, Vanessa had subsequently made a rather nasty-looking cut on her own arm.

"Sure hope we can get a tetanus shot or something at the hospital," Vanessa had muttered before grabbing a handful of snow and mixing it with the blood.

Seth was pretending to ride the saddle that they'd placed in the snow as Addie and Vanessa worked to make two arm cuts look like enough blood to have been blunt force trauma to the head. Once they'd done as much as they could and were teeth-shatteringly cold, they bandaged each other up with the first aid kit that had been in Annabelle's pack.

Addie shot Seth worried glances as they did all this, because despite the layers he was wearing, the snow would make him wet and it was nightfall. The temperature had been dropping steadily, seemingly every minute.

Vanessa used her weakened flashlight to survey their supposed accident scene. It didn't look nearly as gruesome as Addie had hoped, even in the mix of silvery moonlight filtering through the trees and faded yellow glow of a too-small flashlight. "How will they even see it?"

"I imagine they're a little better equipped than we are. High-powered flashlights, headlights if they can get that snowmobile out here. Besides, they might not even be after us yet. Maybe they won't start looking till daylight."

"True." But if that was the case, they might not see it at all, and all this work for nothing. She shook her head. She couldn't think like that. As long as they got to safety without Peter knowing she was alive, they'd succeeded. The rest of the plan could still work.

She scooped Seth off the saddle, much to his dismay. He began to kick and scream. "He needs food. A diaper change."

Vanessa nodded, then moved the faint glow of her flashlight to Annabelle. "Let's get going, then. I think we've done the best we can."

It was some doing getting back on the horse without a saddle and getting Seth situated between them, but eventually they were on their way. Seth fussed and fidgeted, small mewling cries in the middle of a dark forest.

But moonlight led their way, and Addie focused on the hope. She didn't allow herself to consider if Noah and Ty were okay, if Peter knew what was going on.

She didn't think about the future any further than them reaching Bent without problem.

Seth was beginning to doze, something about the rocking motion of the horse soothing him enough to be taken over by sleep. Addie was feeling a little droopy herself, but holding on to Vanessa and Seth between them kept her from nodding off.

Addie wasn't sure how long they trotted through the freezing cold night. The wind was frigid and rattled the trees. The moon shone high and bright and yet gave off no warmth and very little hope.

Seth finally went totally limp in her arms, asleep despite all the danger around them—from people and from the elements. Every once in a while Addie thought it'd be simpler to just lie in the snow and sleep. She was so tired—exhausted physically, tired of fighting a man who'd never give up.

Then Vanessa slowed the horse on a quiet murmur.

"Are we there?"

Vanessa shook her head. "I hear something," she said quietly. Moonlight glinted her dark hair silver, but the dark shrouded her face so Addie couldn't read her expression.

Then Addie heard it, too, and they both winced as a beam of light glanced over the trees. Faint, far in the distance, but coming for them.

"Maybe it's Noah," Addie whispered.

"Not with that kind of light."

Which Addie knew, but she'd just wanted something to hope for. But what would false hope get her? Dead probably. All of them dead. "Let me off. Take Seth. I'll create a diversion."

"No."

"It's the only way. They'll catch us, and I can't let Peter ever get his hands on Seth. I just can't."

"He's supposed to think you're dead."

"Then it'll be even more of a diversion when I'm not. I can't control the horse, Vanessa, and even if I could you have a much better chance of finding Bent than I do. Let me off. I'll scream bloody murder while you ride fast as you can to town."

"They'll kill you, Addie."

"Maybe." She'd made her peace with that in the burning building. She would die for Seth. She had to be willing. "Seth is the most important thing. That was an agreement Noah and I made when we came back here. Peter doesn't care much whether I live or die. I'm a game for him, but he does want Seth or at least convinced himself he does if only to punish me. So we do everything not to give him what he wants. I'll scream— you ride toward town. I'll lead them back to our little scene saying Seth is dead. If I don't make it, I trust you Carsons will make sure Seth is safe."

"Addie…"

But she could tell Vanessa was relenting, so she shifted Seth until she could push him forward into Vanessa's lap. Seth began to whimper and Addie awkwardly slid off the horse. "There's no time. They can't hear him crying. Go. Fast. As fast as you can."

"Cut the little bastard open with that knife of yours. Do whatever you have to do to stay alive. I'll send all the help here the minute I get to town."

"Just go," Addie said. "Keep my baby safe."

Vanessa hesitated. "I'm going to keep Annabelle walking slow and quiet until I hear you scream. Then we'll gallop. Scream as loud and long as you can and hopefully they won't hear me. If you see any split off and come after me, scream 'bear.' It might be enough of a distraction to give me a leg up."

"Okay," Addie agreed. The thought of one of Peter's men breaking off and going after Vanessa scared her to her bones, but splitting up was the best way. The only way. She'd wail and scream and pretend Seth was already dead and pray to God it didn't turn out to be true.

Vanessa urged Annabelle into motion, a quiet walk the opposite direction of the murmuring noise and moving lights. They were definitely closer, but a ways off.

Addie started to walk toward them. Her heart beat hard in her chest, and fear and cold made it hard to move through the snow, but she marched forward. Closer and closer until the swath of light started to hit her.

Then she began to scream.

Noah was tired of the wound on his side holding him back, and yet he couldn't seem to push himself or the horse beneath them harder than he already was. He had no idea where Peter's man had gotten this horse, but it wasn't as adept as his horses back at the ranch.

The snow was deep and the air frigid cold, and while he'd been used to cold his whole life, something about the fear of losing the people he loved made it heavier, harder.

Or was that the gunshot wound to his side that he may or may not have accidentally ripped the stitches out of?

He didn't mention that to Ty. He didn't mention anything to Ty as they rode on, following the trail of Peter's men.

"Don't know where this horse came from, but it's not used to this kind of weather or terrain," Ty said grimly.

"Maybe not, but we've covered more ground than we would've on foot." Noah surveyed the tracks in front of them. Peter's tracks converged with two pairs of horse's tracks not too far from the cabin. They'd been following the horse tracks back down toward the road, but then the tracks abruptly turned back into the trees toward the mountains.

"You think these idiots have any idea what they're doing?" Ty asked disgustedly.

"Doesn't look like it. Doesn't mean they're not dangerous."

"True enough."

Out of nowhere, causing both Noah and Ty to flinch in surprise, a bloodcurdling scream ripped through the night.

They didn't even exchange a glance before they leaned forward in tandem on the horse, urging it to move toward the scream as fast as it could. The horse might not have been experienced or used to the terrain, but it seemed to understand panic.

There was moonlight, but far in the distance an unnatural light moving around as well. And the scream. It just kept going, with only minimal pauses for the screamer to breathe.

He tried not to think about who the screamer was, though there were only two possibilities, and he knew it wasn't Vanessa. But he couldn't allow himself to ponder what Addie might be screaming about, or why.

He only had to get to her. To the screaming, whoever it might be and for whatever reason.

"Stop," Noah ordered abruptly.

"What?" Ty demanded, but he brought the horse to a stop.

"I'll go on foot and sneak around the opposite direction. They have more men, more weapons. We need the element of surprise."

"Agreed, but I should be the one on foot. You're favoring that side, brother."

"I'll live."

"You keep saying that."

"And it'll keep being true." Noah dismounted without letting Ty argue further. "You go straight for the lights, slow and quiet. I'll circle around. I promised Addie we'd keep that baby safe, so he's our first priority. We don't risk him, and you don't risk you."

"But you can risk you, I'm assuming."

"I won't do anything stupid." But if he had to make some sacrifices, then so be it. "Go."

Ty nodded grimly in the moonlight, and Noah took off in a dead sprint. He circled the light instead of going for it, using the moonlight as his guide and the trees as his protection.

Everything in his body burned. His wound, his lungs, his eyes. Still, he pushed forward, adrenaline rushing through him.

He was finally close enough to see people, so he slowed his pace, hid behind a tree and watched the morbid procession of shadows.

Between moonlight and their flashlights, he could make out the odd scene moving toward him. He tried to make sense of what he was seeing. Peter was pushing Addie through the snow, while two men on horseback followed with their guns pointed at her. But they were *following* her, and she was leading them somewhere most definitely not in the direction of the cabin or Bent.

Where was Vanessa? Seth? Had Addie sacrificed herself? Had they escaped undetected? Or had something horrible happened?

Addie slowed, stumbled, and fell to her hands and knees in the snow.

"Get up," Peter ordered. "Or I'll really give you a reason to fall."

Addie struggled to her feet and it took everything in Noah not to jump forward and gather her up in the safety of his arms. But that would only get them both killed.

Still, he and Ty had the element of surprise. They could take out three guys, if they were careful. If they were smart.

"Move!" Peter ordered in a booming yell.

"I'm lost. I don't know where…"

"You better figure it out because if you don't show me the boy's dead body, I'm going to think you're lying, Addie. Then you'll be dead and I'll make sure that boy has the most hellish life you could ever imagine."

"He's your son. He's dead. Don't you have any compassion?"

Dead. Seth, dead. Addie wouldn't be walking let alone coherent if that were true, so it was all part of the plan. To make Peter think Seth was dead, but why hadn't Addie stayed out of it so Peter could think she was dead as well?

"You stole from me, Addie. You lied to me. You caused the death of my son and you dare speak to me of compassion? I should kill you right here and find the boy's body myself, if you're even telling the truth."

Addie stopped her stumbling forward and turned to face him. "Fine, Peter. Kill me."

Noah was so shocked he didn't breathe, and apparently the words shocked Peter as well since he didn't say anything or raise his weapon.

"Do you think I won't?"

"I know you're capable," Addie said. "You killed my sister. She wouldn't run, I realize now. That's why you killed her. I don't know how many other people you've killed, and you've made me into a killer as well. I've been running from you for nearly a year and now here we are and what's the *point*? I'll never have a normal life. You'll always be a black cloud over it, so kill me."

"You will not dictate when or how I kill you."

"I guess we'll see."

Peter raised his hand, presumably to hit Addie, and Noah didn't think, didn't plan, he barely even aimed. He simply raised his gun and shot.

Peter howled in pain, but didn't go down. *Damn it.* His men were already heading toward Noah, so he had to run, rifle in hand.

They were on horseback, so Noah zigzagged through trees, then pivoted suddenly and cut back in the opposite direction. He heard them swear.

"Get off your horse and run!" one of the men yelled at the other.

Noah tried to use the head start to his advantage, but when he circled back neither Addie nor Peter were to be seen. He tried to search the area for tracks, make sense of any of them, but there was a man coming for him and…

A gunshot rang out and Noah dove to the ground. The tree next to him exploded and Noah could only army-crawl through the snow trying to find a cluster of evergreens he could hide from the moonlight in.

"I can't see a damn thing!" one of the men yelled. "Get over here with the light."

Noah heard the horse hooves even over the heavy beating of his heart. He had to get to Addie before these men caught him, but where on earth had she and Peter disappeared to?

Another gunshot, this one even closer, the beating of horse hooves and the shining light of whatever high-powered flashlight they had flashing across him.

But that would give him everything he needed. He zigzagged through trees for a few more minutes before finding a large trunk to settle behind. He pulled the rifle off his back, watched the light move, and then shot.

When the light shook and fell, Noah knew he'd hit his target. But that was only one of the men. He needed to find the one who'd been on the horse. Noah searched the woods for signs of another flashlight beam, but found nothing.

Then, faintly, he heard grunts and followed the sound, finding Ty grappling on the ground with someone next to a prancing horse.

When the man who was decidedly not Ty pulled out a knife that glinted in the moonlight, Noah saw red. He lunged at the man on top of his brother, rolling him onto his stomach and shoving his knee into the man's back as he pulled his arms back. The man screamed in pain, as Noah wasn't very gentle or worried about the natural ways a man's arm should go. The guy's entire body went limp.

Noah didn't believe it at first, but as he eased off the

man he didn't move. He glanced over at Ty, who was struggling to get into a sitting position.

"Stabbed me right in the arm," Ty rasped, and Noah winced as Ty easily pulled a large, daggerlike knife out of where it had been lodged in his biceps.

Noah got to his feet, aches and pains and injuries nothing but a dull ache as fear overtook his body. "He's got Addie."

"Go. I'll bandage myself up and get to you soon as I can."

Noah nodded. "You die, you'll be sorry."

Ty smiled thinly in the moonlight. "I've been through a lot worse. This'll be the last thing that does me in. Now go."

So Noah did.

Chapter 19

Peter pushed her until she fell. Again and again and again. She would lie there in the freezing cold until he kicked her, demanding she get to her feet.

"Get up," Peter demanded, kicking her. She wanted to kick him back. Fight him with everything she had, with everything she was, but *time* was the most important thing. Not revenge. Not yet.

"What for?" Maybe she was going a little over the top, but the more Peter believed she wanted to die, the more her lie that Seth was dead held weight. What was there to live for if Seth was dead?

He kicked her harder, enough she cried out. "Get up and show me his body and then maybe I'll put you out of your misery."

"You don't need me to find him."

When he kicked her again, Addie got to her feet. She

didn't have to fake her shivering or her exhaustion. She didn't have to fake her fear or her sadness, because she had no idea who'd fired that shot at Peter. She had no idea if Vanessa had gotten Seth to safety.

She knew nothing. So all she could do was move forward with the determination this would end. Seth would be safe and this would be *over*, once and for all.

Addie had lost track of where she was in the dark forest, but the longer she and Peter walked in circles, the longer Vanessa had to get safe.

When a gunshot echoed from far away, Addie jerked in its direction. Between the moon and Peter's flashlight, his face was a ghostly silver white as he smiled.

"I don't suppose you think whoever failed at saving you just got shot by one of my men."

"Or whoever shot at you shot at them."

He gave her another hard shove so she fell in yet another icy pile of snow. His gun flashed. "Maybe I will just kill you, worthless as you are."

Addie hesitated a moment, not sure if she should goad him into continuing to believe she had a death wish when she most certainly did not. She couldn't find words as Peter slowly pressed the barrel of the gun to her temple.

Addie swallowed, trying to rein in the shaking of her body. "I'll beg," she offered, her voice a raspy whisper. "I'll get on my knees and beg you to put a bullet through my head." Because it would add time. Everything that added time had to be good.

And if he took her up on it, well…

Peter leaned in close, his lips touching her ear as he spoke. She shuddered in disgust as he whispered. "I want you to *suffer*, Addie. I couldn't take time with

your sister, but I'll take my time with you. Now, admit
you're lying or show me the boy's body in the next ten
minutes, or I'll start breaking fingers for every extra
minute I'm out here in this godforsaken wasteland."

Her patience was fraying and she opened her mouth
to tell him to go jump off a cliff, but managed to swallow the words down before she really did get herself
killed. If only because he'd mentioned her sister. Seth's
mother, who'd died for no other reason than she'd fallen
for the wrong kind of man.

Addie turned away from Peter, trying to study her
surroundings, trying to figure out where she needed
to go. If she led him to the scene she and Vanessa had
created, there'd be no body, but maybe she could convince Peter bears or wolves or some Wild West–sounding animal got there first.

She looked up at the moon and tried to use it as a
guide. Where had it been when they'd gotten on Annabelle? Could you navigate via the moon? Someone
probably could, but she wasn't so certain *she* could.

Still, she moved. Because it ate up time. Time was
the important thing right now. Not her life. Not the
moon. Not Noah or the future. Just time.

"Stop," Peter hissed, yanking her by Noah's coat.
Peter spanned the flashlight over the trees around them
in a circle.

"What is it? Do you think it's a bear?"

He shoved her to the ground and she landed hard
on her hands.

"It's not a bear, you idiot."

"Wolf?" she asked weakly.

He shone the light directly in her eyes and she
winced away.

"Are there wolves?" Peter demanded.

"Yes. Yes. They're nocturnal. Wolves are. A-and here." She thought, maybe. Noah had definitely mentioned coyotes, but wolves sounded a lot more terrifying, and what did it matter if she was wrong? She wanted Peter to be scared. That was all that mattered.

Again Peter slowly moved the beam of light around in a circle. Addie stayed where she was in the snow praying there was no wolf or bear or anything. Just Noah. She prayed and prayed for Noah.

Peter raised his gun and shot. Addie screamed and covered her ears as he turned in a slow circle, pulling the trigger every few seconds.

"What kind of coward hides in the shadows?" Peter demanded. "A man shows his face when he's ready to fight."

"A man doesn't chase an innocent woman and her child across the country, terrorize her and cause the death of his men because of his own stupidity."

Noah. It was Noah's voice in the woods. Peter shot toward the voice, and Addie swallowed back a gasp. Her ears rang with the sound of all the gunshots and she wanted to go running for him. Save him. Hold him.

"*Her* child? Is that what she told you?" Peter laughed. Uproariously. "That boy is *mine.* She has no claim on him."

Silence stretched in the freezing dark, and Addie wanted to cry, but she couldn't allow herself. It didn't matter. If Noah was angry or hurt, or if he believed Peter at all. Nothing in the here and now mattered except Seth's safety, and Noah's getting out of here alive. He shouldn't die for the problems she'd brought to his door.

So if he was hurt that she'd lied about being Seth's mother, it didn't matter. Couldn't.

"What a little liar you are," Peter said cheerfully. "Your big strong man thought you were a doting mother? How adorable."

"I am his aunt," Addie returned. "And his protector."

"If he's dead, you failed."

"I suppose I did fail, but better him dead than with you where you'd only warp and twist him into a sad, pathetic excuse for a human being. Better him gone for good than turn out to be anything like you."

Without warning, Peter snatched an arm out and curled his hand around her throat. The flashlight thumped to the ground, bouncing light against the snow. Addie tried to fight him, kick at him, but he'd holstered his gun and added his other hand around her throat. He was too strong or she was too cold.

"I'm going to choke her to death," Peter called out. "Are you going to just stand there and watch?"

There were only the gurgling sounds coming from her own throat as she clawed at his hands. He'd wanted her to suffer, but now he wanted Noah to suffer by watching him kill her. What was Noah doing? Why wasn't he stepping in to save her?

She began to see spots, everything in her body screaming in agony. She considered how much of a chance she had at running if she stabbed Peter. Panic rose like bile in her throat and she no longer cared what the consequences were. If she failed, she failed, but at least she'd tried not to die.

She kept clawing at him with one hand, but with the other she reached behind her and pulled the knife in her pants out of its sheath. Peter was too busy searching the dark for Noah, so she swung the blade as hard as she could. It hit Peter's side with a sickening squelch and for a moment she could pull in a gasping breath as his hands eased around her throat.

But then she saw Peter's eyes widen, then narrow, and everything inside her sank. The squeezing returned as his lip curled into a sneer.

She hadn't gotten the blade far enough inside him to cause any kind of damage. And now, since Noah was apparently not coming to save her, she was dead.

As long as Seth's safe. As long as Seth's safe. She let her mind chant it as her vision dimmed again.

"You stupid girl. You think that little knife would—" But Peter never finished his sentence, because the sound of a gun going off seemed simultaneous to him falling to the ground.

For a second or two, Noah could only stand where he'd positioned himself behind a tree, rifle still up. But Addie was standing there, next to Peter's unmoving body. Then she collapsed onto her knees, making terrible gasping noises, but gasping noises were alive noises.

Noah's whole body shook as he rushed forward. Peter's body didn't so much as move. Noah didn't bother to look where his bullet had hit. He gathered Addie up in his arms and began to carry her away. He wanted her far away from that man, the ugliness, the violence.

He carried her through the trees, struggling against the exhaustion, his body's own injuries, the cold. But still he moved forward, back toward where he'd left Ty. But his legs only kept him upright for so long.

"I can walk. I can walk," she murmured against his neck as he leaned against a tree, trying to catch his breath. "We can walk, right? If you got away from the other guys, they're… Do you think they're all dead?"

"I don't know about dead, but you're right, we can walk." He set her down carefully, still leaning against the tree, trying to catch his breath and wrap his mind around all of it.

"Seth's alive, isn't he?" Because that was the most important thing, what this had all been for.

"I think so. I told Vanessa to go with him. We were trying…" She choked on a sob, and it hurt to look at her, even in the shadowy light of night. She was pale and bloodied and dripping wet.

"We need to move. Make sure they're safe. I have to find Ty, and then…" He looked around the forest, the starry moonlit sky above. "We'll get to Seth," he promised, holding out his hand for her to take. But when she slipped her hand into his, he had to pull her close again and hold her tight against him for a minute. Just a minute.

"What's a little hypothermia, right?" she asked, her arms around him nearly as tight as his were around her.

He managed a chuckle against her hair, holding her close to assure himself she was alive and well. This was over. *Over.* "We'll survive it, I think. Let's find Ty. He earned himself a little stab wound in the arm."

"So tetanus shots for everyone."

"All these near-death experiences turned you into quite the comedian."

"Or I've just gone insane." She sighed gustily into his neck. "Noah."

She didn't say anything more, so he held her to him, trying to will the cold away. "You're safe now. It's all over."

She sighed heavily. "Not all. Noah, Peter wasn't lying. Seth isn't mine."

"Maybe if you hadn't just almost died I'd care a little bit more about that." But mostly, Noah found he didn't care. Maybe before this had all gone down he would have mustered some righteous indignation, some *hurt*, but after seeing what Peter could do, there was no question everything Addie had done had been done to protect Seth from that monster.

He couldn't hold that against her.

She pulled back, looked up at him, and he couldn't read her expression in the shadows. "I lied to you."

"Yeah. Yeah, well. Maybe Seth isn't your biological son, but he's in your care. He's your blood. To him, and to you I imagine, you're mother and child. A lie to keep Seth safe doesn't hurt me, and I know this whole time all you've been trying to do is keep Seth safe. I won't hold that against you or fault you for that, and no one can make me. Even you."

She expelled a breath. "Noah, I want to go home. I want Seth and I want to go home."

"Then that's what we'll do. Because this is over. You're safe, and once we know Seth's safe, that's all that will matter." Ever.

Chapter 20

The next few days were nothing but a blur. A hospital stay for her due to hypothermia and pneumonia, a hospital stay for Noah and Ty for their respective wounds. Vanessa and Seth were relatively unharmed, and to Addie, that was all that mattered.

The police and the FBI were a constant presence, talks of being a witness and trials. If charges would be pressed against her or Noah for killing men. Addie was almost grateful for being sick and not quite with it.

She was continually grateful for Laurel's presence and help. For Vanessa's bringing Seth to visit whenever the nurses would let her. Carsons and Delaneys working together to help someone who didn't really belong.

Bent is your home. Noah's voice echoed in her head. Bent was her home. But what did that mean? The Carson Ranch? This town? He'd said he loved her once, and she hadn't had the opportunity to say it back.

Addie sat in the passenger seat of Laurel's car, Seth's car seat fastened in the back. Over three months ago, she'd made this exact trek. She hadn't had a clue what would befall her back then.

She didn't have a clue what would befall her now. Noah had been released this morning, and he hadn't come to see her.

"Maybe he doesn't want…" Addie cleared her throat as Laurel turned the car onto the gravel road that led up to the Carson Ranch. "He might not want me here. I did lie to him." He'd said it didn't matter, but that was in the aftermath of hell. Now it might matter.

"He wants you here," Laurel replied. "I am under strict orders."

Addie slid Laurel a look. "From who?"

Laurel smiled. "Too many Carsons to count."

"I don't want to… I brought all these terrible things on him, and he didn't even come see me in the hospital. Why would he want me here?"

"I think that's something you'll have to ask the man yourself. I also think you already know the answer to that, so you might not want to insult him and ask him that in quite those words."

"He could've died. A million times."

"So could you. And Seth. But somehow, you all fought evil together and won. I'd pat myself on the back, not worry about if Noah is overly offended by the sacrifices he willingly made." Laurel frowned. "I am sorry we didn't—couldn't—do more. The police, me personally."

"Peter learned how to outmaneuver the police from

birth, I think. I don't blame you, Laurel. We all did everything we could, and like you said, we all fought evil together and won."

"I suppose." Laurel smiled thinly. "And when you fight evil and win, then you face the rest of your life."

Addie blew out a breath and watched the house get closer and closer to view. "It feels like I've been running forever," she murmured, more to herself than to Laurel.

But Laurel responded anyway. "And now it's time to stop. There isn't anything or anyone to run from anymore, and if there ever is again, you have a whole town—Carsons *and* Delaneys—at your side." She stopped the car in front of the house.

Much like that first day all those months ago, Grady stepped out, his smile all for Laurel. Addie stayed in her seat, waiting for some sign, some *hint* that Noah actually wanted her here. She might have believed it in the snow and the woods at night, but in the light of hospital days and FBI questions, all her fears and worries repopulated and grew.

He'd kept his distance. He was spending his days talking to FBI agents because of her. Maybe it'd had to be done, but that didn't make it any less her fault. She'd lied to him. Maybe once he really thought about it, he'd realized he didn't love a liar.

Laurel had gotten out and was pulling Seth out of his car seat. Grady was unlatching the car seat from Laurel's car. And still Addie sat, staring at the house, wondering what a future of freedom really looked like.

Freedom. No longer a slave to whether or not Peter would find her. She was *free*. Sitting in front of the

Carson ranch house, it was the first time that fact truly struck her.

She stepped out of the car. Laurel handed Seth to her and he wiggled and squirmed, pointing at the house, then clapping delightedly. "No!"

"Yes, we're home with Noah, aren't we?" Because she was free now. Free to take what she wanted, have it, nurture it. Free to do what was best for Seth's well-being, not just his safety. Free to build a life.

A real life.

If Noah was mad at her for bringing Peter to his doorstep, mad at her for lying about Seth not being her biological child, well, she'd find a way to make up for it. She'd find a way to make his words true.

Bent is your home.

I love you.

Grady took the car seat to the front door and Laurel placed the bag she'd brought to the hospital with some of Addie's things next to it.

"We're going to head out," Grady said.

"You aren't coming in?"

"Uh, no. You enjoy your homecoming."

"My…" She glanced at the door. *Homecoming.*

"Call if you need anything, or if the FBI get too obnoxious," Laurel offered, walking back to her car hand in hand with Grady.

Then it was just her and Seth, standing on the porch of the Carson Ranch, alone. It felt like a new start somehow.

And it was. A new start. Freedom. A life to build. But she had to take that step forward. She had to let go of the fear…not just of what her life had been, but of what she'd allowed herself to be. A victim of fear and someone else's power.

Never again.

She took a deep breath, steeling herself to barge in and demand Noah have a heart-to-heart conversation with her. No grunts. No silences. No *I love yous* and then disappearances. They weren't on the run anymore and he couldn't—

The door swung open.

"Well, are you going to come in or are you just planning on standing out in the cold all day?" Noah asked gruffly.

She blinked up at his tall, broad form filling up the doorframe. "I thought I'd stare at the door for a bit longer."

"I see you're still being funny."

"No!" Seth lunged for Noah and Noah caught him easily.

"There's a boy," Noah murmured, the smile evident even beneath the beard. His gaze moved up to Addie, that smile still in place as he held Seth and Seth immediately grabbed for his hat hanging off the hook next to them.

"Come inside, Addie."

Right. Come inside. Conversation. She'd tell him what she wanted. What she needed, and…and…

She stepped inside and Noah closed the door behind her.

"How are you feeling?"

"How am I feeling?" she repeated, staring at him, something like anger simmering inside her. She didn't know why, and it was probably unearned anger, but it was there nonetheless. "That's all you have to say to me?"

"No."

She frowned at him. "You don't make any sense."

"You were just released from the hospital," he said, as if that explained anything.

"So were you!"

"I wasn't sick, though."

"Oh, no, just a gunshot wound."

It was his turn to frown. "Why are we fighting exactly?"

Addie turned away from him. She didn't know why she was arguing or what she felt or…

She stopped abruptly in the middle of the living room when she saw a sign hanging from the exposed beams of the kitchen ceiling. Hand-painted and not quite neat, two simple words were written across the paper.

Welcome Home.

He'd made her a sign. Hung it up. Home. *Home.* She turned back to face him, and all the tears she'd been fighting so hard for the past few days let loose in a torrent of relief.

"But… I lied to you. I made your life a living hell for days, and through the beginning and the end I lied to you about Seth. You've had time to think about that now. Really think about it. You have to be sure—"

"I can't say I *like* being lied to, but I understand it. You were protecting Seth, and there's nothing about *that* I don't understand. But…"

Oh, God, there was a but. She nearly sank to her knees.

"We have to promise each other, both of us, no more lies. Even righteous ones. Because the only way we fought Peter was together. The only way we survived was together. There can't be any more lies or doing things on our own. We're in this together. Partners."

"Partners," she repeated, Seth still happily playing with the cowboy hat as Noah held him on his hip.

"No lies. No keeping things from each other. We work together. Always. I promise you that, if you can promise me the same."

Addie swallowed, looking at this good man in front of her, holding a boy who wasn't biologically her son but was *hers* nonetheless. "I promise you that, Noah. With all of my heart I promise you that." She glanced up at the sign he'd made, this stoic, uncelebratory man. "I do want this to be my home," she whispered.

"Then it's yours," Noah returned, reaching out and wiping some of the tears from her cheeks.

"I love you, Noah."

There was *no* doubt under all that hair and Carson cowboy gruffness, Noah smiled, and when his mouth met hers, Addie knew she'd somehow found what she'd always been looking for, even in those days of running away.

Home. Love. A place to belong. A place to raise Seth, and a man who'd be the best role model for him.

"I hear there's some curse about Carsons and Delaneys," she murmured against his mouth.

"I don't believe in curses, Addie. I believe in us. Hell, we defeated the mob. What's a curse?"

"I'd say neither has anything on love."

"Or coming home. Where you belong."

Yes, Addie Foster belonged in Bent, Wyoming, on the Carson Ranch, with Noah Carson at her side, to love and be loved in return for as long as she breathed.

And nothing would ever change that.

* * * * *